PRAISE FOR HER NOVELS

"[An] emotionally compelling, subtly nuanced tale of revenge, redemption, and romance . . . This flawlessly written book is worth every tear."   —*Chicago Tribune*

"Romance, passion, and thrilling adventure fill the pages."
          —Rosemary Rogers, *New York Times* bestselling author

"A romance you won't soon forget."
          —Sara Donati, international bestselling author

"Draws readers into the romance and often unvarnished reality of life in nineteenth-century America."
                              —*Library Journal*

"Kaki Warner's warm, witty, and lovable characters shine."
                              —*USA Today*

"Filled with passion, adventure, heartbreak, and humor."
                              —The Romance Dish

"Halfway between Penelope Williamson's and Jodi Thomas's gritty, powerful novels and LaVyrle Spencer's small-town stories lie Warner's realistic, atmospheric romances."
                              —*RT Book Reviews*

"Bring[s] the Old West to sprawling and vivid life."
                              —BookLoons

"This is Western historical romance at its best."
                              —The Romance Reader

Berkley Sensation titles by Kaki Warner

Blood Rose Trilogy

PIECES OF SKY
OPEN COUNTRY
CHASING THE SUN

Runaway Brides Novels

HEARTBREAK CREEK
COLORADO DAWN
BRIDE OF THE HIGH COUNTRY

Heroes of Heartbreak Creek

BEHIND HIS BLUE EYES
WHERE THE HORSES RUN
HOME BY MORNING

TEXAS TALL

Texas Tall

KAKI WARNER

BERKLEY SENSATION
New York

BERKLEY SENSATION
Published by Berkley
An imprint of Penguin Random House LLC
375 Hudson Street, New York, New York 10014

Copyright © 2016 by Kathleen Warner
Penguin Random House supports copyright. Copyright fuels creativity, encourages
diverse voices, promotes free speech, and creates a vibrant culture. Thank you for buying
an authorized edition of this book and for complying with copyright laws by not
reproducing, scanning, or distributing any part of it in any form without permission.
You are supporting writers and allowing Penguin Random House to continue to
publish books for every reader.

BERKLEY and BERKLEY SENSATION are registered trademarks and the B colophon is
a trademark of Penguin Random House LLC.

ISBN: 9780425281147

First Edition: October 2016

Printed in the United States of America
1   3   5   7   9   10   8   6   4   2

Cover art by Judy York
Cover design by Lesley Worrell
Book design by Kelly Lipovich

*There is a special place in
heaven for the spouses of writers.
Thanks, Joe, for your support,
patience, and understanding.*

Prologue

———◆———

"I shouldn't have to do this!" Charlotte Weyland swiped a sleeve over her brimming eyes and flung another stick onto the brush piled against the shed door. "But you never listen to me, do you?"

A faint clink of metal.

She stiffened, head cocked, then realized it was the sorrel gelding tied over by the creek, fussing with his bit.

But what if it wasn't?

Stepping closer, she peered through a gap between the weathered slats of the shed wall. "You awake?"

The figure on the cot lay still. The chain binding him to the center pole hadn't moved.

"If you are, you better say something."

Silence.

With a sob, she slumped to her knees and pressed her forehead against the rough wood. "You promised. Remember? You said on my fifteenth birthday, you would take me to Galveston. You said we would chase crabs across the sand, and let the waves lap at our toes, and eat shrimp gumbo. You promised!"

A hot gust of wind whipped up a dust devil, peppering her

face with grit before it swirled on through the drooping trees
along the dry creek where her horse was tied. Withered mesquite pods rattled like dice in a wooden cup, then fell silent
as the wind died and dust drifted slowly back to the parched
earth. The air was thick enough to taste. But to the west,
thunder rumbled and dark clouds churned in the leaden sky.

Charlotte pushed herself to her feet. With a shaking hand,
she fumbled in her pocket for the box of lucifers, opened it
and pulled out one, then dragged the coated tip across the
striker. It broke. Two more snapped before the fourth flared
to life. She dropped it into the nearest pile of brush then ran
to the next as flames licked at the plank walls. Soon all the
piles were crackling.

She hurried to the house.

In the main room, she poured lamp oil over the rags and
brush and broken furniture she had heaped on the floor then
splashed what remained on the walls. Blinking against the
fumes, she took a final look around. But after years of selling
off everything of value, there was little left except a wrench-
ing sense of defeat. Shutting her mind to the despair clog-
ging her throat, she struck a lucifer, dropped it on the soaked
rags, then ran out the front as flames caught with a *whoosh*.

Thunder rumbled again, closer now and heading east fast.
She darted across the porch, her throat burning from smoke
and a new rush of tears, and hurried over to calm the nervous
sorrel pawing at the dirt. "It won't be long now, Rusty."

She watched flames curl around the eaves of the shed.
Tongues of fire shot through the gaps in the walls. With a
crack, a beam fell, bringing most of the roof down with it.
From inside came a groan that was so lifelike it sent her back
a step.

He couldn't still be alive, could he?

The thought was so horrifying for a moment she couldn't
move. Then gripped by mindless terror, she whipped around,
yanked Rusty's lead loose, and flung herself into the saddle.
With a last backward glance at the only home she had ever
known, she kicked the gelding into a gallop.

She was on her own now. She had no family left. No home. All she had to her name was the horse she rode, the contents of the bulging saddlebags strapped behind the saddle, and the twelve dollars she'd taken from her grandfather's desk.

With only a vague destination in mind, she headed east, away from the past and ahead of the storm, her tears turning to salt in the hot, dry wind.

Chapter 1

The morning the Texas Rangers rode into Greenbroke, Texas, Charlotte Weyland—or Lottie, as she called herself now—was sweeping the boardwalk in front of Brackett's Market and Grocery. Normally, it was a task she enjoyed since it gave her a chance to leave the stuffy confines of the store and feel the sun on her face. But this early August day was already blistering hot. Not yet ten o'clock, and the air seared her lungs, drying sweat almost as soon as it rose on her skin. By noon, the streets would be empty. Even the two old checker players outside the Western Union office would move inside.

But this morning there were big doings. Strangers were coming through, and the word "Rangers" rushed along the boardwalk as people braved the heat to watch the tight group of men ride down Main Street. Despite a brief growth spurt after the railroad added two more runs on the spur line to Dallas, Greenbroke didn't draw a lot of visitors. And visitors with badges were rarer still.

Brushing a wave of light brown hair out of her eyes, Lottie paused in her sweeping to watch them approach.

They were five in number, led by a grim-faced man with

a mustache that stuck out more than his nose and covered both lips. Behind him rode three men abreast, followed by the drag rider, a tall, lean man who looked younger than the others. Except for the man in the middle of the threesome, they were all heavily armed with rifles butted on their thighs and pistols in their holsters. The unarmed rider wore manacles instead.

"The Frontier Battalion," Lottie's friend, Becky Carmichael, whispered, suddenly appearing beside her. "They're the ones that got Sam Bass down in Round Rock last month. Heard the old one in the lead is McNelly's Bulldog, Lt. John Armstrong, himself."

"Heard where?"

"The bank." Becky held up a canvas pouch with *People's Bank of Greenbroke* stenciled on the side. "The crab sent me to get change."

The "crab" was Frances Seaforth, Becky's employer and owner of the only dress shop in Greenbroke. Fashions by Fanny—an odd name, Lottie thought. Miss Seaforth was a hard taskmaster, but sometimes Becky needed a firm hand.

Lottie glanced around, hoping none of the others who had come out onto the boardwalk to watch the rangers had overheard. Even though Becky was nineteen and two years older than herself, she didn't always show good sense. "You shouldn't call her that."

"Why not? She is a crab."

"If she hears you, she'll show you the street, that's why." Employment was hard to find in Greenbroke, especially for young women who had no family to watch out for them.

Becky tossed her blond curls. "Then I'll move in with you."

"In the back room at the market? Just you and me and the mice? That'll be cozy." Sometimes Becky's lackadaisical attitude irritated Lottie. They were barely two meals short of starvation as it was. The next stop would be whoring in the saloon or moving on, and despite its slow pace, Lottie liked Greenbroke. There was a welcome hominess to it. Maybe because people had accepted her without questioning why a ragged fourteen-year-old girl would ride into town on her own. Or maybe it was because Greenbroke was the only town she had ever spent time in. Either way, after being here for three years, she felt she belonged.

"That last one's a handsome devil." Brown eyes dancing, Becky puffed out her impressive chest and waved to the young man riding drag.

Handsome? Lottie assessed him over the top of her broom handle as he rode by. A stern, angular face with an unyielding set to his wide mouth. A shadow of beard covering his square chin. Longish dark hair sticking out from beneath his black Stetson. From this distance, she couldn't tell the color of his eyes, but guessed they were more light than dark. Young. Probably barely past twenty. In a few years he might be handsome, once he grew into that jawline and learned to smile a little. But right now, except for the Ranger star pinned to his shirt, he looked like any other big, rawboned farm boy who had yet to flesh out.

Ignoring Becky, he swung his gaze over the other onlookers, then up to the false fronts rising above the overhang along the boardwalk. Looking for what?

Lottie studied the slumped back of the manacled rider as the troop rode past the telegraph office and on toward the depot where Sheriff Dodson waited on the platform. "Wonder what he did."

"The prisoner?" Becky shrugged. "Something bad if they sent the Frontier Battalion after him. Probably taking him somewhere to stand trial."

Outside the depot, the rangers dismounted. The leader went inside with the sheriff. One ranger positioned himself by the water tower, one stayed with the prisoner, and the young drag rider walked back down the street, his head swiveling as he scanned the buildings they'd just ridden past. Did he expect ambushers? Here, in sleepy little Greenbroke?

In the distance, a train whistle blew.

"Lordy, is that the ten-ten already?" Becky tucked the bank bag under her arm. "Better get back before the crab pinches me. Meet for dinner?"

"Mr. Brackett asked me to look over the week's receipts."

Becky gave her a sour look. "It's your own fault. You shouldn't have told him you could tally."

"I'm not complaining. I like it. Working sums is relaxing. Numbers are so . . . predictable." It seemed all her life Lottie had worried where her next meal was coming from. She was tired of it. She wanted more than a hardscrabble life sweeping boardwalks and emptying potato sacks and listening to mice scurry in the night. She had ambitions and a strong conviction that a better future awaited her if she only knew how to get to it.

The locomotive pulled into view, slowing to a crawl as it neared the water tower. Sooty smoke billowed out of the stack. Brakes squealed. Once the train came to a full stop, the conductor stepped off. Only a few passengers followed after him, crossing from the train into the station. It wouldn't be a busy shopping day in Greenbroke.

Becky's voice took on a wheedling tone. "Any chance you could sneak me a can of beans then?"

"Sneak? You mean steal?" Lottie frowned. "Becky, I dare not. The Bracketts treat me good. I don't want to steal from them."

"You did before."

"Once. I hadn't eaten in two days and they hadn't paid me yet." Honesty lost much of its appeal when survival was at stake. "And anyway, I put money in the till after they paid me."

"But I already ran through last week's pay and there's barely enough leftovers to feed Mrs. Ledbetter." Mrs. Ledbetter was the elderly lady Becky watched over. In exchange for room and board, Becky cooked and did light housekeeping. A good arrangement for both.

"You should be more careful with your money." Lottie regretted the words as soon as she said them. Becky was her friend. She didn't want to run her off. But she owed the Bracketts, too.

At Becky's pleading look, Lottie sighed. She hated begging almost as much as stealing, but she didn't want Becky to go hungry. She had suffered a hollow belly too many times, herself. "The Bracketts always feed me when I work late. I'll try to save something for you."

"Thanks. I knew I could count on you."

Becky's grin was slightly off-kilter because of the scar at the corner of her top lip where her daddy had tried to rearrange her face with his fist before she ran off for good. It marred what would have been real beauty, although the cowboys in the saloon didn't seem to mind.

"Come to the back door." Lottie made a last swipe at a manure smear below the display window, then gave up. "I should be done by nine."

"I'll be there." With a backhand wave, Becky headed down the boardwalk.

Lottie started back inside, then flinched when gunshots rang out.

Becky ducked into the doorway of the newspaper office next to Brackett's Market. Shouts up and down the street. Heavy footfalls thudding on the boardwalk as onlookers scrambled to safety.

Heart pounding, Lottie peered around the doorframe.

One ranger lay twisting on the ground by the station platform. The young drag rider was running back toward the train, gun drawn. A stranger with a kerchief over his face fired wildly as he steered the prisoner toward a masked rider holding two sidestepping horses.

Bullets peppered the dirt by his boots, but the drag rider kept going, his dark Stetson flying off as he ran. The sheriff and older ranger ran out of the station and fired at the fleeing men.

The kerchiefed man fell.

More shots from the ranger by the water tower. The second masked man toppled from the saddle. Horses scattered. The prisoner fell to his knees, hands over his head, screaming, "Don't fire, don't fire," in a panicky voice.

Less than ten seconds. A dozen shots. And as suddenly as it had begun, the shooting stopped.

Silence, except for the exhalations of the idling locomotive.

"Sweet Jesus!" Becky peered at Lottie from the newspaper doorway. "Is it over?"

Through the dust and gun smoke hanging in the air, Lottie saw the drag rider sprawled in the street, a bloody hand pressed to his head.

"Get Doc Helms!" she shouted to Becky and jumped off the boardwalk.

As she neared, the ranger tried to rise up, the gun wobbling in his right hand. Blood coated the fingers pressed to the left side of his face and ran down his neck to turn the banded collar of his shirt bright red.

"Lay back!" Lottie knelt beside him. "You've been shot."

He rolled toward her, the gun swinging up.

"No!" She grabbed his thick wrist with both hands. "Stop! It's over! You're safe!"

With a groan, he slumped back, the pistol sliding from his grip.

Lottie pulled his left hand from the wound. Blood matted the dark hair, welling from a long furrow stretching from his eyebrow, past his temple, and back along the side of his head. Not serious, despite all the blood.

"I can't . . . see . . ." He lifted his left hand.

Lottie pushed it away. "Be still." Pulling a hanky from her skirt pocket, she tried to mop up the blood so she could see the wound. "Help is on the way." Starting to panic, she looked around, hoping she was right.

Down the street, the mustachioed leader tied a kerchief around the leg of the other wounded ranger, while the fourth ranger lashed the prisoner to one of the legs of the water tower. The sheriff bent over the would-be rescuers. Both lay motionless in the dirt.

Where was the doctor?

The young ranger groaned. "Why is . . . everything so . . . blurry . . ."

"A bullet grazed your head. You should be fine."

"The others . . ." Breath hissed through clenched teeth as he shoved the hanky away and struggled up onto one elbow. "Have to . . . go . . ."

"No, you don't." She put a staying hand on his shoulder. "They're fine. The shooting has stopped. It's over."

For a moment, he looked around, his gaze unfocused until it settled on her. He looked startled to see her. "Who . . . are you?"

"Lottie. Now lie back until the doctor comes."

His eyes were blue. The bluest she had ever seen. Not as light-colored as a robin's egg or as dark as hill country bluebonnets. More like the glowing blue of a candle flame near the wick where the fire burns hottest. And like all flames, they drew the eye. Only when she heard motion behind her could Lottie look away.

"Make room!"

Lottie stumbled to her feet as the old ranger shoved in beside her. "Ty, can you hear me, son?"

Before he got an answer, Doc Helms and Sheriff Dodson rushed up. Several onlookers crowded behind them, brave now that the shooting had stopped. Lottie found herself pushed back until she lost sight of the young ranger beneath the growing crowd.

"He hurt bad?" Becky moved up beside her, moneybag clutched to her chest. She gaped at Lottie's skirt. "Lordy! You got blood all over yourself. He's dying?"

Lottie wiped her hands on her ruined work skirt, but the blood was already tacky in the dry heat. It stank like hot metal. "I don't think so." At least she hoped not. Something about the farm-boy-ranger had struck a chord with her. A connection. Almost like she knew him already even though she had never seen him before. Probably his youth. He looked only a few years older than she, and that was too young to die.

But Becky was right about one thing. With those eyes, he would be a striking man someday. If he lived that long.

———

By dark, two new mounds graced the little cemetery outside of town. The manacled prisoner was under double guard in one of Sheriff Dodson's cells, the two wounded rangers were resting in the back room at Doc's house, and the saloon was crowded with men anxious to give their accounts of the

"Great Greenbroke Shoot-out." The two unharmed rangers listened from a corner table, accepting congratulations with crooked smiles and cynical eyes.

Or so Becky said that night when she came to the back door of the market for the stew and cornbread Lottie had saved for her.

"What were you doing at the saloon again?" Lottie asked her. "That's no place for a good girl."

Becky grinned through a mouthful of cornbread. "I ain't *that* good. Besides, like I told you a dozen times already, Juno wouldn't let anything happen to me. He likes me."

Juno was the owner of the Spotted Dog Saloon, which also served as the town's gambling house and only brothel. Lottie had never spoken to him but had seen him around town. He made her uneasy. Stern and unsmiling, he volunteered nothing—not even his full name—and had dark, watchful eyes that seemed to cut right through a person's skull to expose all the secrets hidden within. Lottie had the eerie feeling he somehow knew about Grandpa and what she had done, but he never did more than give her a polite nod when he came into the store or saw her on the street. "What Juno *likes* is the idea of you working for him upstairs."

Becky gave a dismissive wave with her fork. "That'll never happen. I've pinned my sights on marriage and he knows it." Setting her empty plate on the floor beside the crate she used as a stool, she gave Lottie a wink. "Maybe I'll get me one of them rangers."

"If you did, he wouldn't be a ranger for long. The Frontier Battalion doesn't allow married men."

"Then maybe I'll go visit the two staying with Doc Helms. Maybe the one with the hurt leg needs a sweet loving woman to help him regain his strength." Becky rocked back, laughing at the notion.

"What about the other one?"

"The kid? Too young. He's barely older than me, I bet."

"I meant how is he doing?"

Becky gave her a sharp look. "Got your eye on him, do you?"

"Just curious. He bled all over my second-best work dress, after all." Hoping to deflect further questions—although she wasn't sure why the subject of the farm-boy-ranger made her skittish—Lottie picked up Becky's plate and set it on the stoop until she could wash it later. She had enough mice running around as it was.

"He's fine, I hear," Becky said when Lottie returned to her seat on the end of her cot. "Should be able to leave with the others tomorrow."

So soon?

"Heard he asked Doc Helms about you." Seeing Lottie's look of surprise, Becky added, "There's no other Lottie in town, so it must be you."

Lottie vaguely remembered telling him her name. It surprised her that he remembered it. She remembered his name, too. Ty, the old ranger had called him. Short for Tyler? Tyrone? Tyson? Tiberius? She wondered if she would ever know.

Becky rose from her crate and brushed cornbread crumbs from her skirt. "Better go. Mrs. Ledbetter doesn't like me staying out too late, and she'll be wanting her night medicine soon."

"How's she doing?" Lottie asked, walking her to the door. The old lady had some sort of female ailment and seemed to be wasting away.

"Poorly. Won't be long, Doc says. Then I don't know where I'll stay. The crab doesn't pay me enough to cover a room anywhere else."

"We'll think of something." Lottie feared that after Mrs. Ledbetter passed on, Becky would become easy pickings for Juno. She didn't want her dearest friend turning whore just to get by.

At the door, Becky paused. "Be sad to see the rangers leave tomorrow. It was nice having a bit of excitement around here for a change."

"Those killed and wounded might not agree."

"Still . . ."

Smiling, Lottie gave her a gentle push. "Good night." As

she closed the door, she wondered if the rangers would leave on the southbound tomorrow morning, and if the boardwalk would need to be swept again.

The rangers took the early train. Lottie was emptying onions into the bin and didn't see them, but Becky did, and said they weren't as impressive going out as they'd been coming in, what with one man limping on a crutch, and another sporting a thick bandage around his head. By the time they'd loaded their horses into the stock car, retrieved the prisoner, and climbed aboard, they were relegated to memory. Main Street was once again nearly empty under the baking late summer sun, and Greenbroke was settling back into its slow routine.

The dog days of August drifted into September with only slightly cooler temperatures. Every day, cloudbanks rolled inland from the Gulf of Mexico, promising rain and relief from the dry heat. Every evening, dry lightning bounced through the clouds as though trying to blast out the moisture.

But no rain came and tempers grew short . . . until September brought another visitor to Greenbroke and things began to change.

Chapter 2

———⋆———

"Lordy, could it get any hotter in here?" Becky grumbled, dragging an arm across her sweating brow. "I can hardly summon the energy to chew."

She and Lottie were in Lottie's sleeping area in the storeroom, sharing a plate of roast chicken, green beans, and biscuits that Becky had cooked for Mrs. Ledbetter. Since the elderly lady suffered terribly from the heat, on hot evenings there were plenty of leftovers to share.

"Why is everything so gritty?" Lottie complained.

"It's from the dust kicked up by the cows," Becky said between bites. "One climbed the boardwalk and charged into the store. The crab had a conniption. I thought she was going to shoot it. I don't know which was worse, the cow or the two cowboys trying to corral it. The heat sure brings out the stink."

And this evening felt hotter than usual, the air thick with dust and the smell of manure left behind by the fifty head of cattle driven down Main Street by riders from the sprawling Bar M ranch outside of town. Even from this distance, Lottie could hear the bawling of the restless animals as they milled about in the pens by the railroad tracks. Hopefully, tomorrow morning, once they were loaded into stock cars bound for the auction barns in Fort Worth, the air would clear. Her eyes and teeth felt scratchy as emery paper.

"Things are hopping over at the saloon." Becky's voice was muffled by the petticoat she was using to blot sweat from her forehead. "Juno's making a killing."

"I don't know why you go over there. You'll get yourself into trouble one of these days when some cowboy mistakes you for a whore."

"Whores make a lot more money than we do."

Lottie looked at her in surprise. "But they're whores."

"Whores who live better 'n us." Becky popped half a biscuit into her mouth. "And Juno treats them good."

"I thought you had your mind set on marriage."

"I do. But whores marry, too. Didn't Bucktooth Maggie get hitched to that patent medicine salesman through town last month?"

"You can do better than that."

Becky looked over with hope in her eyes. "You really think so?"

"Of course I do. You're pretty, smart, hardworking. A man would be lucky to have you. Especially one who had a farm or ranch to run."

Becky finished chewing her biscuit, then shook her head. "My daddy was a farmer. Never had two coins to rub together no matter how hard he worked. Brought out the meanness in him. No, I think I'd rather a city fellow. A man with a future, rather than a plow."

"And you think you'll find him in the Spotted Dog Saloon?"

"Why not? Horace Griffin is in there all the time, and he owns the bank. Even that circuit judge drops by whenever he's in town, and last night a preacher was in there spouting Scripture and dealing cards like the Devil had a hold on him. Not everybody's a drunk cowboy."

"A traveling preacher?" Not many came by sleepy little Greenbroke. Pickings were too thin, Lottie guessed. Even the town's only church—if the Greater Glory to God Assembly could be called a church—met in a barn because they lacked the funds to build their own house of worship.

"He rode in behind the cattle. Been putting up posters everywhere calling for a Sunday come-to-Jesus-meeting." Becky gave her a wink. "You might like him. He's full of advice, too."

Lottie set down her fork. "Am I that hard on you?"

"Worse than my ma." The lopsided grin didn't erase the hurt of her words.

"I—I'm sorry, Becky. I worry about you, is all." A knot of emotion stuck in Lottie's throat and she had to pause until it eased. "I've never had a friend before. I guess I'm not very good at it."

"Don't be silly! You're a great friend!"

Grandpa had called her bossy, too. But the older he got, the more he'd needed someone to look out for him, and who was there to do it but her? If she was bossy, it was because she'd had to be—especially during those last terrible days when she'd tried so hard to get him to eat whatever she could find in their meager supplies.

Becky's laugh broke through her thoughts. "How could you not have any friends? With your looks, you must have had a dozen boys chasing after you."

"Not hardly. We didn't go to town that often." Embarrassed to admit how inexperienced she was, Lottie changed the subject. "Why would a preacher be gambling in a saloon?"

"Said he needed to win money to spread the Lord's word. But I think he likes it. I've seen that wild, hungry look before. Pa would get it and head to town. Then Ma would have to drag all us kids along to help haul him home before he lost the farm, too. But the preacher must have God on his side. He seems to win a lot more hands than he loses."

———

The preacher, Nathaniel Lindz, remained the town's main topic of conversation for several weeks, not only because of his gambling habits, but also because he was excessively handsome. So much so Becky said just looking at him made her teeth hurt.

In addition to a thatch of thinning blond hair that stuck up around his head like a halo, he had a voice that could make angels weep, and a smile that made a girl feel like the most important person he'd met that day.

Or so Becky said.

Lottie had her doubts. She wasn't sure she trusted that flashy smile.

Before moving to Greenbroke, she'd been around few men. Whenever she and Grandpa had gone into the nearest town, San Angela, she was just Old Man Lofton's granddaughter. Boys didn't notice her, probably because she didn't look like a girl with her hair cut short, and didn't dress like a girl in her hand-me-down dungarees. Which was fine with her. She'd never paid much attention to boys, either. Until she'd looked down into the startling blue eyes of the farm-boy-ranger. The connection she'd felt in that moment still haunted her. She didn't understand it. Or understand why her thoughts kept circling back to him. It was confusing. And unsettling. And made her feel things she had never felt before.

It also made her aware of other men. And how they looked at her.

Like Reverend Lindz.

The only other traveling preacher she'd met was one who had come by the ranch years ago. Grandpa had asked him to bless Grandma's grave and that of Lottie's ma, who had died from a bee sting when Lottie was ten. He had been much older than Nathaniel Lindz. Less robust, and certainly more somber. Reverend Lindz had a big smile that crinkled the corners of his hazel eyes and showed a mouthful of strong white teeth. And he had beautiful manners, too. When he saw Lottie studying him the first time he'd come into the market, he'd lifted his hat and given her a flashy bow, his eyes never leaving hers. He might have said something but she was too flustered to remember, much less respond. It didn't sit right—the way he flirted and the way heat rushed into her cheeks when he did. He was a preacher, for heaven's sake.

Apparently, Mrs. Brackett felt the same way.

"It's indecent," she announced to her husband one morning

after the reverend left with a tin of sandalwood-scented hair pomade. "No preacher should be that handsome."

Mr. B. made a noncommittal sound and squinted through his spectacles at the list in his hand.

Undeterred, his wife pressed on. "Such comeliness generates lust in the female parishioners and mistrust in the men, isn't that right, Lottie?"

Lottie gave a vague smile and continued stacking cans on a display table. Was that what she was feeling? Lust? For a man of God? Add another mark on her list of sins.

Mr. B. turned to his wife with a twinkle in his cloudy blue eyes. "Are you feeling lustful, dear?"

"Mr. Brackett!"

"If so, I'm sure Lottie would be happy to watch the store for a spell so we could discuss it further."

Lottie ducked her head to hide her blush. *Lord sake!* The Bracketts were in their sixties, at least. The idea of them even contemplating lust was unsettling.

His wife huffed out her ample breasts. They weren't as impressive as Becky's, but were a good deal longer. "Hush that talk, Mr. Brackett! I've got chores to do." And before her husband could elaborate on his suggestion, she fled into their living quarters behind the front counter. But Lottie could swear she saw a smile on the kindly woman's face.

The Bracketts had been Lottie's salvation since the day she'd arrived in Greenbroke and they'd caught her digging through the refuse bin behind the market. By that evening, they'd given her a hot meal, a place to sleep in the storeroom, a job doing odd chores, and Mrs. B. was altering two of her old dresses to replace Lottie's patched trousers and tattered shirt. A month after that, Mr. B., whose eyesight was failing, learned Lottie could do simple number calculations, and he began teaching her how to keep tallies on the market's expenses and profits. They soon became the parents she'd lost too soon, and she became the child they'd never had. An instant family. Lottie loved them dearly.

"You going to the tent meeting this Sunday?" Mr. B. asked Lottie after a while. When she looked over at him, he gave her a smile. "Pretty girl like you should get out more. Meet some young bucks."

"At a revival meeting?"

"Why not? Services is where I met Mrs. Brackett. Prettiest girl in the choir."

Lottie hadn't been around many married folks. Her father had died in the War of the Rebellion before she was three, and her mother had passed seven years later. She couldn't even remember her grandmother. Mostly, it had just been her and Grandpa, so she had no idea how married folks were supposed to behave. Since arriving in Greenbroke, she'd come to know several couples, but most of them seemed to be people staying in the same house but living separate lives.

Not so the Bracketts. Maybe they'd been together so long they'd merged into one person with the same thoughts and expectations and temperaments. Seeing the way they looked after each other—the teasing words, the gentle pats when they thought no one was looking, the tired smiles across the counter after a long day—was a revelation to Lottie. Watching them made her feel a bit lonely and made her wish for someone special in her own life. Someone other than Becky.

"Yes, sir, I'll probably go to the meeting," she said in answer to his question. "Becky said Mrs. Ledbetter wanted to attend, and I might go with them."

"Be careful." His teasing smile deepened the grooves around his mouth. "Wouldn't want you girls generating any lustful thoughts about the new preacher."

"I'll . . . ah . . . remind Becky."

"Mrs. Ledbetter, too. She was always a rare one."

Lottie couldn't even imagine that. "I'll keep an eye on both of them."

As it turned out, it wasn't Mrs. Ledbetter she had to watch out for when they settled in to hear the reverend preach the following Sunday. Becky nearly threw out her back, waving those bosoms around, and the preacher almost tripped on his tongue when he saw them bob and jiggle. Mrs. Ledbetter mostly dozed.

There were enough people in the crowded tent that Lottie

wondered if the Greater Glory to God Assembly would have
any worshipers that morning. Most had probably come out
of curiosity. And Reverend Lindz didn't disappoint, working
his attentive listeners like a master fisherman, using his voice
to hook them, then promises of eternal glory to reel them in.
His closing message was simple: "The love of money is the
root of all evil." He said it twice for emphasis then passed
around the tin collection plate, adding that it was more blessed
to give than receive and giving to him would help further the
Lord's work as well as keep them safe from Satan.

Seeing how few coins *plink*ed into the plate, he doubled
his efforts. Lifting his voice and hands toward the top of the
tent, he promised fiery damnation to those who refused to
heed God's words, and glorious redemption to those who
gave in His name. That got the money flowing.

It was quite a performance. Lottie wondered if he would
bring out snakes for an encore. Then seeing the slack-jawed
awe on the faces around her, she chided herself for being
such a doubter. She had heard much of this before: Grandpa
had a Bible verse for every occasion and had used them
frequently to keep her in line.

Overall, it was a nice sermon, although Mrs. Ledbetter
seemed unimpressed. Or perhaps the heat in the stifling tent
overrode religious zeal. When Lottie saw her face had gone
pasty gray, she elbowed Becky. "Mrs. Ledbetter is looking
poorly. We should get her home."

Becky stared raptly at the reverend. "Hmm?"

"I'm taking Mrs. Ledbetter home," Lottie said in a louder
voice. "It's too hot in here for her."

"Hot?" When Becky finally tore her gaze from the reverend and looked at the woman beside her, her eyes widened
in concern. "Mercy!" She hopped to her feet, and together,
she and Lottie helped Mrs. Ledbetter from the bench.

As soon as the reverend saw them rise, he pounced.
"Come forth, come forth!" he cried, bounding toward them
down the aisle between the benches. "Let the Lord heal you!
Let Him work His miracles through these unworthy hands!"

"Eh?" Mrs. Ledbetter said, looking around.

Stopping in front of the befuddled old woman, Reverend Lindz boomed in her face, "Do you believe?" Without waiting for a reply, he clapped his hands to her head and scrunched his eyes closed. "By the power of the Father, the Son, and the Holy Ghost," he shouted in ringing tones, "I take away your pain and despair! Rise up and be healed!"

Having already risen, and being unhealable besides, Mrs. Ledbetter did the next best thing and fell dead at his feet, a beatific smile on her face.

———

Some said the reverend killed her. Others said it was a miracle, since her suffering was finally over and she was now at peace with the Lord in heaven. The less pious said the preacher ought to get holsters for those lethal hands.

The reverend offered no comment and added drinking to his growing list of vices.

"I don't care what anybody says," Becky said several days later when she and Lottie left the cemetery after putting wilted flowers on Mrs. Ledbetter's grave. "Nathaniel didn't kill her."

"Nathaniel?"

"He was only trying to help."

"Since when do you call him Nathaniel?"

Becky flipped a curl aside. "Why shouldn't I call him Nathaniel? That's his name, isn't it?"

Lottie continued to stare at her.

"He's heartbroken, you know. He's never killed anyone before."

"And he didn't kill Mrs. Ledbetter," Lottie reminded her. "The poor woman was dying. It was the heat that did her in."

"Oh, I hope so."

They walked for a few more yards, then Becky heaved a despondent sigh. "Her brother is coming from Missouri. He wrote and asked me to stay and keep an eye on the house until he arrives. I think he plans to sell it. If he does, I don't know what I'll do."

"Maybe *Nathaniel* will hire you to pass around his collection plates." It was unkindly said, but Lottie wasn't feeling particularly kindly toward the reverend. He seemed contradictory in a lot of ways, and she hated that he preyed on the vulnerable, like Mrs. Ledbetter and now Becky.

But she could be wrong. She could be hearing her grandfather's voice in the reverend's words. "God casts a jaundiced eye on evildoers," he'd often warned her. "And He's always watching, so you'd best be righteous in His sight."

That ever-present coil of guilt in her stomach tightened. In her head she heard echoes of that inhuman groan as the roof caught. If God was watching that day three years ago, did He understand why she'd done what she had?

Over the next days, Becky continued to console the reverend. She went to every prayer meeting, arriving early to help him set up and staying late to gather the tattered hymnals. She even convinced a couple of whores at the Spotted Dog to attend with her, which caused a ruckus among the more respectable womenfolk and a few awkward moments with their husbands, especially when the whores called out and waved. Even Juno was upset, Becky said.

But not for the reason Lottie would have thought.

On Monday morning of the following week, Lottie was returning from the bank after depositing the previous week's receipts when Mr. Juno stepped onto the boardwalk as she approached the Spotted Dog.

"Miss Weyland."

She stopped, surprised. He'd never spoken to her before. She wondered why he did so now, or if she was about to be pulled into the middle of a conflict between Becky and the saloon owner. "Mr. Juno."

"Just Juno."

She glanced past him down the boardwalk, then across the street, then down at the money pouch in her hands. Anywhere but into those dark, all-seeing eyes. Eyes that reminded her of the color of molasses. His voice, too. Deep and rich and flavored with the cadence of the South.

"I don't mean to embarrass you," he said.

Confusion brought her head up. "Why would I be embarrassed?"

He gave a thin smile that softened the sternness of his features. "You're a good woman. I run a whorehouse. You shouldn't be seen talking to me."

Unsure how to respond to that, she made a vague dismissive gesture. "How can I help you?"

"How serious is Becky Carmichael about Reverend Lindz?"

Now she was even more confused. She studied Mr. Juno, trying to read the intent behind the question. Was he worried he might lose a prospect for his brothel? Upset that Becky had riled up his whores with religious talk?

Then she saw the answer in his worldly-wise eyes. "You care about her, don't you?"

He looked away, his lips clamped in a tight seam.

He wasn't as old as Lottie had originally thought. Maybe early thirties. But there was a hardness about him that made him appear older, as if harsh experience had aged him prematurely, replacing youth with weary cynicism. Would that happen someday to the farm-boy-ranger, too? Would the hard life of a lawman dampen the fire she'd seen in his clear blue eyes?

"Very much," Mr. Juno said, snapping her back to attention.

When he faced her again, she saw a man she could like, possibly even trust, and one who might be good for Becky.

"I don't want to see her hurt, Miss Weyland. That's all."

"I don't, either." Lottie smiled, an idea forming. "But she's at loose ends right now, and looking for something to hold on to. If you want to help her, you might offer her a job—not upstairs," she hurriedly added. "I understand you serve food. Maybe she could work in the kitchen. She's a good cook. Or teach her to deal. I've heard some of the gambling palaces in Dallas have female dealers." And since Becky was in the saloon all the time, anyway, it wouldn't hurt to give her something better to do than flirt with cowboys. "Keep her busy, Mr. Juno. Eventually, the reverend will head to greener pastures."

"Just Juno." He thought for a moment, his dark eyes fixed on a point beyond her shoulder. Then he nodded. "Makes sense. I appreciate the help, Miss Weyland. And I never forget a favor."

"Just Lottie," she said, feeling as if she'd made a powerful ally in the most unlikely of places.

Chapter 3

The days marched on, cooler now as they neared the middle of October. Isolated showers brought on a flurry of last-minute growth in vegetable and flower gardens before the cool nights of fall settled in.

Lottie sensed change—not only in the weather, but in herself, as well. She felt restless and vaguely discontented, as if she was waiting for something she could neither name nor describe.

Nights were long and lonely. As she lay listening to mice scurry and crickets chirp in tempo to the distant plinking of the piano over at the Spotted Dog Saloon, her thoughts often turned to the farm-boy-ranger, and whether he was still alive or if an outlaw's bullet had stolen the glow from his beautiful blue eyes. Did he remember the girl who had tried to help him? Did he think of her as much as she thought of him?

Her preoccupation with him was probably a reflection of her solitary life, always living on the fringes of other people's lives. Yet in the dark stillness of those lonely nights, she wondered what it would be like to have someone of her very own. To have a man show interest in her, kiss her, smile at her the way Mr. Brackett smiled at his wife. Idle thoughts that left her restless and yearning.

But the worst nights were when Grandpa invaded her dreams and she would awaken breathless with fear, dreading the retribution God would exact for what had happened on that terrible day over three years ago.

One week drifted into two, and the sameness of her days added to the restlessness of her nights as she waited for something to change.

Her eighteenth birthday came. Mrs. B. baked her a cake, and Becky gave her a length of green ribbon that she said brought out the green in her greenish-yellow eyes. Becky dropped by less often, spending most of her time at the saloon where she had quickly settled in, doubling as cook and faro dealer. She loved it, and the patrons loved her. Reverend Lindz was less enthusiastic, but managed to keep up his spirits by gambling for God and drinking his guilt away.

Juno continued to watch over Becky and her preacher, which Becky found irksome. But he paid her well, and she was able to quit working for the crab and still pay rent to Mrs. Ledbetter's brother so she could stay in the house. She helped defray the cost by renting out the other bedroom to one of Juno's whores who had gotten pregnant. Juno paid the girl's rent, which surprised Lottie. Most brothel owners would have booted her out since she could no longer work. Or maybe it was his way of protecting Becky's reputation by ensuring she had a chaperone—even if it was a pregnant whore—and making sure the townspeople knew she wasn't staying overnight at the saloon. Whatever his reasons, as far as Lottie was concerned, it was another mark in his favor.

Seeing Becky better herself gave Lottie ideas about improving her own situation. She couldn't stock shelves and sleep in a storeroom forever. The future she dreamed of wouldn't happen on the tiny nest egg she was building. She had to do something.

Early one cool day toward the end of October, she donned her Sunday dress and gloves, took extra care shoving her unruly light brown waves beneath her Sunday bonnet, and marched across the street to the People's Bank of Greenbroke.

"I'd like to see Mr. Griffin," she told the sour-faced, middle-aged man with a permanent squint and a blackened front tooth, who sat at a desk outside the bank owner's office.

"He's busy."

Lottie glanced through the open door behind him. Griffin was dozing in his chair, heels propped on his desk. "He doesn't look busy."

"I can assure you he is."

"Doing what?"

The squint narrowed to a tiny slit.

"I just need a moment of his time."

"He doesn't want to be disturbed."

"You're certain?"

"I am."

"I'll check." And before he could stop her, Lottie rounded his desk and darted through the open door, shutting it behind her with a bang that brought Griffin's feet thudding to the floor and his rotund body bolting upright in his chair.

"Good day, sir. I hope I'm not disturbing you?"

Griffin righted his spectacles and squinted in confusion. "Miss Weyland?"

"I know how valuable your time is, so I'll be quick." Fluffing her skirts, she settled into the chair in front of his desk. "I'm good with numbers," she said without preamble. "I've been doing the books at Brackett's Market for a couple of years now. Have you ever found a mistake in the tallies I deposit?"

"Well, no . . . but . . ." He glanced at the closed door. "Where's Humphries?"

"And have the Bracketts ever offered a complaint about my work?"

Realizing no help was forthcoming, Griffin sighed and rubbed his hands over his face, disturbing his lacquered mustache and knocking his spectacles askew. "Not that I'm aware of," he said, patting everything back in place.

"So you know I'm competent. And trustworthy."

"I do, Miss Weyland." Sitting back in the chair, he laced pudgy fingers over his round belly. A look of regret crossed his face. "Is this about a job? Because if it is—"

"It isn't."

"I would hire you in a minute if I could afford another employee."

"Thank you, sir, I appreciate that. But I don't want your money. I want your knowledge. And your recommendation."

No longer half-asleep, he sat forward, interest sparking in his bleary eyes. "Recommendation for what?"

"I'm starting a bookkeeping business." It was an idea she had toyed with for some time. She liked doing books for the Bracketts, and she was good at it. Why not turn something she enjoyed into a business? "But I'll need your help."

He sat back again. "If this is about a loan—"

"It isn't."

"Then what?" He scratched his balding head. "I don't understand."

"In addition to the bookkeeping business, I want to learn how to invest. I figure you're the man to teach me."

His rapid blinking told her he was shocked by the idea of a woman in the investment business. And maybe a bit flattered that she had come to him.

"What I propose is a trade," she rushed on before he could interrupt with another reason why he wouldn't be able to help her. "I'll work for you two days a week without pay. In return, you'll teach me about stocks, bonds, railroad shares, and so forth."

More blinking. "I will?"

"We'll both benefit. You'll get an honest, hardworking employee for nothing, and I'll learn how to make my earnings grow. I figure it'll take about six months."

"Six months?" A smile peeked beneath the corners of his gray mustache. "Is that all?"

"Meanwhile, I'll be seeing what other businesses might need a bookkeeper. That's where your recommendation comes in." Lottie let out a deep breath and clasped her shaking hands in her lap. "What do you say?"

"Well . . ."

"I can start next Tuesday. On trial, if you'd like. Or I could—"

"Fine." Chuckling, he raised his hands in surrender. "You win, Miss Weyland. Tuesday it is, then."

"You won't regret it, sir."

"I hope not."

Lottie sniffed at Humphries on her way out and refrained from skipping back to the store.

She'd done it.

She had a plan, prospects, and would soon have her own business.

Her grand future was on the way.

The first business she approached was the Spotted Dog Saloon. Mr. Juno had told her he never forgot a favor. She hoped he remembered that.

She went early in the morning, surmising that most of the gamblers, drinkers, and upstairs patrons would have departed by then. But just in case, she went to the back door and entered through the kitchen, as she had seen Becky do several times in the past. Voices drifted down the hall from the front of the establishment. Gathering her courage, she headed that way.

The hallway was narrow, unadorned, and surprisingly clean. The chair rail on the polished wainscoting was free of dust; the plank floor was swept clean. Beneath the masculine odors of whiskey and sweat and tobacco smoke lay the clean scent of lemon oil and a dash of flowery perfume. She continued past several closed doors. The rooms behind them were silent, except for one, from which came the faint sound of snoring.

The voices grew louder, punctuated now and then by soft feminine laughter. Fortified with a deep breath, Lottie stepped through the opening into the main room, then stopped and looked around.

Tables dotted the large open space. The piano she heard in the still of the night sat silently in one corner. Brass cuspidors stood here and there along the floor, and ornate brass lanterns hung from the painted ceiling. Under the morning sunlight slanting through the front windows, everything sparkled and gleamed, and not a single cobweb dangled overhead. If this was a place of wickedness and vice, it was certainly well-kept.

A broad-shouldered Negro man stood behind a long counter, wiping a rag over the polished wooden surface. A mirror spanned the wall behind him, framed on one side by shelves containing tiny glasses and bigger glasses, and on the other, by whiskey bottles of various shapes and sizes. Above it hung a lurid painting of a woman reclining on a couch. What clothing she wore didn't hide much of her ample form. She seemed to be smiling down into the room with an expression of vague contempt, although that might have been the way the morning light struck the canvas.

Suddenly aware that the voices had stopped, Lottie turned to find three women in various stages of undress staring at her from a corner table. Two were young and pretty in a brassy, overblown way. The third looked older, sporting improbable red hair and tired blue eyes.

"You lost?"

Lottie tried not to stare at the speaker, a pretty brunette in a lacy corset and thin chemise that exposed most of her bosom. Was that how men expected women to dress? She wouldn't dare. "I've come to see Mr. Juno."

"He know you're coming?"

"No."

The blonde beside her, who wore a garish patterned robe over her unmentionables, gave Lottie's made-over Sunday dress a sharp look. "You're not a Bible thumper, are you?"

Lottie shook her head.

"If you're with the Temperance Union," the older red-headed woman said around a yawn, "you're wasting your time. He won't see you."

"I came about employment."

Silence. Even the Negro stopped wiping the counter.

"But not upstairs," Lottie added in a rush. "In back. Or . . . wherever." Realizing she was only making it worse, she shut her mouth.

Chuckling, the redhead motioned to the Negro. "Get Juno, will you, Henry?"

"He sleeping."

"Wake him up."

"He be mad."

Lottie's courage deserted her. "Don't trouble him. I can come back later."

But Henry was already disappearing down the hall.

Silence. Aware that the women were staring at her, Lottie pretended great interest in the décor of the room, carefully avoiding the painting over the mirror.

"What's your name, honey?" the older woman asked in a kindly voice.

"Lottie Weyland."

"You're Becky's friend!" The blonde gave a big grin. "She talks about you. I'm Sugar." She pointed to the brunette, adding, "That's Belle, and Red is the redhead. Sally's still sleeping."

Lottie wasn't sure about the proper etiquette when being introduced to whores, so she just smiled and nodded. They smiled back. No matter what Grandpa had said, they didn't seem that evil, even if they were whores. She pointed toward the tables. "Is that where Becky deals?"

"Most nights. Unless she's cooking or chasing after the preacher."

"What are you doing in here, Miss Weyland?" a sleep-roughened voice said from the other side of the room.

Lottie turned to see Mr. Juno standing in the hall doorway, shirt half-buttoned, feet bare, dark hair poking out every which way. And frowning.

"What's wrong?" he demanded. "Is Becky all right?"

"I haven't seen her today, but I assume she's fine."

He let out a deep breath. Dragging a hand through his mussed hair, he looked around as though trying to get his bearings. "What time is it?"

"A little past eight, I believe."

"In the morning?"

Lottie nodded, ignoring the snickers behind her. She might have found his befuddlement amusing, too, if his state of undress hadn't left her so flustered. "I'm sorry to wake you, but as long as you're up, I'd like to talk to you, if I may."

"I haven't even had coffee yet."

"I'll wait."

A disgruntled look. "Talk to me about what?"

"I have a proposition." Hearing more snickers from her audience, Lottie added, "A *business* proposition."

"Hell." He scratched his head and muttered something under his breath, then turned to Henry, who had resumed his position behind the counter. "Give me a few minutes, then bring her—and coffee—to my office."

After he disappeared down the hall, Lottie let out the breath she'd been holding. "That wasn't so bad, was it?" she said to the faces staring back at her. "He didn't seem mad at all."

Which sent the ladies, and even Henry, into hoots of laughter.

Several minutes later, Henry deposited her, a straight-backed chair, and a mug of coffee in Mr. Juno's office—a room crowded with overflowing bookcases, a single upholstered chair beside a small coal stove, a coat rack, and a big, battered desk. No paintings, no knickknacks, no personal items of any kind other than a faded tintype of a woman and child on a bookshelf.

A lonely room for a man who lived a solitary life amidst the chaos of a busy saloon. Rather sad, really.

He waited until she was seated and he'd gulped down most of the coffee before he spoke—and not in a particularly friendly tone. "What's so important that you would come here at eight in the morning?"

"I'm sorry I disturbed you, Mr. Juno. I'd hoped by coming early I would avoid—"

"You shouldn't have come here at all. And it's just Juno."

"Why not?"

"It's a whorehouse."

"You let Becky come."

"That's different."

And she could guess why. But she hadn't come to discuss Becky or his obvious feelings for her. "I'm starting a business."

"Hell." He took another swallow, then sat back, the long fingers of one hand idly turning the mug in circles atop the desk. "Okay, I'll bite. Doing what?"

"Bookkeeping."

"Bookkeeping." He said it the way Griffin had, as if a woman in business was on a par with a talking mule.

"And investing."

That dark, focused gaze made her hands sweat. Eager to fill the lengthening silence, she explained. "I'm very good with numbers, you see. And Mr. Griffin at the bank is teaching me how to invest. I know you're already a rich man, but with wise investments, you could increase—"

"What makes you think I'm rich?"

"You do own the only saloon and brothel in Greenbroke," she reminded him with studied patience. "Between the whiskey and food sales, gambling, and activities in the rooms upstairs, you must be doing very well."

His shoulders stiffened. His face lost all expression. "I let rooms, Miss Weyland. What the women do in those rooms is up to them. Other than what they pay me for rent and board, they keep what they earn."

"Oh."

"I am not a pimp."

Shame sent heat rushing into her face. But before she could apologize, an idea came to her. "What do they do with the money they earn?"

He made an impatient gesture. "Buy fripperies, face paint, I don't know. Nor do I care, so long as they pay me."

"So they might be interested in investing, too?" She hurried on, the idea taking flight. "If we pooled our money, we could broaden our investments and minimize our risks. Mr. Griffin taught me that last week."

"Maybe I should hire Griffin, then."

"I charge less. Especially to those who also hire me to keep their books."

He let out a gust of air. It had the sound of surrender. "You certainly are persistent, aren't you, Miss Weyland?"

"I try." Flush with triumph, she grinned. "Shall I start on your books today?" When he didn't respond, an awful thought arose. "You do have books, don't you? Receipts? Invoices for whiskey and food? A tally of gambling wins and losses?"

"Sort of." Leaning forward, he pulled out a desk drawer.

From what Lottie could see over the desk, it was stuffed with papers—IOUs, bank deposit slips, wadded receipts, and who knew what else. "Those are your books?"

He smirked in challenge. "Still want my business?"

"Of course."

His smirk faded. "I'll get a box."

Over the following days, Lottie made her rounds of the most promising business establishments in Greenbroke. Several had started up after the spur line had come through a couple of years ago. The fact that they were still in business was a sign of Greenbroke's slowly growing economy. Frances Seaforth of Fashions by Fanny agreed to take her on trial. So did Ralph Krebs at the dry goods store. The small auction barn at the edge of town declined, as did the blacksmith, the repair shop, the newspaper, and the Western Union and Wells Fargo offices, all of which had a single owner/employee, limited business, and no interest in investing.

The Petersons, who ran the Greenbroke Hotel and Restaurant across from the depot, were more enthusiastic. Theirs was a small establishment—four rooms upstairs and a three-table restaurant downstairs. They catered mostly to railroad workers, itinerant salesmen, and drifters who couldn't afford the price of an entire night upstairs at the Spotted Dog. The young couple was delighted to hand over their books, since Mrs. Peterson was pregnant again and Mr. Peterson was "not so good with numbers."

Lottie didn't try the barber shop. The owner, Lester Eldridge, who was also the local dentist and mortician, gave her the shudders.

She now had five clients, including Mr. Juno—Juno—and the Bracketts.

It was a start.

Chapter 4

Soon Lottie was so busy she didn't have time to feel lonely or discontented. But she was making progress. And money. Which Mr. Griffin helped her invest as soon as it came into her hands.

And her nest egg grew.

November came in on the heels of a blue norther that whistled through the eaves of the storeroom and had Lottie shivering in her cot. Four days later, the temperature edged back into the pleasantly warm—a short reprieve before the next storm. It was time to start thinking about a new place to stay. After three years of cold winters and stuffy summers in a crowded storeroom, she could finally afford to rent a real bedroom.

Becky's boarder, Sally, with just over three months to go in her pregnancy, had given no indication of her plans after the baby came. If she decided to go back to the Spotted Dog, Lottie could rent her room. But if Sally did go back to whoring, what would happen to the baby?

That was the question that plagued Becky more and more as Sally's belly grew. "It doesn't seem right raising a kid in a whorehouse," she told Lottie one evening after a quick dinner at the Ledbetter house before she had to leave for the Spotted Dog and her dealing duties.

Lottie carried her plate to the sink. "Maybe she'll marry her cowboy. She seems pretty taken with him."

Several days ago, Bar M riders had brought a small herd of late calves to the auction barn since it was doubtful the young animals would make it through the winter. A raw-boned redhead with more freckles than sense who had been one of Sally's Saturday night regulars before her pregnancy, had come by to see her. They'd been stepping out every evening since, whenever the cowboy was in town.

"He won't raise another man's kid," Becky muttered in disgust. "Told her so himself."

Together they tidied the kitchen, then Becky lifted her coat off a peg by the back door and pulled it on. "She hasn't told Juno what she plans to do, either."

"Maybe she hasn't decided yet." Lottie followed her out the door. As they crossed the alley that ran behind Brackett's, she worried that her friend was becoming overly attached to a baby that wasn't even born yet. Becky had a generous and forgiving nature—evidenced by her attachment to the reverend—but this was different. Taking on a baby would change her life forever.

The thought came that the farm-boy-ranger would father beautiful children. Maybe he already had. Maybe he was married and had a passel of kids. She frowned at that, then remembered that men of the Frontier Battalion couldn't marry. That made her feel better. "Maybe Sally will go to San Francisco," she ventured. "She told me whores make a lot more money out there than they do here."

"And take the baby with her?"

Lottie shrugged. She didn't know Sally well, and what she did know wasn't that favorable. It was kind of Becky to let the girl stay here, especially when some of the townsfolk questioned the propriety of it. But Sally had done little to repay that kindness. Nor did she seem particularly interested in the baby she carried. She had yet to try out names, hadn't prepared a single thing for the infant's arrival, and now was out every night doing God knows what instead of eating properly and getting her rest. "You don't think Sally would abandon it or give it away, do you?" Lottie asked when they reached the stoop behind the market.

Anger tightened Becky's features. "If she does, I'll keep it."

"What do you know about taking care of a baby?"

"I was the oldest of seven, remember? So it fell to me to take care of the younger ones. And even though we all flew the coop as soon as we could, we're mostly good people. Because of me. So I sure know more about babies than Sally does."

Lottie was surprised by the grim determination behind Becky's words. "You mean it, don't you? You'd take Sally's baby as your own."

"You bet. If she doesn't want that baby, I'll keep it myself."

Which made Lottie wonder what it would be like to have a baby of her own. Maybe one with bright blue eyes.

Sally was thrilled with the idea of handing her baby over to Becky.

Juno wasn't. He tried several times to talk Becky out of it, but that only brought out the stubbornness in the feisty blonde.

So naturally, he turned to Lottie. "You've got to talk her out of it," he told her early one afternoon when she came by the Spotted Dog to go over his receipts—such as they were.

"I've tried. She won't listen." Thunking the ledger marked DOG on top of the bar, Lottie opened it to a page lined with neat columns of numbers. "See this?" She pointed at figures marked in red.

"She's young." He frowned thoughtfully out the front window. "She'll have her own babies someday."

"And you'll go bankrupt if you keep taking IOUs when you have no intention of collecting."

"She doesn't need to take on some whore's bastard."

Lottie slapped the book closed. "That's an awful thing to say! Luckily, Becky doesn't see it that way." And luckily none of his "renters" were in the room, either, or they would surely have been offended.

He finally looked at her. "She really wants this baby?"

"She wants *a* baby. And since neither the reverend—nor anybody else"—she paused to give him a pointed glare—"has offered to marry her and give her one, she's decided this one will do nicely. And without the bother of a husband. Now, are you going to stop taking IOUs, or not?"

He glowered at her.

But she knew him well enough now to not be intimidated. "Well?"

"I'd lose half of my customers."

"The half that doesn't pay, so where's the loss? And you'll save big on whiskey orders."

"What if the others stop coming around?"

"Where would they go? You're the only saloon in Greenbroke."

A tall figure wearing a dark duster moved through the split front door. Lottie and Juno glanced his way, but with the shadow cast by the brim of his dark Stetson and the glare of light behind him, the man wasn't recognizable.

"We don't open until four," Juno called over to him.

The man continued toward the other end of the counter. Eyeing the mostly naked lady smirking down at him, he began unbuttoning his duster. "Mind if I have a drink while I wait? I've come a long way."

Pushy fellow, Lottie thought. Then she frowned. There was something about him . . .

He took off his hat and set it on the bar, and she saw the thin scar stretching from his eyebrow, past his temple, and back into the black hair along the side of his head.

Her breath caught.

She grabbed Juno's arm. "I know him," she whispered. She nodded toward the circle-star badge pinned to the man's shirt. "His name is Ty. He was one of the rangers in the shoot-out last summer."

Juno glanced back at the stranger then motioned to the Negro polishing glasses behind the bar. "Set him up, Henry. First one on the house."

"My thanks," the stranger—Ty—said.

He'd changed. In three short months, he'd become less of a farm boy, and more of a man, his jaw as square as she remembered, the blue of his eyes still a shocking contrast to his sun-browned face, his shoulders just as broad but now starting to thicken with muscle.

But he still hadn't learned to smile, she noticed.

Juno leaned over the counter and retrieved an empty whiskey box marked *Forty Rod*. "I'll get this week's receipts. And I'll put up a sign saying no more IOUs. But if customers stop coming in," he added as he walked toward the hall, "I'll quit paying you."

"No problem there," she called after him. "You haven't paid me anything yet, anyway."

He stopped. "I haven't?"

"Nary a penny."

"Hell." Retracing his steps, he pulled from his vest pocket a small wad of paper money. He dropped it on the counter. "That should cover most of it."

Lottie studied the bills. "*All* of it, and then some."

"You earned it." With a dismissive wave, he disappeared down the hall.

Henry started on another tray of glasses.

Lottie slipped the money into her skirt pocket then became aware of the young ranger studying her. She gave him a tentative smile, wondering if he remembered her.

"I know you," he finally said. "You're Lottie."

Warmth spread through her. "And you're Ty. I heard the gray-haired ranger call you that." She smiled.

He didn't. But continued to lean against the bar, his dark brows drawn into a disapproving line above his blue eyes. "You work here?"

"Sometimes."

"You're a whore?"

Her jaw dropped. Henry stopped drying. It was a moment

before anger gave her the strength to speak. "Of course not! Why would you say such a thing?"

"I saw the man pay you."

"That means I'm a whore?"

He gestured to the room with a hand the size of a dinner plate. "This is a brothel, isn't it? Why else would you be here if you weren't a whore?"

"Because she's my bookkeeper, you peckerhead!" Juno *plunk*ed the whiskey box on the counter with enough force to send several receipts flying. "And you're done here. Get out!"

The ranger slowly straightened. His frown gave way to bafflement. "She's a bookkeeper?"

Why was that so hard for men to grasp?

"Does she *look* like a whore?"

Those sharp blue eyes swept her from head to toe. "Not in that getup."

Lottie looked down at her brown dress, one of Mrs. Brackett's made-over castoffs. Granted, it was a bit faded and woefully out of style, but it was clean and serviceable and she was grateful to have it. Who wanted to look like a whore, anyway?

"My apologies, ma'am."

Too little, too late. With a huff, Lottie snatched the box of receipts from the counter. She reminded Juno to put up a notice about the IOUs, then with a last glare at the ranger, whirled and marched out the door, desperate to escape before the burning in her eyes turned into tears.

To think she had once admired that man—had even harbored tender feelings toward him. Whore, indeed. She was sorry she had ever tried to help him.

———

"Been looking for you," Becky called later that afternoon when Lottie stepped out of Fashions by Fanny. "Whoa. Is that a new dress you're wearing?"

"It is." Lottie smoothed a hand over the green dimity. The fabric was more of a summer color and weight and wouldn't be much use in winter, but she thought the green suited her eyes. Plus, it had been on sale. "You like it?"

"I do." Grinning, Becky stood back to make a thorough check. "I wonder if your ranger will like it, too." Seeing Lottie's flush, she laughed. "I was going to the store to tell you he was in town. But I'm guessing you already know."

"I talked to him earlier. And found him to be the rudest man alive. I hope I never set eyes on him again."

"Then we'd best get moving." Grabbing her arm, Becky yanked her toward the gap that ran between the dress shop and the dry goods store. "He's headed this way."

"He is?" Glancing over her shoulder, Lottie saw the ranger walking toward them with determined strides. Suddenly, she was the one dragging Becky along. "Hurry," she whispered. "I don't want to talk to him."

"Why not?"

"He called me a whore."

"No!"

"He did. And just because he saw me in the Spotted Dog talking to Juno. Juno was furious."

"Ma'am?" a deep voice called from behind them.

Lottie lengthened her stride.

Becky struggled to keep up.

"Miss Lottie?"

"Hadn't you ought to hear what he has to say?" Becky whispered.

"Why?"

"Because it would be cowardly not to."

"Drat." She released Becky's arm and stopped. "Go on, I'll talk to you later." Crossing her arms, Lottie turned to confront the man who had been following them. "What do you want?"

"To apologize."

Why did he look so irritated? She was the one who'd been insulted. "You already did." She started to turn.

His voice brought her back. "And, to thank you."

"For what?"

This was the first time they had faced each other while

standing and she hadn't realized how big he was. She was
almost five-and-a-half feet tall, herself, and it wasn't often
her eyes were level with a man's shoulders.

"For trying to help me after I was shot."

"Anyone would have done the same."

"But anyone didn't. Only you."

He had a nice voice. Deep and mellow, with a slow drawl
that marked him a Texan, but not enough twang to make
him sound straight off the farm.

He shifted his weight, stared down at his dusty, surprisingly large boots. "And I, uh, wanted to say I made a foolish
mistake earlier and I'm sorry for it."

The pretty phrases had a rehearsed ring to them, but
Lottie nodded anyway, just to put the ordeal behind her.
"Fine." Again, she started to turn.

This time he stopped her with a hand near her shoulder.
A hand that completely encompassed her upper arm. "Could
I buy you dinner to make up for it?" Not a very gracious
invitation, since he was frowning when he issued it.

She gave his hand a pointed look.

He released her arm.

"No."

If possible, his frown deepened. "You won't have dinner
with me?"

"No."

"Why not?"

Did he truly think she would enjoy a meal spent with a
man who didn't smile, barely looked at her, and acted as if
every word he spoke was dragged out of him by force? "It's
not necessary."

Ignoring her refusal, he pressed on. This time, there was
a hint of desperation in his tone. "I hear the restaurant at the
hotel sets a fair table."

"Passable. But as I said, it's not necessary."

He let out a deep breath and scratched the whiskers on
his square jaw. "Well, that's the thing. It *is* necessary if I
want to go into the Spotted Dog again."

And suddenly it made sense—his irritation, the forced

words, his inability to even look at her. "Juno's making you do this, isn't he?"

"Well . . . he does own the only saloon in town."

"And brothel."

At least he had the grace to blush.

She didn't know whether to laugh or hit him with her reticule. And maybe hit Juno, too. The absurdity of the situation put the Devil in her mind. If the ranger was being browbeaten into taking her to dinner then, by God, she'd make sure he had a miserable time of it. He didn't like talking to her? Well then she'd *make* him talk by asking him every question she could think of. Then she'd go after Juno.

"Fine. The hotel it is." Smiling through clenched teeth, she tucked her hand at his elbow. "Shall we?"

He wasn't a talker, was even worse as a smiler, and wasn't anything like the handsome hero her imagination had painted him to be. But his arm felt solid and warm beneath her hand, and his sturdy form made her feel almost dainty.

She was glad she'd bought a new dress.

———

As he towed the woman called Lottie down the boardwalk, Ranger Ty Benton tried to figure out what had just happened. He'd thought he was off the hook then suddenly she'd changed her mind. Now he was stuck trying to talk to a woman he hardly knew, when all he wanted was to knock back a few drinks, look over the whores, then get some sleep.

He wasn't much of a womanizer. Mostly, he did his job and stayed to himself. Not that he didn't like women. He liked them fine. But he steered clear of women like the one beside him because they didn't fit into the ranger lifestyle. The Frontier Battalion didn't allow married men or those with children. There were already too many widows and fatherless children running around Texas since the war, and being a ranger assigned to patrol the Nueces Strip carried a high death rate.

What in the hell was he going to talk to her about?

"What are you doing in Greenbroke?" she asked, jarring him back to attention.

"I was on my way to pick up a prisoner but got word he died in an escape attempt, so I got off the train here."

"What had he done?"

"Robbed a bank."

She studied him for a moment, her head tipped slightly to one side. It made him nervous. What did she see when she looked at him that way?

"Do you like being a ranger?" she finally asked.

"Most of the time."

"But not always."

"Not always." Luckily, his clipped tone discouraged further questions and they walked in silence the rest of the way to the Greenbroke Hotel. But after they'd taken seats by a big window and the pregnant waitress had taken their orders, Miss Lottie resumed her interrogation.

"What would you do if you weren't a ranger?"

"Try ranching."

"That's a costly undertaking. Land is expensive."

He'd forgotten she was a bookkeeper. "My uncle left me a few acres up near the panhandle."

"How many acres?"

"Eight thousand, or so. You sure ask a lot of questions."

She smiled. It was less disturbing than the smile she'd given him earlier, but still made him uneasy. "Do my questions bother you?"

He shrugged, unwilling to admit they did. Her curiosity put him off. Plus, he hadn't used so many words in weeks, especially to a woman—paid or not.

"I know your first name is Ty. What's your last?"

Those pretty hazel eyes bored into him with unnerving focus. She would have made a fine interrogator. "Benton."

"Is Ty short for Tyson? Tyler?" That smile again. "Or maybe you were named after the corrupt Roman emperor, Tiberius?"

That surprised him. Not many people knew about Roman emperors. She was smart, no doubt about it. He would have admired her for it if she hadn't been so nosy. "Tyree. It's the name of the island in Scotland where my mother was born."

"She must have been homesick."

"I suppose."

"Do you have brothers and sisters?"

"One brother. He died in the war."

"Parents?"

"They're dead, too. Does it seem hot in here to you?"

Luckily their food came and the grilling stopped for a while. By the time they pushed their plates aside, he'd come up with a question of his own. "Why did you decide to become a bookkeeper?"

"I like working with numbers. How do you think Hayes is doing?"

"Who?"

"Our president."

He was starting to sweat. "Doing about what?"

She laughed in genuine amusement, although Ty had no idea what was so funny. Dropping her napkin beside her plate, she picked up her drawstring bag and held it in her lap. "I see my questions have made you uncomfortable, Ranger Benton. I'm glad for it. Perhaps you'll remember this wretched evening the next time you give a woman false apologies and ask her to dinner when you obviously don't want her to accept."

He blinked in astonishment. She'd played him, and so thoroughly he wondered if there were puppet strings coming out of his back. "You thought it was wretched?"

"You didn't?"

She had him there. "My apology was sincere. Both of them."

Rising, she smiled down at him. A real smile that brought a sparkle to eyes that nearly matched her dress, and a flush to her pretty face.

Remembering his manners, he stood, too.

"Then I appreciate the apologies, Ranger Benton. Both of them. And the meal . . . if not the company. I'll be sure to tell Juno you did your duty. No need to walk me back. Good evening and safe travels."

He watched her walk away, so bemused he didn't realize he stood there grinning like a fool until the waitress gave him an odd look.

Chapter 5

The following morning, Lottie was transferring pumpkins from bushel baskets into a bin outside the market's front door when she saw Ranger Benton coming down the boardwalk.

He walked with determined strides, coming down hard on his heels, hips rolling, wide shoulders swaying with every step. Almost a swagger. A horseman's gait. When he spotted her, he quickened his pace.

She finished emptying one basket and started on another, wondering why he was still in town, and why breathing was suddenly so difficult.

"We're starting over," he announced, coming to a stop beside her.

Lottie set another pumpkin on the pile then straightened.

He loomed over her, a tall dark form backlit by the morning sun, close enough that she could smell coffee, horses, a faint trace of sweat.

"Starting what over?"

"This. Us. And this time no one's making me ask you."

"Ask me what?"

"To dinner."

Was this a joke? Pushing a loose wave from her eyes, she squinted up at him. He didn't appear to be jesting, although how could she tell since the man never smiled? "You're asking me to dinner. Again."

"I am."

"With no threats from Juno."

"All on my own."

"Why?"

He spread those big hands in a palms-up gesture. "To get it right. I might have handled it poorly last time."

"Might have?" Hiding a smile, she added the last two pumpkins to the bin, then dusted her hands. "You'll probably leave on the train tomorrow, Ranger Benton, so why go to the bother?"

He almost smiled. She could tell by the crinkle at the corners of his eyes and the slight twitch of his lips. "So you'll have fond memories of me?"

She snorted. "Don't put yourself out on my behalf." Picking up the empty bushel baskets, she went back inside.

"I'm not trying to court you, Miss Lottie," he called after her through the open door. "Just ask you to dinner."

At the front counter, Mrs. Brackett and Mrs. Jarvis stopped chatting to stare at the ranger. Then at Lottie. Then grin.

Oh, Lord. Now the gossip will start. Defeated, yet oddly not that upset about it, Lottie gave the man in the doorway a backhand wave. "Fetch me at seven, then. And wear a smile if you have one."

As soon as he left, she asked Mrs. Brackett to excuse her for a minute then rushed over to Fanny's to look for a new dress. She wasn't sure why—after their dinner tonight, she would probably never see Ty Benton again. But for some reason she wanted to look her best when they parted. Maybe to send him off with fond memories of *her.*

She knew nothing about attracting men. In fact, most of them steered clear as soon as they learned she could read and write and work numbers. So why would Ranger Benton show interest? And why was she so pleased that he had?

Because she was loco, that's why.

She wished Becky was awake so she could ask her advice. The pretty blonde could twist men around her finger with little more than a smile and a jiggle of those bouncy breasts. But Becky rarely rose before noon after a late night dealing at the Spotted Dog.

Lottie would have to charm the ranger all by herself—which must not be too hard, if he had already come back for an encore. Wondering if she'd have anything left to invest after this day was over, Lottie pushed open the door of Fashions by Fanny.

An hour later she left, her new and very expensive dress wrapped and tucked beneath her arm. It was the prettiest thing Lottie had ever owned—a deep gold poplin with tiny embroidered flowers on the ruffled ivory collar, cuffs, and underskirt that showed below the hem. Miss Fanny said the color brought out the highlights in her hair and gave an amber cast to her hazel eyes. Lottie wished she had new slippers, too, instead of her worn walking shoes, but the store had nothing suitable in her size. Hopefully the ranger would be too dazzled by her dress to check her feet . . . and well he should, since it had cost her almost a month's wages.

After hanging it on a peg in the storeroom, she spent the rest of the morning avoiding Mrs. Brackett's questions by tallying receipts and checking invoices in the back room.

And fretting.

It still puzzled her that the ranger had invited her to dinner a second time—he certainly hadn't seemed to enjoy their first outing. He must have realized she'd asked all those questions just to needle him. Was tonight his chance for payback?

If so, she'd be ready. She liked a challenge.

He arrived at precisely seven o'clock. Through the thin walls of the storeroom, Lottie heard his deep voice greeting the Bracketts, and suddenly all her doubts rose to the surface.

What if she was overdressed? Or her upswept hairdo was too fancy—he'd only ever seen it coiled up in a braid. What if he thought she'd spent all this time and money fixing up just to impress him? Or even worse, what if he wasn't impressed?

She felt like vomiting.

Instead, she ran a trembling hand over her hair one last time, pinched her cheeks for color, and fluffed her skirts. Then, pressing a hand against her stomach to calm the butterflies, she stepped into the store, hoping her smile didn't look as shaky as it felt.

———

Ty wasn't sure what he expected . . . certainly not the vision moving toward him. Miss Lottie had surprised him again. Last night she had looked real pretty in that green dress. But tonight, she was beautiful. Maybe because this time her smile carried more shyness than anger. Or because the light from the overhead lantern shimmered off her hair, giving it an almost golden glow. Or because she had bought a new dress just for him. He knew it was new because the price tag was still pinned beneath one arm. He wasn't sure what had changed between yesterday and today or why she had softened toward him. But it pleased him.

She pleased him.

"Evening, Miss Lottie," he said with a tug on the brim of his Stetson. "You're looking right pretty tonight."

"Thank you." She looked him over and smiled her approval. "You clean up nicely yourself."

He was glad she'd noticed. He would have been disappointed if his bath, fresh shave, and clean clothes had gone unnoticed.

This morning, when he'd asked her to dinner a second time, he had only intended to show her that he could behave better than he had the previous night. She'd set him down soundly. Not that he didn't deserve it—probably—but he wanted to leave her with a better impression of him.

And leave her he would. He already had a ticket in his pocket for tomorrow's train to Austin. But that didn't mean he couldn't have an enjoyable dinner tonight, did it?

Before he could escort her to the door, Mrs. Brackett pushed forward, a worried look on her round face. "Could I speak to you for a moment, Lottie?"

"Now?"

"It won't take long." With a quick smile in Ty's direction, as if to assure him their chat wouldn't be about him, Mrs. Brackett pulled Lottie behind a tall cabinet displaying guns and knives.

After a rapid, whispered exchange, which he and Mr. Brackett tried to ignore, the ladies reappeared . . . Lottie showing high color, but minus the price tag.

"I hope you don't mind eating at the hotel again," Ty said, trying to put her at ease.

"Not at all."

"Good." He offered his elbow.

Leaving the Bracketts grinning after them like possums eating persimmons, they finally escaped to the boardwalk.

"What am I to call you? Ranger Benton? Mr. Benton?"

"Ty."

"All right, Ty Benton."

It occurred to him he didn't know her last name. But it was probably a bit late to admit that, so he stuck with Miss Lottie. It suited her.

"The Bracketts seem a nice couple," he ventured as they headed toward the hotel.

"They are."

"Work for them long?"

"Over three years."

"You must have started pretty young."

"Fourteen. But a very capable fourteen."

Ty didn't doubt it. She was disturbingly capable now. "It's a nice night."

"Yes, it is."

"A little nippy, though. Winter's definitely on the way."

"You're right about that."

Having exhausted his range of meaningless conversation, Ty gave up. She didn't speak, either. It wasn't a comfortable, companionable silence, but rather the stiff reserve of two people who had last parted on a sour note, and now didn't know what to say to each other to get past it. Ty was starting to regret his impulse to ask her to dinner, and almost wished

she'd start with her questions again, just to give them something to argue about.

She must have felt the same way. When she finally spoke,
it was with the tone of someone trying to start something.
"I thought I asked you to wear a smile."

"You did."

"So why aren't you?"

"Say something amusing and I will."

He hadn't meant it to be funny, and was surprised when
she laughed out loud. But it broke the stilted mood, for which
Ty was grateful. He let out a deep breath and allowed his
shoulders to relax. Maybe the evening wouldn't be so bad,
after all. "What's your last name?"

"Weyland. Why do you sometimes not like being a
ranger?"

He gave her a look. "You're not fixing to pester me with
questions again, are you?"

"You could ask me questions," she suggested.

"I already did."

"My last name? That's all you're curious about?"

"I also asked if you'd worked for the Bracketts long."

She didn't respond.

Fearing another prolonged silence, he posed another question. "Did you grow up in Greenbroke?" Although he'd come
through Greenbroke occasionally on his runs between Austin
and northeast Texas, he didn't remember ever seeing her. But
then, whenever he was in town, he rarely strayed far from the
Greenbroke Hotel and the sheriff's office. And the saloon.

"Only since summer of '85."

"Your family still live here?"

"No. They never have."

"Ever?" He looked down at her in surprise, but she didn't
meet his gaze. "You came here alone? At fourteen?"

"You needn't make it sound like they booted me out. They
died. And I'd rather not talk about it, if you don't mind."

Ty wished he'd thought of saying that when she'd questioned him. But respecting her wishes, he moved on to another topic. "Why did you pick this town?"

"My grandfather had mentioned it a couple of times. He'd been through here years before and thought if ranching didn't work out, he'd come back here to teach. I came, instead."

"He was a rancher?"

She nodded with a wry smile. "Not a very good one. When he died, we were down to one horse and less than a dozen cows."

"How'd that happen?"

She shrugged. "The usual. Indians, rustlers, poor graze, and bitter water."

Ty knew how that went. He'd lost the family ranch to similar causes.

"Grandpa had been a teacher back east, but he'd always been fascinated with the West. When it looked like war was coming, he and my grandma moved to Texas. She died soon after. My mother and I moved here after my father went to fight the Yankees."

"Is your grandfather the one who taught you about Roman emperors and how to bookkeep?"

"Mostly. Mr. Brackett taught me some, too. What made you decide to be a ranger?"

"I didn't have anybody around to teach me to bookkeep. Here we are." Grateful to have the burden of conversation lifted from his shoulders, Ty held open the door into the restaurant of the Greenbroke Hotel.

———·———

After they'd settled at the same table where they'd dined the previous night and given their orders to Mrs. Peterson, Lottie was over most of her nervousness.

But not her curiosity.

Ranger Benton was making a concerted effort to be more sociable tonight, and she couldn't help but wonder why. At first, when he started asking so many questions, she'd thought he was paying her back for her interrogation of him. But every now and then, she caught a flash of genuine interest. Which only confused her more. "You're being very talkative tonight."

"I'm trying."

"That big an effort, is it?"

Again, he almost smiled. "Not as big as I thought it would be."

"I'm gratified to hear it." The man had a wickedly dry sense of humor. She liked that. And the intelligence behind it. "May I ask you a question?"

He raised one dark brow. "Could I stop you?"

"I'm curious about something you said last night."

He sat back, hands resting on his thighs, a wary look in his striking blue eyes. "What did I say?"

"You said you didn't always like being a ranger. I've been wondering why."

Instead of speaking, he looked out the window beside their table. She thought he wasn't going to answer. Then his gaze swung back to hers, and she saw a wealth of sadness in his eyes. "I don't always like command decisions."

"But you obey them, anyway."

"So far."

She waited for him to elaborate.

It was a long time before he did. "You probably heard about that business with Sam Bass in Round Rock last July."

Lottie nodded. "Rangers shot him after he'd gunned down that Williamson County lawman."

"Deputy Grimes. A good man." As he spoke, Ty idly toyed with the knife beside his plate, rolling it back and forth across the folded napkin. "What you probably didn't hear was how we made one of Bass's own men turn against him. Ever heard of Jim Murphy?"

"Was he a ranger?"

"One of Bass's men. We'd been tracking Bass and his gang for a while. When we learned Murphy's father lived in the area, we brought him in for questioning. He wasn't well." Ty quit fiddling with his knife and frowned out the window as if watching unpleasant memories unfold in his mind. "John Jones was commander of the Frontier Battalion back then. A hard leader with a stone for a heart. He decided not to let the sick man see a doctor until he answered his questions. But Murphy's father tried to protect his son by keeping his silence. So he got worse and worse. When Jones realized he couldn't break the old man, he decided to use his illness to break the son."

Lottie swallowed back her distaste. "How?"

"He sent word out that rangers had Jim Murphy's sick father and wouldn't allow him medical help unless Jim turned himself in."

No wonder Ty was upset. Lottie had heard whispers about questionable practices involving Leander McNelly, leader of the Frontier Battalion, and the brutal executions carried out in the lawless country along the Nueces River. But she'd hoped the rumors weren't true. That Ranger Benton might have been involved saddened her. "What did Murphy do?"

Ty's troubled expression became one of disgust. "What could he do? He didn't want his father to die, so he came in and told Jones what he wanted to know. That's how we found out Bass planned to rob the Williamson County Bank."

"Did the father go to the doctor then?"

He shrugged. "We didn't stay to find out. As soon as Jones got what he wanted, we left to set up an ambush. Deputy Grimes blundered into the middle of it and got himself killed. Then everybody started firing at once. Bass tried to make a run for it and caught a couple of bullets. We tracked him to a pasture west of town, but he died the next day. It was his twenty-seventh birthday." Ty let go a deep breath and shook his head. "Not our finest mission. But at least we put a killer in the ground, even if the way we went about it wasn't altogether aboveboard."

Lottie could see the episode had left a bitter taste in Ty's mouth, which spoke well of his honorable character. She knew what it was like to make hard choices. She'd faced the same with Grandpa. And even if setting that fire three years ago had been the right thing to do—and her only option—guilt still left a hole in her heart. She understood what Ty was going through.

Their food arrived, and she was glad to put the conversation behind them. Ty looked relieved, too. They ate without speaking. But it wasn't as awkward as previous silences between them had been and as the food on their plates disappeared, the somberness of the mood eased.

"That was delicious." Lottie leaned back with a sigh. "I don't know when I've enjoyed a meal—or the company—more."

"Me, too."

She looked up to find him studying her, the muscles in his cheeks bunching as he chewed. She saw the smile in his remarkable eyes, and was glad they would be parting on friendlier terms. But sad, too.

She liked Ranger Tyree Benton. She liked that he regretted his earlier treatment of her and wanted to do better this time. Liked that he was troubled by his commander's treatment of a sick man and his son. And she especially liked that he had remembered the girl who had tried to help him on that hot summer day months ago. She would miss him.

When they left the hotel a while later, a full hunter's moon hung in the night sky, haloed by lacy clouds that reflected back its pale glow. It had a lonesome feel to it, reminding Lottie that her time with Ty was almost over.

"Where do you live?" he asked when they neared Brackett's Market.

"In the storeroom."

"Here? At the market?" He seemed troubled by that.

"For now. I'll probably move soon."

They went around to the back stoop then stood in awkward silence for a moment. She studied him in the moonlight, wanting to remember every arc and plane of his chiseled face. A sense of loss stole over her. "One thing before you go," she said on impulse. "Will you smile for me?"

He studied her for a moment. Then in a voice so soft she scarcely heard it, he murmured, "I'll do you one better," and bending, pressed his lips to hers. Once. Then again. And again. "I'll never forget you, Lottie Weyland." And before she could think of anything to say, he faded into the darkness.

Chapter 6

Lottie slept little that night and was up and dressed long before the morning train was due. Not that she intended to go to the depot to see Ty off. What would be the point? He might come through Greenbroke again someday. Or he might not. Either way, their lives pointed in different directions so it would be foolish to fan the spark that had flared between them last night when he'd kissed her.

Her first kiss. Short and sweet. Not the dizzying reaction she had expected, but something much more tender. A good-bye kiss. Whatever had happened between them was over. Best she accept that.

And she was able to . . . until she heard the train whistle announce the arrival of the southbound. She tried to ignore it and stay busy straightening store shelves. But the refrain *he's leaving he's leaving* kept circling her mind.

The train was already pulling away when she reached the depot. She feared she'd missed him, but as the last car rolled past, she saw a man wearing a dark hat and duster leaning against the railing on the rear platform. When he caught sight of her, he slowly straightened and lifted a hand.

Rising on tiptoes, grinning even as tears filled her eyes, she waved back.

And there it was—the smile she had been seeking. And she was totally lost.

An hour later, Becky found her in the back room that served as the store's office, staring blankly at invoices she had already gone over twice. "I came by earlier, but you weren't here." Dragging her crate from a corner, she plopped down. "So, how'd it go?"

"How'd what go?"

"Dinner with your ranger. I would have come by yesterday, but I was painting a rocker for when the baby comes."

Lottie gave a brittle laugh. "Which dinner?"

"You went twice? Two days in a row? You sly thing!" Leaning forward, Becky rested her crossed arms on her knees. "Start at the beginning and tell me everything."

Trying to look busy, Lottie shuffled through the invoices. "What's to tell? We ate, we argued, he apologized, we went to dinner again. That's the end of it."

Becky tipped her head down to study Lottie's face. "Good Lord! You're crying! You never cry!"

"It's the dust."

"What happened?"

"I don't want to talk about it."

"Oh, honey. What did he do to you?"

Giving up all pretense of working, Lottie swiped a hand over her leaking eyes. "He kissed me is what he did."

Becky made a face. "That bad, was it?"

"It was awful. And wonderful. And now he's gone back to Austin and I'll probably never see him again."

"Oh, dear."

Lottie struggled to bring her emotions under control. She hated to cry. All she gained from it was a headache and puffy eyes.

"You really care for him, don't you?"

Lottie picked up the invoices again. "I might have, but now we'll never know."

"Would it make you feel any better if I told you that some foreign woman paid cash money for that old dance hall by the tracks?"

Lottie wasn't sure how that would make her feel better, but she was glad of the distraction. "When did you hear that?"

"Last night. Griffin told Juno who told me she plans to turn it into a fancy dining and gambling palace."

Now that did perk up Lottie. A place like that could probably use a bookkeeper. "I hope it's not another brothel."

"I guess we'll know soon enough. They're starting renovations next week. Folks are already hiring on. I might, too."

"You'd leave the Spotted Dog?" *And Juno?*

Becky avoided her gaze. "Nathaniel doesn't like me working there. Says a good woman shouldn't be in such a place."

"But it's okay for a preacher?"

"He's only watching out for me."

"And gambling away the collection plate."

"Don't you start, too. I get enough nagging from Juno." Rising, Becky moved restlessly around the small room, finally stopping at the tiny window on the back wall. She wiped at a smear then looked at her hand in disgust. "You ought to clean this place. I can hardly see out the window for all the fly specks and grime."

"Then don't look. Juno nags you about the preacher?"

"All the time." With a sigh, Becky plopped down on the crate again. "If he's not carping about Nathaniel, he's on me about keeping Sally's baby, or accusing me of flirting with the cowboys. There's no pleasing that man."

"Maybe he's jealous."

"Jealous?" Becky laughed at the notion. "He's old enough to be my father."

At first, Lottie had thought so, too. But after spending time with him she'd come to believe the hard shell he presented might be due to past disappointments rather than age. "I doubt he's much over thirty."

Becky snorted. "Well, he *acts* older. Man's got the disposition of a snapping turtle."

Lottie recalled the small tintype in the saloon owner's office. A lost wife and child, perhaps? "Maybe he has reason," she suggested. "There's a lot about Juno we don't know."

"You've got that right. But being jealous over me ain't one of them."

They sat in silence for a few minutes. Lottie tried to get up the gumption to tackle the invoices. Becky stared thoughtfully at the far wall.

"You really think he could be jealous?" she asked after a while.

"Maybe. I know he cares about you."

Becky grinned. "Wouldn't that be a hoot."

The foreigners arrived the next afternoon in two overfilled wagons, led by a man so big he made the Greenbroke blacksmith look like a citified dandy.

Or so Becky said when she stopped by on her way to the Spotted Dog. "And they talk funny," she added, as she helped Lottie stack cans on a shelf. "Real hoity-toity-like. The crab thinks the woman who bought the place is in the English upper crust since the folks she brought with her bow and scrape whenever she opens her mouth. Even the big scary fellow running the show calls her 'my lady.'"

"Aristocrats in Greenbroke. We're in high cotton now, aren't we?" Yet Lottie had to question why fancy folks would settle in a small town like this. Especially since Greenbroke already had gambling at the Spotted Dog and a restaurant in the Greenbroke Hotel. Unless they were anticipating more visitors.

"And she wore the most beautiful dress I've ever seen, Lottie. All ruffles and bows, with a skirt tucked up on the sides to show a ruffled underskirt, and one of those new low-slung bustles. The crab says it's the latest in French fashions. Too fancy for the likes of Greenbroke, but I'd trade my eyeteeth for a dress like that."

Lottie thought of the gold dress she'd paid too much for and would probably never wear again. Then she remembered the way Ty had looked at her when he'd seen her in it. No regrets about that. Simply knowing it was in the wardrobe made her feel pretty.

Smiling, she bent to load cans onto a low shelf. "What's the lady like?"

"A real beauty. Dark hair and pale skin. Cheeks as rosy as a fresh peach. The men in town can't stop staring at her."

After sliding the last can into place, Lottie straightened and wiped her hands on her apron. "Sounds like she's just the distraction you need."

"What do you mean?"

"If Juno is busy ogling her, he can't be nagging you, can he?"

"I guess not." Becky didn't look particularly pleased with that idea.

As it turned out, it wasn't Juno who was distracted, but Reverend Lindz. Which was exactly what Lottie had suspected would happen. The preacher was as predictable as a hound on a scent. If he couldn't be true to the morals he preached, how could he be trusted to stay constant to anything—or anyone?

But Juno was steady as a rock. In the time Lottie had spent with him, she had never once seen him waver in his loyalty to Becky, even when she was arguing with him, or flirting with cowboys, or chasing after the reverend. Maybe now Becky would see that, too.

The new arrivals had the Bracketts in a dither of excitement, too. Foreseeing new orders coming their way, Mrs. B. insisted they stock more exotic items, like India tea, English marmalade, and canned sardines, which were the closest thing to kippers she could find. But it wasn't until after Thanksgiving—which the English didn't celebrate— that the foreigners came to the market.

Lottie was in the office doing paperwork when Mrs. B. rushed in, her color high and her chest pumping. "Quick, Lottie! I need you to write everything down! They talk so odd and fast I can't keep up, and my hand is shaking so bad I can hardly read what I write. Hurry! And bring a tablet!"

Lottie didn't know who "they" were until she saw the slim brunette woman talking to a red-faced, grinning Mr. B., and the giant standing guard beside the front door. The mysterious Jane Knightly and her man of all trades, Anson Briggs.

An interesting pair. Lottie had seen both around town, but only from a distance. Up close, they were even more striking, not only because of her beauty and his size, or the way they spoke and dressed, but because they were so alien to anything ever before seen in Greenbroke. They were like exotic birds blown off course that, by happenchance or poor luck, had landed in a sleepy Texas town. Why they continued to stay was the big mystery.

"Here Lottie is, ma'am—my lady—oh, dear!" Mrs. B.'s hands fluttered like the wings of a frantic moth. "I don't know what to call you."

The brunette smiled and patted the older woman's arm. "Jane will be fine, Mrs. Brackett. No need for formality amongst friends, is there?"

Mrs. B. looked ready to swoon. Mr. B. continued to grin. The giant seemed to be fighting a yawn.

Realizing the Bracketts were too addled to do business, Lottie stepped in, tablet and pencil ready. "Good afternoon. Mrs. Brackett said you wished to place an order?"

They must be rich as Midas, she decided later as she looked over the list of items they had requested. She wasn't sure she could find everything they wanted, and even if she could, the cost would be high. They must anticipate a large clientele, she surmised. Which would require a competent bookkeeper. She decided to give them a couple of weeks to settle in before offering her services.

The dance hall renovations continued at a rapid pace, hammers pounding from dawn to dusk as carpenters struggled to complete the work before the weather turned. New shipments arrived regularly, and townsfolk with nothing better to do crowded the depot to see what treasures would be uncrated each day. Fringed lamps, brocaded couches, inlaid tables with tiny claw feet. Chandeliers draped with crystal beads, tall paintings, high-backed chairs upholstered in burgundy velvet, and gilded mirrors of every size and shape. There were even wide beds with framed canopies a foot thick and matching walnut wardrobes. It was as if Christmas had come early to Greenbroke.

But not everyone was feeling festive. Things had cooled somewhat between Becky and her preacher—which had Juno smiling for a change. Sally was having second thoughts about giving up her baby, even though she still talked about going to San Francisco. And Mrs. B. and Mrs. Jarvis were at odds because Mrs. B. was on a first-name basis with the Englishwoman and Mrs. Jarvis wasn't.

Lottie did her best to avoid all the turmoil by hiding in the office, going over her clients' accounts and thinking of Ty.

Like her, the ranger had no family left. How did he celebrate the coming holiday season? Would he spend it alone? Christmas was hard for Lottie. Thoughts of Grandpa always intruded, tainting what should have been a joyous time. But at least she had Becky and the Bracketts to spend Christmas day with. Who did Ty have?

A week before Christmas, flyers showed up in doorways and shop windows, announcing that Lady Jane's Social Club was now open for business, offering *"fine dining, gambling, and luxurious accommodations for the enjoyment and relaxation of discerning guests."*

Lottie wondered if those luxurious accommodations came with whores.

When she mentioned that to Juno several afternoons later while she dug through his desk drawer for the latest receipts, he said probably not, since Lady Jane's would attract a neater, cleaner, better behaved clientele than the drifters and cowboys who usually hung around Greenbroke.

"Maybe," Lottie said, doubtfully, wondering where that clientele would come from. "And I still don't see how a town the size of Greenbroke can support two gambling places and another hotel and restaurant. Or why she would even open such a fancy place in the middle of nowhere."

"As I said, the social club will draw a different set of cus-

tomers than the ones who come to the Spotted Dog or the
Greenbroke Hotel and Restaurant. We cater more to ranch
hands, railroad workers, cattle drovers, and peddlers passing
through. The club aims for fancier folks like those who make
the run between Austin or Houston and north Texas. Besides,
Greenbroke won't be in the middle of nowhere for long."

"Why do you say that?"

Pulling an atlas from his bookshelf, Juno opened it to a
map of Texas. "Here's where we are." He pointed to a blank
spot in the northeast quadrant of the state. "Smack on a rail
line running from the ports on the gulf up through the capital in Austin, and on to the money and cattle interests in
Dallas and Fort Worth, as well as the growing oil speculation areas around Oil Springs and Nacogdoches. Stands to
reason Greenbroke would be a stopping off place between
all those points." He closed the atlas and slipped it back onto
the shelf. "Jane Knightly is a smart lady. She's done her
homework, and she knows Greenbroke is set to boom. Cheap
land, cheap labor, good access, and lackadaisical leadership.
The perfect fertilizer for rapid growth."

Lottie looked at him in admiration. "How do you know
all this?"

"I wasn't always a saloon owner."

"What were you?"

"Something else."

Seeing he wouldn't give out more information on that
topic, Lottie resumed digging. As she stuffed the receipts
into the whiskey box, she thought about all he'd said about
Greenbroke's future.

Suddenly an idea exploded in her mind. The perfect investment! Exactly what she had been looking for.

She slammed the drawer shut and grinned at Juno. "If
what you say is true, and if Lady Jane is that smart, she
shouldn't be wasting her money on a glorified saloon."

"Why not?"

Warming to the idea bouncing through her head, Lottie
paced the small office, plans coming so fast she could hardly
sort them out. "Cattle prices rise and fall, don't they? Oil

fields play out or come up dry. But there's one thing that'll always be in demand." She stopped pacing and turned to face him, excitement bubbling in her veins. "If Greenbroke is as well-situated as you think it is, then it's a sure bet! The perfect place to put your money."

"Why?"

"Because it's got the one thing growing businesses, cattle, and oil fields all have to have."

"Which is . . . ?"

"Land. Or the rights to what lies beneath it."

"That's long term," Juno argued. "It might take years to pay off."

"I've got years. I'm only eighteen. What I'm missing is money. The kind needed to buy enough land to make it worthwhile."

"Don't look at me." Leaning back in his chair, he lifted his hands in a slow-down gesture. "I don't have that kind of money, either."

"I know. I do your books, remember?"

"And aren't eighteen-year-olds supposed to be thinking about new dresses instead of buying land?"

She began pacing again. "But if we joined together and formed our own investment group . . . you, me, the Bracketts, maybe even Lady Jane . . . we might be able to pull it off."

"And you know all about forming an investment group, do you?"

"They're called consortiums. Mr. Griffin told me about them last week. He even has the papers to set one up. I bet I could get him to invest, too." She stopped in front of the desk, hands on hips. "What do you think?"

"I think you're scary."

Despite his sour expression, she heard surrender in his voice. "It's settled then. I'll go see Griffin tomorrow."

"Tomorrow's Christmas."

"The day after then." Picking up the box of receipts, Lottie headed out the door. "Merry Christmas!"

"Don't tell him you're only eighteen," he called after her.

She was so excited about her idea she laughed out loud.

Her plan could work. It could actually work and make them all rich! She could hardly wait to talk to Griffin and the others.

When she walked into the market a few minutes later, the Bracketts were standing at the front counter. When Mrs. B. saw Lottie, she elbowed her husband and shoved an envelope across the counter. "This came for you today." She sounded excited . . . but not especially happy.

"From Austin," Mr. B. added, his blue eyes dancing.

Lottie almost dropped the box of receipts. *Ty?*

Mr. B. winked at her.

Mrs. B. sniffed. "Man has no business writing to an unmarried woman."

Lottie snatched up the missive and raced to the storeroom. Setting the whiskey box on the floor, she sank onto the foot of her cot and stared at the bold writing across the front of the envelope. "Miss Lottie Wayland, Brackett's Market, Greenbroke, TX." Who else could it be, but Ty?

With shaking fingers, she carefully pulled out the note, unfolded it, and checked the signature. *Ty!* Heart pounding, she began to read.

Dear Miss Lottie,

I hope I spelled your last name right.

(He hadn't, but she didn't care.)

   And I hope you remember me, Ranger Tyree Denton.

(As if she could forget!)

   I sure remember you and how pretty you looked in that fancy gold dress. The green one, too.

(He thought she was pretty? Suddenly she felt so giddy she had to stop and take a deep breath before she could continue reading.)

*I've been promoted to Lieutenant and assigned to
escort duty. With the 1880 Presidential Election coming
up, politicians will be swarming the state like biting
flies, trying to drum up support. The Rangers are
charged with their protection, so I might be coming
through Greenbroke before long. If I do, will you go to
dinner with me again? I promise I'll behave.*

(Yes! She felt like laughing, crying, dancing around the
room. Of course I'll go with you!)

*You can probably tell I've been thinking of you a
lot. I hope you've been thinking of me, too. Well, that's
all for now. Merry Christmas, Miss Lottie.*

> *Until we meet again,*
> *Lt. Tyree Benton,*
> *Texas Rangers*

Eyes burning, Lottie pressed the letter to her chest. Her
first kiss, and now her first letter from a boy—a man—and
a Texas Ranger, to boot.
This just might be the best Christmas yet.

Chapter 7

1879 brought with it a week of warmer temperatures and bright sunshine that promised an early spring. It fit perfectly with Lottie's optimistic mood.

Everything was going according to plan. Mr. Griffin helped her set up a consortium that included himself, the Bracketts, Juno, Fanny Seaforth, Ralph Krebs of the dry goods store—who seemed to do everything Fanny did—and Becky, although she didn't have much to contribute yet. And now, proposal in hand, Lottie was on her way to Lady Jane's Social Club to see if she could interest the Englishwoman in joining the group or, failing that, perhaps hiring Lottie as the club bookkeeper. Or both

After talking it over with Mr. Griffin and Juno, Lottie realized that land speculation would be less risky if they bought in areas of rapid growth. A solid investment. But like Juno said, one that was expensive and might take years to pay off. But if they went in a new direction—like oil speculation—and only bought the rights to what lay *beneath* the land—it would be cheap enough that they could afford to sit on it until oil production became more feasible. The key would be to find the right place to invest, and Mr. Griffin was already working on that.

It probably would have been better if Lottie had asked Mr. Griffin to present the proposal to Lady Jane. After all, he was the owner of the bank and had helped finance the Social Club. But the consortium was Lottie's idea, and she feared if she gave up the reins at the onset, she would never be able to regain control. It wasn't that she distrusted Griffin. She just trusted herself more.

The doors leading into the restaurant and gaming rooms of the Social Club didn't open until mid-afternoon, but the hotel portion of the establishment had its own entrance, manned by a blue-and-gold-uniformed doorman—Fred Kearsey, a dignified middle-aged man who had arrived with Lady Jane. Rumor had it he had been in service on an English estate but thought his prospects would be better if he emigrated. Now he served as doorman and hotel concierge. Lottie wasn't sure he'd improved his status much, but he took his duties very seriously and executed them with great style.

"Good morning, Miss Weyland." Sweeping off his top hat, Kearsey swung open the door with a flourish that would have made a carnival barker proud.

"Same to you, Mr. Kearsey. Is Lady Jane available?"

The doorman motioned toward the burgundy couch flanked by two leather wingback chairs near the crackling fireplace. "If you would care to wait, Miss Weyland, I'll inform Mr. Briggs that you're here."

"I came to see Lady Jane, not Mr. Briggs."

He gave a polite smile. "And he will be happy to escort you to her."

The message was clear: to see Lady Jane, you go through her watchdog, Anson Briggs. "Fine."

With a nod, Kearsey left.

As Lottie settled into one of the wingback chairs, she looked around. This was the first time she'd been in the Social Club, and she had never seen such a grand place. The hotel lobby was an oasis of green and gold and burgundy in the drab, winter-withered landscape of Greenbroke. She wondered if this was where Ty and his politician would stay if they came through town. It was certainly impressive enough.

"Miss Weyland."

Startled, Lottie looked up to find Anson Briggs looming at her elbow. How did a man his size move so soundlessly? She rose, a smile plastered on her face.

She didn't exactly dislike the Englishman. She knew too little about him to form an opinion one way or the other. They had never spoken directly, although he was always present whenever she saw Miss Knightly. He was simply there, like a bear in the shadows, silent and watchful and unpredictable. A person never knew what he might do if crossed, or if Lady Jane was threatened. Plus, he had scary eyes—pale gray with a black ring on the outside of the iris and very dark lashes.

"If you'll follow me, Miss Weyland, I will take you to Miss Knightly."

Lottie followed.

His accent was different from Lady Jane's. Not as refined. A few consonants dropped, a few vowels broadened. Lottie knew little about English society, but she guessed Anson Briggs and Lady Jane Knightly were of different classes. Perhaps he was a loyal servant who had come to America with his employer and, when the time was right, planned to strike out on his own. Or maybe he was a distant cousin charged by the family to keep an eye on her. Lottie doubted they were a couple. Nothing they said or did indicated anything of a romantic nature. Nonetheless, there was still something odd about them.

Miss Knightly's office was a reflection of the woman herself. Elegant, richly appointed without being showy, feminine without being frilly. It was a room that clearly stated a person of refinement and consequence resided within.

Lottie took note. Having grown up dirt-poor and never wanting to suffer such again, she intended to be rich someday. And when she was, she wanted to convey the same sense of power that Lady Jane did. But in Lottie's case, she wanted that power to come from *her*, rather than her surroundings or the giant standing guard at her back.

Lady Jane came forward, her hand extended. "Miss Weyland, I'm so delighted to see you again."

Lottie hesitated, not sure if she was to kiss the hand or shake it. She shook it and was surprised to find a firm grip on such a fragile-looking woman. "Thank you for seeing me, Miss Knightly."

"I've been wanting to know you better. And please do let's not be so formal. Call me Jane. May I call you Lottie?"

"Of course."

"Excellent." Jane motioned to two gold velvet chairs before the marble-framed fireplace. "Please join me. We'll be warmer by the fire."

As they took their seats, Lottie studied the room more closely, taking in the mahogany curio cabinet, the castle painting over the fireplace—Lady Jane's home, perhaps?—the delicately carved desk, and the thick floral rug beneath her feet. Someday she would have a room like this.

"I was told Texas was hot," the Englishwoman said with a smile. "But I've never been so cold, except in Scotland, of course. It's the constant wind, I think. Briggs, would you have Cook send in a tea tray, please? Unless you'd prefer coffee, Lottie?"

"Tea will be fine, ma'am—Jane." Lottie kept on her Sunday gloves but removed her bonnet and set it atop the folder containing the proposal on the floor beside her chair.

As Briggs silently left the room, Jane sat back. "So, what do you think?" She spread her hands in a motion that encompassed the room.

"It's quite opulent." Lottie was surprised by her own words. She never used "quite" and wasn't even sure she'd used "opulent" right. For some reason, whenever she was around the English people she became very—quite—conscious of the way she talked—spoke. She'd gotten lazy without Grandpa around to correct her grammar all the time. As a someday-rich person, it would be to her advantage to speak correctly.

Jane smiled, exposing the one flaw in her beauty. Her two front teeth overlapped slightly. Certainly not a big flaw, but enough to make the Englishwoman seem more like regular folks. And since her own teeth were perfectly aligned, it also made Lottie feel less intimidated.

Jane's blue gaze took in the room. "I daresay it's a bit much for Greenbroke. But perhaps our little town won't always be in back of beyond."

Seeing her opening, Lottie pounced. "My thoughts exactly. Which is why I've come to see you today."

But before she could continue, the door opened and Briggs entered, followed by Bea Davenport, bearing a silver tray loaded with a teapot, china cups and saucers, a tiny creamer and sugar set, and a plate of muffin-looking things. Beneath the starched white apron, Bea wore the same blue and gold colors that Kearsey did—minus the gold braid, and with a mop cap in place of the top hat.

Lottie had heard that Bea had left the family ranch outside of Greenbroke to hire on as cook's assistant. It was apparent the poor girl was struggling. The china cups rattled on the wobbly tray, and the sweat of concentration dampened the girl's brow. As soon as she set the tray atop a footstool between the chairs, Bea straightened with a sigh of relief. Lottie gave her an encouraging smile, and received a shaky grin in return.

"Thank you, Bea," Anson Brigs said. "That will be all for now." He held the door open, closing it softly behind her after Bea left.

Lottie wished he had left, too. She didn't want to discuss business with him hovering in the background. But he remained, taking a position behind Lady Jane's chair, feet braced, hands behind his back, his cold gray gaze fixed on Lottie.

Once Jane poured the tea and passed around the plate of muffin things, which she called scones, she sat back with a smile. "You were explaining why you've come, Lottie?"

Lottie glanced at Briggs. He stared back, his face revealing nothing of his thoughts. Pushing her irritation aside, Lottie retrieved the folder she had set at her feet. "There's been a lot of talk about why you would build this fancy hotel and gaming palace in a backwater town like Greenbroke. I think it's because you know it presents a fine investment opportunity."

When there was no response, Lottie elaborated, repeating Juno's words about access, labor, and cheap land. "When the growth comes, you and your Social Club will be ready. As will I. And this is how." Lottie held out the folder.

As Jane opened it, Briggs stepped closer to look over her shoulder.

Lottie thought that odd, since he wasn't included in the offer. But she made no comment. While they read over the proposal she and Griffin had put together, Lottie explained about the consortium and their plan to invest in two ways.

"First, as we feel Greenbroke and the surrounding areas are well positioned for future growth, our long-term plan is to buy land in anticipation of rising real estate values." Griffin's words, not hers. But after repeating them over and over in her room, they felt comfortable on her tongue.

"Second, and more risky but with greater possible rewards, we plan to invest in the budding oil industry. You may have heard of the wells being drilled throughout Nacogdoches County. So far, they don't produce much, but even so, anticipation of other finds has pushed up land prices throughout east Texas. And there are other places to invest. Griffin and I are collecting land surveys of the entire state, and we've also been in contact with John Carill, a man well-known for his expertise in oil engineering and exploration."

Briggs looked up, pinning her with eyes the color of smoke—and about as readable, too. "What does he say?"

Again, Lottie wondered why the man was inserting himself into the conversation. Was he the brains as well as the brawn behind Lady Jane?

She deliberately kept her answer vague. "He says areas in Texas are very promising." She didn't mention which areas. Until Jane Knightly came on board, Lottie wanted to keep her cards close.

The Englishwoman closed the folder. "Oil speculation is risky."

"It is," Lottie agreed. "Which is why we aren't interested in drilling for oil."

"Then in what are you investing? Surely not the land itself."

"Only what lies beneath it." Seeing their surprise, Lottie explained. "Rural folks are very protective of their farms and ranches. Not many can be coaxed into selling. But when told they can keep their land and continue to work it as they've done for generations, they're more willing to consider selling or leasing the rights to what might, or might not, lie under the surface."

"And once you have a promising lease," Jane surmised, "you sit on it until oil drillers come calling."

Lottie nodded. Juno was right—Jane Knightly was a smart lady. "And as holders of the oil rights, we take a share of production profits."

Briggs nodded in understanding. "But without the risk or expense of drilling a well and coming up dry."

"Exactly."

"But what if no one wants to drill on your lease?" he pressed.

"Then we'll mark that one a loss and move to another. That's why we're researching surveys and consulting with Carill. With enough investors, we should be able to buy oil rights in several promising areas. And we only need one to bring in enough black gold to make us all rich."

They discussed it a few minutes longer, then Jane asked if she could keep the folder for a few days.

"Of course." Lottie tried to keep elation from her voice. But even as a sense of triumph surged through her veins, nagging questions arose. How did Anson Briggs fit into all this? He seemed overly interested in Jane's business dealings. Was he protecting her or managing her? And why did Jane need such an ardent watchdog? Shaking off those troubling thoughts, Lottie put on a smile. "Talk to Griffin at the bank. Write down any questions you might have. We can discuss it all again after you've had a chance to think it over."

"I will. And thank you, Lottie, for including me in this investment opportunity. It sounds most interesting."

Briggs left.

Lottie gathered her bonnet, then hesitated.

"Was there something else?" Jane asked.

"I don't suppose you need a bookkeeper?" Realizing how unprofessional that sounded, she took a breath and tried again. "What I meant to say is I'm an experienced book-keeper, and if you find that you need one, I'll be happy to supply references." Better. But still weak.

Jane smiled. "As a matter of fact, I do need a bookkeeper. Briggs was complaining just the other day that he couldn't watch over me, the hotel guests, the restaurant staff, and the gaming rooms, and still keep up with the accounting. When can you start?"

"As soon as you need me."

"Perfect! A woman who knows her own mind. I knew I would like you. Tomorrow, then. That will free Briggs to bring the club up to snuff." Jane rose and, linking arms with Lottie, walked her toward the door. "We have an important visitor coming in on Wednesday and we hope to make a good impression. Perhaps you've heard of him? Royce Palmer?"

"The politician? Yes, I've heard of him. He helped draft the new Texas constitution, and I read he's supporting Win-field Hancock in the upcoming presidential election. Do you know if he's coming alone?"

"I don't think he is. He specifically asked for two rooms."

A few minutes later, Lottie was charging down the board-walk, her mind spinning. *Ty is coming! Ty is coming!* At least she hoped he was. And in two days!

She almost laughed out loud. Another client for her book-keeping business, possibly another investor in the consortium, and maybe another visit from Ty. Life couldn't be better.

Which dress should she wear to her dinner with him? She hoped they would be dining in the fancy blue-and-gold

Social Club restaurant. She had never eaten there but had heard it was wonderful. Apparently Lady Jane had brought a French chef all the way from England. If they dined there, she would wear the gold since it would match the décor. But if the weather turned warm again, the green would be cooler. But would it clash with the blue?

Mr. Brackett looked up from his stack of lists as Lottie came through the door. "How'd it go?" As an investor, he took a keen interest in all the consortium doings.

"Good, I think." She stopped at the front counter to give him a brief rundown of her meeting with Jane. "She seemed interested. Plus she's hiring me to bookkeep."

"Soon you'll be too busy to work here," he chided.

"Never!" With a backward wave, Lottie started toward her sleeping quarters in the rear of the store. "Give me a minute to change and I'll come help you with your lists."

"No chance of that."

Lottie hesitated. "Why do you say that?"

He lowered his voice to a whisper. "Best prepare yourself. You've got a visitor. A weepy one." Before she could question him, he made a shooing motion. "Go. I don't want her coming out here, blubbering and scaring off the customers."

Figuring it must be Becky, and wondering what had gotten her in such a state, Lottie hurried toward the back.

"There you are!" Becky rushed forward as soon as Lottie opened the door. "I've been waiting and waiting and—oh Lottie, she's leaving! What am I going to do?"

It took a moment to calm Becky down so Lottie could understand what her friend was saying. Apparently, Sally had decided to go to San Francisco after all. And she intended to leave on the Friday eastbound.

"And she's taking the baby with her!" With a wail, Becky collapsed, sobbing, into Lottie's arms.

If Sally intended to leave so soon, it stood to reason that she would take the baby with her since it wasn't due to arrive for at least another month. Lottie patted Becky's shoulder. "Are you certain she plans to leave right away? Traveling this close to the birth could harm both her and the baby."

"If she takes that baby away from me—"

"It's not your baby, Becky."

"It should be!" Pulling away, Becky brushed a hand over her damp cheeks then went to sit on the foot of Lottie's bed. "She won't take care of it right. You know she won't. She won't even name it!"

Unsure how to comfort her friend, Lottie sat down beside her and put an arm around her shoulders. "She's not leaving for five days. Maybe we can convince her to—"

"I could give her something." Becky sat up, a hopeful look on her tear-streaked face. "Something that would make the baby come before she left. Then once she had it and saw the bother it was, she would leave it with me. Don't you think that would work?"

Lottie was too horrified to respond.

"Why are you looking at me like that? I wouldn't do anything that could hurt the baby!"

"But forcing it to come early might do exactly that."

Becky looked away, her mouth set. But as Lottie's words sank in, her defiance crumpled. "I'm going to lose the baby, aren't I?"

Lottie remained silent, tears of sympathy clouding her eyes. She'd been afraid this would happen. Becky had been so set on keeping Sally's baby she hadn't allowed herself to consider the possibility that Sally would change her mind. Now she was heartbroken. Even though Lottie had never spent time around babies, she felt a sense of loss, too.

Becky blotted her eyes with the hem of her petticoat. "I just wanted to love it and take care of it."

"I know."

"I thought I could give it a better chance than Sally could. Now we'll never even know if it's a boy or a girl."

Hoping to stem a new flood of tears, Lottie said, "I think it's a girl."

"Do you?" Becky gave a wobbly smile. "I've thought so, too. I was going to name her Prissy, after my baby sister who died. That's a nice name, don't you think?"

"I do. And I also think someday you'll give that name to your own daughter."

"Maybe I'll have a son."

"Then name it Pisser, instead."

Laughing despite the tears, Becky bumped her shoulder against Lottie's—a gesture that said she was all right now. "You always know how to cheer me up, don't you?"

"You're the sister I never had, Becky. I'd do anything for you."

Fearing another emotional outburst—this one from herself—Lottie rose and walked over to the small wardrobe in the corner. "But now I need you to do something for me." Pulling out her two new dresses, she held them up, one in each hand. "Tell me which would go best with the colors in the restaurant of Lady Jane's Social Club."

Chapter 8

As early as she dared the next morning, Lottie arrived at the Social Club to begin her duties as bookkeeper.

Briggs was waiting for her. "Good morning, Miss Weyland. If you will follow me, please."

Without waiting for a response, he led her through the lobby and down the hall to the room across from the one where they had met the previous day. Opening the door, he stepped aside so she could enter first.

The room was Spartan compared to the elegance of Jane's office. A neat bookcase, a tall oak filing cabinet, a table and chair in one corner, a coal stove in another, and a large desk in the center of the room. Atop both the table and desk were neat stacks of folders and ledgers.

"Is this your office?" she asked, untying her bonnet.

"It is. We will share it for now." Closing the door behind them, he stood in front of it, feet braced, hands behind his back. He nodded toward the table and straight-backed chair in the corner. "That is where you will work, Miss Weyland. In those folders are invoices, orders placed and received, as well as a payroll list."

What? No whiskey boxes of receipts and IOUs to dig through? Juno could take a lesson.

"For now, your duties will only involve expenditures and receivables relating to the restaurant and hotel. I will continue to handle the gaming aspects of the club."

Lottie set her bonnet and gloves on the worktable beside a tray of sharpened pencils and a stack of blank work tablets. She had to give Briggs credit for being thorough. And neat.

"Until you are familiar with the way we do things here," he went on, "I will review your work each day. Have you any questions?"

"What's that?" She pointed to a slate chalkboard marked in a bold, masculine script.

"Our scheduling chart. You needn't concern yourself with that. Anything else, Miss Weyland?"

Lottie studied him for a moment. "Were you in the military, Mr. Briggs?"

"British Light Infantry."

"An officer?"

"Aide to Lord Bellingham. Now if you will excuse me, I must be about my duties. I will return later to check on your progress." With a curt bow, he left the room.

An odd man, Lottie thought, watching the door close behind him. How did a British soldier end up in America with a proper English lady? Was it simply an extension of his duties? Or something more personal?

She soon forgot about Anson Briggs and Jane Knightly and lost herself in tallies, entries, credits, and debits. Working with numbers relaxed her, creating a shield around her mind and channeling her thoughts into the simple task of adding, subtracting, and placing numbers in neat lines on a blank page.

An hour after she had begun, Jane swept in with a tray of tea and biscuits, and wearing a pale lavender morning gown that put Lottie's expensive gold poplin to shame. "Good morning, Lottie. I hope you don't mind if I hide in here for a while. Briggs has been a proper tyrant all morning, drilling the staff and inspecting the least little thing. It's his military background one presumes, but really, this is a social club not a battle campaign. Shall I pour?"

"Yes, please." Lottie set a biscuit on the saucer Jane handed her, then settled back in her chair while Jane sat at Briggs's desk. "Is he usually so exacting?"

"He can be," Jane admitted. "But today he's worse than usual. He wants the club to make a good impression in hopes that Congressman Palmer will carry a favorable report back to his colleagues at the capital."

"He does seem to take his duties seriously." Lottie admired that, even if she wished he were more amiable. "Have you known him long?"

"A little over three years. He served with my brother in India and Africa, and when Roger was injured, Anson brought him home. It was a difficult time. I don't know how I would have managed without him."

Lottie thought it odd that Jane would refer to Briggs by his Christian name. A slip? Or an indication of something more personal? "Is your brother well now?"

A sad look came over the Englishwoman's pretty face. "He died of his injuries. And after . . . well, things were in a bit of a muddle. But that's all in the past now." They spoke for a while longer, then Jane gathered their empty cups and picked up the tray. "I've dallied long enough. Cook is almost as big a tyrant as Briggs, and he's nervous about the menu for the congressman."

Lottie held open the door for her. "When do you expect Mr. Palmer?" She had heard nothing from Ty, and didn't know if the ranger would be coming with the congressman, or not. But in case he did, she wanted to be prepared.

"On tomorrow's train. He has a busy schedule. After meeting with local merchants and pushing for their support for his presidential candidate, he's to dine with Mr. Griffin to discuss campaign donations then enjoy the gaming rooms for an hour or two before retiring. A few more visits the next morning, then he's off to the next stop. Now I must run before Briggs tracks me down. I enjoyed our chat. If you're here tomorrow, perhaps we can visit again. Oh, and by the way, do please sign me up for your investment group. It sounds like a wonderful opportunity."

It was almost midday before Briggs returned. Lottie had finished the books for the hotel, and was reconciling expenditures for the restaurant when he walked in. After dumping a stack of letters atop his desk, he settled into his chair and began slicing open the envelopes with a long bladed knife, rather than the ornate letter opener one might have expected from such a proper English gentleman.

Lottie waited for him to say something. When it was obvious he wasn't going to, she cleared her throat and said, "You're paying too much for beef."

He looked up in surprise, as if he'd forgotten she was there. "How so?"

"If you bought your meat from local ranchers rather than bringing it in from Kansas City, you'd not only pay a lower price, but you'd gain loyalty, too."

"We were told Kansas City beef is superior."

"It is. But that's because most of it comes from Texas."

A flicker of a smile crossed his face. "I see." He continued sifting through the mail, arranging it in neat piles. "Any other ways we can cut costs?"

"Laundry. It's apparent from your notes that the women you've hired can't keep up with both the laundry and their housekeeping duties."

"You're suggesting we fire them? Or hire more?"

Knowing how hard it was to find employment in Greenbroke—especially for older ladies— Lottie shook her head. "Neither. But there are other alternatives."

He put aside the letters and sat back. "Explain."

"Confine your current chambermaids to making up the hotel rooms, and hire out the laundry." Seeing he was about to object, she raised a hand. "I know that would increase the housekeeping budget. But if you had to hire more chambermaids, you would have to pay them the going rate. Laundresses are cheaper—especially if you used the Chinese laundry outside of town."

He studied her in silence.

"They're fast and do good work. With an order this size, if you included the restaurant linens along with the hotel bedding, you'd pay less than if you hired more chamber-maids."

"Where is this place?"

"Out Main Street about a mile. Mr. Chang and his wife run it."

"I'll look into it." He went back to sorting through the letters.

She went back to the restaurant ledger.

They worked in silence for a few minutes, then he asked if she had finished with the hotel receipts.

"Yes. Since it's only been open for a short while, there wasn't much to do."

Without looking up, he held out a hand. "The ledger, please."

Irritated at having her work checked as if she was a child on her first day of school, Lottie walked over and dropped the thick book atop his desk with a satisfying *thump*.

He didn't even look up.

Rankled, she returned to her table.

He opened the ledger. A few minutes later, he closed it and sat back again. "How old are you, Miss Weyland?"

She stiffened. Had he found an error? Or was this another instance of a man holding her age and gender against her? "Why do you ask?"

"Curiosity."

Ire bubbled to the surface. "I'm older than I look." Then, reminding herself that she needed this job, she softened the snapped words with a weak smile. "Or so people say."

He continued to look at her.

She had once thought Juno's molasses-colored eyes lacked warmth. But they were warm and toasty compared to Briggs's icy stare. Her smile faltered. "Eighteen."

"I see." He pushed back his chair and rose. "Carry on, then."

"Yes, sir." She almost saluted, but caught herself in time.

He opened the door, then paused and looked back at her. "Thank you for your suggestions. And for your fine work, Miss Weyland."

Then before she could respond—curtsy, salute, or tell him "you're welcome"—the door closed softly behind him.

———

"Briggs gives me the jitters," Becky said later that afternoon when Lottie crossed paths with her outside the apothecary shop. "When I went to hire on at the club, I had to talk to him, and I didn't like the way he looked at me. Man's got eyes as hard as flint. Just as well they didn't need dealers. Nathaniel doesn't want me working there, anyway."

"Briggs was rude?" Lottie looked at Becky in surprise as she fell into step beside her. Although he could be curt and dismissive, Briggs had been nothing but gentlemanly around her.

"No, but he's so big and mean-faced. And those eyes give me chills."

"He was a soldier. He seems to approach everything like a military campaign. Lady Jane called him a 'proper tyrant.'" Which he was, of course. Lottie glanced at the parcel in Becky's hand. "What'd you get from the chemist? Not something to bring the baby early, I hope." She said it in a joking tone, but there was real worry behind the question.

"Hair grower."

Lottie had to laugh. Becky had enough hair to fill a mattress. "Where are you planning to grow it? I doubt there's any more room on your head."

"It's for Nathaniel. He thinks his hair's falling out."

"Probably singed from all that fire and brimstone he preaches."

Becky gave her a look.

Lottie grinned innocently back.

They walked on toward the market, nodding to folks they knew and studying displays in storefront windows. It was a warm day for January, and shoppers were out and about, running late errands before the stores closed.

"Bea Davenport thinks there may be something between the two of them," Becky said, gracing the old checker players outside the Western Union with a smile that made their day.

"Between Briggs and Lady Jane?" Lottie had seen no indication of that.

"Says he watches her like a fox scouting a hen house."

"He is rather protective." Lottie thought of what Jane had told her about Briggs bringing her brother home to die. That could create a strong bond. "Maybe he's a family friend trying to look out for her."

"And travel all the way from England to do it?" Becky snorted. "Men don't usually put themselves out that much for a woman. As they say, 'in the dark we're all pretty much the same.'"

An awful thought. Admittedly, Lottie had little experience with men, but she hoped they were more constant than that.

"Did you see Nathaniel hanging around the club while you were there?" Becky asked.

"No. But I was in Briggs's office most of the time." She looked over at Becky, worried that her friend might be about to lose both the baby and Nathaniel. "Things still cool between the two of you?"

Becky shrugged and kicked a clod of dirt off the boardwalk. "He says he still wants to marry me, but I—"

"Marry you!" Lottie grabbed Becky's arm and jerked her to a stop. "You never told me he asked you to marry him!"

Another shrug. "He never actually *asked*. He just assumes I will. Like, 'When we marry, you can lead a women's group at the revival meetings,' or 'It'll be a big help having a pretty wife to bring in more men,' or 'As an evangelist's wife, you'll need new clothes.' Talk like that."

"What's wrong with your clothes?"

"He says bright colors give the wrong impression."

Lottie thought that was ridiculous. She also wondered if Becky noticed that Nathaniel was more concerned about what he wanted, rather than what he could offer his bride.

As they passed Fashions by Fanny, Lottie slowed to study the dresses in the window. Nothing new since she'd walked by earlier. Not that she could afford another new dress, but it never hurt to look.

"Oh, I forgot to tell you," Becky said. "Sally's staying until after the baby's born. Doc said it would be too dangerous to travel this late."

"That's good news."

"She's still talking about taking it to San Francisco. And now, Nathaniel's looking to move on, too. He keeps pressing me for an answer whether I'll go with him or not. Maybe I should. With Sally taking the baby, I should probably just marry the reverend and get one of my own." She didn't sound particularly enthusiastic about the idea.

"Do you want to marry him?"

"Maybe. I'm just not sure I want to be a traveling preacher's wife—moving around all the time, having to be nice to wild-eyed Holy Rollers I don't know, never settling down in one place and making a real home. Bad as the farm could be sometimes, at least I always knew where I belonged." She gave a crooked smile. "I guess I'm not very pious."

"Pious is overrated," Lottie said, thinking of Grandpa. They had reached the market and she knew the Bracketts would be expecting her to help uncrate today's shipments after she did the day's tally, but she didn't want to leave Becky when she was feeling so low. "Does Juno know you might marry Nathaniel?"

"He's probably guessed, seeing the way Nathaniel hangs around when I'm working at the saloon. I know he doesn't want me to leave. Says I'm the best dealer he's ever had."

Lottie doubted that was the only reason Juno didn't want her to leave. But what more could she do? She had planted the idea in Becky's head that Juno had feelings for her, but so far, nothing had changed. Either Becky discounted the notion, or didn't care enough about Juno to pursue it.

"Well, I better go. Juno gets cranky when I'm late."

As she watched Becky walk away, a feeling of panic

gripped Lottie. She didn't want Becky to marry Nathaniel. She didn't want her only friend to move on and leave her behind. It might be selfish, but she needed Becky in her life.

She would just have to convince Juno that he needed Becky, too.

When Lottie walked into the store, Mr. B. held up a thick white envelope. "This came for you today. And no, it didn't come from Austin."

Disappointed, Lottie took the envelope and saw by the return address that the letter had come from San Angela. The law offices of Ridley Sims, to be exact.

A quiver of alarm shot through her. San Angela was the nearest town to the home she'd left behind. Why would a lawyer from there be writing to her? And why three years after she'd left?

Her mind raced, trying to make sense of it. She vaguely remembered her grandfather talking to an old man named Sims or Simmons or something like that on the few occasions they'd attended church in San Angela. Was he this lawyer? Before he died, Grandpa had spread word around town that he and his granddaughter were moving. He didn't say where or when. It was all part of his plan to protect her after he died.

But if everybody in San Angela thought she and Grandpa had moved to some unnamed place, how had Sims tracked her to Greenbroke? And why would he write to her instead of Grandpa? Surely he didn't know Grandpa was dead.

Unless someone had found his bones in the shed.

Oh God.

Her chest felt caught in a vise. She could hardly draw in air and her heart pumped so hard it made her dizzy.

She should have changed her last name. She'd thought shortening it to Lottie would be enough, since few people in San Angela knew her last name was Weyland and not Lofton like Grandpa's. And she should have waited to make sure the storm didn't put out the fire before it destroyed everything. But the horror of what she'd done had sent her fleeing in terror.

"Aren't you going to open it?" Mr. B. asked.

"What? Oh. Sure." With trembling hands, Lottie tore open the envelope and scanned the contents. Words jumbled in her mind. She had to read everything twice before she could make sense of it.

"You in trouble?" Mr. B. asked, watching her from behind the counter. "You've sure gone pale."

"No, I . . ." Lottie shook her head. Struggled to keep the terror from her voice. "Someone wants to buy my family's property in Concho Valley."

"That sounds like good news. Why the long face?"

"I'm just surprised, is all. It's pretty poor land." A tangle of emotions coiled in her chest. Fear of being caught. Fury that all she had done to put the ranch and those horrible memories behind her might amount to nothing. Shame that she had been too frightened to bury her grandfather like she should have.

"Maybe it's got oil under it." Mr. B. gave her a wink.

Lottie forced a smile. "Maybe." But she didn't care if it had a vein of pure gold two feet below the surface. She wanted nothing more to do with that place.

"Best close shop," Mr. B. said, crossing to the front door. "Mrs. Brackett has her quilting ladies due."

After emptying the fancy brass cash register that was Mrs. B.'s pride and joy, Lottie carried the receipts and the lawyer's letter back to her office to start on the day's tally. But it was a long time before that feeling of dread eased and she was able to concentrate.

———

She hardly slept that night and awoke with a feeling of being smothered. Not surprising since it felt like her worries were closing in on her: Becky maybe leaving, a lawyer from home tracking her down, Ty coming and what that might mean. A week ago she'd felt like she had the world by the tail, but this morning everything was crashing down around her.

By the time she was dressed, she'd calmed down enough to face the day. She wrote to Mr. Sims that she had no interest in selling the home place. After dropping the letter in the mail slot at the Western Union office, she returned to the store and worked a couple of hours tending chores. Then, needing something to focus on rather than her own troubles, she picked up the whiskey box and headed to the Spotted Dog to gather the latest receipts. She found Juno in his office, feet propped on his desk, reading the latest week-old newspaper.

She dropped the whiskey box on the floor, plopped into the chair in front of his desk, and said, "The reverend wants Becky to marry him."

He continued to read, his face hidden behind the paper. "Half the men in town want her to marry them."

"But this time it might actually happen."

He lowered the paper. "What makes you say that?"

"He's fixing to move on to richer pastures and wants her to go with him."

The crease between his dark brows deepened into a scowl. "She wouldn't do that, would she?"

"She might. She hasn't decided yet."

"Hell."

"You could stop her."

He looked at her.

She raised her brows.

"You're loco." He picked up the paper again.

"Why not? I know you care about her."

He continued to hide behind the paper.

Lottie refrained from snatching it out of his hands. She glowered at him, arms crossed, trying to come up with a way to convince him. Then her gaze fell on the framed tintype on the bookshelf. An awful thought arose. "You're already married, aren't you? That's why you won't make your move. Lord's sake, Juno—"

He slapped the paper onto the desk. "What are you talking about?"

"Them!" She pointed at the portrait of the woman and child. "You got a family hidden away somewhere, Juno? Is that why you won't act on your feelings for Becky?"

"No!" He jerked forward, his eyes fierce, his jaw so tight she could see a muscle jumping in his cheek. They glared at each other for a moment, then the fight seemed to drain out of him. Slumping back in the chair, he rubbed a hand over his face. "No," he repeated in a weary voice. "I don't have a family. Not anymore."

Lottie regretted ever opening her mouth. "Juno, I'm so sor—"

"Don't!" With a vicious slash of his hand, he cut her off. "Don't speak of them." For a moment, he looked around like a man seeking escape, then his eyes swung back to hers. The desolation in them was terrible to see.

"You want to know why I don't act on my feelings?" he asked in a hard, flat voice she didn't recognize. "I'm thirty-two years old, but I feel a hundred. I fought a war I didn't believe in, killed kids I didn't know, and led men I loved to their deaths. I watched my wife and son die, then buried them beside the charred remains of our home. I've got nothing left but regrets and lost hope, and Becky deserves better than a man just waiting out his time. That's why I won't ask her to stay." He sat back, his expression bleak, his face pale except for the dusting of whiskers along his jaw. "And don't ever ask me about it again."

His pain was so thick it filled the room. Filled with remorse, Lottie gathered the receipts and put them in the whiskey box. Juno was a friend, too, and she wanted to help. But how? She walked to the door, then stopped and turned back. "I'm sorry for what you suffered, Juno. But I won't give up on you."

"Then you're a fool." He picked up his paper, "Go."

She went, her thoughts in a muddle, her emotions so raw she felt abraded. She wished she could crawl back into bed, pull the covers over her head, and start the day over.

Then she caught sight of the long figure slouched on the bench outside the market and the world tilted again. "Ty!" she called, quickening her pace.

He stood as she came up the boardwalk steps, his amazing blue eyes dancing in his rough-hewn face. "I thought maybe you were avoiding me."

"How could I avoid you? I didn't know you were here."
No need to tell him she'd already picked out the dress she
would wear in case he did come to town. "How long will
you be here?"

"Until tomorrow. I'm escorting Congressman Palmer."

Lottie nodded, that awkwardness rising up, stealing
thoughts from her brain. He was too big. Too handsome.
Too real. Why couldn't she be flirty like Becky? "I got your
letter," she finally said.

"You didn't write back."

Heat rushed into her cheeks. "I wish I had."

"Then I'll let you make up for it."

She saw the almost-smile lurking at the corners of his
wide mouth and lost her thoughts again.

"Go on a picnic with me. Anywhere you want. I'm off
duty all afternoon."

It wasn't what she had expected him to say. It was late
January. Who went on a picnic in the winter? But the idea
of an afternoon away from all her fears and worries . . . an
afternoon spent with Ty . . . made her heart sing. "I'd love
that."

"Good. I'll take care of the food. Buggy or horses?"

"Horses." Even though she had sold Rusty long ago, Lottie still rode whenever she could. "Gus, at the livery, will
know which horse and tack I prefer."

"Fifteen minutes, then?"

"I'll be ready."

And there it was—that smile she'd been waiting for. And
suddenly everything steadied and the world felt right again.

Chapter 9

It was the perfect day for a ride. Cool yet sunny, the earth already starting to show signs of the coming spring. Compared to the panhandle, warm weather came early to east and central Texas. By February, azaleas would bud, and little more than a month after that, bluebonnets would turn the rolling hills into a carpet of blue.

But today, Lottie hardly thought of weather, or flowers, or where she'd be in a month or two. She felt freer than she had in weeks, and this moment in time was as perfect as any had ever been.

She glanced over at Ty. He rode with calm assurance, his shoulders swaying with the horse's gait, his big hands relaxed on the reins. Athleticism, grace, and strength. Masculine beauty carved with a steel blade.

Again, she wished she could flirt like Becky could. She wished she could come up with a quip or an amusing observation that would make him laugh. She wished she had blond curls and bigger bosoms.

He caught her staring and gave her a questioning look.

And in that dumbstruck moment, while a part of her mind cast frantically about for something to say, another part realized he wasn't assessing her bosoms, or her boring light brown hair, or the schoolgirl flush on her cheeks. Instead, he looked directly into her eyes, as if none of the rest mattered. And the smile that slowly spread across his mouth told her he liked what he saw.

She was in such trouble.

But she reveled in it. After the fears and worries of the last few days, sudden, intense joy sent her spirits soaring. With a challenging laugh, she kicked her horse into a run.

Caught off guard, Ty was slow to catch up. But seconds later, she heard him racing up behind her. She bent low over her gelding's mane. Wind made her eyes water. Her bonnet strings tugged at her neck. The pounding of the horses' hooves against the winter-dry ground matched the drumbeat of her heart.

She let him win, of course. She wasn't stupid. And when they slowed to let their horses blow, she led him to one of her favorite places, where a small creek meandered through a grove of native pecan trees. In spring and summer, the grove would be cool and shady, but by fall, hard-shelled pecans would litter the ground. She and Becky had come here to gather a bushel of nuts that eventually made their way into Thanksgiving and Christmas pies. But today, the sun shone warmly through the bare branches, and what pecans remained underfoot had been broken open by hungry squirrels.

After tethering her horse to a sapling, Lottie walked over to scout the creek while Ty untied the picnic basket lashed to the back of his saddle.

The bank was dry, the grass not too tall—Lottie hoped there wouldn't be chiggers out this early—and there was enough sun coming through the leafless branches to warm the air.

Ty walked up with the basket under one arm. "This looks like a good spot." He kicked a few rocks and pecans shells out of the way, then looked around. "You didn't happen to bring a blanket, did you?" When she shook her head, he pulled off his duster and spread it across the ground. "Have a seat."

She sat. The oiled canvas still carried his scent and warmth, and as she drew it in, it created within her a sense of intimacy that made her nerves hum.

He stretched out beside her. Leaning on one elbow, his long legs crossed at the ankles, he dug through the picnic basket.

"Let me know if you get cold," she said, feeling a slight shiver herself, although not from the chill.

He stopped digging and looked at her, those blue-flame eyes carrying invitations to sin. "If I do, will you keep me warm?"

She bit back a smile. "Sure. I'll lend you my bonnet."

His exaggerated sigh told her that wasn't the answer he'd hoped for. He resumed foraging. "Not near as appealing."

She tipped her head to see his face more clearly. "Are you flirting with me, Ranger Benton?"

He gave her a grin and a chicken leg. "I might be."

It was a moment before she could speak. "Why?"

He bit into a roll. "Why not?"

"You're in the Frontier Battalion. They don't allow members to have wives." When did watching a man swallow become so fascinating?

"Flirting's not courting."

Forcing herself to take a bite of chicken, she chewed thoughtfully, hoping she could get it down. And keep it down. His nearness was playing havoc with her digestion.

He seemed to suffer no such malady, having devoured the roll, a wing, a thigh, and most of another roll before she finished half the chicken leg.

"Then I guess you'll have to explain the rules to me," she finally managed. "I know little about flirting and even less about courting. Why would an honorable man—which I assume you are—flirt with a good woman—which I assure you I am—when he has no intention of ever marrying?"

"It's fun."

Oh, that smile! She took a moment to catch her breath. "And that's all you hope for? A bit of fun?"

His smile faded. He dropped the half-eaten roll and rose off his elbow. In a single unbroken movement, he grabbed the ties of her bonnet, pulled her face to within a breath of his, whispered, "That . . . and this," and kissed her.

At first, Lottie was too stunned to move. Then she didn't

want to, fearing if she did, he might stop doing what he was doing. His first kiss had been sweet and tender. This one was more urgent . . . more involved . . . more everything. He tasted of chicken and coffee and yeasty roll. His whiskers pricked her cheek. His lips were firm, yet soft, and his tongue—*oh, Lord*—it was in her mouth.

Somehow her bonnet came off and cool air swept over her heated scalp. She wondered what would come off next, and if she should allow it. Then she stopped thinking altogether and sank into the heady sensation of a man's fingers threading through her hair, his tongue sliding across her lips, his heat making her pulse pound in her ears.

When finally he lifted his head, she was breathless and reeling.

He seemed no better. He drew back, his hands falling away, his eyes riveted to her mouth. "I've been wanting to do that since I saw you on the platform when my train pulled away."

What could she say to that? What was she to do? He was so far removed from her experience she was a bundle of unraveling nerves.

Still watching her, he leaned back on his elbow again.

Something had changed. This was no longer a lighthearted flirtation. They had moved into a different place and Lottie didn't know where she was or how to find her bearings.

"You're frowning," he said, breaking the long silence. "Why? What are you thinking, Lottie?"

"I'm thinking if I'm not careful, you could break my heart, Tyree Benton." She tried for a teasing smile, but the muscles in her face couldn't seem to manage it.

He didn't smile back. "Not on purpose."

"Well." She gave a shaky laugh and brushed a leaf from her skirt. "That makes all the difference, doesn't it? Are there any rolls left?"

He handed her a roll and they continued to eat in silence. Lottie scoured her addled mind for something to say to dispel the sudden tension—why did words always desert her whenever he was near?—when she remembered why he had come to Greenbroke. "What's the congressman like?"

"A politician. All hat, no head. You want this last piece of chicken?"

"No, thank you."

So polite. So cautious. Where had the smiles gone?

He finished the chicken, then closed the basket and rose to carry it back to where his horse was tethered.

Lottie watched him, admiring the way muscles bunched and flexed beneath his shirt as he tied the basket behind his saddle. Although still young, he was already a powerful man and wore the ranger star well, with quiet authority and a calm demeanor. An honorable man, troubled by the dishonorable actions he had been forced to take. A man easy to trust. Maybe easy to love.

But he wasn't for her.

She wasn't the slave-over-a-hot-stove type of woman, and he'd made it clear he wasn't the whitewashed-picket-fence type of man. Their lives were pointed in opposite directions. So why was she sitting here, watching him and wishing for something that wasn't to be?

He unhooked the canteen strap looped over the saddle horn, then walked back and sat down beside her again. He uncorked and held out the canteen. "Water?"

She drank, trying to ignore the warm, tinny taste of it, then handed it back.

He drank, took a moment to work the cork back into the opening, then set the canteen aside. Resting his right forearm across his bent knee, he stared off past the creek to the straw-colored horizon rising to meet a low band of wispy clouds.

"Earlier, you asked why I wanted to be a ranger. It came about by chance. And it's not a pretty story." He waited, as if expecting—or hoping—she would tell him he needn't go on.

She didn't. In truth, she was desperate to know all she could about this guarded and reticent man.

Faced with her silence, he continued. "I was five when my brother rode off to join Lee's army. The last thing he said to me was, 'Watch over the folks while I'm gone.' Which I did, such as I was able. Two years later, the war ended and we learned he had fallen at the Battle of Appomattox. The folks took it hard, especially Ma. Mindful of what my brother had asked of me, I did the best I could to look after them. But south Texas was a brutal place back then, and every year we lost more stock to Indians and Mexicans raiding across the border."

He glanced over at her. Maybe to see if she was still listening, or what effect his words might be having, or if he should go on.

Moved by his loss, she reached out and touched his arm where it rested across his knee. She wasn't sure why he was telling her this, but she sensed it was important for him to talk about it and for her to listen.

His gaze dropped to her hand. Before she could pull it away, he covered it with his own. His palm felt rough and warm against her chilled fingers. Heavy.

For a moment, he said nothing, his mind drifting away from her as he absently ran the pad of his thumb along the sensitive skin of her wrist. When he spoke again, his voice was low and gravely and his gaze stayed fixed on some point in the past she couldn't see.

"I was fifteen when Indians tortured and killed my parents. I'd been out rounding up strays when I saw smoke. By the time I got back to the house, there was nothing left but charred timbers and their mutilated bodies hanging from a cottonwood. After I buried them, I started hunting those who had done it. I found McNelly's Frontier Battalion instead."

With the weight of his hand pressing her fingers against his forearm, she felt the muscles go rigid with tension. She wanted to comfort him, soothe the tautness away, bring him back from that painful time.

But he wasn't finished.

"The rangers had been tracking me," he went on, "thinking I was part of the band they were hunting. When McNelly realized I knew the country as well as the men they sought, he gave me a choice. Work with them, or stay out of their way and let them handle it. I couldn't do that. I had failed my brother and left my parents unprotected. I had to make it right. So I joined the battalion. Eventually we caught the killers and I did what I had set out to do. There wasn't a trial."

He took a deep breath and let it go. Some of the tension left with it.

"That was almost five years ago. I stayed with McNelly for a while, but when he started brutalizing and executing prisoners, I figured I had enough blood on my hands, and transferred to another command. It's been downhill since. First the Sam Bass fiasco, then getting wounded here last summer. Today, I nursemaid politicians."

Finally he looked at her, and the bleakness in his eyes reminded her of Juno. "Now you know all my secrets. So tell me true, Miss Lottie. Even if I could, would you really want a man like me to court you?"

Yes. Always. "Perhaps." She gave his arm a gentle squeeze then slid her hand from beneath his. "But he'd have to ask me nicely, first."

A foolish thing to say, but it seemed to lighten the solemn mood. Or maybe it was relief that put the spark back in his eyes. Either way, his lips tilted in a crooked half smile. "How about we start with supper, first."

"At Lady Jane's restaurant?"

"The best table in the house. Anything you want."

Sadly, what she wanted wasn't on the menu. But she smiled and hopped to her feet. "Come on then. We have to get back so I can finish my chores at the market and change clothes before we go."

———

As soon as he saw her in that gold dress three hours later, Tyrce knew he'd made a grave mistake. He shouldn't have asked her to dinner. Or gone on the picnic. Or come to Greenbroke again. And he definitely shouldn't have kissed her.

Ever since the shoot-out last summer when she'd been the only one to try to help him, he hadn't been able to stop thinking about her. No matter how contrary she was—like dressing him down for thinking she was a whore, and later, smirking when he'd tried to apologize, then today, pestering

him about flirting and courting, and making him dredge up
all that past history he'd locked safely away in a corner of
his mind—he still couldn't get her out of his thoughts. She
kept him constantly off balance.

But the biggest mistake was that kiss.

He hadn't intended to do it. It was apparent she was inexperienced. But when she looked at him in that innocent,
earnest way she had, how could he not?

You could break my heart, Tyree Benton.

If he was the honorable man she seemed to think he was,
he would walk away now. Instead, he stood gawking like a
green kid as she glided toward him, her hair done up in fancy
waves, lamplight bringing out the gold in her eyes, and that
shy smile telling him she was pleased he was staring, but
embarrassed by the attention, too. She would have looked good
in a potato sack, but in that gold dress she was so beautiful Ty
forgot all the reasons he shouldn't have been standing there.

She'd dropped a rope on him, for certain.

"A suit!" Her eyes raked over him in a way that made
hairs rise on his arms. "You look so dashing, Ranger Benton,
I feel quite plain in comparison."

Liar. She had to know how beautiful she was. And what
she was doing to him with that look. And in front of the
Bracketts, too. "You leave me speechless, Miss Lottie."
What are you up to?

"And yet . . ." She tilted her head to the side. He watched
a wave slide across her bottom lip and nerves twitched to
life all through his body. "You spoke."

"I try." *You'll pay,* his look warned.

We'll see, her smile answered.

They chatted with the Bracketts for a moment, then she
held out her hand. "Shall we?"

But instead of tucking it under his elbow, as proper manners dictated, he took her hand in his. An inspired move.
Even the Bracketts seemed impressed. He gave a slow smile
and a hard squeeze. *Propriety be damned.*

She didn't flinch, although a flush climbed up her throat.
You won't win, those innocent eyes said, and she upped the

intimacy by lacing her slim fingers through his. Palm against palm. Smooth against callused. Cool against . . . starting to sweat.

She was shameless.

Before he embarrassed himself entirely, he told the Bracketts good-bye and hustled her out the store. As soon as the door closed behind them, she broke into laughter. "Mercy! Did you see their faces? It was mean of you to scandalize them that way."

"Me?" He looked down at her in mock anger, charmed by her unguarded laughter even if it was directed at him. "You started it, looking at me that way."

"I'm sure I don't know what you're talking about, Ranger Benton."

"I'm sure you do, Miss Lottie. There isn't a woman alive that naïve."

"Or a man so easily bested."

He had no answer to that. So he gave her hand another squeeze and quickened his pace.

Ty didn't know what game she was playing, but he liked it. Liked that she felt comfortable enough to tease him. Liked that she was in a frisky mood and wouldn't let the dismal story he'd told her that afternoon cast a pall over what time they had left. And he especially liked that he had made her laugh.

What he didn't like was the way things were shifting in his mind. Convictions were starting to waver. Ideas never before considered demanded he take notice. Because of this woman, the orderliness he worked to maintain was sliding into chaos. Yet even as he struggled to regain his balance, one thought kept ricocheting through his mind.

What if?

———

Lottie felt giddy. Triumphant. She was actually flirting! Becky would be so proud. She glanced up at Ty. Apparently he wasn't as moved by their teasing exchange. But she wouldn't let that frown ruin her evening. He would leave her again in the morning, maybe not to return for months, and she was determined to enjoy the few hours remaining.

By unspoken agreement, they stopped holding hands as they neared the Social Club. After he left, she would still be here, and as a good woman and someday-rich person, she needed to guard her reputation.

At the hotel and dining room entrance, Doorman Kearsey waved them through with his usual flourish. Several men lounged before the fire in the lobby, chatting in serious tones. Lottie knew all but one, who she assumed was Congressman Palmer. Luckily he was too engrossed in the conversation to notice Ty, so they were spared a delay and introductions. Lottie was glad. With their time together so limited, she wanted Ty all to herself.

Briggs stood guard in the dining room, his watchful eyes tracking every waitress, every diner, every plate whisked in and out of the kitchen. The man must never sleep. Just to needle him, Lottie gave him a bright smile as the hostess, Missy Harris, looking even more beautiful than usual in the club's blue-and-gold livery, led them to a corner table between the fireplace and a window overlooking Main Street. Definitely the best table in the house.

As they took their seats, Ty frowned at the Englishman. "You know him?"

Was that jealousy in his tone? *If only.* "Since I'm the hotel and restaurant bookkeeper, our paths cross frequently." Lottie was aware of Briggs watching them, but refused to look his way and studied the room instead.

She had been in the old dance hall only once—two years ago when the town had put on a Christmas rummage and bake sale to benefit a family whose home had burned. The place was unrecognizable now.

Wainscoting and fabric-wrapped panels had replaced unpainted plank walls. The lighting was still kerosene, but instead of tin lamps on hooks along the walls, ornate brass chandeliers with a dozen globes each hung overhead. The ceiling was a marvel of shiny pressed tin that reflected back the light, bathing the entire room in soft, golden hues. Damask drapes, the same blue as the walls—and slightly darker than Ty's flame blue eyes—boasted gold fringe and tasseled ropes holding them open in a graceful arc against the sparkling windows. Settings of crystal and china and polished tableware sparkled atop tables dressed with pristine white cloths and elaborately folded napkins.

Lottie had never seen the like.

"I feel like I'm in a fairy tale," she whispered to Ty. "Don't you?"

His lips twitched. "Haven't seen the elephant, I'm guessing."

"Maybe not. But I didn't just fall off the turnip wagon, either. And you don't have to be worldly-wise to know this is a beautiful room. Especially for sleepy little Greenbroke."

"You're right." He studied the room for a moment, then his eyes swung back to lock on hers. "But then, I've discovered that the prettiest things are often found in the humblest settings." A smile rife with meaning spread across his chiseled face. *"Especially* in sleepy little Greenbroke."

Lottie blinked. Was he talking about her? Pretty? The idea of it brought on such a rush of heat her scalp tingled with tiny beads of sweat. *Oh, please. Don't do this to me. I'm lost enough as it is.*

Luckily, their waitress—a local girl from a hardscrabble farm north of town—came with their menus and Lottie was able to fix her attention on that, rather than the man across the table.

She could make out less than five words on the entire menu. Had it been written in Spanish, she might have had a chance. But French? Hardly.

Setting the menu aside, she looked up at the farm girl who probably had as little understanding of the offerings as Lottie did. "Do you have one written in English?"

"Bring two," Ty said, closing his own menu.

The poor girl blushed and started stammering when a large form suddenly loomed behind her. Startled, she whipped around, saw who it was, and fell into a stricken silence.

"May I be of help?" Briggs asked.

Lottie tapped the menu with a fingernail. "It does seem rather much, doesn't it, Mr. Briggs? This is Texas, after all. We fought wars to maintain our independence, and have little fondness for countries that tried to interfere, such as Spain and France—"

"Don't forget Mexico," Ty added, helpfully.

Briggs's expression never wavered, but she saw mischief in his gray eyes. "Are you saying you can't read our menu, Miss Weyland? Shall I translate it for you?"

Braggart. But rather than admit she was ignorant, she gave the Englishman a gracious smile. "That's not necessary. Any well-prepared chicken dish will do . . . assuming you have a well-prepared chicken dish?"

"We do. It's listed as *poulet provençal et sa ratatouille.*"

Was that a wink? Surely not.

He turned to Ty. "And you, sir?"

"Steak, medium rare, all the trimmings."

Briggs nodded and repeated the order for the waitress, who fled to the kitchen as if her skirts were on fire. "Enjoy your meal." He started away, then swung back. "Oh, and Miss Weyland." Devilment became a smirk.

Lottie braced herself.

"We anticipate a busy weekend. Please be at your desk early Monday to work on the receipts . . . *assuming* your busy schedule will allow it?"

He'd gotten her again. "I'll check, but I believe I'm open at that time."

"Carry on, then." And with as close to a grin as Lottie had ever seen on his stern face, Briggs marched back to his post by the door.

She should have known better than to do battle with an ex-soldier.

Chapter 10

"What was that about?" Ty asked, his gaze pinned to Briggs's broad back.

"I'm not sure." Yet Lottie had to smile. A wink and a grin—two things she had never expected to see from the taciturn Englishman.

Ty looked back at her, his brows drawn into a dark ridge above deep-set eyes. "Is there something going on between the two of you?"

He *was* jealous! That giddy feeling came over her again. "He's my employer, more or less." Seeing that didn't satisfy, she leaned over and said in a whisper, "Rumor has it he's got his eye on Lady Jane. That's why he followed her from England and watches over her so protectively." She sat back, her gaze flicking to Briggs, who was deep in conversation with the lady in question. "I think it's romantic."

Ty snorted. But the scowl had lifted and he was no longer glaring at the Englishman. "Keep an eye on him anyway. He seems odd."

"He is odd. He's British."

The waitress brought their meals, and they spoke of inconsequential things as they ate. He recounted an amusing incident involving the congressman and an incontinent dog. She told him about the reverend preaching Mrs. Ledbetter to death. Ty was easy to talk to and even though he revealed nothing more about his years as a ranger, he did share several touching memories about the big brother he had obviously worshiped.

It was a wonderful evening—the food was delicious, the setting was beautiful, and the company couldn't have been better. Lottie was having an evening she would never forget.

Then they finished their pie, and he started asking about her family.

"There's not much to tell," she hedged. The less she said about Grandpa and her past, the better. "My father died in the war shortly after I was born, so all I know of him came through stories my mother told me. She passed when I was ten, and from then on it was just me and my grandfather."

"Must have been lonely."

"Maybe. But I didn't know that until I moved to Greenbroke." She smiled, remembering how strange it had been at first. "I felt like a kid in a candy shop with so many people to talk to. Luckily, my friend Becky reined me in."

"She's the blonde I saw you with?"

Lottie nodded. Adopting a scolding voice, she quoted Becky the day she'd found Lottie chatting with a group of cowboys outside the saloon. "'Girl, you've got to be more careful. You're too young and trusting, and that could get you in big trouble someday.'" Odd how she and Becky had reversed roles over the years. "I fear my curiosity drove me to make a complete nuisance of myself."

"That accounts for all the questions you pestered me with."

She laughed and shook her head. "That wasn't curiosity, Ranger Benton. It was pure punishment for accusing me of being a paid woman."

"I wasn't accusing, Miss Lottie. I was hoping. As I recall, I was feeling pretty lonely at the time."

Scandalized, Lottie glanced around. "Hush. Someone will hear."

"You started it." He sat back as the waitress cleared their dessert plates then settled those piercing blue eyes back on her. "What was your grandfather like?"

"Strict. He definitely didn't spare the rod."

"He was hard on you?"

"When I needed it. He knew he wouldn't be around forever and he wanted to make sure I kept to the straight path after he was gone." Seeing the troubled look on Ty's face, she added in Grandpa's defense, "He wasn't mean. He just had his way of doing things." And she had learned early on that his way was the only way . . . even at the end.

"Whatever his methods," Ty said, "he taught you well. I never met a smarter person than you." Before Lottie could stammer out a response, he asked how he died.

She shrugged to hide a sudden nervousness. "He got sick." A man as honorable as Ty wouldn't understand why she'd set that fire. It was something she could never talk about . . . especially to him. "So where are you and the congressman headed next?" she asked, changing the subject.

"Wherever there's money and votes."

From there, the conversation moved to her bookkeeping business, the investment consortium, and how she hoped to travel the entire state someday.

In answer to her questions, he told her about the country he'd seen as a ranger, cities he'd visited, and people he'd met along the way. It made her aware again of how isolated her childhood had been and added fuel to her dream of becoming rich enough to see and experience it all.

They must have talked for hours. By the time the waitress came for the third time to ask if they needed anything else before they closed, the room was empty. Even Briggs was gone.

Ty signed his room number to the tab, dropped some coins on the table for the waitress, and they left.

The night was cool and still, lit by a nearly full moon hanging overhead. The air carried a hint of spring and the scent of hyacinths blooming nearby. As they walked slowly back to the market, Ty took her hand again as if it was the most natural thing in the world. Which to Lottie it was.

"I envy you," she said.

"Why?"

"For all the things you've done and the places you've been. I envy that freedom."

"Sometimes freedom carries a high price."

She looked up at his face, all shadows and planes in the moonlight. Tyree Benton was a striking man, not only for his beautiful eyes and powerful physique, but for his strength of character, too. "You have regrets?"

"There are always regrets, Lottie. Especially in my line of work. But sometimes, on the good days, there's a sense of accomplishment, too."

"And when the time comes that the bad days outnumber the good?"

"Then I'll turn to ranching. I thought you were moving."

Lottie saw they had reached the back stoop of the market. Sudden panic assailed her. She didn't want this magical day to end. She didn't want him to go and send her back to her sterile life. "You're leaving in the morning?"

He nodded.

"I'll miss you." Such a simple statement to describe the turmoil in her heart.

His hand tightened around hers. "I wish I could ask you to come with me."

Tears burned behind her eyes. It was only through pride and tremendous effort that she kept them from falling. "And I wish I could ask you to stay."

"Lottie . . ."

Fearing he might say something she didn't want to hear, she released his hand and reached up to rest her palm against his cheek. It felt hot and faintly rough with new bristles against her cold fingers. She gave a wobbly smile. "You take care of yourself, Ranger Tyree Benton. I won't always be around to save you."

With a harsh sound, he pulled her into his arms. She breathed in the smell of coffee and chocolate pie and the warm musky scent of a healthy male. She felt the thudding vibration of his heartbeat against her ear. The strength of his arms. The tremble in hands that skimmed up her back to cup her face. "I don't want to leave you."

Then stay and make a home with me here in Greenbroke.

Instead, he kissed her, his mouth insistent on hers, his body tight with tension. When he pulled back, his expression was fierce and his eyes glowed silver in the moonlight. "Will you wait for me?"

Until when? You tire of being a ranger? Or an outlaw's bullet finds its mark? She couldn't bear that. But she couldn't bear the idea of him walking away from her forever, either. "Until when?"

"I don't know. I . . . I'll write to you. Will you write back?"

Because she didn't trust her voice, she rose on tiptoe and pressed her lips to his. *Good-bye, Tyree Benton.* Then before she burst into tears, she opened the door and went inside.

———

She didn't go to the depot the next morning. Not with half the town there to see the congressman off, and Ty standing guard behind him. He looked stern and a little sad, his eyes scanning the crowd, probably hoping to see her.

Or so Becky said when she came to Lottie's room after the train left.

"You've been crying again," she accused. "Don't bother denying it."

Lottie didn't.

"He shouldn't be stringing you along this way."

"He's not. He made it clear from the beginning he couldn't take a wife."

"It isn't right." Becky sat beside her on the bed and gave her a one-armed hug. "I'm so sad for you. You deserve better."

Lottie agreed. But even the little bit of Ty she did have was worth all the pain of his parting.

Becky gave her another squeeze then took her arm away. "Maybe it's for the best that he's gone. You know how people talk. Nathaniel saw you walking down the boardwalk, holding hands, and thought it was unseemly. Others might, too."

Lottie glared at her through puffy eyes. "Is this the day for sermons on morality? If so, tell Reverend Lindz I've got a few for him."

"I would, but we're not speaking right now."

Lottie wasn't in the mood to hear about Becky's man troubles. But being the dutiful friend she tried to be, she asked anyway. "What'd he do this time?"

"Ran up a bunch of IOUs at the Spotted Dog. Juno told him to pay up or else. Since he's got no money, he's thinking it's time to move on."

Coward. Lottie blew her nose, then stuffed her hanky into her skirt pocket. "An idle threat. As his bookkeeper, I know for a fact that Juno never collects his IOUs." And she also knew Juno wouldn't risk upsetting Becky by doing anything to Lindz . . . no matter how much the reverend might deserve it. "Nathaniel's safe enough." The words came out nastier than she intended.

Becky didn't seem to notice. "I hear this Sunday is his last meeting."

"He'd leave without paying Juno?"

Blinking hard, Becky nodded. "And without taking me. He said he'd come back, but I'm not sure if I want him to."

Lottie refrained from dancing a jig. "You don't want to marry him?"

"Not now. Maybe not ever. And it's all your fault."

"My fault? What'd I do?"

"You told me about Juno. Oh, Lottie . . ." With a mewling cry, Becky dropped her face into her hands. "Everything's falling apart."

Now it was Lottie's turn to offer comfort. "We're a pair, that's for sure," she said, giving her a hug. "But we'll figure this out. I promise."

The following Sunday, after a rousing sermon on the evils of loose behavior—either aimed at Lottie or as a warning to Becky—Reverend Nathaniel Lindz stuffed his tent into his wagon, and with promises to Juno that he'd be back by summer to pay off his debt, and assurances to Becky that when he returned they would marry, he climbed into the driver's box.

Lottie doubted they would ever see him again. Nonetheless, she stood with the other smiling townspeople to bid the preacher *adios* and safe travels.

Becky took the parting well. Maybe too well. But Lottie didn't press it. She could barely manage the chaos in her own life, much less someone else's.

After another restless night of *if only*s and *what if*s, she headed to the club to work on the hotel and restaurant books. She hoped Briggs would be tending duties elsewhere, but when she arrived, she found him at his desk, counting the weekend's take from the tables and tying the bills in neat bundles.

"Good morning, Miss Weyland."

"Good morning, Mr. Briggs." After stuffing her winter gloves into her coat pocket, she hung her coat and scarf on the hat rack by the door and crossed to her desk.

"I relayed to Lady Jane your comments about the menu," he said, without looking up.

Lottie studied his bent head, wondering if Jane was mad at her.

"You'll be pleased to know she is having them reprinted in English."

"Oh." Still confused, Lottie eased down into her chair. The menus looked very expensive. Reprinting them would be costly.

When she didn't respond, he finally looked up. "You *are* pleased, aren't you? I certainly am." He must have found her bewilderment hilarious. He almost smiled. "I've always thought the French menus were a mistake. But I'm relieved she heard that from you, rather than me."

"Am I in trouble?"

"Not as much as I would have been." He went back to counting and tying.

Lottie admired Jane. She'd hoped they could become

friends. Had she ruined any chance of that? "I should have kept my mouth closed."

"Don't be too hard on yourself, Miss Weyland. Leave that to me." He flashed a sudden, teasing grin that almost rocked her back in her chair, then on the next breath, his expression settled back into its usual somber lines. It had come and gone so fast Lottie wondered if she had imagined it. "In truth, Lady Jane tends to overlook practicalities. It falls to me to rein her in, which I don't enjoy doing. I'm grateful this time I didn't have to." Rising from his chair, he gathered the tied bundles and crossed to the door. "I'll return later to check your progress." He opened the door, then hesitated. "Miss Weyland, I'm curious."

Lottie was learning to dread his turn-back remarks. "Yes?"

"That young ranger you had dinner with . . . is there an understanding between the two of you?"

Heat flooded her face. "No. Maybe. I'm not sure. Why do you ask?"

"Before he left with the congressman, he made a point of warning me away. I'm puzzled as to why he thought I was a threat to you."

Oh, Lord. "N-not a threat. Exactly." She needed to sew her mouth shut.

"Then what . . . exactly?"

"He thought you and I . . . we . . . he didn't know about Lady Jane, or that you were my employer." She was almost gasping by the time she got the words out.

"Know what about Lady Jane?"

"That you and she . . . you know."

"No, Miss Weyland, I do not know. Explain."

Could those gray eyes look any more furious? "It's just talk, Mr. Briggs. That's all."

"About me and Lady Jane?"

Lottie nodded. Despite the chill, she was starting to sweat.

"I see."

"I wouldn't worry about it, sir."

"Carry on, Miss Weyland. And please don't mention this conversation to Lady Jane."

"I would never."

———•———

Over the following days, Lottie went from missing Ty so much she doubted she would ever feel whole again, to anxiously anticipating the letter he'd said he would send. Gradually, her restless nights improved, mostly because she stayed so busy with her bookkeeping tasks, chores around the market, and consortium investments she fell into bed each night numb with exhaustion.

Somehow, the sun set, the moon rose, February came, and her life went on without him.

Becky wasn't faring much better. No matter what she did, Juno stayed at arm's length. Early into the second week after the reverend left, she couldn't take it anymore.

"Either I've lost my touch," she announced, plopping down onto the crate in Lottie's office, "or you're as big a liar as Titus Curlew."

Biting back a sigh, Lottie closed the store ledger and turned in the chair to face her scowling friend. "What did I lie about and who is Titus Curlew?"

"Never mind Titus. Why did you tell me Juno had feelings for me? I might as well have the clap for all the distance he keeps between us."

"What's the clap?"

"Lord." Becky pressed a hand to her forehead. "I can't believe I'm taking love advice from a girl who doesn't know the first thing about men."

Lottie bristled. She might not be as experienced as Becky, but she wasn't the naïve ninny everyone seemed to think she was. She'd let a man put his tongue in her mouth, for heaven's sake. "Juno does have feelings. He admitted as much to me. The truth is he's convinced he's not good enough for you."

"Not good enough?" Becky's stunned expression gave way to a speculative frown. "Why not? What'd he do?"

Suddenly furious, she leaped from the crate. "If that man already has a wife somewhere—"

"He doesn't."

"Then what? Did he rob a bank? Kill someone?"

"Of course not!" Striving for patience, Lottie waved Becky back to her seat. "I'll tell you what I can, but you have to promise you'll never let Juno know where you heard it. Do I have your word?"

"Okay, sure. Talk."

"He's disillusioned."

Silence. Blinking. Then, "That's it? He's disillusioned?" Becky said it like she'd never heard of such a thing. "About what?"

"Life. The past. The future. He's gone through some difficult times. They've left their mark on him. Plus, he's twelve years older than you."

More blinking. "You're jesting. That can't be all there is to it." And before Lottie could answer, Becky was off the crate again, pacing and waving her arms in vexation. "That's the poorest excuse I ever heard! My uncle was twenty years older than me, but that didn't keep him from nosing around whenever he had the chance. Poor Juno's had difficult times? So what! Does he think I've been hiding in the cabbage patch all my life? I'll match scars with him any day."

Lottie let her rant until she ran out of steam, then calmly said, "It's not me you have to convince."

Becky stopped pacing and let her arms fall to her sides. She looked on the verge of tears. "Then what do I do?"

Lottie patted the crate. "Sit down and we'll figure it out." Once Becky was seated, Lottie said, "First, you have to decide if you really want him."

"Of course I want him. He's handsome, generous, rich, and one of the nicest people I know."

Lottie didn't tell her that most of those riches were tied up in uncollected IOUs . . . many of which were signed by Becky's last admirer who was, hopefully, halfway across Kansas by now.

"Is there anything about him you *don't* like?"

"I don't like the way he ignores me. Or pretends to."

"What about the Spotted Dog? Would you want him to give it up?"

"Heavens, no! I love the saloon. I love dealing there. It's a fun place."

"What about his whores?"

"I love them, too. And don't give me that look, Lottie Weyland. They're just people trying to get by as best they can. And they're not *his* whores. They rent rooms from him. That's all."

Lottie kept her opinion of that arrangement to herself. "You don't want a cozy cottage with a chicken coop out back and flowers along the front walk?"

Becky snorted. "That's what you want, not me. I want to be where the fun is. Where people go to have a good time and set their troubles aside for a while. Like the Spotted Dog."

"What about babies? You wouldn't want to raise them in the saloon, would you?"

That stumped her for a moment. Then she gave a shrug and said, "I'll worry about babies when I have babies to worry about. He may be too old, you know."

Even Lottie knew better than that. Plus, she'd seen the way Juno looked at Becky. "So there's nothing you'd change?"

She made a face. "I'd get rid of the bottled pig's feet and maybe have the girls clean up a little. Everybody already knows they're whores. No need for them to dress the part."

Lottie was amazed. How could she and Becky be so different and still be closer than sisters? It was a good thing her friend hadn't married the reverend. With her unconventional views, the two of them would have been doomed from the start.

Chapter 11

Lottie was on her way to the club several mornings later when Sugar, the pretty blond whore from the Spotted Dog, stopped her on the boardwalk.

"Sally's baby's on the way," she said, struggling to catch her breath. "Been at it most of the night, so it won't be long. Becky sent me to tell you."

"Does she want me to come?"

The girl must have seen Lottie's panic. She laughed. "No need. She's got plenty of help. She just wanted you to know."

Lottie let out a relieved breath. She'd never been around a birthing before—other than horses and cows—and the idea of assisting at a human birth made her slightly queasy. "I'll be at Lady Jane's most of the morning. Let me know how it goes, or if she needs anything."

Promising she would, Sugar hurried on toward the house where Becky and Sally lived.

When Lottie entered the club, Jane smiled at her from the lobby window overlooking Main Street. "Who was that you were talking to? I don't believe I've seen her around town before. She's very pretty."

"She works at the Spotted Dog." Lottie hoped Jane

wouldn't hold her association with a whore against her.
There were many who would.

Jane crossed toward her. "A dealer, like your friend,
Becky? I wonder what he pays. We're busy enough now we
could use more help in the gaming rooms."

"Ah . . . no. She's not a dealer."

Comprehension dawned. "You mean she's . . ."

Lottie nodded, sparing Jane the horror of saying the word
aloud.

"Oh, my." The Englishwoman looked more intrigued
than insulted. "I don't believe I've ever spoken to a light
skirt. You Americans are so . . . democratic."

Lottie smiled. "We try."

Linking her arm through Lottie's, Jane led her toward
the offices in back. "It was suggested—and by our own
banker, no less—that we offer such services here. But Anson
wouldn't hear of it. For a military man, he can be quite
prudish about such things."

"What things?" a deep voice said behind them, startling
them both.

"Light skirts." Jane pushed open the door into Briggs's
office. "And I do wish you would stop lurking about, Anson."

"I do not lurk. And why were you discussing prostitutes?"

"You most certainly do lurk. Doesn't he, Lottie? Shall I
send for tea?"

With a disgruntled look, Briggs crossed to his desk. "She
has work to do."

"Oh, pish, Anson. Even if you don't know how to enjoy
a relaxing moment, there's no reason to deprive others."

Watching them out of the corner of her eye, Lottie dis-
posed of her outer wear then took her seat at the worktable.
It was fascinating to see the two of them go at each other.
Especially if there was a chance Briggs could come out the
loser.

"As I've stated many times, Lady Jane," he said in his
sternest voice as he stood at the desk sorting his mail, "it is
highly improper for you to address me by my Christian
name. Briggs will do."

Jane grinned at Lottie. "See what I mean? Provincial to the core."

"I am simply trying to maintain proper decorum. Something you would do well to observe yourself, milady."

Jane rested a hip on the edge of his desk beside his thigh. "Oh, Anson. Do let up. We're practically family. My brother would never have asked you to look after me if he knew you would be such a bossy old thing." Turning to Lottie with a mischievous grin, she added in a whisper loud enough for Briggs to hear, "But I must admit, when he stomps about in his uniform issuing orders, he cuts as fine a figure for a tyrant as I've ever seen. The upstairs maids at home practically swooned when he passed by."

"I do not stomp."

"Oh, dear." Laughing, the pretty Englishwoman reached up and patted Briggs's red-flushed cheek. "I see I've upset you, darling, so I shall go. Lottie," she added with a wink as she rose and headed to the door, "we'll have tea and chat about prostitutes another day. Ta-ta."

Lottie was too astonished to respond. *Darling*? Who was pursuing whom? Had she been wrong all this time? She had only been around Briggs and Lady Jane when they were discussing business. This teasing banter was altogether new . . . and enlightening. Although Briggs didn't seem to enjoy it as much as Jane, which made it all the more fun to watch.

With a deep sigh, he settled into the chair at his desk. "Miss Weyland, you will not repeat anything you see or hear in this office. Is that understood?"

Struggling to hold back a smile, she opened the hotel ledger. "Of course."

"Lady Jane is above reproach. I would not have you think differently."

"I don't."

"She's impulsive and high-spirited and often says things she doesn't mean."

"Like calling you 'darling'?" She couldn't help herself.

"I should dismiss you for that."

His threat left her unmoved. With Jane as an ally, she felt safe enough as long as she didn't push it too far. "That won't be necessary, Mr. Briggs. Your secret is safe with me."

"I have no secrets."

"Of course not. If you're finished with it, may I have the restaurant ledger?"

A few minutes later, Bea brought in a tray sent by Jane, bless her. Briggs—as always—wore a vest and wool suit, and seemed impervious to the chill, but Lottie could definitely have used a warming cup of tea.

For an hour she and Briggs worked in silence, then Kearsey appeared in the open doorway with a message for Lottie. "I'm to inform you that the baby has arrived. A girl."

"A girl! Wonderful! And everyone is okay?" Lottie might not know much about birthing, but she was aware that it often ended badly.

Kearsey nodded. "Both are resting. Miss Carmichael suggests you come this evening after they awaken."

Lottie let out a relieved sigh. "Thank you, Mr. Kearsey."

After the doorman left, she became conscious of Briggs studying her. "What?"

"Who had a baby?" he asked.

"Sally."

"One of the prostitutes you and Lady Jane were discussing?"

A shocking thought arose. "You *know* her?" Was Briggs one of her regulars?

The corner of his mouth twitched. "No, Miss Weyland, I do not . . . *know* her. But I make it my business to be aware of the people around me. Miss Carmichael is the blond woman I've seen you with?"

Lottie nodded, another thought taking shape. "You were a spy, weren't you?"

"I beg your pardon?"

"In the British army. That's why you watch everybody the way you do and creep around—"

"I do not creep. Or stomp. Or lurk. And we call them forward riders, not spies." Pushing back his chair, he rose.

"Now if you will excuse me, I have a meeting with our banker."

Sally's baby was red and wrinkled and crowned with downy pinkish hair as soft as the fuzz on a new foal's belly. The instant Lottie cradled the tiny bundle in her arms she realized why Becky was so desperate to keep her. "Oh, Sally, she's beautiful. Have you named her yet?"

"Anna," the new mother said from the bed. Even resting most of the afternoon, she still looked exhausted. "After my ma."

Lottie knew better than to ask who the father was. Sally was a whore, after all. But as she studied the baby's hair, she wondered if maybe Tim, Sally's freckle-faced cowboy and one of her long-time regulars, might be the father after all.

"She's starting to fuss." Becky hovered anxiously nearby as if she expected Lottie to become so upset with the crying she tossed the baby out the window. "Jiggle her a little bit. Not that hard. Like this." All but snatching the infant from Lottie's arms, she held her close and began to sway and jiggle and croon in a soft musical voice.

It didn't seem to work.

"Maybe she's hungry." Sally held out her arms. "I'll try to feed her. Doc Helms said to keep at it until my milk comes in."

With reluctance, Becky returned Anna to her mother. As she watched the baby nurse, she had such a look of longing on her face Lottie had to turn away.

"Has Tim been by to see her yet?" she asked. Becky had told her he'd made it clear he wanted nothing to do with another man's baby. Hopefully, once he saw little Anna— and her pink hair—he might relent. If he was smart enough to figure it out.

Sally yawned. "I sent word to the Bar M. I suspect he'll be in when he can."

"When are you going to San Francisco?" Becky asked, worry in her voice.

"Not for a while. Doc says I shouldn't travel for a few

weeks. Oh, did I tell you?" Sally looked up with a bright smile, despite the weariness on her wan face. "Tim wants to go with me. He thinks there may be a better job for him out there, too. He's tired of wrangling cows all day."

Becky frowned. "What about Anna?"

"We haven't decided. Here." Sally held out the baby. "I think she's wet. Would you change her for me?"

Before Lottie could move, Becky rushed forward to take the baby.

A few minutes later, Lottie left. It saddened her how emotionally fixed on Anna Becky had become. It was an attachment that had been building for months and now that the baby had arrived, it seemed even worse. If Sally took the child with her to San Francisco, it would break Becky's heart. Lottie had hoped Juno would come around by now, but he was still dragging his feet, and now she sensed Becky was headed for heartache. She had to do something.

Her opportunity came several days later. She was digging through Juno's bottom desk drawer for receipts when Becky came in with the baby.

"Where's Juno? Sally's sleeping so I brought Anna to meet him."

"I haven't seen him." Closing the drawer, Lottie went over to grin at the baby, who was sucking on a rag wrapped around a stub of sugar cane and attached to a string. "She looks so bright-eyed this morning."

"She should. Last night, she slept five hours straight, God love her. Doc says she'll do even better once Sally starts making more milk. Meanwhile, she's stuck with this sugar tit." Becky tugged on the string, which renewed Anna's efforts on the sweetened scrap of cloth. "Poor thing's hungry all the time."

"Has Tim been in to see her?"

"Last night." Becky settled in Juno's chair with a sigh. "I never saw a man change his mind so fast. You'd think Anna was his, the way he's carrying on."

"He might be, considering he's the only redhead around Greenbroke."

"That doesn't mean she's his."

"His what?" Juno asked, coming through the open door. When he saw Becky, he came to a dead stop. "What's that?"

"Sally's baby. Come see. She's adorable."

With dragging feet, Juno moved closer.

Lottie thought that for a man who had once had a child in his life, he seemed strangely reluctant to get near the baby.

He peered warily over Becky's shoulder, his expression unreadable. "What are you doing with it?"

"She's not an 'it,'" Becky chided. "Her name is Anna, and I'm nursemaiding her while Sally gets some rest. You want to hold her?"

"No thanks." He held out a finger. A tiny hand bumped into it and quickly latched on. For a moment they played tug-of-war. "She's strong," he said, one corner of his mouth tipping up in a smile.

The baby kicked her legs.

Becky grinned up at him. "She likes you. You sure you don't want to hold her?"

His smile faded. He gently pulled his finger free and stepped back. "I just came in to get something." As he spoke, he gathered up a stack of loose papers piled in the bookcase behind his desk, then crossed to the door. "You want me to send Henry in with coffee or something?"

Becky didn't answer, her gaze drawn to the small tintype on the shelf where the papers had been.

"We're fine," Lottie answered.

Juno left.

Becky continued to study the photograph. "Who's that?" she finally asked. "The boy has the look of Juno around his eyes."

It was a subject Lottie had dreaded. But she figured it was time Becky understood the things that had shaped Juno into the lonely man he was today, and why he was so reluctant to open himself to the possibility of a second chance with Becky. "They're Juno's wife and son."

Becky's head whipped toward her. "You said he isn't married."

"He's not now. They died long ago."

"How do you know?"

"He told me."

That seemed to surprise her. "He never said anything to me about them." She studied the tintype again. "They're both so beautiful. He must have loved them very much to keep their photograph so close after all these years."

"I think it's less about missing them than having a reminder of the life he once had."

Becky continued to study the tintype. "What do you mean?"

"The war, and then their deaths, changed him. Took away his hope. He told me that now he's just waiting out his time. Sad, really."

Becky tried to pretend she didn't care, but Lottie saw the quiver in her chin. "That's ridiculous. He's not that old."

"Certainly not too old to marry again. And father more children."

"Maybe." When Becky turned, Lottie saw anger on her face, but sadness in her eyes. "Yet what woman can compete with a ghost?"

Lottie had no answer to that.

A few minutes later, Becky left and Lottie settled at Juno's desk to record the receipts in the Spotted Dog ledger. She wished Juno would come back—she had some prime words for him—but he never did.

From the Spotted Dog, she went to Fashions by Fanny, the dry goods store, then on to the Greenbroke Hotel to bring their accounts current. She'd finished the club's books yesterday, so all she had left was the market. Mr. Brackett had been in bed, battling a cold over the last few days, and stocking chores were lagging behind.

When she came through the door, Mrs. Brackett pushed a letter across the counter. "This came while you were out," she said in a disapproving tone. "Probably from your ranger."

Lottie curtailed the impulse to run over and snatch it up. Mrs. B. had been suspiciously quiet about Ty since Lottie and "her ranger" had gone to supper almost two weeks ago, no doubt critical of the way they had behaved—holding hands, and all. Until now she hadn't said anything, but Lottie guessed that was about to change, judging by the pinched look of Mrs. B.'s mouth.

"A man shouldn't be writing to a single woman unless his intentions are honorable," the elderly woman announced in a righteous voice. "Much less holding hands with her."

Lottie hung her head. "You're right, Mrs. Brackett. But Ranger Benton is a dear friend, and I asked him to write and let me know he was all right. After the shoot-out here last summer, I worry about him."

Unable to maintain her stiff posture, Mrs. B. reached over the counter and patted Lottie's hand. "You're such a kind person, Lottie. Too sweet for your own good, I fear. I'm only watching out for you as I know your mother would have had she been able. I'm sure your ranger is an honorable man. But we shouldn't allow others to get the wrong impression, should we?"

"No, ma'am." Lottie gave a sniff—not completely fake. She loved the Bracketts and dreaded the idea of disappointing them. But she wasn't about to give up Ty. "I promise I won't tell anyone he's writing to me. They can't gossip about it if they don't know, can they?"

Mrs. B. gave a worried sigh. "I suppose not. But no more handholding, Lottie. That goes too far."

She would probably faint if she knew Ty's tongue had been in her mouth. Lottie was still a bit shocked herself. "Yes, ma'am. I'll remind the ranger of that if I ever see him again." Another sniff for effect, then she picked up the letter and happily escaped to her room.

Dear Miss Lottie,

I hope you are well. I am, although I'm so bored I'm building houses in my mind. I miss you a lot, and probably think of you more than I should. But nursemaiding a congressman is so dull I have to do something for fun. Like remembering our picnic and

*dinner and how pretty you looked. I felt so proud
knowing you were with me.*

*I do not know when I will get to Greenbroke again,
but until I do, I hope you will write back like you said
you would. You do know how to write, don't you?
(That's a joke.)*

*Give my regards to the Bracketts and stay away
from Briggs.*

> *Waiting to hear from you,*
> *Lieutenant Tyree Benton,*
> *Texas Rangers*

Lottie wrote back immediately.

Dear Ranger Benton,

*I am sorry you're so bored, but glad you are out of
harm's way. I, too, fondly remember our time together.
I have not had such an enjoyable day in a long time.*

*I will share with you all the news from Greenbroke,
but I warn you there isn't much. One of the "girls" at
the Spotted Dog had a baby, Briggs has kept his
distance, and Mrs. Brackett warned me away from
men who have not professed "honorable intentions"
but still insist on holding my hand. You rogue. I am
still shocked that you would do such a thing. I
probably won't feel better about it until I see you
again and we can discuss it in more detail.*

> *Until then,*
> *Charlotte Weyland,*
> *Bookkeeper Extraordinaire*

Chapter 12

Spring stormed into Greenbroke with branch-snapping winds in a daylong deluge that sent the creek south of town over its banks and turned Main Street into six inches of churned up mud and manure. Several townspeople complained to the mayor, Pete Spivey, who said the town couldn't afford paving stones. Dissatisfied, they went to Sheriff Dodson to complain about the mayor, but he was busy hunting his chicken coop that had washed downstream. By week's end, most of the mud had dried into a mountain range of ruts, the stink had faded, and things were back to normal. Meanwhile, Juno saw a rise in whiskey sales, Sally and her freckle-faced cowboy started talking marriage—which threw Becky into a panic—and Lottie took Griffin's advice and invested in a new venture called the Edison Electric Light Company, which had begun operation the previous October.

And life went on.

In late March, another letter came from Ty. He was through squiring the congressman around, and had been assigned to prisoner escort. He seemed to like it no better.

*It is just as boring, but at least I feel I am doing
something useful. Local law enforcement issues the
warrants, then rangers find the suspects and deliver
them to their jurisdictions. Thus, there is a lot of
travel involved, which gives me too much time to
think. And I am starting to think maybe it is time to
leave the Frontier Battalion and try my hand at
ranching the property my uncle left me. It wouldn't be
an easy life, but I would be building something for the
future. What do you think?*

Lottie thought it was a wonderful idea . . . for him. For
her, it was terrifying. It wasn't the hard work. Striving toward
a goal that would better one's life was something she understood. But struggling just to stay alive was a different matter.

Bitter memories flooded her mind. Sharing what food
she had with their rail-thin hound. Wrapping her feet in rags
to protect blisters caused by boots that were the wrong size
and already worn out by the time they came to her. Putting
patches over patches on clothes Grandpa found in the charity
bin at the church. Watching half-starved cattle pawing for
water in the dry creek bed, and wondering what they would
do when their well finally went dry. "God will provide,"
Grandpa always said. But God also helped those who helped
themselves. So Lottie had found her own way out of the hole
she was in by setting fire to all that misery and escaping
into a better future. She'd survived. But now, if she wanted
Ty, she might have to go back to that life again.

She couldn't do it. She had worked too hard to build
something worthwhile here in Greenbroke. She couldn't toss
it all away. Even for Ty. Yet the thought of a life without him
felt like a blade ripping into her chest.

It wasn't until two evenings later that she was able to
write him back. She kept it light, telling him about the storm
and flooded creek, and how well baby Anna was doing, and
how upset Becky was that Sally and the baby might be leaving soon.

*I won't be that sorry when they go, since I plan to
move into Sally's room at the house Becky rents. It
will be a sight more comfortable than a cot in a
storeroom. Meanwhile, things at the club have been so
tense lately that Lady Jane and Briggs are going at
each other like two cats in a bag. Whatever it is, it has
Lady Jane in a tizzy. I will tell you more when I find
out what is going on.*

She thought hard about how to respond to his question
about taking up ranching. She didn't have the courage to
tell him the outright truth, so she only brushed up against
it with careful words.

*I have lived the ranching life. And you're right—it
is hard. For me and Grandpa, it was an endless, daily
struggle toward failure, so my memories are not
happy ones. But you are a stronger man than
Grandpa was, and wise for someone so young. Unlike
him, I think you know the difference between a dream
and what is real. If you decide the ranching life is for
you, I know you have the fortitude to make it work.*

She stopped before adding, *But don't expect me to be
there beside you.* It sounded too final, too much like good-
bye. She wasn't ready for that. Knowing how easily she
might change her mind, as soon as she sealed the envelope,
she hurried to the Wells Fargo office before it closed and
dropped the letter into the mail slot. Then she went back to
her lonely room and cried for most of the night.

———

The problem at the club wasn't financial. As the bookkeeper
for the restaurant and hotel, Lottie knew they were turning
a nice profit. Nor were there issues with the employees or
she would have heard. No complaints on food or accommodations, either. So it must be something personal. Briggs
was as tight-lipped as ever. So if she was to discover what

was troubling them and maybe find a way to help, she would have to go to Jane. Hoping to talk to her, Lottie went to the club the following day.

"Morning, Mr. Kearsey," she said as the doorman opened the door. "How's it going today?"

It was a code they'd begun using as tensions had built. If he mentioned the weather, it meant all was clear. If he complained about his bunions, she was to lie low and avoid Briggs, who had been in an especially foul mood of late.

"This wet weather makes my bunions ache."

Lottie sighed. "Pick one," she said in a low voice. "Weather or bunions."

Kearsey leaned closer. "Both."

That couldn't be good. As Lottie started down the hallway to the back rooms, she was almost run over by Briggs, who stomped by with a furious expression. She continued on, then heard a loud crash from Jane's office. She hesitated but, concerned that something had happened, she cracked open the door and peered inside. "Jane?"

The Englishwoman stood at the mantle, the shattered remains of a vase showing on the unlit hearth. "That man!"

Lottie didn't have to guess who she was talking about. "Is there anything I can do?" she asked, stepping farther into the room.

Jane whirled. If Lottie had expected tears, she'd have been disappointed. Jane's face fairly glowed with fury. "Do you have a bat? A rock? *Anything* I could use to beat some sense into his thick head?"

"I assume we're talking about Mr. Briggs?"

"Who else is that hardheaded?" Jane began to stomp to and fro, her hands fisted at her sides. "I won't return to England, no matter what he says!"

Return to England? Lottie stared at her in shock. The town wouldn't be the same without Jane and her band of English misfits. What would happen to the Social Club? "You can't leave Greenbroke, not after all the work you've done."

"Precisely what I said. But Anson insists. 'Go back,'"

she mimicked. "'Assume your rightful position in society.'"
She threw her hands up in agitation. "What position? Spin-
ster cousin? Wallflower at local assemblies? I am too old to
be a blushing debutante at her first season. Besides, I have
struggled too hard to build a life here to simply walk away.
I love Greenbroke." Her voice broke. Pulling a lace hanky
from her sleeve, she pressed it against her eyes. "I don't want
to go."

Lottie was on the verge of tears, too. She didn't want Jane
to go, either. Or Kearsey, or even Briggs. They'd become
her family. How could she bear losing all of them, and
maybe Ty, too? "Why does he want you to go back?"

"He's a tyrant, that's why." Jane dabbed her face one last
time, then slipped the hanky back into her sleeve. With a
sigh, she slumped into one of the gold velvet chairs before
the marble-framed fireplace. "I left England under difficult
circumstances. But now that things have changed, Anson is
convinced I should return to my former life. What life? My
parents are gone. My brother is dead. My cousin and his
vicious wife have made it impossible to return home, no
matter how many apologies they offer. What's left for me
there?"

When Lottie moved toward the second chair, Jane held
up a warning hand. "Mind the glass." She gave a brittle
laugh. "I'm afraid I had a bit of a tantrum."

Lottie toed several shards aside then took the chair opposite Jane's. "What's changed? Why did you have to leave
in the first place?"

"Scandal, of course. English society feeds on scandal the
way a starving man gobbles up bread." She made a dismissive gesture. "It's complicated. And sordid. Suffice to say, I
shan't ever return, no matter what Anson says." Tipping her
head back against the chair, she closed her eyes as if to distance herself from unhappy memories. "If only he could see
how much better things are here, where anything is possible
and class distinctions don't matter. If he could just . . ."

"Just what?" Lottie prodded.

Jane gave a hopeless shrug. "See me for who I am, rather

than the title before my name. See past all the rules that were pounded into him as a vicar's son. But apparently, some things can't be overcome."

Lottie had the feeling that Jane was alluding to something more personal than their argument about her return to England. "Is there anything I can do?"

She gave a weak smile. "Simply having a sympathetic ear to listen to my complaints helps. I so value our friendship, Lottie. That's what I miss most about my life in England—the company of other women. Even servants."

"You've already made many friends in Greenbroke."

"I'm trying." With a falsely bright smile, she straightened in the chair. "I could use a cup of tea. How about you?"

After tea and scones and lighthearted gossip about the storm and Sally's baby and Fanny Seaforth's supposedly secret courtship with Ralph Krebs, the owner of the dry goods store, Lottie left Jane sweeping up broken glass and headed across the hall to Briggs's office with the excuse that she needed to work on the accounts.

He wasn't there. Which was probably for the best. She was bursting with curiosity, even though she knew that whatever scandal had driven Jane from England, and whatever reasons Briggs had for wanting her to go back were none of her business. Besides, confronting Briggs would only get his back up and might make things worse for Jane. She didn't want to risk that.

———

Baby Anna continued to thrive. As Sally improved, she spent more and more time at the Spotted Dog with Tim, who had quit the Bar M in anticipation of their move to San Francisco. Becky insisted that a smoky, noisy, whiskey-stinking saloon was no place for an infant and happily volunteered to watch Anna while they were out—which was most afternoons and into the evenings. Lottie worried that her friend's attachment to the baby had grown so intense that when the time came for Sally and Anna to leave, it might be too strong to break without breaking Becky, too.

It all came to a head in early April when Sally announced that she and Tim were getting married and would be leaving the following week. "Tim won big at the tables last night," she told Lottie and Becky as she sorted through the clothing she wanted to take—Lottie was relieved to see she was leaving her more garish outfits behind. "He made enough to get me this nice valise and pay for train tickets for the three of us all the way to San Francisco."

"You're taking Anna?" Becky shot Lottie a stricken look. The last they had heard, Sally hadn't yet decided if she would take the baby with them.

"Tim insisted. With that red hair, he's pretty sure she's his, and he's determined to be a good father. Isn't that sweet?"

"But it's too soon for her to be traveling," Becky argued. "Trains are filthy. She might catch something."

Sally waved the objection aside. "It's been almost a month. Doc said she should be okay. Could I have one of your old work dresses, Lottie? You hardly wear them anymore, and I need something that won't be ruined by soot or cinder burns."

Lottie nodded, glad she'd used some of her earnings to spruce up her wardrobe. She'd had no idea her made-over work dresses were such an eyesore.

"Why don't you leave Anna here?" Becky pleaded. "Once you're settled, you can come get her. Or I could bring her to you."

Sally wouldn't hear of it. Apparently, her maternal instincts had finally emerged, and she couldn't bear the idea of being without her "sweet little Anna."

Lottie had her doubts. But unwilling to stay for a continuation of the argument, she went to the Spotted Dog, hoping to convince Juno to do something.

"Like what?" he said sullenly, after she had cornered him at his desk in his office. "Steal the baby for her?"

"It's killing her, Juno." Lottie slumped into the chair across from him. "She cries all the time, she hardly eats, she's a mess."

"She'll get over it."

That got her back up. "Like you got over the loss of your son?" She could tell by his expression that she'd hit a nerve but she didn't care. "She loves that baby as much as you loved him. Lord's sake, Juno! Have some compassion!"

"I do have compassion! But what can I do?"

"You can give her hope."

"Of what?"

"Of something better than what she's got now. Just talk to her. She needs you. And if you let her down, you'll never forgive yourself." Without waiting for a reply, she rose and stomped from the office.

Sally and Tim were married two days later. They celebrated with a rowdy send-off at the Spotted Dog, which neither Lottie nor Becky attended—Becky, because she was watching Anna, and Lottie, because she was watching Becky. Also, Mrs. Brackett would have been scandalized if she'd found out they had attended a party for a whore. Lottie preferred not to add fuel to that smoldering issue.

The day of departure dawned with cloudless skies and gentle breezes. A betrayal, Lottie felt, considering her dark mood. But she kept a cheerful countenance as she walked with the newlyweds and Becky down to the depot.

It was a heartbreaking leave-taking. Not that Becky made a scene, but Lottie knew she was crumbling inside. After the last good-byes were said and the train began to pull away, Becky still stood on the platform, staring blankly after the last car, tears streaming.

"Come along." Lottie tried to lead her away.

Becky dug in her heels. "I-I don't want to go back to the house right now. It will seem so empty without her."

"You'll have to go back sometime."

"I know. But not now. Not just yet."

"Okay. Then we'll go to Juno." About time the man saw what a shadow of herself Becky had become. Maybe then, he would relent enough to offer solace. Or if not consolation, at least a shoulder for Becky to cry on.

The moment they walked into his office and Juno saw how broken Becky was, he rose and silently held out his arms.

Weeping soundlessly, Becky stumbled toward him. "Sh-she's gone, J-Juno. Anna's gone . . ."

"I know. I'm sorry, sweetheart," he whispered against her hair. "Let it go. I've got you." As he wrapped his arms around the sobbing woman, he closed his eyes, but not before Lottie saw the mixture of pain and confusion and defeat reflected there. Yet she also saw tears, and knew she had done the right thing in bringing Becky to him.

She didn't know if Becky went home that night and she didn't ask. She had never suffered the loss both Juno and Becky struggled with, and knew she had nothing to offer that they couldn't find in each other.

In some odd way, their troubles brought up thoughts of Grandpa. What she'd felt—and still felt—about his passing was all twisted up in guilt and duty and confusion. She might never come to terms with what she'd been required to do, but she was learning to move past it.

Maybe with time, Becky and Juno could move past their pain, too.

———

The next morning, another letter came from the law offices of Ridley Sims of San Angela. Just seeing the return address made Lottie queasy. This time he wrote about back taxes. Lottie hadn't even thought of taxes. How much did she owe? After the usual salutations, he wrote . . .

I do not know if you are aware, but prior to his death, your grandfather had the foresight to pay the taxes on your land three years in advance. However, the three years have passed, and now payment for the current tax year is past due. If left unpaid, this will put the property in jeopardy of foreclosure. I have enclosed the amount you owe, should you wish to pay it, and the county offices where it should be sent. I also wish to inform you that several people have been seen around the property. I do not know their intent, but if they express interest in purchasing the aforementioned

*tract, I will be happy to handle the paperwork in your
absence. Please advise.*

Panic swamped her. Had Grandpa confided in Sims? Did
the lawyer know what her grandfather had asked her to do?
And who were these people nosing around the home place?
What would they find?

She bent over, gasping, yet unable to draw a full breath.
Regrets that had plagued her for weeks rose to the fore. She
should have stayed to make sure the fire destroyed everything. She should have changed her name. She should never
have answered Sims's first letter.

The urge to run sent her circling the storeroom on trembling legs. She had to do something. She had to leave. And
go where? How could she give up everything she'd worked
so hard to build, and start all over again?

Sudden nausea sent her grappling for the chamber pot.

After she'd emptied her stomach and the mindless terror
had passed, her first thought was to tell Mr. Sims to sell the
property for whatever he could get. Then she thought of the
tombstones by the creek that marked the resting places of
her mother and grandmother. It shamed her that she hadn't
put her grandfather there beside them. But she'd been barely
fourteen, and heartsick at losing Grandpa, and so horrified
by what she had done she had been desperate to get away.

She looked at the letter crumpled in her shaking hand.
But she could never get away, could she? The past would
track her down. This letter was proof of that.

Once she got her thoughts in order, she wrote, thanking
Mr. Sims for notifying her that the taxes were due—which
she paid—and repeating what she had written before: that
at this time, she had no interest in selling the property.

Yet, even as she posted the letter, the terror persisted,
and she knew no matter how fast and far she ran, she could
never outdistance what she had done.

Becky dropped by just before noon. She looked weary,
but more settled.

"I'm still afraid to go back to the house," she said.

Which answered the question in Lottie's mind about where she had spent the night.

"I'll go with you," Lottie offered. "If it's still all right that I move into Sally's bedroom, I could take some things over when we go."

"Oh, I definitely want you to move in with me. I couldn't bear staying there alone."

Which answered Lottie's next question about what future arrangements she and Juno might have made. None.

"What do you want to take?" Becky asked. "I'll help you pack."

An hour later, they were hauling boxes up the walk to the clapboard house Becky rented. It wasn't much different from other homes in the area, with a wide, covered front porch that butted up against the front bedroom on one side, and was open on the other. If it had belonged to Lottie, she would have livened it up with window boxes in the front bedroom windows and rockers on the porch. The inside was filled to the point of being crowded, since Mrs. Ledbetter's brother hadn't removed any of the old lady's furniture or her lifetime accumulation of knickknacks.

"Not in there," Becky said, when Lottie started toward Sally's bedroom in back. "You take the front bedroom." Seeing Lottie's look of surprise, her gaze shifted away on a shaky laugh. "After I thought about it, I realized her room is all I have left of Anna. You'll probably think it silly, but I'll feel closer to her if I stay where she did."

"Okay, then," Lottie said with determined cheer. "Let's get your things moved. These boxes are heavy."

It didn't take long. Neither of them had a lot of possessions. Lottie would continue using the office at the market so she didn't need to move the ledgers or boxes of receipts. Once everything had been put away, they went into the kitchen for a late lunch.

Becky ate little. When Lottie joked about that, saying Juno wouldn't want her to turn into a bag of bones, the blonde gave a wry smile. "You probably think since I didn't come home last night, we were busy knocking boots."

"I thought no such thing," Lottie lied. "Juno is too honorable to take advantage of your grief over Anna."

"It had nothing to do with honor. I wish it did. But I'm beginning to think he just doesn't find me attractive."

"He called you 'sweetheart,'" Lottie reminded her. "When he hugged you. And he wasn't wearing the face of a man comforting someone he didn't have feelings for. It hurt him to see how upset you were."

"I don't remember much about that. What I do remember is that after I quit crying, we talked a lot. Or rather, I did. He mostly listened while I babbled. Until I asked him about his wife and son." Her gaze took on a pensive, faraway look.

"What did he say?" Lottie prodded.

"They married as soon as he came home from the war. He was nineteen, she was seventeen. They barely knew each other, and both had changed a lot during the war years. But promises had been made, so they stuck it out. Within a year, their son, Jacob, was born. Juno adored him. He was determined to give him a good life and worked hard to do that. When Jacob was six and Juno was out of town, setting up his railroad freight company, their house burned down. No one was hurt, but his wife and son spent several nights in the barn waiting for him to get home. They caught influenza. Right after he arrived, they died. I think there might be more to it, but that's all he would say."

Lottie blinked back tears. "Poor Juno. How sad for him."

"It was." Becky still had that distant look in her eyes. "But I think he was saddest about Jacob. He didn't say much about his wife. Never even mentioned her name. But he really loved that boy."

Later that afternoon, when she returned to the market to make sure she hadn't left anything behind, she found Mrs. B. waiting for her.

"I can't believe you've left us," she accused with ominously damp eyes.

Lottie put an arm around the older woman's ample waist. "I haven't *left* you, Mrs. B. I'm just across the street in back.

And I'll be here every day to do my chores and work on my bookkeeping."

"It won't be the same."

"I know." A quick hug, then Lottie put some space between them. "But Becky can't stay there all by herself. She's taking Anna's leaving hard, and I don't think she should be alone right now."

They had discussed her move to Becky's several times. Lottie had made it clear she was anxious to trade the storeroom for a real bedroom of her own. Mr. B. understood. But Mrs. B. had never taken to the idea. Which was part of the reason Lottie wanted to do it. The dear woman was becoming a bit too involved in Lottie's business. Especially her growing relationship with Ty. Lottie appreciated the concern. She dearly loved the Bracketts, and owed them so much. But she was over eighteen now, and after eight years without a mother's guidance, she'd grown accustomed to making her own decisions.

"Go on then and get the rest of your things." Mrs. B. dabbed at her eyes with the hem of her apron. "And remember the storeroom will always be here if things change or you want to come back."

"I'll remember. And thank you." She kissed the older woman's cheek then headed toward the back.

"Stop by the counter before you go," Mrs. Brackett called after her. "I've packed a box of groceries for you to take. No telling what you'll find at Becky's."

Chapter 13

——◆——

After fourteen years of having her sleeping area defined by a ratty blanket tied across a corner in their cabin, then three more years sharing a drafty storeroom with a family of mice, having a bedroom of her own was heaven for Lottie. And living with Becky was a whole lot easier than having to account for everything she did to the Bracketts, God bless them. She wondered if this was what normal people felt when leaving their parents—delighted to be free but sad to go, even if it was only a street away.

Becky was a wonderful housemate—neat, a good cook, quiet when she came in late, and crying for only about three hours a day. Lottie was there when needed, but mostly she let Becky work out her grief on her own.

Slowly, they adjusted—Lottie got over her guilt at leaving the Bracketts and Becky recovered her spirits enough to resume dealing at the Spotted Dog. Since their work hours were opposite, they rarely saw each other except at supper, which became a treasured time for Lottie, having someone to talk to while they shared kitchen and cooking chores.

Juno, on the other hand, was elusive as mist. Every time Lottie went to collect receipts, he managed to be gone.

Probably afraid she would pester him with questions about him and Becky. Which, of course, she would have.

When Lottie commented on his absences over supper one evening, Becky said he was always around when she was there and seemed the same, although he did hover more. "I think he's worried I'll have another crying fit and scare off the customers."

"So nothing has changed?" *In almost two weeks?* Did the man need a slap upside his head?

Becky thought for a moment. "The other night, I noticed him glaring at something behind me. When I turned to see what, I found a cowboy standing at my shoulder, trying to see down the front of my dress. I thought it was funny. Juno didn't. I've never seen him look so fierce."

That sounded promising. "Did he say anything?"

"Oh, yeah." Becky made a face. "He told me to wear high-collared dresses from now on."

"That's it?"

"I know, it's ridiculous. A saloon full of half-dressed whores strutting around, and he's worried about *my* dresses? Ha!"

"I hope you didn't do anything rash." For all her kindness, Becky had quite a temper. Lottie had seen her call to accounts more than one pushy cowboy.

"I laughed in his face, is all." Seeing Lottie's look of disappointment, she sighed. "I know you're trying to read romance into all this, but I doubt he was doing anything more than looking out for me. He's still too stuck in the past."

Dimwits, both. Lottie mentally washed her hands of the two of them. She had enough to worry about. Like what was going on between Jane and Briggs, and how she could keep dear Mrs. B.'s nose out of her business without causing offense, and figuring out who was sneaking around her old home, and why she hadn't heard from Ty in almost a month.

Things at the Social Club didn't improve. Unsure what to do about it—other than punch Briggs—Lottie pretended all was fine, and that Jane's strained smiles and her English bulldog's morose silences didn't keep her constantly on edge.

But in the back of her mind, she had that sense of change coming, and feared her happy life in Greenbroke was beginning to crumble.

The days warmed. Leafless trees budded, bluebonnets laid out a carpet of blue on greening hills. And still no word from Ty.

Lottie got through the days by staying busy. But once supper was over and Becky left for the Spotted Dog, the empty house seemed to close in on her. If the night was warm enough, she would sit on the steps of the front porch just to hear the distant *plink* of the saloon piano and know she wasn't entirely alone.

Those still evenings were when she missed Grandpa most—his whiffling snore as he dozed in his chair, his low voice when he read aloud from his worn Bible, even the musty old man smell of him that seemed to have soaked into the plank walls through the years. All those hard days and long nights surrounded by the sounds of cattle and horses and yodeling coyotes. The music of her youth. She didn't miss the hardship, but she did miss that.

Greenbroke had a different song. Fewer coyotes, more people. The rattle of wagons passing by, the saloon piano, sometimes the sound of laughter and voices. And later, if she was still awake and it was running on time—which it rarely was—the late train coming through with its lonesome whistle signaling the end of another day.

The sameness of it was both stultifying and comforting.

But one perfect spring evening in late May, when the Milky Way hung like distant smoke across the moonless sky and the gentle breeze was heavy with the perfume of spring flowers, Lottie stayed on Becky's porch longer than usual, rather than retreat to her lonely bedroom. Sitting on the top step, she leaned against the porch post, eyes closed, enjoying the cricket and whip-poor-will serenade. The late train came and went, the chuffing heartbeat of the departing locomotive fading as she drifted into a light doze.

"You sleeping, or what?" a familiar voice asked.

She jerked upright, eyes flying open.

And there he was. Standing at the bottom step, saddle-bags thrown over one broad shoulder, a pale slash of white teeth in his shadowed face.

"Ty!" she cried, flying down the steps.

"Whoa." Startled, he dropped the saddlebags as she plowed into him. Strong arms pulled her tight. Deep laughter ruffled her hair. "Hell of a welcome."

Her joy was so big it filled her to overflowing. She couldn't speak. Could hardly think. All she wanted to do was hold on, drowning in his scent and the feel of his warm, sturdy body against hers.

He must have sensed her clinging desperation. After a moment, he stepped back. Hands resting on her shoulders, he bent to look into her face. "What's wrong?"

She struggled to rein in her emotions. "N-nothing. I'm just glad to see you."

"Then why are you crying?"

"I'm not." Dragging a hand across her eyes, she felt the dampness and tried to smile. "I've missed you, is all. I thought . . . since I hadn't heard from you . . . I thought . . ." Her voice grew higher and wobblier with each word until finally it gave out altogether.

"Aw, honey," he murmured, pulling her close again. "I didn't forget to write. I was busy. And I have a lot to tell you." A squeeze, a quick kiss that ended too soon, then he loosened his grip and looked up at the house. "When I went by the market and saw the lamps were out, I hunted down Becky at the Spotted Dog. She told me you'd moved in here."

"Several weeks ago."

"She's working tonight?"

"Yes."

"Good." Picking up his saddlebags, he took her hand and led her up the steps.

"But she'll be back later," she reminded him as he opened the front door.

"I wasn't planning on staying the night." He dropped his saddlebags inside the door, closed it, and looked around.

"Nice place. Cluttered some, but much better than a store-room, I bet. Got anything to eat?"

After being apart for weeks, the first thing he wanted was food? Hiding her disappointment, Lottie led him toward the kitchen. "Leftover stew and cobbler." Luckily she'd had little appetite earlier, so there was plenty left, even for a man with Ty's prodigious appetite.

After hanging his black Stetson on a peg by the door, he sat in the chair facing the stove and tracked her every move as she heated the stew. It reminded her of Grandpa's hound who was always hungry. Except Ty's eyes were flame blue, rather than soulful brown, and showed a different kind of hunger. One that made her feel clumsy and breathless.

But as soon as she put a coffee mug and loaded plate in front of him, he forgot about watching her and attacked the stew like a man on the brink of starvation.

They didn't speak. He focused on getting food into his stomach as fast as he could, and she focused on him, enjoying his appreciation of the meal, and the way his dark hair slid across his brow, and how his Adam's apple bobbed when he swallowed. When had a man's throat become so alluring? And for the first time in weeks, a feeling of contentment stole over her, pushing aside all the worries that had dogged her since she'd seen him last.

"That was tasty." He pushed aside his empty plate after demolishing two days' worth of leftovers for both her and Becky. "You said you had cobbler?"

In no time, he finished that, too, along with a slightly shriveled apple Mrs. B. was going to throw out. After her hungry childhood, it pained Lottie to waste food.

"How long has it been since you've eaten?" she asked, piling his dishes into the sink.

"I got a box lunch at one of the train stops." As he spoke, he rose and came up behind her. Sliding his arms around her waist from behind, he pulled her back against his chest. "I've missed you, Miss Lottie," he whispered in her ear.

Apparently, the big meal hadn't satisfied *all* of his appetites, which he proved by turning her around and taking her mouth with his. It was a long, lingering kiss that demanded a response, then soothed, then teased, then grew hungrier. And this time when his tongue touched hers, she wasn't shocked, but joined in the play until they were both breathless and trembling.

After several minutes, he pulled back, breathing hard. He gave her a hopeful lopsided grin that did odd things to places she couldn't name. "You said Becky wouldn't be back until later?"

Despite the hammering of her heart and the tingles racing up and down her body, Lottie knew she had to stop this before it was too late. Part of her was frightened by the feelings he awoke in her. Another part wanted to see where those feelings would lead. But a lifetime of restraint held her back. Good girls didn't.

"You said you had a lot to tell me?" she countered.

He sighed and, with a chiding look, grabbed a towel from a peg. "You wash, I'll dry." After they'd put away the dishes, she poured more coffee, and they carried their mugs out onto the porch.

A sliver of moon sat on the eastern horizon. The crickets were quiet now, drowned out by drunken Bar M cowboys, shouting out the lyrics of "The Yellow Rose of Texas" and happily spending their paychecks on bad cards, rye whiskey, and willing women. The air was cooler now, and Lottie was glad for the coffee.

"How long will you be in town?" she asked, as they settled on the top step.

"Not long. I have to be back in Austin tomorrow." As he spoke, Ty looped an arm around her shoulders and pulled her against his side. "I had to see you. And to tell you I went to my uncle's ranch."

Lottie felt a chill that had nothing to do with the coolness of the evening. She carefully set down her cup and clasped her hands in her lap. "Oh?" She kept her tone light, but inside, she was terrified that a decision she didn't want to make was rushing toward her. "And how did you find it?"

"Dismal. The house is useless, the barn has no roof, all the fences are down, and the well has caved in. I guess twenty years lying idle takes its toll."

Lottie tamped back her relief. "What are you going to do?"

She felt his shrug in the arm across her shoulders. "I don't know. I don't have the money to fix it right now. Wouldn't even know where to start."

"But the land is good?"

"Fair. It can maybe support one cow per acre. Half the number you could graze on an acre around here."

Lottie stared down the front walk, her mind racing through ideas, picturing survey plats, and trying to remember recent land prices. All the things she had been studying with Griffin.

"I should probably sell and buy somewhere else."

Her first reaction was, *Yes! Sell and buy land here so we can stay in Greenbroke!* But the practical side of her couldn't allow him to make what might very well be a costly mistake. "Where exactly is your uncle's land?"

"West. Near the base of the panhandle."

She didn't remember if Carill had surveyed that area. But she did know the value of holding on to land. Any land. Which was partly the reason she didn't want to sell her grandfather's ranch unless it was absolutely necessary. But if selling the land Ty's uncle had left him would give them a start here . . .

"You wouldn't need as much acreage per cow if you bought around here."

"True. But the land would cost more."

"It would be a better investment. Land around Greenbroke has already gone up almost fifteen percent in the last five years. Plus, with the railroad coming through three times a day now, you'd have a much easier way to get your stock to market than if you had to drive them so far their weight fell off."

He tilted his head so he could see her face. "How do you know all this?"

"The banker, Mr. Griffin, told me. He says land in central and east Texas is a better investment than gold. They can always dig more ore, but they'll never make more land. Especially along the rail lines."

He studied her with that look men often wore around her—like she was speaking in tongues, or had grown an extra ear. "You're really smart, aren't you?"

Did that mean she was a freak? Undesirable in a man's eyes? Lottie hid her irritation behind a thin smile. "Does that bother you, Ranger Benton?"

"No. It's different, is all. I never met anyone as smart as you, and . . ." With a sheepish grin, he tugged at the knees of his Levi's with his free hand.

"And what?" she challenged.

"And it makes me wish Becky wasn't coming home tonight."

She blinked in astonishment, then burst into laughter. If she hadn't already been tucked against his side, she might have thrown herself on his neck. "So you don't care?"

"Oh, I care. No man likes being at a disadvantage. Especially around a woman he cares for. But as long as you remember that no matter how smart you are, I'm bigger and stronger and can bend you to my will at any time, we'll do just dandy." Even though he said it with a grin, she wasn't sure if he meant it or not.

"Bend me to your will?"

"Sure. As it should be between a man and his woman. Like this."

And before she knew his intent, he had her on his lap and was kissing her again. Only this time, he was touching her, too. In unexpected places. Soft, circling touches on her breasts, long strokes up her back, gentle nips on her neck and ears.

"You're driving me loco." His teeth tugged at her earlobe. "I can't stop thinking about you. And this." More kisses in a hot trail down her neck. "I want to lay you down. Feel your heartbeat against my tongue. Watch your skin flush when I kiss you here." A gentle squeeze on her breast had her back arching. "I want you so bad."

"Yes," she whispered, her mind spinning in circles. *Do it. Do it now.*

Ty stilled, then carefully removed his hand from her breast and straightened her off his chest. "No." Breathing deep, he dropped his forehead to hers. "Damn."

Lottie froze, not sure what she'd done. "What's wrong?"

Muttering under his breath, he lifted her off his lap and set her back on the step beside him. "I don't have the right to do this."

"Do what?"

"This. Us. Treat you this way when I'm not even free to court you." He turned his head and looked at her, his beautiful eyes reflecting back the pale starlight. "But, Lord knows, I want to, Lottie. I've never wanted anything as much as I want you right now."

Tears burned in her eyes—relief, joy, a nameless wanting she didn't fully understand. Reaching over, she cupped his cheek. "Then we'd better think of something soon. Because I feel the same way."

That elusive smile stole the breath from her lungs. A quick kiss then he tucked her against his side again. "So start thinking. You're the smart one, remember."

But she didn't know what to think about this breathless urge to forget all the rules and let him continue to bend her to his will. It was illogical. Something that went so much deeper than thought or reason. Something almost unstoppable. Was this the way it was between men and women? Or was she one of those wanton women Grandpa had warned her about?

She decided she didn't care.

Once her nerves had settled, she said, "If you want to buy land around here, I'm sure Griffin would give you a loan." She'd make sure of it.

"Enough to build fences, buy horses and cattle, and put up a house?" Ty shook his head, sending that fall of dark hair over his brow. "I doubt he'd want to finance a shoestring outfit, especially since it would take me years to pay him back." He gave her a thoughtful look. "Is that what you

want? To start another ranch? Your last letter didn't sound
very enthusiastic about the idea."

This was the conversation Lottie had dreaded. Without
stomping on his dreams, how could she make him understand how determined she was to avoid the poverty she'd
known on her grandfather's ranch? Rising, she held out her
hand. "Come. I want to show you something."

She sent him on to the kitchen while she ducked into her
bedroom. When she followed a few minutes later, he was
feeding kindling into the kitchen stove. "There's still coffee
left. Want some?"

"No, thank you." She set the dented tin box she'd retrieved
on the table, then sat down and waited.

Once he'd filled his mug, he took the chair across from
her. "What's that?" He nodded toward the box.

"Our family treasures." Opening the lid, she lifted out a
pair of round, wire-rimmed spectacles and set them on the
table. "These belonged to my great-grandfather. In his last
years, Grandpa wore them when he read."

Next, she removed a chipped cameo and set it beside the
spectacles. "This was my great-grandmother's. After she
died, it went to Grandma, then Mama, and now me."

"This was Grandpa's." She pulled out his dog-eared Bible
and set it beside the cameo and spectacles. "He read from
it every night. Even taught me my letters from it."

After lifting out the last two items—a simple gold ring
and a curl of dark brown hair—she pushed the box aside.
"These are my mother's wedding band and a lock of my father's hair she cut before he went to war." She laid them beside
the other items then folded her arms and sat back. "And that's
it, Ty. Along with a tract of near worthless land and a burned
house, this is all our family has to show for three generations
and almost twenty years of backbreaking work." She looked
up, met his gaze straight on. "I want more."

He studied her for a long time, those striking blue eyes
revealing little of his thoughts. Then sadness settled over
his chiseled features. "I don't know if I can give you more,
Lottie. Much as I might want to. Or how hard I might try."

"Not alone, maybe." Sensing his withdrawal, she leaned forward and gripped the wrist of the hand holding his coffee cup. "But with my help, Ty, you can." She felt his resistance, saw it in his face. But before he could reject the idea out of hand, words tumbled out of her in a rush.

"Ever heard of the Standard Oil Trust? Their stock dividend has a payout ratio of over sixty percent and climbing. The Edison Electric Light Company is talking about joining with several other Edison companies, and maybe merging with Thomson-Houston Electric, which would make them the most powerful electric company in the country. Griffin has helped me buy stocks in both. And our investment group is also investing in land. And mineral rights. And government land grants the railroads don't want anymore."

That wary look was back in his eyes. Realizing she was about to lose him, she skipped to the important part. "We've only been at this a few months, Ty. But our group is already making money, which we reinvest. If just a quarter of our investments pay off, we could be rich." Flush with excitement, she gave his wrist a squeeze. "You want a ranch? I can get it for us, Ty. With a little patience, and a lot of luck, within a year or two, I could have enough money to buy you a nice spread not far from Greenbroke."

"Buy *me* a nice spread?" Pulling his arm away, he sat back as though trying to distance himself from her and her words. "You plan to support me, do you, Lottie? Keep me around like a lap dog?"

The sneer in his voice shocked her. Is that what he thought of her grand plan? "No! Of course not! The ranch would be *ours*, Ty."

"Except your name would be on the papers."

"Not just mine. Yours, too. We'd be equal partners."

"Two ramrods?" He shook his head. "That won't work."

"Fine. Then you handle the operation."

"While you second-guess my decisions and dole out the money? That won't work, either."

Now anger was churning through her, too. Why was he being so unreasonable? Didn't he see that if they worked together, they could have it all? "Then what, Ty? We work like dogs for most of our lives and *maybe* get by? Is that what you want?"

"What I want is to be my own man, Lottie. I don't mind hard work, or taking a risk, or even failing. But I won't be beholden."

Shortsighted fool! She felt like screaming. Slapping some sense into him. Stomping from the room. How had this gone so wrong?

For long minutes, they sat at the table, unable to look at each other. Lottie saw no way to salvage this. She had offered a solution, and because of foolish male pride, he had rejected it without even giving it a chance.

The realization that he wouldn't even consider her as a partner hurt so bad she could hardly breathe.

"So tell me, Ty," she said, once the tightness in her throat eased. "What do you object to most? The idea of owing a bank? Or owing me?"

"Either way, it's charity. Can't you see that?"

"It's *business*! And if we can both profit from it, what's the harm?"

In his blue crystal eyes, she saw a reflection of her own disappointment and hurt. "If I can't earn it on my own, Lottie, I don't deserve it. Or want it."

My way, or no way. First Grandpa and now Ty. Was that every man's motto? "Then we're at an impasse, it seems."

"We don't have to be. Just give me time. If you believe in me, give me a chance to make it happen."

Another "someday" dream. Grandpa had fed them to her like candy. "I do believe in you, Ty. More than anyone I know. But even you can't change reality. And the reality is that unless a starting rancher has money backing him, odds are he won't last more than a few years, no matter how much he believes or how hard he works. I know that failure. I lived it. And I won't go back. Not when I hold the way to an easier future in my hand."

Anger had deserted her. She was crying now, but didn't care. Her heart was in tatters, her hopes and dreams a tangled mess at her feet. But resolve gave her enough strength to rise on trembling legs. "So, if you won't accept my help and take me on as an equal partner, then I see no way past this."

Ty stood, too, his big body tense. "Lottie . . . honey . . ."

She shook her head, not wanting to hear sweet words or for him to try to talk her out of what she needed to do. "It breaks my heart to face a future without you in it, Ty. But I've worked too hard to go back now. Even for you."

"Don't do this, Lottie. Give me time. I'll think of something."

"If you do, you know where to find me." Lifting his Stetson off the peg by the door, she held it toward him. "Goodbye, Ranger Benton. See yourself out." And while she still could, Lottie turned and walked from the room.

Chapter 14

———————

For two hours, Ty sat slouched on a bench outside the deserted depot, waiting for the early train and watching the crescent moon crawl slowly across the night sky. He'd cursed and argued and tried to convince himself it was for the best. But he still couldn't accept that he'd lost Lottie.

What was she thinking? Didn't she know they belonged together?

She was his woman—and had been from the moment he'd opened his eyes and found her kneeling beside him in the street, trying to tend his wound. She confounded him at every turn, argued with him every chance she got, and wouldn't accept his word on anything without questioning it first. But he admired her anyway.

In fact, he loved her.

Loved her? The ground seemed to shift beneath him. Admiring Lottie was easy. Loving her was terrifying. But inescapable. And the longer he thought about it, the more comfortable the idea of it became.

He loved the courage that had sent her charging into the middle of a gunfight to help a downed man. Loved her fine mind and strong character and her refusal to back down— even to him. So why was it so hard for him to accept her help?

It unmanned him, that's why. When she'd offered to buy him a ranch, she might as well have patted his head like he was a little kid, or hung his balls on a string around her neck.

Disturbed by that last image, Ty rose and began to pace along the edge of the platform.

He could accept that she was smarter than him. Probably. And better-looking. And had a warm and caring nature that drew people to her like bees to honey. A man could move mountains with a woman like her at his side.

But what did he have to offer her?

A strong back. Determination. Loyalty. A willingness to do everything he could to please her. He slowed to a stop. *Damn.* He sounded like a plow horse. With a deep sigh, he thrust his hands into his front pockets and watched a dying star streak across the sky.

That's how he felt. Burned to a cinder and racing nowhere as fast as he could go. *Damn that woman.*

He couldn't let this happen. He couldn't let it end like this. He'd have to find a way to win her back. By God, she owed him at least a chance to do that.

With grim determination, he kicked the saddlebags out of sight under the bench then started walking down Main Street toward Becky's house.

No light showed when he arrived. Not surprising, since the whole town was dark except for a faint glow to the east that signaled the coming of a new day. He tried the front door and found it unlocked. Reminding himself to scold her about that and to lock it on his way out, he slipped silently inside. He took a moment to let his eyes adjust and get his bearings, then he threaded his way through tables loaded with knickknacks toward the bedroom he'd seen her enter earlier when she went to get that tin box of mementos.

The door stood ajar. Hoping the hinges wouldn't creak, he slowly pushed it open. He could make out a bed and a bureau, but not much else. The room smelled like her. Something flowery. Feminine. And he could hear a faint snuffling sound coming from the bed. A stuffy nose? Had she been crying?

Good. Maybe she wasn't as set on cutting him loose as she'd made out.

He moved toward the sound, saw a dark head on a pale pillow, and reached down to where he thought her mouth was. As soon as his hand closed over it, she reared up, fists swinging.

Luckily her arms were shorter than his, or he might have gotten a split lip. As it was, she caught him a glancing blow on the bridge of his nose that made his eyes water and his nose run. "Stop, Lottie," he hissed. "It's me."

She froze. Then shoved his hand aside. "Ty?"

"Shh. You'll wake Becky."

"What are you doing? Why are you in here?"

Between the watering in his eyes and the darkness of the room, he couldn't see well enough to tell what she was wearing, but it felt like a lot more than she usually wore in his dreams. Just as well. He didn't need any distractions until he said what he'd come to say. Watching for another roundhouse, he eased down on the edge of the bed. "We're starting over."

"Again?" He couldn't see the smirk, but he heard it.

"I care about you, Lottie. And I think you care for me, too. So we've got to find a way to work this out."

"You care about me?"

"I might even love you. And since I'm not as smart as you . . . maybe . . . I'll need time to think about all you said. But I'm sure we—"

He almost toppled off the side of the bed when she threw herself against him. He thought she was attacking again, then felt her kissing his ear, his cheek, his nose, his chin— apparently she couldn't see him that well, either, because she never found his mouth.

"Oh, Ty. Your face is wet. Have you been crying?"

"What? Me? No. But I think you might have given me a bloody nose." He dragged a sleeve over his top lip, but couldn't tell if it came away wet.

"That's your blood I'm tasting?"

"Shh. You'll wake Becky." It pleased him she sounded so horrified about hitting him, until he heard spitting noises off the other side of the bed.

A second later, she was climbing on him again, saying how sorry she was that she'd hurt him, and how glad she was that he'd come back, and that she'd do anything to make it work between them.

Not a declaration of undying love, but he took what he could. And as soon as he felt her arms slide around his neck, and her soft, round breasts pressing against his chest, it was like coming home. He would have laid her down then and there but was determined to do this right. Plus, he didn't have time—he could already hear the distant whistle of the early train. "Lottie," he whispered when she finally loosened her grip and he could talk again. "This isn't the end of it. It can't be. I won't let it be."

"You love me? Truly?"

Surprised, he drew back. But in the dimness, he could only see the pale blob of her face. "Of course I do. Don't you love me?"

"Well, I—"

"Never mind." He wasn't ready to hear another rejection. "You will. Just give me a shot. That's all I ask."

He felt her body—her really soft, lush, sweet-smelling body—go tense. "I don't want to fight with you again, Ty."

"Then don't. Just tell me you'll wait. If I can't find another solution, we'll do it your way." He'd apologize to his balls later. They'd believe damn near anything.

Instead of speaking, she grabbed ahold of him again. Which was all the answer he needed. He would find a way. He couldn't lose this woman. "Now kiss me good-bye, honey, and go back to sleep. I'll return soon."

It wasn't a short kiss. But it wasn't long enough, either. And when it was over and he stood up, he was glad it wasn't light enough yet for her to see what condition she'd left him in. "Wait for me," he said, and quietly left the room.

———

Of course, after all that hugging and kissing, there was no chance that she could go back to sleep. She felt like she'd been caught in a cyclone. Her head was still spinning.

He loved her. The last time she'd heard anyone say that

to her she'd been ten, a week before Mama died of a tiny little bee sting. Grandpa had never said it, and over the years she had wondered if anybody ever would again. And now, Ty. She couldn't wait for Becky to wake so she could tell her.

But by the time dawn gave way to bright morning sunlight, she realized nothing had really changed. Ty was still reluctant to take her on as a partner, and she was still determined not to spend the rest of her life scraping out a living on a failing ranch. And both of them were too hardheaded and prideful to give in.

An impasse.

She stayed in bed until she heard Becky moving around, then forced herself to get up. By the time she'd splashed most of the puffiness from her eyes, dressed, and pinned her braid in a thick coil on the back of her head, Becky had coffee going and biscuits warming.

"Hey, sleepyhead," she said when Lottie came into the kitchen.

"Morning." Lottie set the table, poured coffee into two mugs, then took her usual chair.

Becky eyed her as she pulled the biscuits from the oven. "Rough night?"

"Do I look that bad?"

"Worse."

"I feel it." Hoping to deflect questions she wasn't yet ready to answer, Lottie asked how things had gone at the Spotted Dog the previous night.

"Nothing unusual." Becky kicked the stove door closed with a clang, set the pan of biscuits on the table beside the butter crock and jar of honey, then took the chair opposite Lottie. "Not like around here."

"How do you mean?"

"Somebody snuck into the house last night, ate all our leftovers, then snuck back out and locked the door behind him. I had to go around to the back window to get in. Know anything about that? Or where he might have left the key?"

"It was Ty. I don't know where he put the key. Probably somewhere so high only he can reach it."

"We never lock up anyway. Why was he in Greenbroke?"

Lottie hadn't intended to tell Becky about Ty's visit. But as soon as she opened her mouth, it all came rushing out—his refusal to take her help, their fight, his later return. "He even said he loved me, Becky. Now what am I supposed to do?"

"Grab him while you can." She drizzled honey on a biscuit and took a bite. "He's a good man."

"Haven't you been listening? I don't want to live poor again. But that's how it'll be if he won't accept my help."

"You mean accept your money. Oh, sweetie . . ." With a sigh, Becky set down her biscuit. "He's a man. They don't think like us. Sometimes they don't think at all." She winked and tapped her temple with her pointer finger. "At least not with this head." Seeing Lottie's look of confusion, she waved the thought away. "What I mean is a man doesn't care if his clothes are patched, or the curtains are ratty, or if there are even any curtains at all. As long as he's got food, a dry place to sleep, and a woman to cuddle up to at night, he's as happy as a pig in poop. All the rest is just window dressing."

"My life was hardly window dressing."

"I know. I don't want to be poor again, either. But if you want your ranger, I say give him the time he's asking for. He might surprise you and come up with something that will work."

Lottie hoped so. She felt trapped between two terrible choices: a life of poverty with Ty, or a life of ease without him. Neither was acceptable.

Her troubled mood didn't improve when she went to the club later that morning to find Briggs at his desk. Scowling, as usual. "Good morning, Mr. Briggs."

"Good morning, Miss Weyland."

Thankfully the conversation ended there. Lottie had a grinding headache—probably from crying so much the previous night—and was in no mood for idle chitchat.

After a long silence, she heard the squeak of Briggs's swivel chair. "Are you well, Miss Weyland?"

She looked up to find him studying her with an expression of concern. "Why do you ask?"

"And why must you always answer my questions with another question?" Before she could answer that, he continued. "You've been sighing a great deal. It makes me wonder if I've done something wrong."

He did have the most remarkable gray eyes—the color of polished mother-of-pearl, except for the dark ring around the irises. In her fragile state, the kindness she saw reflected in them weakened her. Feeling a sudden sting of tears, she looked down at the blurry numbers in the ledger. "I'm fine."

A pause, as if he expected her to say more.

She didn't.

"Deception doesn't become you, Miss Weyland."

She stared mutely at the ledger, willing the tears—and him—away.

"It's been my experience," he went on in a kindly voice, "that when a woman uses the word 'fine' to describe her feelings, it means just the opposite. What's wrong, Miss Lottie?"

His use of her nickname almost undid her. Raising a warning hand, she said in a wobbly voice, "Don't be nice to me."

"Why not?"

"It'll make me cry."

"Oh. Well. Thank you for the warning." He turned back to his desk.

It was some time before she trusted her voice enough to speak again. "Have you ever been poor, Mr. Briggs?"

"Do you mean impoverished?"

"I mean constantly worrying if you'll have enough to eat, or clothes to keep you warm."

The chair creaked as he sat back, his broad hands with their long, tapered fingers clasped at his waist. "Conditions on a battlefield can be quite harsh. As soldiers, we were often cold and wet, with scarcely enough food to keep us going. But if you are asking if I was ever *destitute*, then my answer would be no."

He waited.

She didn't say anything.

"Have you been poor, Miss Weyland?"

She'd started this conversation. She might as well

continue. "Yes, I have. Although, at the time, I didn't know I was poor. Not until I saw the way people in town looked at my patched clothes and hand-me-down boots. I thought everybody lived day-to-day."

He said nothing, but she imagined she saw understanding—maybe even sympathy—in his eyes. But this time, instead of weakening her, it strengthened her.

"I don't ever want to be that poor again, Mr. Briggs. I'll do anything to escape it. Does that sound greedy, or make me a selfish, shallow person?"

"Not at all, assuming you do nothing illegal or harmful to avoid it. In truth, I admire your determination to rise above a disadvantaged beginning."

More stinging. She blinked it away. "But the scars of that poor beginning remain. As do the fears of ever living that way again."

"Fears? You, Miss Weyland?" He almost smiled. "I cannot imagine it."

Some of her melancholy eased. Despite his stiff aloofness, Mr. Briggs was very likeable. She hoped someday to count him as a friend.

"Does any of this have to do with your ranger?" he asked.

The question sent that telltale flush into her cheeks. But Briggs was being so nice, and he did sound concerned, and she needed so desperately to find some answers. "He wants to try his hand at ranching, but he has no money to get started. And he won't accept any help from me."

"I see. And by 'help,' do you mean funds?"

What was so terrible about offering money to someone who needed it? "It's illogical. Why does he think I've been working so hard? Just to put money in a sock? No, to build a better life. Maybe even a future with him. But that can't happen unless he lets me help him. It's so unreasonable!" She threw up her hands in aggravation. "Why won't he listen? Why are men so bullheaded?" With every word her voice rose until Briggs's expression of sympathy became one of alarm.

"Please sit down, Miss Weyland."

Lottie wasn't even aware she had risen from her chair. "It's stupid is all."

Briggs waited until she was seated again. Then, in what she thought of as his military voice, he said, "Men are simple creatures, Miss Weyland. We are driven by two needs. Well, three, but we won't discuss that. To protect and to provide. By offering your ranger money, you effectively told him you would be a better provider than he would be. That's a mortal blow to a man's pride."

"Hogwash. At the Spotted Dog, men offer money to women all the time. Why can't women offer the same to men?"

"That's an entirely different thing, as you are well aware."

She waved a hand in dismissal. "I know. Services rendered. But I prefer to think of it as a negotiation where each side gets what he wants. Men offer money, and in exchange, women—"

"This conversation is over, Miss Weyland. Return to your duties."

Lottie slouched back in her chair, arms crossed. "Then what am I to do? How do I negotiate this with Ty so that we both get what we want? Becky says all a man needs is food, a dry place to sleep, and a woman to cuddle with. Surely, that can't be all there is to it."

When Briggs didn't respond, she glanced over to see him thumbing through the stack of mail on his desk.

"What's a rogering?"

His head flew up, eyes round with shock. "Where did you hear that word?"

"I overheard one of your countrymen use it. He said you needed one."

"Good God."

"What is it? Maybe if I got one for Ty, he'd be more open to my idea."

For a moment, he seemed at a loss for words. Then, in his sternest voice, "I cannot believe a woman as smart as you, Miss Weyland, can be so bloody ignorant."

Bloody. Wasn't that a cuss word? Why was he so angry? Not angry. Embarrassed.

Understanding dawned. As Becky so happily—and

often—pointed out, Lottie's "ignorance" usually had to do with men. If so, then "rogering" must mean . . . that.

She almost laughed. No wonder prudish Mr. Briggs was red in the face. To have his employees speculating on such a private matter must be awful for a man as guarded as he was. Still, he shouldn't have called her ignorant. That wasn't fair. Or true. And it demanded retaliation.

"Why would he say that about you, I wonder?"

No response.

"And how does one present a rogering? Wrapped and tied with a bow?"

"Miss Weyland."

"Do you know of a store where I could buy one?"

His eyes were positively fierce. "I am not having this discussion with you."

Laughter burst out of her. Poor Briggs. He might look as mean as a caged bear, but inside, he was soft as plum pudding. "Okay, I'll stop teasing you, Mr. Briggs. But you deserved it for calling me ignorant. And don't worry. I won't tell Jane. Your secret is safe with me."

"You are dismissed, Miss Weyland. Leave. Now. And don't ever come back."

"Of course, sir. As soon as I finish with the books."

An hour later, she left the club, her steps considerably lighter than when she'd arrived. Sparring with Briggs always put her in a good mood. There was nothing quite so satisfying as putting a bossy male in his place, even if she came out a bit battered in the exchange.

Yet, despite the teasing, she had learned something important today about how fragile a man's pride really was. And how desperately he might try to protect it, even if it led him to make rash decisions and say things he didn't truly mean. Like Ty refusing her help, or Briggs calling her ignorant. She would have to be wiser about how she handled future negotiations with men. She was just grateful Ty had come back last night to give her a second chance.

Chapter 15

The following weeks were busy ones for Lottie. The growing season was in full production in south Texas, and soon trains were heading north, loaded with fresh produce. By mid June, traveling greengrocers had set up booths outside the depot, and twice a week Lottie and Mrs. B. combed through the offerings to restock the produce bins at the store.

A newspaperman from Dallas wrote a flattering article about Lady Jane's Social Club and Greenbroke, and before long, business throughout town increased as more and more passengers stopped off for a visit or to try their luck at the tables. Lottie worried how that would impact Juno's profits, but as he'd said, he and the club catered to entirely different clienteles.

Increased business meant additional work for Lottie, but she didn't mind. She had a grand plan now, and needed every penny she could earn to make it work. The consortium investments were beginning to pay off, too, as word of Greenbroke's pleasant surroundings and easy rail access started bringing in land speculators and folks looking to move. It wasn't exactly a boom yet, but the future looked promising.

Lottie still worked at the bank, but only one afternoon a week now. Like in most towns, the local bank was the center of business, and Lottie liked knowing what was going on around her.

Which was how she found out about the Buck place.

The Buck and Reynolds families had been among the first to homestead in the Greenbroke area. The Bucks had settled along the east bank of Middling Creek—the same one that ran south of town and flooded whenever it had the chance. The Reynolds had homesteaded on the west bank. For a time they had prospered. But after decades of Indian attacks, bouts of small pox, complications of childbirth, childhood accidents, war, and general bad luck, the two families were down to Delbert Buck, his wife, Nadene Reynolds Buck, and their simple-minded daughter, Ruby. And poor Delbert, with his failing heart, wasn't long for this world. Worried what would become of his wife and daughter after he was gone, Delbert—who could no longer take care of the place anyway—was talking about taking his family back to Missouri where they had distant relatives.

Which meant he would probably sell.

Which meant Lottie was interested.

She cornered Griffin late one afternoon before the bank closed. "How does one go about buying land?"

He stopped stuffing papers into the drawer of his desk and gave her an amused look. "You buying land now?"

"Maybe."

"The Buck place?"

That surprised her. Maybe Griffin did more than nap at his desk in the afternoons. "I might. Thought I'd take a look-see first."

"It's good land." Griffin pushed the drawer closed, locked it, yelled for Humphries, and started shoving the papers atop his desk into neat piles. "Don't know what the house is like now. Probably run-down some since Delbert took sick. But as I recall, it was built sturdy."

Humphries came in, dressed to leave and looking more sour than usual. Probably irritated at the delay in his drinking plans. "Yes, Mr. Griffin?" he asked, squinting down at his pocket watch.

"What do you know about the Delbert Buck place?"

Despite his sullen attitude and the permanent squint that made him look slow-witted, Humphries had a memory any card sharp would envy. He could store a wealth of facts in that round head of his and, when primed, could spew them back out with remarkable accuracy.

"Just over five thousand acres, including both the Buck and Reynolds parcels. One useable house, two sheds, a barn with four paddocks. Some fencing. Year-round creek with seasonal flooding. Limited timber, but good graze— although Mr. Buck is more of a farmer than a rancher."

"Liens?"

"Free and clear."

"Make sure the safe is locked on your way out."

"Yes, sir."

After Humphries left, Griffin rose and lifted his bowler off the hat rack. "So there you have it, Miss Weyland." He set the hat at a jaunty angle on his balding head, herded her out of his office, then locked the door behind them. "Still interested?"

"If so, what would I do?"

"Settle on a price with Buck then come see me."

"About a loan?"

"Unless you've got that much cash or Buck decides to carry the note himself. Good night, Homer." He nodded toward the night guard who slept in the barred cell that housed the bank's safe, then walked Lottie toward the exit.

"What do you think he'll ask for it?"

Griffin named a figure.

Lottie thought about it while he locked the front doors. It wasn't a bad price for decent land but it was still a lot more than she had. "Is it worth it?"

"Depends on how bad he wants to sell and how bad you want to buy."

Lottie nodded, excitement building. This might be just

what she was looking for. "I'll ride out tomorrow and look it over, then let you know."

Early the next morning, following the directions Gus at the livery had given her when she'd rented Daisy, her usual horse, Lottie rode south out of Greenbroke. The day was already growing warm, but the air didn't yet have that dusty, lung-searing dryness that would come later in the summer. She breathed deep, enjoying the isolation and that sense of freedom she always felt when she left the bustle of town and all her troubles behind.

Not all her troubles. It had been almost three weeks since Ty had left her with the promise that he would soon return. And still, no word. Perhaps after today, if she got the news she hoped for, she would write to him. The thought made her smile. By putting her ideas in a letter, maybe she could explain it better. And hopefully, it would give him time to get over his initial resistance and think about what she was proposing.

The eight miles out to the Buck ranch went by fast, even though she kept the mare at a fast walk. She'd never been to their place, although she had seen the family in the market many times over the years. They were quiet folks, bent with age and hard work, and deeply devoted to the slow-witted child that had arrived late in their lives. Ruby was a sweet girl— woman, actually, since she was older than Lottie—and always had a ready smile for anyone who passed by. Remembering her fondness for peppermints, Lottie had brought two sticks from the store, as well as a potato sack of fresh produce for Mrs. Buck, and a tin of the tobacco Mr. Buck usually bought.

After fording shallow, meandering Middling Creek for the third time, Lottie saw the house ahead. It sat on a rise a quarter mile from the creek and at least sixty feet above flood level, as seen by the debris line stretching several yards above the low bank. Lottie thought it wise of Buck to build his house and buildings on high ground, since the creek had a tendency to flood after heavy rains.

About thirty yards from the house stood the barn and paddocks and two sheds. The sheds had fenced areas around them—stout wood and poultry mesh. Maybe a chicken house, and a garden shed or pig sty. Both needed work. Rising behind the house was another hill, topped with a cluster of wind-bent live oaks that probably shaded the house somewhat from the late afternoon sun.

The house was a big two-story box with evenly spaced windows along both levels and a small inverted V roof over the front entrance. Plain, but sturdy. Lottie's imagination filled in the first change she would make. Since the house faced east, she would add a wide, covered porch and balcony all across the front, so she could sit in a rocker or a bench hung from the eaves, and enjoy the sunrise in the morning and escape the heat on summer evenings.

As she drew closer, she studied the barn. Barns were almost as important as houses in rural areas and, by their condition, could give a fair indication of the prosperity of the holding. Buck's barn showed no sags in the roof, although a few shingles were missing and some of the plank siding on the sides would have to be replaced. One of the double front doors had busted off its hinges and several paddock rails were almost chewed through. All that would be easy to fix. What couldn't be fixed was the land itself.

And it wouldn't need to be. Judging by the fat cattle she saw as she rode up from the creek, it was as good as any grazing land she had seen around Greenbroke.

She tried not to get too excited, but it was hard not to. This could be the place. This could be a home.

The house had a small front yard enclosed by a three-foot picket fence, once whitewashed but now almost obscured by a riot of day lilies poking through the slats. Sweet Ruby was waiting at the gate, smiling and bouncing on her toes. "Hi-do, Miss Lottie," she called, waving vigorously. The elder Bucks watched from the small front stoop, smiles of welcome on their faces.

"Hi, Ruby. How are you today?" Lottie dismounted. After looping the mare's reins over a rail outside the picket fence, she loosened the horse's girth a notch then untied the potato sack hanging from the saddle.

"What you got in that sack, Miss Lottie?"

"Some things I brought from the store for your mama and papa."

"Nothing for me?"

Lottie pulled the candy sticks from her pocket. "Nothing but these. And this." She lifted a small rag doll from the sack. It wasn't much. A sand-stuffed figure in red gingham with yellow yarn hair, blue button eyes, and pink painted lips and cheeks. An impulse buy. But it had reminded Lottie of the doll her mother had made for her that she'd dragged around until the seams split and the stuffing fell out. Nothing to it, really. But seeing the girl's joy awakened bittersweet memories—Mama smiling and giving the rag doll to her. And years later, Grandpa saying, "You're too old for toys now," and throwing the tattered remains into the stove.

"Pep-mints! And a dolly!" With a squeal of delight, Ruby snatched them from Lottie's hands and raced up the dirt walk to show her parents her treasures.

Lottie followed. Once she'd handed over the sack of produce and tin of tobacco, and the Bucks had expressed their gratitude, they led her into the kitchen where Nadene had coffee warming and oatmeal cookies fresh out of the oven.

While Ruby played with her new doll in the front room, the adults sat at the worn kitchen table, Lottie munching on warm cookies and sharing the latest doings in Greenbroke. Although their place wasn't that far from town, even short trips had become an ordeal for Mr. Buck, so they didn't get into Greenbroke as often as they once had. Lottie knew from her own experience how the smallest tidbit of news could feed lonely people for weeks. So she talked until she ran out of gossip and the cookies were gone and her coffee cup was empty. Then she told them the purpose of her visit.

The old people looked at one another—sort of a sad look, heavy with meaning—then Delbert Buck nodded. "Sure, and we've talked of moving back to Missouri. Still have family there. And with no one around here to leave the place to . . ." He glanced toward the front room where Ruby was playing and shook his head. "Just hadn't figured on doing it this soon."

Lottie watched tears fill Nadene's faded eyes and felt a rush of sympathy. She knew how it felt to leave everything behind.

Seeing his wife's distress, Delbert patted her hand. In a falsely hearty voice, he said to Lottie, "You think you can run a place this size all by yourself, missy?"

Lottie smiled. "Not by myself."

"Got a fellow, do you?"

"Maybe."

"He better have a strong back."

"He does."

Nadene leaned forward, her earlier sadness forgotten. "Someone from town?"

"No, ma'am. But he comes through now and then. He was one of the rangers in the shoot-out last summer."

"A ranger! My word."

They discussed the shoot-out and rangers for a time, then Delbert planted his gnarled hands on the tabletop and pushed himself to his feet. "Nadene, why don't you show Miss Lottie through the house. When you're done, give a holler, and I'll give her a tour of the barn and such."

The Buck house was as Griffin had described. Worn, but sturdy. The central staircase led up to four bedrooms, although the Bucks used one of them for storage and another as a play area for Ruby. If it was up to Lottie, and there was enough water pressure, she would install indoor plumbing and convert one of the unused bedrooms into a dressing area and water closet.

Downstairs was a parlor and a big kitchen with an eating area. Lottie liked the roominess of the house but could see it needed refreshing.

Mr. Buck's tour of the outside area didn't show Lottie anything she didn't expect. The barn held four stalls, a tack and feed room, and plenty of space in the overhead loft for hay. Everything seemed solid. What wasn't, looked repairable.

The paddocks off the barn would have to be replaced, but the rest of the fencing—what there was—was barbed wire and seemed in passable shape except for a few rotted posts.

The well was in good condition, and the water Buck pumped for her was sweet and clear. But the creek was the biggest asset. A ranch couldn't operate without ample water. Mr. Buck said it ran year-round, and the seasonal flooding wasn't a big problem unless he was in a hurry to get to town, which he rarely was nowadays.

Excitement built. Plans raced through her mind. The place was perfect for her and Ty.

Not wanting to appear too eager, Lottie let Mr. Buck bring up price. It was higher than she'd hoped, but not high enough to put her off. They danced around it for a while then Lottie admitted she only had enough for a down payment of fifteen percent, and asked if Delbert would want to carry the balance for five years at low interest.

He said he'd think about it.

She said she'd do the same.

And that was the end of their first negotiation.

Lottie thought it went well. She would know how well if Buck made a counter offer she could live with. She would discuss it with Griffin and see if he could do better with a bank loan, but so far, it was looking good.

As she rode back to town, she dreamed of all the changes she would make. Flowers and a porch across the front. Fresh paint and new curtains. A windmill to pump water up to a tank on the hill behind the house so they could have gravity-fed water for indoor plumbing. A bench swing hanging from the eaves that was big enough for her and Ty to cuddle together on cool evenings.

She couldn't wait to write him about the wonderful place she'd found. Then the next move would be up to him. If he was serious about trying his hand at ranching—and her—he would know exactly what he had to do.

———

Three days later, Lt. Tyree Benton stepped off the train onto the loading platform of the Greenbroke railroad station, the knot of dread in his belly as tight as a clenched fist. He'd thought about sending word that he was coming, and why.

But he was still reeling from shock and wasn't sure what to say. Besides, it might have complicated things. Or made them even worse. If that was possible.

Hearing footsteps behind him, he looked back to see Lt. Tom Millsap approaching, his saddlebags over one shoulder and a surly look on his deeply lined face.

"So where do we look first?" the older man asked, stopping beside him. "I want to get this over with as soon as possible."

"Brackett's Market."

As Ty started up Main Street, that feeling of dread hardened into anger. He felt betrayed. Confused. Furious that he was having to do this—that he'd been lied to—that he'd been so easily fooled. He had questions. And by God, he would get his answers.

Ignoring the curious stares directed their way, he and Millsap strode purposely down the boardwalk, the thud of their boot heels signaling they were men in a hurry and not to be detained. Ty wished he could outdistance the man plodding along beside him. He didn't like or trust Millsap. Especially since the older ranger was in charge of this detail, even though he and Ty were of equal rank. Now Ty would have to keep an eye on him, too.

They had both ridden under Captain Leander McNelly years ago when the Frontier Battalion patrolled the lawless Nueces Strip. But while Ty had been put off by their captain's questionable and sometimes brutal tactics, Millsap had seemed to enjoy them. After McNelly's retirement three years prior, Millsap had served in various capacities until he settled into prisoner escort last year. Since then, more than one prisoner had complained of harsh treatment at his hands. Which is why, when Ty heard about this detail and that Millsap had been assigned to it, he had volunteered to come along. He was determined there would be no harsh treatment this time. The idea of it sickened him. A sign of weakness that only added to the anger bubbling in his mind.

She should have told him.

She should have trusted him enough to let him help her.

Damn that woman.

The Bracketts hadn't seen Lottie that day. When they realized he wasn't going to tell them why two grim-faced Texas Rangers were looking for her, they suggested he check at Becky's.

When they didn't find her there, Ty crossed over to the Spotted Dog.

"This is more like it," Millsap said, stepping through the swinging doors of the saloon.

Ty spotted Becky and the owner, Juno, talking at a table against the back wall. "Why don't you have a drink while I ask around?"

Millsap didn't need urging. When he headed to the bar, Ty walked toward the back table.

Becky grinned when she saw him. "Ty! What are you doing in town? As if I didn't know," she added with a wink.

"Where's Lottie?"

Her grin faded. "What's wrong?"

"I need to find her."

Juno glanced at Millsap then back at Ty. "What is this about, Benton?" Those sharp eyes didn't miss much.

Ty had come for answers, not more questions. He started to turn away.

Becky grabbed his arm. "She's at Lady Jane's. But I'm going with you."

Juno pushed back his chair. "Then I guess I am, too."

Ty couldn't stop them. In truth, he was glad to have them along. This would be difficult for all of them, but mostly for Lottie, and she would need her friends around her. He just hoped they didn't try to interfere with what he had to do.

When Ty asked Kearsey at the club where Lottie was, he told them to wait in the lobby and he would get Briggs. Millsap wouldn't hear of it. So, the four of them walked past the doorman and down the narrow hallway to the offices in back.

When they came through the door, Lottie looked up from the ledger she was working on, saw Ty, and jumped to her feet. "Ty!" she cried with a smile of welcome surprise.

"What are you doing here?" Then she noticed Becky and Juno and Kearsey crowding behind him, and something in their faces alerted her. "What's wrong?"

Briggs had risen, too. As Millsap shoved forward, the Englishman came around his desk and planted his big body at Lottie's side. "May I ask the reason for this intrusion?" His tone was calm, but Ty could see the steel in his gray eyes.

Ignoring him, Millsap addressed Lottie directly. "Are you Charlotte Weyland?"

Lottie looked at Ty. The confusion and fear he saw in her face ripped a hole in him. He almost went to her, desperate to shield her from what was to come. But he didn't dare.

She looked back at Millsap. "Y-yes, I'm Lottie Weyland."

He pulled manacles from his coat pocket. "Hold out your wrists, ma'am."

"Why?"

Becky charged forward. "What are you doing?"

Ty put out an arm to stop her. "Don't interfere."

"You're letting him do this? Juno, do something!"

Ty braced himself, half expecting the saloon owner to rush him.

Then Briggs's voice cut through the room. "Kearsey, get the sheriff. Now!"

"Have him meet us at the jail," Ty told the doorman without taking his eyes off the furious ex-soldier.

Becky began to cry. "Ty, what's happening? Why are you doing this?"

Color left Lottie's face as Millsap snapped the metal cuffs on her wrists. She looked at Ty in panic, but he couldn't help her.

"Charlotte Weyland," Millsap said in a rehearsed tone, "by the authority of the Texas Rangers and the State of Texas, I arrest you for the murder of William Franklin Lofton." Then he took her arm in a firm grip and led her past the stunned onlookers.

Chaos erupted.

"Who's William Franklin Lofton?"

"Ranger Benton, what is this about?"

"I'm going with her!"

When Becky tried to follow, Ty stepped into the doorway and blocked her from leaving. "There's nothing you can do. And making a scene will only upset her more."

"But she didn't do anything! She's not a murderer!"

"You better have a damn good reason for this, Benton," Juno warned, "if you expect to leave this town alive."

Ty felt like howling. Slamming his fist into the wall. But he couldn't protect Lottie if he was in jail, too. He fought to remain calm, as he'd been trained to do in tense situations. "Are you threatening me, sir?"

"Bloody hell. Stand down, Juno," ordered Briggs.

Ty looked from one furious face to another. He knew how they felt. The shock, the confusion, that sense of betrayal. But events were now in motion that none of them could stop. All they could do was watch helplessly as they unfolded and hope for the best. "I know you have questions. And I'll answer them—"

"Then start talking," Juno snapped.

Ty looked back to check the hall and saw that Millsap and Lottie were already in the lobby. "Later. I need to see her safely settled then I'll come back and talk to you."

"Safely settled?" Briggs advanced, his bull neck red with fury. "Don't you trust your own man?"

Ty had no doubt the ex-soldier could do serious damage with those clenched fists. He almost wished the Englishman would try, so he could act on the rage churning inside. But he couldn't. He had to see this through. It was the only way to protect Lottie and get the answers he needed. "I have to go. Now." He started down the hall.

"Who is William Franklin Lofton?" Juno called after him.

"Her grandfather. I'll be back as soon as I can."

Chapter 16

Lottie sat stiff-backed on the cot in the back corner of her
cell and watched the late afternoon sun slide past her
barred window. Low voices drifted down the narrow hall
from the sheriff's office in front. Probably the ranger who
had handcuffed her and brought her here. Maybe Sheriff
Dodson. Was Ty there, too?

She pictured the look on his face—the hurt, the bewilderment. The anger. She should have told him. But after waiting
so long for the past to catch up with her, when it didn't, she
had allowed herself to believe the danger of being found out
was past. Why bring up something that was behind her forever? But when she saw his face, she knew she'd made a
terrible mistake.

She should have told him. Another *if only* strewn in her
wake.

Angrily, she brushed her tears away. Crying wouldn't help.
She would have to wait and explain everything to him later.
But for now, she had to think. Figure out what to do next.

It was a struggle to focus her thoughts. She could hardly
grasp what was happening to her, even though in the back
of her mind she feared this day might come. But why now?

Almost four years after she'd set the fire and when everything she had worked toward was almost within her reach? What had changed?

The people nosing around Grandpa's ranch must have found his body and reported it. But wouldn't the flames have destroyed everything? Unless the fire had burned out too soon or the storm had doused it. Did they find his blackened bones? A charred skeleton with a chain around its neck?

The images were so vile they sent bile shooting up the back of her throat. Gasping, she bent over and retched. Nothing came up. After a moment the cramping stopped and she sagged weakly against the wall that the cot was pushed up against.

Would she be hanged? Locked in a tiny cell for the rest of her life? Would she have to stand up in front of everyone and tell what happened? Shame rolled through her. The staring. The questions. Having to dredge up every wretched detail of those last awful days and her grandfather's endless suffering. Unable to face it, she dropped her head into her hands.

Grandpa . . . I'm so sorry.

From the office came the sound of a door opening and closing. Heart thudding, she lifted her head as a new voice joined the two others. She recognized the low rumble. Hope shot through her. She tried to make out what Ty was saying but couldn't. Awareness that he was near filled her with both dread and longing. He knew now what she had done. Did he know why? Would he forgive her? She waited, praying he would walk back to her cell and tell her that they were wrong, it was all a mistake, and she was free to go.

Instead, the outside door opened and closed again, and hope died.

What would her life have been like, she wondered, if not for that one awful decision—command, really. What if she had simply said no? But if she had, there would be no Greenbroke, no farm-boy-ranger, and a different kind of guilt.

Silence pressed against her, making it hard to breathe. Had they left her? Needing distraction, she looked around, saw names scratched into the stone, and felt the despair that had seeped into these walls. The air smelled faintly of urine, sweat, alcohol. Desperation. Was she doomed to this for the rest of her life?

Tears threatened again. This time, she hadn't the strength to hold them back. Slumping onto the stained mattress, she curled into a ball and wept for Ty and for Grandpa and for all that she had lost.

———

Ty stood in the shadows under the boardwalk overhang and watched Millsap walk toward the Greenbroke Hotel to get something to eat. When he saw him disappear inside, he waited a few more minutes to make sure he didn't come back out, then hurried on to the Social Club. After he dealt with Lottie's friends, he would go back and relieve Sheriff Dodson. He didn't trust the elderly sheriff to stay awake through the night and Ty couldn't leave Lottie unguarded with Millsap around. Plus, with both men gone, he could get the answers he sought.

When he walked into Briggs's office a few minutes later, he found it empty. Then he heard voices across the hall.

"In here," Briggs called. "Lady Jane's office is more comfortable."

And more elegant, Ty noted when he entered. Becky and Jane Knightly sat in upholstered chairs that had been turned to face the room, rather than the cold marble fireplace. Briggs and Juno stood beside a delicate table topped with a silver tray holding three glasses and a cut glass decanter. "Drink, Ranger Benton?" Briggs asked, pouring amber liquid into one glass.

Ty shook his head. He needed to stay focused when he questioned Lottie. "It's Lieutenant Benton now."

After pouring drinks for him and Juno, Briggs pulled the chair from behind the desk and set it in the middle of the room and facing the women. "Have a seat," he ordered, then took up a position behind Miss Knightly, while Juno stood beside Becky's chair.

An inquisition. Dreading what was to come but knowing he couldn't avoid it, Ty took off his Stetson, set it on the desktop, then sat. He looked at the hostile faces staring back at him and waited for the questioning to begin. At least no one was crying. Yet.

"What is the basis for these murder charges against Miss Weyland?" Briggs asked, signaling he was in charge of this interrogation.

Ty was glad. Even though Briggs might be a dangerous man, he also seemed levelheaded, which was good. If they were to help Lottie, they would need to think calmly, and not get sucked into an emotional shouting match.

"She's accused of setting fire to her grandfather's ranch then disappearing."

"There's no law against torching your own place," Juno argued.

"There is if a man is left chained inside one of the burning buildings."

Shock. Disbelief. Disgust. Ty recognized them all. Felt them all.

Jane Knightly made a sound of distress and pressed a hand over her mouth.

Briggs murmured something, his big hand resting on her shoulder.

Juno would have comforted Becky, too, but she was already out of her chair.

"That's ridiculous! She didn't do it, Ty! You know she didn't! Why are you doing this to her? I thought you cared about her!"

"Sit down, Becky." Juno put a hand on her arm.

She shook him off. "But he said he loved her! How can he do this if he loves her? This is wrong! You know it is! Lottie would never hurt anybody!" Her voice ended on that screechy high note women make when they try to talk and cry at the same time.

So much for calmness.

Ty crossed his arms and waited for the shouting to stop. It was disconcerting to have his private declarations made public—especially now, when he was so confused he didn't know what he felt anymore.

Once Juno had Becky under control and back in her chair,

Briggs asked how they knew the body was her grandfather's, especially after so long. "What's it been—four years?"

"About. The fire didn't burn everything. Lofton had distinctive false teeth. Two were metal and survived the flames. So did his pocket watch. It was a gift from the school back east where he had taught before the war and was inscribed on the back with his name. Reportedly, he never went without it. Then there's the fact that Lottie ran." Which was the part Ty didn't understand. She must have known how that would look. And if she was innocent, why didn't she report the fire?

Juno's voice cut through his thoughts. "How did they track her here?"

"Mr. Lofton had been through Greenbroke in the past. He mentioned it to several parishioners at the church he attended in San Angela, saying he might want to move here someday when he tired of ranching. After they quit coming to town, folks figured they'd left. It was a long shot. But when your Sheriff Dodson was contacted by investigators after the remains were found, he confirmed she lived here."

Becky looked at him, tears streaming down her face, her eyes reflecting the same bewilderment Ty felt. "But why you? Didn't they know what it would do to her to send you to arrest her?"

"No one sent me. I volunteered. That's the only way I could ensure that Lottie would be safe."

"That's the second time you've mentioned her safety," Briggs said. "What's your concern?"

Ty hesitated, not sure how to answer. Millsap hadn't said or done anything of a hostile nature. Still, Ty didn't trust him. Or maybe, he was just using that as an excuse to stay close to Lottie. "There's been no threat. But it's a long way to San Angela, and she doesn't know Ranger Millsap. He's a rough old cob and might not treat her as courteously as she deserves. I'm there to see that he does."

"The poor dear." Miss Knightly dabbed a lace handkerchief to her eyes. "Someone should go with her."

"I will!" Becky shot to her feet again. "If she has to stand trial, she'd want me to be there."

Ty shook his head. "You can't travel with her, Becky. She's not allowed to associate with anyone outside of law enforcement while she's in transit."

"You mean I can't see her at all?"

"You can see her at the jail. But I'd appreciate it if you wouldn't tell anyone about her arrest until after we leave. Even the Bracketts. She's like a daughter to them. They'll take it hard, and the last thing Lottie needs is a weepy send-off or to be bombarded with a bunch of questions."

With tearful reluctance, Becky returned to her seat.

Juno asked when they were leaving.

"On the morning train. But I'll stay on guard all night."

"Is there anything we can do?" Jane Knightly asked.

"There is." Leaning forward, Ty rested his forearms across his bent knees. "Tell her not to discuss what happened to her grandfather with anyone. Especially Millsap and the sheriff. And me. We have to report anything she says to us, and it could be used against her if this goes to trial." He would tell her that, too, if he had the chance. But if Millsap overheard and thought Ty was interfering, he might use that as a reason to kick Ty off the detail, which would leave Lottie unprotected.

"*If*? You mean there's a chance there won't be a trial?"

"It depends on how the preliminary hearing goes and what the judge decides. If he thinks there's not enough of a case against her, he'll drop the charges."

"What are the chances of that?" Juno pressed.

Ty shrugged. "So far, there are no witnesses, no proof that she even set fire to the shed, much less knew her grandfather was chained inside. Remember, the charge against her is murder, not arson."

Jane Knightly looked at the others. "That sounds hopeful, doesn't it?"

"It would if she hadn't disappeared right after," Juno told her. "That makes her look guilty."

"The grisly nature of the crime doesn't help, either," Briggs added. "If she set the fire, she needs to give a plausible explanation why. If she didn't set it, she'll have to explain why she ran."

Such logic was wasted on Becky. "But we know she didn't do it! She would never murder anyone, much less her own grandfather. If she did set the fire, she had a good reason and once the judge hears it, he'll have to let her go."

Ty admired her loyalty. It was apparent that Lottie had kept her friend in the dark, too, yet Becky never wavered.

"I'm sure you're right, Becky." Juno gave her shoulder a reassuring squeeze then turned again to Ty. "Is there anything else we can do, Lieutenant?"

"She'll need a lawyer. A good one. Sheriff Dodson doesn't have much confidence in the one here in Greenbroke."

"Because he's a drunk."

Becky sat up, her brown eyes sparking with interest, rather than tears. "You're taking her to San Angela?" When Ty nodded, she rushed on. "She's gotten a couple of letters from a lawyer there. Has an odd name. I could probably find the letters in her room."

"If you do, wire him about the charges against her and tell him she'll be arriving in San Angela day after tomorrow. I'll pay his fees."

"Wouldn't that be in conflict with your ranger duties?" Briggs asked.

"I won't be with the rangers then. The minute we get her to the San Angela jail, I'm quitting." He had no stomach for this job anymore. Whether she was guilty or innocent, everything had changed.

His announcement caused a stir, but Ty impatiently waved aside their questions. Millsap would be finishing his dinner about now and Ty needed to get back to Lottie. "One last thing," he said to Becky. "She'll need clothes and personal items to take with her. Can you get that together and bring it to the jail?"

Becky nodded.

"What about food?" Jane Knightly asked. "I can bring something from the club's kitchen. Have you eaten dinner, Ranger Benton?"

Ty shook his head and thanked her for the gesture, although he wasn't sure either he or Lottie would have much appetite. He rose and picked up his hat. "See you at the jail."

When Lottie heard the door into the sheriff's office open, she felt such relief her knees shook. She could tell by the heaviness of the footfalls that it was Ty. Sheriff Dodson was older and had a slow, shuffling gait. Braver now that she was no longer alone with Millsap, she glared at the smirking ranger, still shaken by his suggestion that if she cooperated he'd see that things went easier for her. She wasn't sure what he meant by "cooperate," but by the look in his piggish eyes when he said it, he wasn't referring to legalities.

When Ty walked up to her cell, he must have seen her panic. "What's going on, Millsap?"

"Just trying to get a confession and save us the trouble of a trial." Millsap glanced from Ty's furious face to Lottie's frightened one. A look of speculation settled over his weathered features. "You two got something going between you?"

Ty didn't answer, but Lottie recognized the struggle for control behind the icy glare.

The older ranger saw it, too. "So that's how it is. Do I have to watch you now, too, Benton?"

"Do what you want," Ty said through tight lips. "But I'll be watching you, too."

They glowered at each other for a few seconds, then Millsap shrugged. "Suit yourself." He turned back to Lottie. "I'll tell you what I tell all my prisoners, Miss Weyland. Try to run and I'll put a bullet in your back. Give me lip and I'll gag you. Escape and I'll hunt you down like a dog." His gaze shifted to Ty. "And if you sweet talk Benton here into helping you, I'll do the same to him. Understand?"

Neither answered.

He studied them a moment longer. "We leave on the early train." And without another word he left.

As soon as the door closed behind him, Lottie stepped closer and grabbed the bars of her cell. They felt cold and greasy in her hands, making her wonder how many other desperate prisoners had clutched them before her.

"Ty, I'm so sorry I brought you into this."

He didn't respond. She could feel that intense gaze studying her, could read the questions and doubts he was struggling with, saw the anger that made the blue in his eyes burn even hotter.

"Just tell me one thing, Lottie," he finally said in a hard, cold voice. "Did you do it? Did you kill your grandfather?"

That he would ask that question told her how his thoughts ran. She shouldn't blame him. And yet she did. "I don't know."

"How can you not know?"

His fury sent her back a step, yet the distance between them seemed to stretch an immeasurable distance. She'd lost him. Her silence had cost her his trust, his faith. His love. The sudden sense of loss almost doubled her over. Only pride kept her upright. He deserved the truth, even if it was too slow in coming, and no matter how painful it might be. "I don't know if I killed him. When I set—"

"Stop!" He thrust up a shaking hand. "I don't want to hear it. I *can't* hear it."

"But I thought you—"

"You're not supposed to talk about this to anyone—not Millsap, not the sheriff, not even me—unless your lawyer is with you. I shouldn't have asked."

"But I want you to know, Ty. I want to tell you what I should have told you months ago." How could she fix this if he wouldn't even listen to what she had to say? "I know you would never repeat—"

"No." Shaking his head, he stepped back as far as the narrow space outside her cell would allow. "I'm an officer of the court. I have to report anything you say to the judge."

"But it's just me, Ty. You and me. Can't we—"

"No." She hardly recognized the harsh tone of his voice, the trapped look in his eyes. "I took an oath, Lottie. If you don't say anything, then I won't have to lie to protect you."

Lie? So he thought she did murder Grandpa? Without even hearing her side of it?

Ty started to say more when the door opened.

"Lottie!" Becky shouted.

"Back here," Lottie called.

A moment later, Becky burst through the doorway between the cells and the sheriff's front office, Juno right behind her. "I've been so worried! Are you all right? I sent a wire to that lawyer in San Angela and told him that you were coming, and look!" She held up a small bag and nodded toward the larger valise hanging from Juno's han . "We brought you clothes and your reticule, and a brush, and some hairpins, and . . . are you sure you're all right? You look like you've been crying."

Becky did, too. "I'm worried and a little frightened, but unharmed. I see you brought reinforcements." She greeted Jane and Briggs, embarrassed that they should see her like this, but grateful they had come to show support. "Thank you so much for being here. It means a lot to me to see friendly faces."

Sheriff Dodson had returned, and came into the hallway behind the others. He seemed surprised to see so many people crowded outside Lottie's cell. "Party?"

"Just saying their good-byes," Ty told him.

Jane stepped up to the bars, her arms laden with a cloth-wrapped basket. "I brought you something to eat. There's enough for Ranger Benton, too." When she looked for a way to shove the basket between the bars, Dodson put out a hand.

"I'll have to check that, ma'am. Just to make sure you haven't slipped a six shooter in there with the vittles." He said it with a smile, but they all knew he wasn't joking. Nodding to the bags Juno and Becky held, he added, "I'll need to see those, too. If you'll carry them into the front office, I'll inspect them there."

It was humiliating to have her personal things pawed through. But Lottie was glad to have them. She would need fresh clothing in the morning. The thoughtfulness of her dear friends almost undid her. Especially when they didn't ask if she was guilty of the charges against her. Unlike Ty, who seemed to have made up his mind already.

"Miss Weyland." Briggs frowned at Ty, obviously wishing

to speak to her privately. When Ty didn't move, he went on. "You mustn't say anything about your case in front of—"

"I know. He already told me." Peering toward the office to make sure Jane couldn't hear, she waved the Englishman closer. "I don't know when I'll see you again, but I—"

"You must soldier on, Miss Weyland. I'm sure you will be back home in—"

"I'm not talking about that," she cut in impatiently. "I'm talking about the way you've been bullying Jane. You've got to stop it, Mr. Briggs. I know you think you're doing the right thing, but you're only hurting her."

"I see." He stiffened, shoulders back, hands clasped behind him. "And you'll explain to me why that is any of your business?"

"Don't play the soldier with me, Briggs. It's my business because I care about both of you and want you to be happy." Nothing was quite as trite as jailhouse avowals, but Lottie meant it. She loved all these people. They were her family now and she wanted their happiness—even if she might not be around to manage it for them. "Jane doesn't want to leave. And I don't think you want to go back, either."

"Go back where?" Jane asked, walking up behind Briggs.

"To the club," Lottie hedged. "I appreciate what you've done. All of you," she added as Becky and Juno crowded behind Jane. "But I'm very tired. And I can see how this ordeal has wearied you, too. So please go home, say a prayer for me, and hold good thoughts."

Becky began crying, promising she would. As she turned to go, Lottie grabbed Juno's arm. "Don't let her be alone," she whispered. "She really needs you now, Juno."

He started to argue with her, then gave a curt nod and followed Becky out.

Jane moved closer to the bars. "Take heart, dearest. In England, I, too, was accused of something I didn't do. It was terrifying. I doubt I would have gotten through it without Anson." She shot the big Englishman a fond smile, which he tried to ignore. "But I did. And you will, as well. Trust your ranger, as I did my soldier, and he'll see no harm befalls you."

Lottie glanced at Ty.

He stared back, those flame blue eyes so intense they looked lit from within.

"Now, try to sleep." Jane reached through the bars and patted Lottie's arm. "I'll send another basket of food to the station in the morning. Ranger Benton, make certain she eats. We don't want her getting sick, do we?"

"Yes, ma'am. I'll see she's taken care of."

"I have no doubt of it." A pat on his arm, too, then she swept down the hall, Briggs at her heels.

Lottie felt tears welling. She was terrified she might never see any of them again.

After the outside door closed behind them, Ty glanced into the office to see that Dodson had finished inspecting the basket and two bags her friends had brought. "I'll get your dinner. And while you eat, maybe you should worry about your own problems, rather than trying to manage everyone else's."

A mean thing to say. But he was right. If she was to get through this, she had best start thinking about what she should do next.

It promised to be a long, horrible night. She hardly had the strength to swallow the delicious food Jane had brought, and wondered how she would ever be able to sleep in this dismal place. As soon as Ty had devoured everything she couldn't eat, he convinced Sheriff Dodson he needn't stay the night, sent him on his way, then moved a chair from the front room to the hallway outside her cell.

"Sleep," he ordered, slouching down, his ankles and arms crossed. "I'll see that no one disturbs you."

In view of his anger and lack of faith in her, Lottie wondered why he bothered. Or why he'd come to Greenbroke in the first place.

If only he would let her explain what she'd done and why. But even if she did, would a man as honorable as Ty—one who saw the world in black and white and put duty to the ranger star above loyalty to the woman he professed to love—ever be able to forgive her?

Chapter 17

———•———

Lottie managed to get a few hours' rest before Ty called through the bars that it was time to wake up. After returning her valise and allowing her privacy to change, he brought in the dreaded handcuffs.

"It's only a formality," he explained, obviously as upset about the manacles as she was. "I don't want to give Millsap any reason for complaint."

Lottie looked at him in surprise. Ty was younger, stronger, bigger. Surely the paunchy ranger posed no threat to him. "Are you afraid of him?"

He snorted at the idea. "I don't trust him. He's got a mean streak. Several prisoners have complained." The click of the cuffs locking over her wrists sounded loud in the small, stone room. "We'll use the back door." Taking her elbow, he steered her out of the cell.

Lottie remembered the way Millsap had looked at her when he'd suggested she cooperate. She didn't doubt he could be a threat to her. But she was tall for a woman and agile and Grandpa had taught her how to drop a man to his knees with a well-placed kick. "I can take care of myself."

Ty gave her a look. "And everybody else, it seems."

"What's that supposed to mean?"

He stepped ahead of her onto the back stoop, scanned the alley, then led her toward the small outhouse standing in the weeds at the edge of the rutted road behind the jail. "Just stay clear of Millsap and do what I tell you. I don't want to give him any excuse to send me back. I wouldn't be able to help you then."

It pleased her that he still cared enough to worry about her. But she didn't need the warning. She'd already had one confrontation with Millsap and knew if he came at her again, she might not have metal bars to keep him at bay.

At the reeking outhouse, Ty removed the manacles and waited by the door while she tended to her needs. When she stepped out, gasping for fresh air, he replaced the cuffs and escorted her back to the jail.

Another humiliating experience. She supposed she had best get accustomed to them.

Once in her cell, he removed the cuffs again and left, only to return a minute later with a small bar of soap, a scrap of towel, and a pan of cold water to wash in. He also gave her the hairpins the sheriff had confiscated during his search. "We'll head to the depot in ten minutes. You'll be handcuffed again and Millsap will walk with us, but I'll try to make it as easy on you as I can."

"Thank you."

They were back to stilted politeness, all the warmth between them gone. She almost wished he would shout at her or leave so she wouldn't have to suffer his cold withdrawal. But that same sense of honor that wouldn't allow him to talk to her, also wouldn't allow harm to befall her. She took comfort in that. "Did you get my letter?" she asked as he started back toward the front office.

He stopped. "Recently? Where did you send it?"

"Austin. But I only posted it a few days before you arrived, so it probably never reached you." Just as well. If things went south in San Angela, she might never see the Buck place again. Or Ty.

"I'll send word to have it forwarded to San Angela."

"It's not important."

He studied her for a moment. "Any letter from you is important."

Lottie tried to smile, but feared her face might crack. "You can say that now, after all this?"

"Lottie . . ." He rubbed a hand along the back of his neck, frustration apparent in the way he avoided her eyes. "Why didn't you tell me?" he finally burst out. "I might have been able to help you if you had."

"Like you're helping me now?" *Unfair.* She knew it. But he wasn't the only one suffering disappointment. She had expected better of him, too. "I did try to tell you," she reminded him. "But you said you couldn't talk to me about it."

"*Now* I can't. But I could have if you'd told me earlier." She could see the uncertainty in his face and wondered if it would stand between them forever.

"I just wish you'd told me, Lottie. It was a shock, finding out the way I did. Made me wonder if I knew you at all."

"I'm the same person I was before you knew about Grandpa. You're the one who's changed."

"I still love you." It sounded less like a declaration than a grudging admission.

"*Still*?" Should she dance a jig across the cell floor? "Even though you don't know if I'm guilty or not? How loyal of you."

"Damnit, Lottie! What am I supposed to think? I walk into ranger headquarters, see your name and a drawing of you pinned to the wall—'*Charlotte Weyland, Wanted for Murder*'—what the hell am I supposed to think?"

"That I might be innocent?"

He gave a long, heavy sigh. "I know you're not a murderer. Any woman who would charge into the middle of a gunfight to help a wounded man could never be a cold-blooded killer. Whatever happened between you and your grandfather was not by your design. But you should have trusted me enough to tell me. That's what I can't get past. I don't need you to buy me a ranch, or shield me from the truth, or keep secrets you think I won't want to hear. I'm the one who should be protecting you, not the other way around."

"I wasn't trying to protect you. I was protecting myself. I was ashamed. And I was afraid if I told you . . ." She spread her hands in a gesture of defeat. "This would happen."

She waited for him to say something. When he didn't, she gave up. "If we're leaving in ten minutes," she said, wearily, "I need to wash and tidy my hair."

Lips pressed in a thin line, he whirled and walked out.

Lottie wasn't a praying person—at least, not since Grandpa's death. But this June morning, as she walked to the train station between Ty and Ranger Millsap, with manacles locked over her wrists and the stares of curious townsfolk tracking her every step, she offered up her first prayer in over three years. A simple chant that circled around and around in her head.

Help me get through this. Help me get through this.

God must have heard and taken pity. From the moment she boarded the train in Greenbroke until she stepped off the stagecoach in San Angela the following afternoon, she was numb to thought, to sound, even color. The world was reduced to an endless, silent, sepia vista rolling past the window beside her seat.

She functioned. She did what she was told, ate when food was set before her, slept when she could. She didn't complain about the handcuffs, or being locked in a cell overnight in some small railroad town before boarding a stagecoach bound for San Angela the next morning. It was as if she moved through knee-deep mud. Even breathing was an effort. The only thing she remembered about those exhausting hours was that Ty was there beside her or within sight.

Thank you, God.

The journey seemed to take forever, yet ended too soon with their arrival early in the afternoon the day after she'd left Greenbroke. When the stagecoach rolled to a stop outside the Overland Stage office in San Angela, a small,

dapper, white-haired man with thick spectacles, a kindly
smile, and a satchel bulging with papers came forward. He
studied Lottie as if they might be acquainted. But after being
stared at so often throughout the trip, it seemed everyone
looked at her in speculation, as if word of the infamous
Weyland Murderess had raced ahead of her across the wires.

"Miss Weyland?" he asked, doffing his bowler as she
stepped onto the boardwalk.

Lottie drew back, fearing he was one of those scandal-
hungry newspapermen Ty had warned her about.

"Stand aside," Millsap ordered, resting his hand on the
butt of the pistol holstered at his hip. "Don't approach the
prisoner." Positioning Lottie between him and Ty, they
started down the street.

The old man pulled a small card from his suit pocket,
handed it to Millsap without looking in his direction, then
fell into step with the three of them.

"Allow me to introduce myself, Miss Weyland," he said,
leaning forward to speak across Ty. "My name is Ridley
Sims. I received a wire that you would be arriving and might
need my assistance?" He had to hurry to keep up with Ty's
long strides.

Lottie relaxed enough to smile. "Oh, yes, Mr. Sims. I'm
so happy to meet you."

"Actually, we met many years ago. I attended the same
church you and your grandfather frequented whenever you
were in town."

"Yes, I recognize you now." But Lottie hadn't known he
was a solicitor. "Thank you for meeting us. Are you ac-
companying us to the jail?"

"I am. We will say no more for now, but be assured, Miss
Weyland, I will do everything I can to straighten out this
mess as quickly as possible."

"I hope so."

The next few hours went by so fast Lottie hardly knew
what was happening. Thank goodness Mr. Sims was there
to get her through the legal procedures. As soon as they
arrived at the San Angela jail, Millsap and Ty left to

complete the paperwork relating to her arrest and transport. The San Angela sheriff searched her belongings for weapons, told her the circuit judge was in town so she would probably go before him that afternoon, then took her to her cell. Another dim, dank cage.

After locking her in, he set a chair for Mr. Sims outside the bars then retreated to his front office so they could discuss her case in private.

"The trial is today?" Lottie thought she would have more time to ready herself. Everything was happening so quickly.

Sims shook his head. "Only the arraignment. All you have to do is enter a plea of guilty or not guilty after the judge reads the charges against you. I will handle the rest."

"The rest?" Lottie wanted no surprises. Knowing what to expect would keep her from panicking.

"I will ask for bail, which he will deny. Then I will request a preliminary hearing to be held at a later date, which he will grant. The hearing is similar to a trial—open to the public, with lawyers and witnesses and a judge. But instead of a jury deciding your guilt or innocence, the judge will decide if there is enough evidence against you to take you to trial. I'm hoping there is not. But I'll be better able to assess the situation after you answer a few questions. Shall we begin?"

Things became muddled for Lottie after that. Exhaustion, fear, and lack of sleep had begun to take their toll. Most of his questions centered around what she remembered about that awful day. Especially after she admitted she didn't know for certain if Grandpa was dead when she lit the fire.

"I know that sounds improbable," she added, remembering Ty's reaction when she'd told him the same thing. "But the shed was locked. And since I couldn't get inside, all I could do was call to him. Which I did for a day, maybe two—I don't remember exactly, but it seemed a long time. When he didn't answer or eat the food I brought or move, I assumed he was dead and lit the fire."

Should she have waited longer? Would she ever know?

He wrote everything down then gathered his papers and

shoved them into his case. "I was aware of your grandfather's situation," he said, surprising her. "He came to see
me soon after the hound died. I'm sorry he chose to involve
you this way but I understand his reasoning."

Lottie didn't. But before they could discuss it further, the
sheriff returned to escort her to the arraignment in the courtroom next to the jail.

Apparently Mr. Sims was well acquainted with Judge
Yarborough—another older man, with a hairless dome of a
head and a curling, lacquered mustache permanently stained
with tobacco along his top lip. After they argued for a minute about which of the two forks of the Concho River had
the best fishing, Judge Yarborough read the charges and
entered her plea of not guilty into the record. He then ruled
against Mr. Sims's request for bail since she had run off
once already, but agreed to a preliminary hearing, which he
set for first thing in the morning two days hence.

And that was it.

Mr. Sims left to prepare for the hearing and a guard escorted Lottie back to her cell, where her valise, a ratty blanket, and a plate of cold stew awaited her.

But no Ty.

Sadly, she was too exhausted and discouraged to care.

———————

From what Ty could see from the window of his rented room
across from the building that housed the jail and courtroom,
San Angela was a bigger, wilder version of Greenbroke—
more brothels, more saloons, more gaming houses, although
none so fine as Lady Jane's Social Club. Like most Western
towns, it had begun as a fort, charged with protecting pilgrims
from hostile threats. And as he had learned while patrolling
the Nueces Strip, wherever there's a fort, a settlement will
soon follow.

This one was founded by Bartholomew DeWitt and
named after his wife, Carolina Angela. The name was later
shortened to San Angela, which made little sense gram-
matically. Ty heard that the Post Office department was

trying to correct that by changing the name to San Angelo. But no matter what it was called, the town was a fairly boring place unless you were a cowhand with a month's pay to spend, a gambler, a drinker, or horny enough to try the local talent.

Which was probably why Lottie's hearing drew so much attention. In addition to the scarcity of female murderers—especially pretty ones—and the gruesome nature of the crime, Lottie and her grandfather had been known around town, at least among those who attended the Concho Valley Pentecostal Church. Still, it surprised him that a half hour before her hearing was due to begin two days later, people were already lining up, waiting for the courtroom doors to open.

Ty tried to read their faces, hoping to see sympathy rather than anger or ghoulish interest. It wouldn't matter today, since there would be no jury at the hearing. But if the judge decided to hold Lottie over for trial, many of these curious onlookers would become the jury that would decide her fate.

That helpless, nameless fury that had plagued him over the last trying days settled into a hot knot in the center of his chest. He didn't know how to get rid of it. Where to focus this anger. What he was supposed to do next.

He hated indecision.

All his life—ever since his brother had charged him with watching over their parents—he had felt driven to protect. That's what had sent him into the ranger service. What had fueled his need for revenge against his parents' killers. What now had him clenching his teeth so tight his jaw ached.

Despite his confusion and frustration about what she might or might not have done, he was desperate to protect Lottie. Because no matter what she thought, he still loved her. And because he didn't believe she was a murderer. And because if he couldn't keep her safe, it would be a worse failure than when he'd lost his parents. But mostly, because his life would have little purpose without her in it.

So he stood at the window and waited and watched and prayed like he never had before.

Ranger Millsap escorted Lottie to the hearing. Since she
hadn't seen him since they'd arrived in San Angela, she had
hoped he had gone back to Austin. She had also hoped Ty
would be the one to lead her into the courtroom. Despite
the tension between them, she felt safer with him than with
anyone else.

It shocked her to see the pews were full, with more people
standing shoulder to shoulder along the back wall. Some
faces she recognized. Most she didn't.

Except for Ty.

He was easy to spot, standing a head taller than those
beside him. He had his arms crossed and wore that shuttered
expression she had come to dread. Even though he didn't
smile when she glanced his way, she could feel that intense
blue stare following her down the aisle to the railed-off
section in front of the judge's bench. It strengthened her.
Knowing he was there gave her the courage to keep her head
high and ignore the stares and murmurs as she walked past
the pews.

Mr. Sims rose to greet her when Millsap led her to one
of the two tables set before the judge's bench. At the other
table sat the prosecutor, a short, round man wearing a garish
plaid suit and a strip of false hair across his bald scalp that
looked like a beaver's pelt. As she took her seat, he played
to his audience by making a show of studying her with an
expression of horrified disgust.

Lottie gave no indication she noticed and somehow managed to keep her expression calm, even though her heart
drummed so loudly she could hear little else but the fast
hard pulse of it in her ears.

At her attorney's insistence, Millsap reluctantly removed
her manacles before taking his place in the first pew, directly
behind her chair. She could feel the heat of his animosity
against her back, and was thankful Ty was near.

"All rise," a uniformed guard ordered as Judge Yarborough entered with a flourish, the hem of his long black robe

whipping around his legs. After stepping onto the raised platform and taking his seat, he frowned at the many faces staring back at him, apparently not expecting such a turnout for a simple hearing. "Bailiff, read the charges."

When nothing happened, Yarborough glared down at the guard who had earlier given the all rise. "I'm talking to you, Chester."

"Oh. Yes, sir." Stepping forward, the nervous man read from a paper that court had been convened to determine if there was enough evidence to hold one Charlotte Weyland over for a trial for the murder of one William Franklin Lofton. Judge Herschel Yarborough presiding.

"Step back, Chester."

"Yes, sir."

Yarborough waited until the bailiff had returned to his post, then addressed the onlookers in a stern voice. "Here's what's going to happen. If any of you folks gasp, snicker, pass wind, or even yawn too loud, you're out of here. If you shout out, or act up in any way, you'll be carted off to jail. You're here to observe, not participate. Any questions?"

There were none.

"Then let's begin. Ramsey, you're first."

The man at the other table rose, tugged his vest over his bulging belly, then spun toward Lottie, arm extended, his index finger aimed at her face. "There she sits! A woman so depraved she chained her own grandfather in a filthy shed, piled brush against the walls, and set it on fire! Her own grandfather! Do you know what we call a woman who does that?"

"Murderess!" a man in the pews shouted.

Sims bounded to his feet. "Your Honor!"

Judge Yarborough's gavel came down with a crack like a gunshot. "Bailiff!" he shouted over the murmuring crowd. "Remove that man!"

When the guard started toward Sims, the judge barked, "Not him! Him!" and pointed the gavel at the onlooker who had spoken.

After the bailiff took the protesting man out and returned

to the courtroom, Yarborough glowered at the spectators. "One more outburst and I'll clear the room. Understand?"

"It's a public hearing," someone called. "We got a right to be here."

"Chester, take out that man, too." As the bailiff led out the second protestor, Yarborough eyed those remaining. "Anyone else got something else to say?" When no one did, he nodded in satisfaction, waited for the bailiff to close the door and return to his post, then crooked his finger at Ramsey.

The prosecutor stepped forward. "Yes, Your Honor?"

"Are you aware, Mr. Ramsey, that this is a hearing and not a trial?"

"Yes, Your Honor."

"Then address your remarks to me, rather than the rabble, or I'll have you thrown out, too. Is that clear?" When Ramsey gave a red-faced nod, Yarborough waved him away and sat back. "Call your witness."

Facing the pews, Ramsey shouted, "Jerry Krispin, you're first."

As the bailiff swore in the witness, Sims asked Lottie if she knew Krispin.

"He owns the tract of land next to ours. He would drop by now and then. He and Grandpa would play checkers for hours," she added with a catch in her throat.

"When did you see him last?"

Lottie thought for a moment. "About a week before the fire. Grandpa didn't want to see him, so I said he wasn't home."

Krispin told the judge almost the same thing. "I thought it odd, though," he added, "that she said he was gone, since their only saddle horse was still in the paddock."

Next, Ramsey called Curly Joe Adkins, one of Krispin's riders. He testified that he had been hunting strays near the Lofton place on the day of the fire.

"Did you see anything unusual?" Ramsey asked him.

"Other than the fire?" When Ramsey nodded, Adkins said he'd seen Lofton's granddaughter. "Heading east, hell-bent for leather, saddlebags flapping like buzzard wings. Figured she was going for help, or leaving, one."

"What happened then?"

"I rode to tell Mr. Krispin about the fire. We gathered some boys and went back."

"And what did you do when you arrived?"

"Not much we could do. But we seen a cloud coming up, and waited to see what it would bring. Turned out to be a real frog-strangler. The sound of the rain hitting those hot coals was like all Satan's snakes hissing at once. Gave me the jumps. Didn't last long, but it did the trick. When the fire died down to steaming smolders, we hightailed it across the creek before it busted its banks."

"And where was Miss Weyland—Lofton's granddaughter— during this time?"

"Dunno. Never saw her again 'til today."

From there, Ramsey called other witnesses, starting with the land broker who had found Grandpa's remains, the deputy who had ridden out to verify a crime had been committed, and the ranger who had come to investigate. One by one, witnesses came forth to tell the story of Grandpa's death and her part in it.

It seemed to go on forever—damning testimony seen from a single perspective and manipulated by Ramsey to show her in the worst possible light. The tooth-puller describing how he'd added metal cuspids to Grandpa's dentures because he kept breaking off the ones made from animal teeth. The jeweler who had repaired the hinge on her grandfather's pocket watch, saying, "Yep, that's the one," when Ramsey held up the blackened timepiece. "Even got Lofton's name scratched on the back." The mercantile clerk verifying he sold Lottie the chain and two heart-shaped padlocks, and the sheriff affirming that he had found those items tangled with the skeleton in the burned shed. "Never seen the like," he added with a glare at Lottie.

And Sims never objected or posed a single question of his own.

Battling nausea, Lottie tried to block the horrible images their words painted. *It wasn't like that*, she wanted to shout. *I didn't do it because I wanted to*. She could feel the hostility building at her back and wondered what Ty was thinking. Or if he was still there. She hadn't the courage to check to see if he was.

After several hours, people in the pews grew restless. Lottie could hear them rustling about behind her and hoped the judge would call a break soon. She had been too nervous to eat the cold oatmeal sent to her cell before they'd left for the hearing and now her stomach churned and ached.

Yarborough asked Ramsey how many more witnesses he planned to call.

"Only one, Your Honor. Dr. Tillips."

"All right, but make it quick. My ass is killing me."

Tillips was the local doctor who also served as medical examiner when required. He was a kindly man who always had strings of rock candy for children who came to see him. Lottie had been to him only once, when she was twelve, to have an embedded mesquite thorn removed. It had surprised her that Grandpa would take her to a doctor for such a minor thing. But the true reason for the visit soon became apparent when Dr. Tillips began talking to her about monthly courses, wombs, bloody cycles, changes to expect in her body, bees and pollination, and how she needed to stay away from boys until she was married. She remembered it had been embarrassing and confusing. But the rock candy had been tasty.

Today, the good doctor brought with him a large box that he set on the floor at his feet when he took the witness chair beside the judge's bench.

Ramsey asked him about his duties as medical examiner then told him to describe what he had found when he was summoned to the Lofton place.

Again, Lottie tried not to listen. Tried not to see the ruin of her home through a stranger's eyes. The shed. Her grandfather. But his words pierced the brittle shell of numbness that surrounded her and demanded she listen.

"Please remove the item marked exhibit one," Ramsey told Tillips.

Her dread intensified as Lottie watched the doctor pull out a length of chain with padlocks at both ends. "Found this chain in the burned shed. One end was around the neck of the skeleton. The other was locked around the center pole."

Ramsey laid the chain on his table. "And item number two?"

Her heart speeded up when Tillips reached into the box. Her lungs burned. Each breath felt like it was ripping through her chest yet she never seemed to draw in enough air. Unable to look away, she watched in horror as he lifted out a blackened skull, eye sockets empty, mouth open in a silent scream, the metal cuspids fused to the upper jaw in a predator's evil grin.

No more, she begged silently. *Please . . . no more.* With a strangled sob, she dropped her head into her hands and wept in soundless despair.

Chapter 18

Pandemonium exploded in the courtroom.

Cries, gasps. Wild-eyed spectators climbed onto pews to get a better look at the charred skull. Others crowded the aisle.

"Move!" Ty snarled, pushing aside those who blocked his way to Lottie.

Up front, Sims shouted objections and tried to protect her from the surging crowd, while Judge Yarborough pounded his gavel against the sound block like a demented carpenter.

By the time Ty had worked his way to the front, the bailiff was herding Sims and Lottie out the door the judge had come through earlier. Ramsey watched the chaos with a smug expression, and the judge continued to shriek and wave his black-robed arms as if attempting to take flight.

Ty vaulted the low railing at the front of the pews and raced to the door where Lottie had disappeared.

A narrow hall ran the width of the courtroom, with two doors on the far side. One carried a brass plate: *Office of the Circuit Judge*. The other was unmarked.

Ty flung open the unmarked door.

A small room. One window. Sims consoling Lottie at the far end of a skinny table.

"See to the judge," Ty ordered the frightened bailiff standing inside the door. Without waiting to see if he obeyed, Ty rushed forward. "Lottie?"

At the sound of his voice, she whirled and ran into his arms. His relief was so great he had to remind himself not to hold her too tight.

"It's okay, honey," he murmured over her broken sobs. "I'm here. Breathe. I've got you."

She clutched at him, her nails digging through his shirt. "D-did you see, Ty? Grandpa's head . . . how c-could they do that?"

"I don't know." Rage burned through him, searing a path through his belly, his lungs, to lodge like a closed fist in his heart. "I'm sorry. I'm so sorry."

"Lieutenant Benton," Sims said, hovering at his elbow. "Might I say—"

"Now?" Ty whipped his head toward the old man, a ready target for his fury. "You want to say something *now* after you said nothing all morning? You call that a defense?"

The smaller man retreated a step. "I regret she had to hear all that. I tried to get Miss Weyland to wait in here until Ramsey finished with his witnesses, but she insisted on being present."

She would. *Damn hardheaded woman.*

"I can hear you," Lottie mumbled against his tear-dampened shirt.

Ty pulled her closer, not aware he had spoken aloud. Were it possible, he would have pulled her inside his chest to shield her from this farce of a hearing. "She can't take any more of this, Sims."

"I'll decide what I can take," Lottie muttered, obviously feeling better.

"She won't have to," Sims assured him. "An hour more. That's all."

"Then what?"

The lawyer smiled, his faded hazel eyes twinkling behind his wire spectacles. "Then she'll be free."

Her head flew up, clipping his chin. "Free?"

"You can guarantee that?" Ty demanded.

"Of course. I have proof of her innocence right here." The attorney patted his coat pocket. "Now if you don't mind watching over Miss Weyland, I'll see what's going on in the courtroom and send for lunch. How does that sound?"

It sounded grand to Ty. Especially the part about watching over Lottie. And now that he had some small hope that she might come through this relatively unscathed, lunch sounded grand, too.

As soon as the door closed behind Sims, he bent down and kissed her like he'd wanted to do since he'd walked into the courtroom hours ago. He felt the quiver of her response. Tasted the salt of her tears. Sensed within her the same connection that had driven him back to her every time they'd been apart. This was where he belonged. Whatever she had done, or thought she had done, he didn't care. She was his woman.

And once he had rebuilt her trust in him, she would realize that, too.

The door opened.

Lottie jumped out of his arms.

Ty whirled, thrusting her behind him.

Lt. Millsap grinned from the doorway, thumbs hooked in his gun belt. "Figured this is where you'd run, Benton."

"Her lawyer asked me to watch over her while he brought her lunch."

"Now I can watch over her, so get out."

Ty didn't budge. "I'm not leaving until her lawyer returns."

"You're a civilian now. You're not allowed in here."

Lottie shot him a surprised look.

Ty ignored it. He wondered how far to take this confrontation when he saw the San Angela sheriff standing behind Millsap. "Sheriff." He motioned him into the room. "Since the rangers have signed off and this is no longer our case, will you stay with Miss Weyland until her lawyer returns with lunch?"

"Well . . ."

"I think he's bringing enough for you, too."

"Then sure. I'll keep an eye on her."

Ty looked past him at Millsap, saw the sneer as the ranger turned and headed back down the hall, and knew this wasn't over. "Lock the door after I leave," he instructed the sheriff. "Don't let anyone in but her lawyer or the bailiff. Especially don't let in Lt. Millsap. Understand?"

"No."

"Do it anyway. Miss Weyland's safety depends on it. Lottie, I'll see you at the hearing." Without waiting for a response, he slipped out the door and headed in the direction Millsap had taken.

The bailiff escorted Lottie and Sims back to the courtroom shortly after they ate. While they waited for the judge, Lottie looked for Ty. He hadn't returned to the small conference room for lunch and she didn't see him now. But she might have missed him with all the people filing in. There seemed double the number of spectators than had been there for the morning session. Yet despite the stares aimed her way, Lottie felt stronger now that she knew Sims had a plan—whatever it was—although she would have felt better if she knew Ty was behind her, ready to come to her aid should she need it. Worried where he might be, she scanned the pews again.

"Miss Weyland," Sims said, drawing her attention. "I didn't tell you this before because I didn't want to add to your nervousness."

Oh, God. Lottie braced herself.

"If the judge is to hear the full account of your grandfather's passing, you will have to explain what happened and why Mr. Lofton asked you to do what you did."

Lottie was afraid of that. She just didn't know if it would make a difference. "It will only be my word against all of Ramsey's witnesses. Why would he believe me?"

That crafty smile again. "He'll believe you, my dear. I'm certain of it. Just be truthful. You have nothing to hide."

Before she could question him further, the bailiff called

"All rise," and the judge came into the courtroom—this time with more glower and less flamboyance. Probably still mad about the disruption earlier. Or maybe it was the late-day droop in his mustache that made him look so dour.

After taking his seat, the judge frowned at the empty table reserved for the prosecutor. "Where's Ramsey?"

"Celebrating at the Golden Doe," someone called out. "He figures he won."

"Bailiff, find the sheriff and have him arrested."

Chester gave him a fish-eyed look. "Have the sheriff arrested?"

"For God's sake, pay attention! Not the sheriff! Ramsey!"

"Yes, sir. Okay. Why?"

"Just do it. I'll think of a reason later."

After the bailiff left, Yarborough told Sims to call his first witness.

"I have only two, Your Honor. And one piece of evidence, which I will present later. Miss Charlotte Weyland, please come forward."

Lottie rose on trembling legs. Her time of reckoning had finally come.

In a way, she was glad. She had dreaded this moment for so long it was almost a relief to finally be able to unburden herself. She had thought about it a great deal while she lay too nervous to sleep, waiting for dawn to bring light into her dark, stifling cell. In her heart, she knew the only thing she had done wrong was not telling anyone what had happened, no matter what Grandpa said. Out of cowardice and guilt and shame, she had run. For that, she must answer. The rest of it, she would do again.

As she took the chair beside the judge's bench, she looked again for Ty, and found him standing against the back wall again, arms crossed and shoulders tense. Just seeing his face calmed her. As long as he was nearby, she could do this.

Don't leave me.

As if reading her thoughts, he nodded and gave one of his rare smiles. *I'm here.*

Sims began with a series of questions that were easy to answer. He asked about her father's death when she was three and her mother's death seven years later. Grandpa stepping in to raise her rather than putting her in a church home. Their struggles to keep the ranch going. His strong faith in God and the teachings of the Bible.

"Would you call your grandfather a hard man to deal with? Or an easy one?"

Lottie gave a wry smile. "Hard to please sometimes. But easy to love."

"You loved him?"

"Very much." Just saying that aloud brought up a catch in her throat. "He raised me, taught me my lessons, provided for me, protected me. I owed him everything."

"Did he treat you well?"

"Yes."

"He never harmed you in some heinous, unforgivable manner?"

"Of course not."

"Did he beat you? Refuse you food and water? Force his attentions on you?"

Lottie scowled at the solicitor, incensed by his insinuations. "Never!"

"Never," Sims repeated. He paced for a moment as if trying to make sense of that. Then he faced the pews, his hands lifted in a gesture of confusion. "And yet, you chained in a shed the man who raised you—the man you professed to love and to whom you owed everything—locked the door, and set it on fire?"

"Yes."

He turned to study her, his head tilted to one side as though trying to understand. "Why would you do such a thing, Miss Weyland?"

"Because he asked me to."

Murmurs of surprise rippled through the pews. Judge Yarborough called for order, then gave Sims a hard look. "You playing to the rabble, Ridley?"

"Sorry, Your Honor. It simply got away from me."

"I bet. See that it doesn't happen again or you'll be rooming with Ramsey."

"Yes, Your Honor."

"Continue. And watch your step."

Mr. Sims took a moment to consult his notes, then he turned again to Lottie.

"Mr. Lofton asked you to chain him and lock him in the shed? Is that correct, Miss Weyland?"

"Not precisely. I purchased the chain and locks at his request, but he put them on. He was already becoming erratic by that time and was afraid he might hurt me, so I wasn't allowed to go into the shed."

"Why would he hurt his own granddaughter?"

"He wouldn't have done so on purpose. He was a gentle man. A good man. But he was ill. It made him violent sometimes. So to keep me safe and prevent harm to anyone else, he locked himself in."

Despite open windows, no breeze stirred the stagnant air in the courtroom. It stank of too many people crowded into too small a space and felt heavy against Lottie's skin. Hard to breathe. The smell reminded her of the odors seeping through the gaps in the walls of the shed. Sweat, urine, the stink of madness and decay. She could almost hear his cries of frustration. The crashes as he tried to free himself. The screams—

"Miss Weyland?"

Lottie startled. Saw Sims and the judge staring at her, and forced her mind away from the horrors of the past and back into the courtroom. "I'm sorry. Would you repeat the question, please?"

The kindly lawyer studied her with an expression of deep compassion. He didn't like doing this, she realized. He had been Grandpa's friend, and this was hurting him as much as it hurt her.

Ty looked concerned, too. He had come off the back wall and looked ready to charge forward. She tried to smile to reassure him. *I'm all right.*

He stepped back against the wall again. But the concern in those beautiful blue eyes remained.

"I asked you how long your grandfather remained locked in the shed," Sims said.

"Until he died."

"And how long was that?"

"I'm not sure. A week. Maybe a little longer. It was a difficult time."

"Did you bring him food and water during that time?"

"I did. But he had little appetite and was deathly afraid of the water. Sometimes he didn't even know me and thought I had come to attack him." Feeling wetness on her cheek, she wiped it away.

"He was that ill?"

She met Ty's gaze and drew strength from it. "He was dying."

"You know this for a fact, Miss Weyland?"

She nodded.

"How? Do you have medical training?"

"No, but our hound had died of the same sickness. After Blue bit Grandpa, he was worried he might die the same way. That's when he started making preparations."

"Like sending you to purchase the chain and locks so he could imprison himself in the shed."

"Yes."

"Did he also ride into San Angela himself?"

Lottie frowned, trying to remember. "Yes, I recall he did. Before he took sick. He wouldn't let me come with him and it made me mad. I wasn't aware at the time that Grandpa had been bitten."

"Do you know why he went to San Angela?"

"He never said. And once he got sick, I forgot to ask."

Sims made a dismissive gesture. "We'll come back to that later. For now, let's move on to the day you set the fire. Is that something he asked you to do, as well?"

Lottie nodded. "By then, I knew what was wrong with him and that there was no hope he would recover."

"And what was wrong with him?"

"He'd caught the same sickness that killed the hound."

"Which was what?"

"Rabies. It's also called hydrophobia because those stricken with it are afraid of water even though they have a terrible thirst. It—it's a horrible way to die." Tears rose again, but she willed them away. She needed to stay strong. She owed that to Grandpa.

"Can you describe for Judge Yarborough your grandfather's last days?"

Her mind recoiled. She hated to even think about that time, and the idea of recounting Grandpa's ordeal to strangers made her stomach churn. She turned to the judge. "Must I? His suffering was terrible. I know he wouldn't want others to remember him that way."

"All right, Miss Weyland. But you need to explain why you set the fire and how you knew for certain your grandfather was dead when you did."

She had dreaded this part the most. The uncertainty. The guilt. The horror of never knowing for sure if he was still alive when she struck that first match.

"Miss Weyland?"

She took a deep breath, let it out.

At the back wall, Ty gave an encouraging nod. *You can do this.*

Some of the tension eased. "We talked about it. At first, I wouldn't listen. I was only fourteen. I had already lost a father and a mother. I couldn't imagine a future without Grandpa, too. But he kept at me. Told me he didn't want strangers messing with him and was afraid if anyone handled his body or prepared it for burial, they would be exposed to the disease. Fire was the only way. Burn everything after he died so there was no sickness left. He said if I helped him do this one last thing, he could meet his Maker with an easy heart.

"Eventually, he wore me down. Made me promise on his Bible to burn everything after he died, then leave and never look back. He said the ranch was failing anyway, but I was smart enough to start over somewhere else. I didn't want to do it, but he begged and begged. I was still a child. I didn't know how to disobey him. Or what else I could do. He had given me everything and all he asked of me was to help him die in peace."

The tears fell unchecked now. She couldn't stop them. Couldn't escape the ache spreading through her heart, the grief flooding her mind. But she needed to finish this and end the secrecy so she could put all this behind her and build a life with Ty.

"What happened then, Miss Weyland?" Sims asked.

"For two days, I sat outside the shed and talked until my voice gave out, trying to get him to let me know if he was still alive. He never ate the food I brought. Never spoke. Never made a sound. When I looked through the gaps in the plank wall, I could see he never moved. So I did what he had told me to do. I gathered rags and broken furniture, stacked them in the house, and doused them with lamp oil. I piled brush along the sides of the shed. Then I gave him one last chance to call out. When he didn't, I set everything on fire and rode away."

Sims gave her a handkerchief and waited while she blotted the tears. Once she had regained control, he asked where she went after leaving the ranch.

"East. To Greenbroke."

"Why there?"

"I felt that's where Grandpa would want me to be. He had mentioned the town several times in the past. Told me when he tired of ranching he might go to Greenbroke and take up teaching again. I didn't put much credence in it at the time—he had a lot of grand plans—I called them 'someday' dreams. But when I saw the signpost pointing the way, I knew that's where I should go. I thought being there might bring me closer to him and I wouldn't feel so alone."

Sims stepped back. "I have no more questions for this witness," he told the judge.

The courtroom was silent. Lottie saw faces that had once been hostile, now showed sympathy. Perhaps even forgiveness. Only one was smiling.

Ty. When he caught her eye, he mouthed the words, *I love you. Still.* And she almost burst into tears again—tears of joy, relief, gratitude. Love. Her ordeal was over. It would be in the judge's hands now. But no matter his decision, she felt free at last.

Lottie started to rise when Judge Yarborough said, "I've got a question." He waited for her to sit back down, then leaned forward and studied her through skeptical eyes. "That was a compelling story, Miss Weyland. It had the ring of truth to it. But it would help if you had someone to back it up. Did anyone ever come visiting or see your grandfather while he was sick?"

Sims started to say something.

The judge waved him off. "I'd like to hear from the accused, not her paid solicitor. Miss Weyland?"

"No, Your Honor. The only one who came by was Mr. Krispin, and Grandpa wouldn't see him. He was in pain and out of control most of the time, and was too prideful to let anyone see him that way. But I think the main reason he didn't want anyone to know he was dying was because he was afraid of what would happen to me. A fourteen-year-old girl on her own can be easy prey. He had taught me to take care of myself, and thought I'd be better off making my own decisions rather than becoming a charity case for well-meaning folks. And he was right. I've done well in Greenbroke, mostly on my own, but also with a lot of help from very kind people."

The judge studied her for a moment, then sat back. "You're excused, Miss Weyland. Sims, proceed with your next witness."

Grateful that she no longer had to face the stares of curious spectators, Lottie returned to the defense table. As she took her seat, voices rose at the back of the courtroom. She turned to see Ty disappear out the door. Odd, that. But before she could puzzle it out, Sims was announcing his next witness.

"I call Ridley Sims to give testimony, Your Honor."

"That's you."

"It is, Your Honor."

Muttering under his breath, the judge motioned for the bailiff to swear him in. "You going to ask yourself questions, too?" he asked snidely.

Sims fought a smile. "I'll simply tell what I know firsthand to be the truth, Your Honor. But should you have questions, feel free to ask."

"Oh, I will." One corner of Yarborough's lacquered mustache quirked. "Well, get to it. The fish won't wait forever."

Lottie wasn't sure if he was referring to the folks in the pews or actual fish.

After giving the oath and taking the witness chair, Sims began. "I didn't know William Lofton well, although we had spoken at church several times. I found him to be a virtuous man of great intellect and exacting standards. Before his death, he came to me seeking legal advice. His hound had recently died of rabies, and Mr. Lofton was certain he had contracted the disease through a bite the animal had given him while sick. At that time, Mr. Lofton showed no symptoms of the disease, but wanted to make preparations just in case."

"You believed him?" Yarborough asked.

"I had no reason not to. And he certainly had no reason to lie about something like that. In addition, he had an obvious dog bite on his arm that was already showing signs of infection."

"Continue."

"He told me he wanted to protect his granddaughter as best he could. To do that, he entrusted me with the money and paperwork to pay the taxes on his land three years in advance."

"Where'd he get the money?" Yarborough asked.

"I believe he sold some family belongings, but I don't know to whom. He also gave me this." Sims reached into his coat pocket and extracted a folded piece of paper. "He signed it in my presence." As he handed it to the judge, he added, "If you deem it necessary, Your Honor, I will be happy to provide witnesses to verify that the signature is indeed that of William Lofton."

Lottie wondered why Sims hadn't told her about this paper.

Judge Yarborough scanned the letter then frowned at Sims. "This sounds as if he expected his granddaughter to be charged in his death."

Lottie's jaw dropped. He did?

"He felt it was a possibility," Sims said. "As you see in the letter, he describes in great detail what he wanted Miss Weyland to do, including the disposal of his remains by fire so that even in death he could not infect others."

"Is that even possible?"

"There are some who think it is. I read extensively about rabies after Lofton came to see me. Many think the disease can be transmitted from one person to another through saliva and lesions of the skin. It's unproven at this point, but he felt it wasn't worth the risk. Especially to his granddaughter."

Lottie was stunned. Why hadn't she known about this? She thought of what she had gone through when all the while, Sims had carried the key to her freedom in his pocket. If he'd been within range she might have struck him.

Yarborough set the paper aside.

"Anything else?"

"No, Your Honor."

"I'll present my ruling at nine tomorrow morning." Lifting his gavel, the judge brought it down with a crack. "Court is dismissed." In a lower voice he told Sims to be at his office in half an hour. "And bring bait."

"Before you go, Judge," Lottie said, "could I ask what will happen to my grandfather's remains? I'd like to take them home for burial if possible."

"Chester, ask Dr. Tillips to seal them in a box or something. Miss Weyland has been through enough without having to deal with that."

As soon as the judge left the courtroom, Lottie rounded on Sims. "Why didn't you tell me about Grandpa's letter?"

"He asked me not to. He was afraid you'd worry."

"And going through all this was better?" She truly did almost strike him.

"Miss Weyland, you have been the soul of courage. Don't fail me now."

Lottie pressed fingertips to her brow where a headache was forming. "All right. Now what? Am I free?"

"Not yet. The judge will give his decision tomorrow—which I'm hopeful will be in your favor—then you'll be free. Take heart. It's only one more night."

Chapter 19

While Sims stuffed papers back into his case, Lottie looked around for the sheriff to take her back to her cell. Instead, she saw Lt. Millsap lurching through the departing crowd on unsteady legs, the ever-present handcuffs dangling from his hand. His shirt was torn. Blood oozed from a split in his lip and a bruise darkened the swollen skin across his cheekbone. What in the world had happened?

"Hold out your arms," he ordered, slurring his words.

She drew back, repelled by the stench of whiskey on his breath. "The sheriff said he would take me back."

"The sheriff's busy. Hold out your arms."

"But he—"

"You'd rather do this the hard way? Fine with me." In a move so sudden Lottie had no time to react, he grabbed her right arm in a bruising grip, snapped the manacle over her wrist, and reached for her left.

Sims stepped forward. "Is that really necessary, Lieutenant?"

"Move!" Roughly elbowing the elderly solicitor aside, he snapped on the left cuff. "Interfere again, old man, and I'll put you down hard. Now get out of my way!"

Sims got out of his way.

Gripping the back of Lottie's neck, the ranger steered her through the small gate in the railing and past the empty pews.

She tried to call back to Sims, but Millsap's fingers dug in so deep she couldn't turn her head. Yet what could the lawyer have done against a man half again his size, especially when that man had the power of the Texas Rangers behind him? And where was Ty?

"Let me go!" She tried to twist free, but he tightened his grip, sending arcs of pain across her shoulders. "Why are you doing this? I thought you weren't involved with my case anymore."

Instead of answering, he pushed her out of the courtroom and into the sheriff's office next door. Shoving her inside, he slammed the door closed behind him.

When she saw the room was empty, panic exploded. "Where's the sheriff?"

"Shut up."

Grabbing the ring of keys off a nail in the wall, he herded her ahead of him toward the cells in back. "Party time, son," he called out and laughed.

Lottie saw movement in the middle cell next to hers, but it wasn't until Millsap unlocked her barred door and thrust her inside that she got a clear view of the occupant. "Ty?"

"Lottie!" Jumping from his cot, he charged to the bars separating their cells, gripping them with knuckles that were scraped and swollen. More blood trickled down his jaw from a swollen gash on his forehead. "Are you all right?"

"Y-yes. What happened?"

His gaze shot past her to Millsap. His eyes were terrifying. Menace radiated off his tense body like sweat. "Get out of her cell!" he snarled, his lips drawn flat against clenched teeth.

"Not yet." The ranger kicked her cell door closed, stuffed the ring of keys into his front pocket, then started unbuckling his gun belt. "Thought I'd have some fun before my train comes."

Lottie stood frozen in the middle of the cell. *Do something!* her mind screamed. But her body wouldn't obey. Where was the sheriff?

Ty yanked on the bars like a madman. "You hurt her, I'll kill you!"

"I doubt it. You don't have the guts for it." The belt dropped to the floor beside the door. "But to show there's no hard feelings, son, I'll let you watch." Grinning, he reached for Lottie.

Finally jarred into action, she darted for the door.

He caught her, swung her off her feet, and flung her toward the cot against the back wall.

She landed in a sprawl, banging her forehead against the rough stone. Above the ringing in her ears, she heard Ty's panicked voice.

"You'll never get away with it! They'll take your badge. They'll hang you!"

"They haven't yet. Lie down, bitch!"

Lottie tried to scramble out of reach but he grabbed her ankle and yanked her back. Head still reeling, she reared up, kicking and flailing. Heard him grunt when her fist landed on his bruised cheek.

"Be still!"

His palm cracked against the side of her head, drove her back down. Panting, she twisted, desperate to free her legs so she could kick.

"Millsap!" Ty yanked so hard on the bars the metal rattled against the stone sockets. "You touch her, I'll kill you. I'll put you in the fucking ground!"

Then the ranger was on top of her, his big belly pushing against her stomach. She smelled stale sweat, alcohol. Felt his fingers dig into her thighs, trying to force her legs apart. In mindless terror, she fought him, clawed at his face, his eyes.

"You like it rough, do you?" Planting his knees on either side of her legs, he rose up, one hand pressing against her throat, the other drawn back and clenched in a fist.

Freer now that he was kneeling over her rather than lying on top of her, she brought up her knee. Heard his grunt as it struck him between his legs. Kneed him again, then again until he doubled over with a rasping groan and collapsed on top of her, trapping her beneath him.

Over the drumming in her head, she heard Ty shouting, kicking the bars.

She couldn't breathe. Lungs burning, she twisted and bucked, frantic to get Millsap off. Something sharp and hard dug into her side. *The keys!* She wrestled them free and with the last of her strength, flung them toward the sound of Ty's voice. Then everything began to dim.

Dimly, she heard Ty calling her name. The clang of the barred door. Shouts. Curses. The thud of fists striking flesh.

And suddenly, the weight was gone.

She gasped, her chest on fire as she sucked air down her bruised throat and into her starved lungs. Then she was being crushed again, but this time it was Ty, and he was shaking as much as she was, and she knew she was finally safe.

"Is he—"

"Taken care of." With a trembling hand, Ty brushed back hair that had escaped her pins during the struggle. "You're safe. He won't bother you anymore. Jesus, honey . . . I should have taken better care of you. Are you hurt? Did he hurt you?"

Hearing a groan, she looked past Ty's shoulder to see Millsap curled in the front corner of her cell. One hand clutched his groin, the other was handcuffed to the bars. He was retching. "What did you do to him?"

"Less than he deserves." He gave a shaky laugh. "Remind me never to make you mad."

She shuddered, terror rising to the surface again. "That's not funny."

"It wasn't meant to be. You're an amazing woman, Charlotte Weyland. I wish I could thank your grandfather for his part in that."

"Holy hell!" The sheriff gaped from the hallway, Sims and Yarborough at his back. "What happened? Is that Lieutenant Millsap?"

Ty bolted to his feet as Sims pushed past the sheriff into the cell. "Are you all right, Miss Weyland? I would have come sooner but I couldn't find the sheriff."

Realizing she was still stretched on her cot, Lottie shoved down her skirts and struggled to get up, only to sag back when the movement made her head swim. She made it to her feet the second time, although it took a moment for her to find her balance. Lifting a hand to her head, she felt a lump where her forehead had banged into the wall. "Battered, but fine."

"No thanks to you, Sheriff," Ty accused, his big body still planted between her and the men crowding through the cell door. "Where were you? And where's my gun?"

Sims ignored him. "Perhaps you should fetch Dr. Tillips, Sheriff. Miss Weyland seems a bit more than battered, and Lieutenant Benton should have that cut tended."

"Not before I find out what happened here," Yarborough snapped. "Benton, explain."

In clipped tones, Ty told them he had followed Millsap to the Golden Doe Saloon to confront him about the ranger's poor treatment of Lottie. "We argued, made a few threats. I thought that was the end of it and went back to the hearing. But Millsap kept drinking and finally worked himself up enough to come roust me out of the courtroom. He was mean drunk by then and itching for a fight. So I gave him one. Until he hit me in the head with his pistol. Next thing I knew I was locked up."

Yarborough turned to the sheriff. "And where were you all this time?"

"In the courtroom with most of the rest of the town."

Ty glared at him, hands fisted at his sides. "Then why didn't you escort Miss Weyland from the courtroom like you were supposed to?"

Color flooded the lawman's face. "I was sent to check on a stolen horse."

"Sent by whom?" Sims asked.

"Him." The sheriff nodded at Millsap. "But I didn't know nothing about any of this until now." He gave a nervous smile.

"Good thing you insisted that me and the judge come with you to check on Miss Weyland before y'all went fishing."

Muttering something about incompetent fools, Yarborough dragged a hand over his hairless scalp. "Then what happened?"

Wanting to get this over with, Lottie stepped around Ty. "Perhaps I can explain." Which she did, as succinctly as possible, despite her pounding head and aching muscles from her struggle with Millsap. "He would have forced himself on me," she concluded, "if not for Lieutenant Benton's intervention."

"And your knee," Ty reminded her.

The sheriff looked from Ty to Lottie. "What about her knee?"

Yarborough waved the question aside. "But if Benton was locked in another cell, how did he get into yours, Miss Weyland?"

"I threw the keys to him."

"After she kneed him," Ty added, proudly.

"Kneed him?"

"In the privates. Three times. She's a helluva fighter."

All four men looked at the ranger still moaning and retching on the floor.

"I want my gun back," Ty said again.

"Not if you're going to use it on him," the sheriff muttered.

Sims turned to the judge. "A clear case of self-defense, Your Honor. Two cases, if you count Lieutenant Millsap's attack on Ranger Benton."

"Just Benton," Ty corrected. "I'm no longer with the rangers."

Lottie frowned at him. "You keep saying that. Why? And since when?"

"Since I delivered you to the San Angela jail."

"But why? I don't understand."

"You can argue about that later," Yarborough said impatiently, obviously still hoping to get in some fishing before dark. "Either of you got any proof it was self-defense? Other than parroting what the other says? Any witnesses?"

Lottie was losing patience, too. She had just gone through a horrifying court hearing, had watched strangers handle her grandfather's remains, had been attacked by a drunken brute in her cell, and now she was being interrogated again? It was beyond belief. But before she could give Judge Yarborough her views on his insistence that they provide witnesses for every little bitty thing, a voice called from the cell on the far side of Ty's.

"There's me."

Startled, they all turned to see Prosecutor Ramsey smiling hopefully through the bars.

"I saw everything. And I'll be happy to testify to that once I'm released. If it pleases the court, of course. Your Honor. Sir."

Judge Yarborough sighed and muttered and sighed again. "Aw, hell. Charges dropped on all of you. Except for Millsap. Sheriff, release Ramsey and Miss Weyland from their cells."

"What about me?" Ty asked.

"You, too. But I expect all three of you in my courtroom at nine o'clock in the morning for the official ruling. Understand?"

Lottie nodded, sudden relief making her dizzy again.

"Yes, Your Honor," Ramsey called. "And thank you for—"

"Shut up, Ramsey. I'm still mad at you. Sheriff, send a wire to Ranger Headquarters that we're holding Lieutenant Millsap until his arraignment in a year or two, or when I'm back in San Angela, whichever comes first. Meanwhile, get him a bucket unless you want him puking all over your floor. The rest of you get out of my sight. I've got fish to catch. Ridley, bring the bait."

———————

Because Lottie couldn't tolerate the thought of spending the evening locked in a hotel room no matter how much more luxurious it was than a cold jail cell, Ty suggested a picnic along the banks of the Concho River that ran through town.

This time, they went by buggy. It was a perfect June evening—not too hot, the sunset sky awash with fiery colors and tattered purple clouds, and a breeze so gentle she could discard her bonnet, but steady enough to keep the mosquitoes away.

Ty picked a beautiful spot. Secluded and quiet, yet within view of town. She hadn't realized how much people noise had filtered through her small cell window until she felt the soft, still evening close around her.

While he tied the horse to a lanky mesquite, she looked for a soft, dry place to spread the blanket. The rhythmic drone of frogs and the smell of wild mint growing along the bank drew her to the river. Lightning bugs danced through the grass, and crickets added their song to the plaintive calls of bobwhites and the distant lowing of cattle. The air smelled of wildflowers and damp earth—a vast improvement over the stink of her filthy cell.

She took a deep breath then let it out on a long sigh. Never had she valued her freedom more. She was still shaking, still half-afraid it would be snatched away. She had to keep telling herself that it was over. Done. The past was behind her, where it belonged. She was safe.

Hearing footsteps behind her, she turned and gave Ty a weary smile. "Thank you for bringing me here. I needed this."

He smiled but said nothing.

Together they spread the blanket on a grassy spot, sat down, and set the picnic basket between them. He had been silent since they'd turned onto the river road and she could tell he had something on his mind. She hoped he wasn't still angry that she hadn't told him. But if so, she would give him the space he needed to come to terms with it. It was time for a new start . . . no matter how long it took.

He'd brought a simple meal of cold ham slices, deviled eggs, carrots, and bread pudding that had gone soggy during the ride from town. This time, Lottie ate her fair share, having gone without decent food since she'd finished the contents of the basket Jane had brought to the train station the morning they'd left Greenbroke.

Her dear friends. How she longed to see them. "After the ruling, assuming it goes my way, we should send Becky a wire telling her I've been cleared."

"You'll be cleared. No one in their right mind could hold what you did against you."

They ate without speaking, both more interested in food than conversation. After they finished, Ty tossed what scraps were left into the bushes while she returned their plates and utensils to the basket so he could carry it to the wagon.

Lottie watched him, arms wrapped around her shins, cheek resting on her bent knees. She loved the way he walked, assurance showing in every line of his long, muscular body. Loved the way he looked at her, those flame-bright eyes drawing her in, sending heat coiling low in her body. Loved the way he seemed to know what she was thinking, what she needed, and what she needed him to do to bring balance when she felt unsteady and confused. She loved *him*.

She knew that now. Had known it for some time. He was her anchor—her lost self—the part that had been missing from her life that made her whole. But was it too late? Had she ruined their chance at happiness with her silence?

The events of the day unraveled in her mind, awakening the terror that still hovered just below the surface. She felt raw, as if her skin had been scraped away and all her nerves were exposed. Even now, tears pressed behind her eyes and her bruised limbs felt wobbly and weak. But she dared not complain and add more worry to the regrets Ty was obviously battling. He had been so solicitous all evening. A rare thing in her life. Grandpa had wanted her tough, so he had never fussed over her. She liked that Ty did.

But she needed to know why he was fretting. If they were to move past this, there could be no more secrets, no unspoken words hanging between them.

He returned to sit beside her, one leg drawn up, his forearm resting across his bent knee as he stared out over the slow-moving river. That fall of dark hair shadowed his deep-set eyes and partially hid the bandage Dr. Tillips had put on his gash.

"We should probably talk," she said.

Avoiding her gaze, he plucked several long blades of grass and idly worked them into a loose braid. "About what?"

"About what happened. What I did."

"That's in the past now. We should leave it there."

She studied his strong profile, the high, intelligent forehead, his straight nose and square chin, the muscular slope of his neck. In the months she had known him, Ty had grown into a handsome and powerful man. Even his poor scraped hands looked bigger and stronger. Yet she knew how gentle they could be when they moved over her body.

"I'm sorry I didn't tell you."

He tossed the grass aside and looked at her, a crease of worry between his dark brows. "I never doubted you, you know. It bothered me that you didn't tell me—bothered me a lot—but I never doubted you."

"Doesn't it upset you at all, what I did?"

He shook his head. "Now that I know, I admire you for it. It took courage to do what your grandfather asked you to do."

"Then what's troubling you?"

Unable to remain still, he plucked two more blades of grass, tore them into long strips, then tossed them aside. Leaning back on his elbows, he looked up into the night sky. "I'm not a killer, despite what I did to my parents' murderers. Millsap knew that, which is why he dared do what he did. I should have realized that and protected you better."

How like Ty to see Millsap's attack as his failure. "You did protect me, you silly man. You stopped him from forcing me."

His looked over at her. "Silly?"

In the fading light, his eyes looked more gray than blue, but that shock of awareness that sent blood thrumming through her veins was the same. She felt something loosen inside—that last knot of resentment and hurt that had clogged her thinking over the last days. In its place came a feeling of such contentment she felt new all over again. "I love you, Ty."

For a moment he didn't move or speak. Then a slow smile

spread across his chiseled face, showing a flash of white teeth and deep grooves where those elusive dimples dented his cheeks. "Sorry. I didn't catch that."

Laughing, she rolled over and pushed him flat, pinning him down with an arm over his chest and her knee trapping his. He went utterly still, except for the steady thump of his heartbeat against the breast pressed against his side. "I said I love you, Tyree Benton." Stretching up, she kissed the thumb dent in his chin then slid higher to run her tongue along his bottom lip. "And I think I have for a long time."

"Have you?"

"I have."

"Since when?"

"Since we started over the second time."

"Third time lucky." And in the next instant, he flipped their positions until she was on her back and he was nuzzling her under her chin.

"Stop!" she choked out and tried to shove him off.

He drew back. "What?"

"That tickles!"

Surprise gave way to an evil grin. "You're ticklish here?" He nuzzled her neck again, sending her into thrashing giggles. "How about here?" A finger bounced along her ribs.

"You're mean," she cried, caught between laughter and suffocation.

"But you love me anyway."

"I can't breathe!"

"Let me help." He kissed her with an open mouth, his breath mingling with hers, his tongue sliding inside.

Giggles gave way to a different kind of hysteria, and suddenly it was too much—the tickling, the weight of him pressing her into the ground, the days of terror and uncertainty. She felt like she was flying apart and the only thing holding her together was Ty.

Her mind splintered. Tears flooded her eyes. She began to shake.

"Lottie? What's wrong?"

Words caught in her throat. She didn't know what was

wrong with her or how to answer. She only knew if he let her go she would shatter into a thousand jagged pieces.

"Shh. It's okay, honey. I'm here." Arms locked around her, he rolled them onto their sides and tucked her against his chest, his strong body curled protectively around hers. "I've got you. I won't let you go. Breathe."

It was a long time before the tears and shaking stopped. It seemed she had been weeping for days. Ordinarily such uncontrollable emotion would have embarrassed her. But not with Ty. He understood. Only with him could she let the fear go and simply let herself *be*.

It grew late. The air cooled. Even the crickets tucked in for the night and lights were beginning to dim in town. The dampness of the ground had seeped through the blanket and into her bones. Her bruised muscles were so sore she could scarcely move. "We should go."

Cooler air rushed into the space between them when he lifted a hand to brush hair from her eyes. "You're staying with me tonight." He wasn't asking.

"At the hotel?" He'd already taken their belongings there after the judge had released them from jail. "I thought you booked two rooms."

"I did. But you're staying with me tonight."

She looked up at him, not sure what to do. Then she realized this was what she needed, what she craved from this man. To be held for a while. To feel safe.

She smiled. "Are you courting me now, Mr. Benton?"

"I do believe I am."

"Then I'll stay."

Chapter 20

"Why did you leave the rangers?" Lottie asked him on the road back to town.

He gave the simplest answer, not wanting to bring up her arrest or his run-in with Millsap, although, in truth, he'd decided to leave the battalion long before he knew about the charges against her. Before he'd decided to marry her, too. Assuming she'd have him. "I felt it was time to move on."

"I had nothing to do with it?"

The woman was too smart to let him get away with half answers. He might as well get used to it. "You had everything to do with it." He saw her frown as she digested that. Simple answers were never enough for Lottie.

And sure enough . . .

"I don't want to be the cause of you giving up a job you love."

"*Loved*," he corrected. "I didn't mind hunting down miscreants, but I do mind nursemaiding prisoners and politicians. I need a better purpose in my life."

"Like what?"

"Ranching. And you," he added with a grin.

She didn't smile back, her sharp mind racing ahead of

him to someplace he couldn't see. He'd better get used to that, too.

"So you don't have to get back to Austin?"

"Not right away. I'll have to go in to sign papers and turn in my badge. But I have time to take you back to Greenbroke, if that's what you're asking."

"Would you have time to take me to my grandfather's ranch, too? The judge said he would have Dr. Tillips seal his remains in a box for me. I'd like to put him to rest beside my mother and grandmother. I feel bad I didn't do that before."

He could tell by the tremor in her voice that the subject was a hard one for her. Not surprising. She was probably still seeing her grandfather's skull in Ramsey's hand. "I'll see Tillips and make arrangements for a wagon first thing in the morning."

"And wire Becky that we should be home in a couple of days."

Home. Where would that be? Greenbroke? Her grandfather's ranch? Someplace new to both of them? That smothered feeling crept over him again—the one that came when she started making decisions without him. But now wasn't the time to argue about it. She was still too brittle, and he wasn't yet sure what he wanted to say. Or do. Or where he wanted to settle.

The hotel lobby was empty when he escorted her up to his room. "The water closet is downstairs at the end of the hall. Your valise is in the wardrobe. I'll be back as soon as I drop the basket by the kitchen and return the rig to the livery."

By the time he entered the room a half hour later, she was already asleep.

He studied her in the light of the lamp she'd left burning. A fierce need to protect her rose within him, bringing with it a rage so consuming he almost shook with it. She looked exhausted and battered, purple smudges below her eyes. The bump on her head was starting to go down, but the bruise on her cheek where Millsap had slapped her showed darker in the dim light. He wished he'd killed the bastard.

He wanted to wake her up and tell her that. He wanted
to hold her and kiss the bad memories from her mind, and
brand her body with his. But now wasn't the time.

After unbuckling his gun belt, he set it on the nightstand
within easy reach, then pulled off his boots. Leaving on his
shirt and trousers, he slipped beneath the covers and gently
pulled her back against his chest. She sighed and wiggled
for a minute, then settled into the slow rhythmic breathing
of deep sleep.

It took him an hour longer.

Ty awoke early, quietly dressed, and left Lottie sleeping while
he tended to a few last-minute details. When he returned later,
the room was empty, her valise gone. For one terrible moment
he feared she had left him, then realized she wouldn't do that.
At least not without an explanation. Thinking she must have
gone to the washroom, he hurried downstairs. When she
emerged a few minutes later, he was waiting outside the door,
weight on one hip, his shoulder propped against the wall.
Trying to look unconcerned.

"You shouldn't have left the room without me," he
scolded. Millsap was still in jail, but others might see her
as easy pickings.

"I didn't want to be late to the hearing."

Taking her valise, he steered her out the back door to
avoid as many curious eyes as possible. She was probably
the most recognizable woman in town since the hearing,
and there might have been some who thought what she'd
done was wrong—no matter the circumstances—and try to
render their own form of justice. He was there to see that
didn't happen. Rather than march her through the lobby, he
led her out the back door to where he'd left the wagon and
horse in the shade of the trees behind the jail. As he tossed
in her valise beside his saddlebags and the borrowed shovel,
she stared at the fancy pine box in back. "That's Grandpa?"

He nodded. "The judge told Tillips to bill Ramsey for it.
The bastard never should have done what he did."

Lottie didn't respond, but he saw a slight easing in the tension across her shoulders.

"I'll get a blanket to cover it," he said. No need for her to look at a coffin all day. "How far is the ranch?"

"Not far. If the ruling doesn't take too long, we should be back in time to catch the afternoon stage to the rail line."

Ty smiled, his thoughts jumping ahead. *Or we could spend the night under the stars in the back of the wagon.* He reminded himself to bring two blankets. Or three. And maybe something to cook over a campfire.

Sims was waiting when they arrived at the courtroom. Hopefully his smile meant something other than yesterday's fishing had been good. While Lottie took her place at the table, Ty pulled him aside and spoke to him privately for a minute. Reassured that all would be well, he patted the elderly lawyer's shoulder and asked where the judge was.

"Running late," Ramsey answered from the prosecutor's table. "He can't find his fish creel."

Ty nodded and bent by Lottie's chair. "I have an errand to run but I won't be long." Before she could interrogate him, he told Sims not to let her leave the courtroom without him, shot her a don't-argue-with-me look, then walked quickly back down the aisle between the pews.

———

Lottie grinned after him. He was so adorable when he acted bossy.

"Have you thought any more about selling your grandfather's land?" Mr. Sims asked, turning Lottie's attention from the way muscles rippled up Ty's back when he pushed open the courtroom door.

"You have a buyer?" She hadn't thought about it lately, but if there was an interested buyer, she would definitely consider selling. Grandpa's land was a small tract—less than three thousand dusty acres—and on its own, would never be profitable as a working cattle ranch. After receiving the solicitor's earlier letters about possible buyers, she had gone over Carill's surveys more carefully. There was a possibility of oil in the area, but since she'd seen the Buck place, she'd been leaning more toward selling the Concho Valley land and investing near Greenbroke. Now she was rethinking that, too. If Ty wouldn't let her buy a ranch for them, perhaps he would allow her to make improvements on the land his uncle had left him. It would be her gift—no strings attached—a way of showing faith in him without bruising that fragile male pride.

"Mr. Krispin, your neighbor, has expressed interest," Sims went on. "I believe he's been running cattle on your land during your absence, and has strung several miles of barbed wire to enclose it. Since he's made those improvements and increased the size of his herd, he would like to continue to use the land."

"Has he made an offer?"

"Not yet. But he's thinking about it."

Lottie weighed her options like Mr. Griffin had taught her. She had always thought of the ranch as her safety net. But if she sold, she and Ty could use the money to get started somewhere else. On the other hand, holding on to the land wasn't costing her anything but the annual taxes, which would be covered and then some if she leased, rather than sold. She wasn't sure what to do. Best she talk to Ty before making up her mind.

"I don't know if I want to give up the ranch altogether," she told Sims. "But I might consider a lease that would grant Krispin first rights of purchase if I do sell."

"He didn't seem interested in a lease. He spoke only of buying outright."

"Well . . ." She did some quick calculations. "As long as it's a good offer. Four years free use of the land should balance what he spent on fencing, so that's a wash. But I'd need to retain the mineral rights. A hundred percent, if possible. Seventy-five if he balks. That needs to be written into the purchase agreement, along with his assurance that our family cemetery won't be disturbed."

"I will tell him of your wishes."

If Sims thought it odd to be discussing leases and rights

of purchase with a woman, he showed no sign of it. Which made her like him all the more.

Behind them, the courtroom began to fill. Lottie dared a glance and was gratified to be met with more smiles than glares, and several people nodded encouragingly.

"If it pleases you," Sims said, regaining her attention, "I will handle all the paperwork pursuant to Mr. Lofton's passing, as well as the transfer of ownership of the land to you. That way, should Mr. Krispin make an acceptable offer, the documents will be in order."

Lottie gave an appreciative smile. "Thank you, Mr. Sims. You've been a lifesaver throughout this mess. I don't know what I would have done without you. Be sure to send me an accounting of your expenses. Although I feel I owe you so much more than money."

"That won't be necessary, Miss Weyland. It's being taken care of."

Lottie blinked at him in surprise. "By my grandfather?"

"An anonymous party." When she started to ask who, he held up his hand. "I'm not at liberty to say. But you should know, Miss Weyland, that despite the unfortunate circumstances that have led to your incarceration and this difficult court hearing, you have many friends who care about you."

Lottie was stunned. Her mind raced through possibilities. Friends here? She hardly remembered anyone. It must have been her friends in Greenbroke. Juno? Jane? The Bracketts? All of them?

Ty. In his determination to protect her, it was exactly what he would do. But where had he gotten the money?

Sims must have seen her worry. "It won't be much," he assured her. "Two days, no witnesses, no exhibits. What I did hardly even warrants a retainer."

"What you did was save me," she corrected.

"And it was my pleasure, my dear."

"All rise," Chester called.

The door behind the judge's bench swung open and Judge Yarborough swept in. He seemed in a hurry. The remaining dozen hairs on top of his head stuck out in wild disarray, his robe was half-buttoned, and his mustache showed only a dash of lacquer. Plus, he was wearing rubberized boots. He seemed in exceptionally high spirits.

Turning to Mr. Sims, she whispered, "Going fishing again?"

He gave a sheepish smile. "There's been an early hatch and the fish are hitting anything that moves. How could we not?"

The judge plopped down in his chair, impatiently waved the spectators back into their seats, and cracked the gavel against the sound block. "Court is now in session. Charlotte Weyland, please step forward."

As Lottie and Mr. Sims moved around the defense table, she heard the courtroom door behind her open and glanced back to see Ty taking his place against the back wall. He was grinning like a cat with a mouthful of feathers. Bolstered by his presence and the capable solicitor beside her, she faced the judge.

"After careful consideration of the evidence put before me, I find insufficient cause to pursue the charges against you, Miss Weyland." He said it so fast it sounded like one long word. "Have you anything to add, Ramsey?"

"No, Your Honor."

"Then charges are dismissed. You're free to go. All of you. Now."

There was scattered applause from the pews.

Lottie grinned, hardly daring to believe she was really free.

Sims beamed back. "Congratulations, my dear."

"All rise," Chester called.

Before exiting the courtroom, Yarborough motioned Lottie and Mr. Sims closer. "I'll see you in my chambers," he whispered. "You, too," he added as Ty came up. Then he swept out the door, unbuttoning as he went.

The whole thing had taken less than three minutes.

"Why does he want to see us?" Lottie asked. "I thought it was over."

"Mr. Benton, perhaps you should explain. I'll await you in Judge Yarborough's office. Try not to be too long. He's not known for his patience." Picking up his satchel, he hurried after the judge.

Ty still wore that grin, although it was starting to fray at the corners.

"What was all that about?" she asked him.

He looked back to see that most of the spectators had left, gave Chester a look that made the timid bailiff get busy with his paperwork, then faced Lottie. "I realize this is short notice and you might want more time to think about it—which is okay. But since we'll be traveling together, and knowing what a stickler you are for the rules—"

"What are you talking about?" she cut in.

He took a deep breath, then taking her hand in his, got down on one knee. "Lottie Weyland, will you marry me?"

She stared at their clasped hands, not knowing whether to burst into laughter or tears. "You're serious?"

"I'm on my knee, aren't I?"

"But we've only been courting a day."

"Leave it to you to count. A day's plenty. What do you say?"

Elation made her giddy. Plans swirled through her head. "I need to make a dress, pick out the—"

"We don't have time for that. Sims and the judge are waiting."

"What? Now?" She gaped at the door behind the bench as if the two men might burst through at any moment. "You mean get married *now*?"

He gave a disheartened sigh. "This isn't going like I expected."

"But Becky will be furious if I marry without her."

"We can have another wedding with all the trimmings in Greenbroke." He was sounding less enthusiastic with every word.

"Two weddings? But wouldn't that be—"

"So your answer is no." He started to rise.

She shoved him back down. "Of course, I'll marry you. I'm dying to marry you! You really mean it, don't you?"

"Now who's being silly?" He was halfway up when she

flung herself against him, almost pulling them both off balance.

"Yes! Yes! A thousand times yes!" Throwing her arms around his neck, she planted kisses all over his face.

He gently pushed her away. "You better stop that, or we'll both be embarrassed when we stand before the judge. If he's still there." Taking her hand again, he pulled her past the wide-eyed bailiff and through the rear door of the courtroom.

———

Lottie made it to the door marked *Office of the Circuit Judge* before reason asserted itself. "Wait!"

He stopped. "What? Regrets already?"

"You said since we'll be traveling together and I'm a stickler for the rules. That's why you want to marry me now?"

"That, and you need a caretaker, and I'm in love with you."

"But it's so quick. We hardly know each other."

Dropping her hand, he stepped back, hands planted low on his gun belt. "How can you say that?" he challenged, eyes snapping, chin jutting. "Do you have other secrets I don't know about?"

"No, of course not!"

"Then what?"

Her mind raced, trying to come up with a way to put her fears into words that wouldn't hurt him more than she already had. "It's so soon," she said lamely. "Grandpa always told me I should never make a decision when I was upset. And after what I've just been through I'm definitely upset."

He let some of his anger go on a weary sigh. "But you said yes. You said you wanted to marry me. A thousand times over, in fact. Now you don't?"

"No! I want to marry you, Ty. I want it so much it's like a fire inside of me. But there are things . . . obstacles we need to deal with."

"Such as?"

"Where are we going to live? Do you want a big family

or a small one? Can I continue to bookkeep or do you expect me to stay home and cook and wash and chase children all day?"

"But that's what wives do."

Was he joking? Would *he* do it? "To a point," she hedged. "But I also want to continue doing accounts, manage my investments, travel, learn more about business and stocks and . . . well, everything. I need to do something that challenges my brain, or it'll eat me from the inside out."

"Oh."

Oh? That's it? Fearing she might have pushed him too far, she softened her tone. "I love you, Ty. And I do want to marry you. I can't imagine spending the rest of my life with anyone but you. But let's work through some of these issues first so we can start with a cleared slate. Let's give ourselves a little more time."

His disappointment was painful for her to see. But Lottie knew she was right. If they married in haste, they might end up resenting each other because of misdirected purposes. "I know we can work this out, Ty. We love each other too much not to. But it may take time."

"So your answer is no," he said again.

"For now."

"And you'll let me know when I'm supposed to ask you again?"

He said it with a nasty edge, but she let it pass. "How about I ask you next time?"

"That'll be the day," he muttered, apparently needing to have the last word.

Which she couldn't allow. "I look forward to it."

"You're the one telling the judge."

She had no comeback to that.

———

The judge took it better than Ty had. No man liked being turned down, especially after maneuvering so hard to get the deed done without the hoopla of a fancy wedding so he could get straight to the loving part. Seems he'd been standing at the ready for months. Now he'd have to wait God knows how long before he could get her under him where she belonged.

Yet she did have a point. Living with Lottie would definitely require some adjustments. Like breaking her of that troubling habit of trying to manage everybody. And needing to have the last word all the time. And being so bossy.

But if he was honest with himself, he'd have to admit that the main reason he'd tried to rush the wedding was because the idea of spending the night loving Lottie under the stars tonight had a strong appeal, especially to a man who had thought of little else for a long time.

"You're still fretting," she observed about an hour into the ride to her grandfather's ranch.

"More like reconciling." Seeing that worried frown, he reached over and twined his fingers through hers. "Don't worry. We'll figure this out."

She gave a grateful smile. "I know." Putting her other hand over his as if she expected him to bolt, she silently studied the country rolling slowly by. He sensed her sliding into old memories. Rather than disturb her, he used the silence to look around at land not too different from what his uncle had left him.

It wasn't a particularly pretty place. Cactus, mesquite, buffalo grass, sage, and a few shinnery oaks dotting the gently rolling ground, with greener areas around the occasional sinks and water tanks. A land of extremes, molded by freezing winters, blistering summers, wind, drought, and wildfire. The main thing it had going for it was there was plenty of sky. Ty admired the openness of it, that unfettered feeling of being able to see to the distant horizon with only a few puffy clouds overhead, and maybe ten thousand jackrabbit ears and two skinny cows blocking the view.

No wonder her grandfather's ranch had failed. Charlie Goodnight had the right of it—gobble up as much land as you could, populate it with feral cattle, then drive them north at the end of the season. That's the only way to make ranching pay off in hard country like this.

An hour later, Lottie pointed to a string of stunted mesquite marking the banks of a creek. "There it is."

It was a dark, squat structure, which Ty identified as the charred remains of a house as they drew closer.

Lottie wore a sad expression when the wagon rolled to a stop between the barn and what was left of the house. "I can't believe anything is still standing."

A generous assessment. Ty doubted either structure had been sturdy, even in its prime. "You want to stop here or over by the creek?" He hoped by the creek. If they were lucky they might find water in it and graze for the horses nearby.

"The creek. You can cross there." She indicated a small gap in the brush. "There's a little fenced cemetery on the other side. We'll put Grandpa there." As she spoke, she stepped down from the wagon. "You go on. I want to look around."

"We're in no rush to get back. We can even stay the night if need be." Although if they did, Ty doubted Lottie would go for what he had in mind.

———

After Ty drove off, Lottie stood for a moment in the middle of what had once been the yard and tried to gather her courage. She wasn't sure what she expected to see: she only knew she had to look.

Stepping around cow pies left by Krispin's cattle, she approached the tilting barn. It was a wind gust away from collapsing, so she stopped at a safe distance. There wasn't much to see. The only things she recognized were a few harness parts, the buckboard springs, and the metal rims of its spoked wheels, all showing a coating of rust over the blackened metal.

Disheartened, she moved on to the shed.

It was a scorched skeleton, but seemed stable enough. Stopping short of going inside, she surveyed what was left.

Most of the roof was gone. Rubble littered the floor and the center pole was burned through. Yet despite the destruction, there were signs of rebirth. Weeds grew through the twisted metal springs of Grandpa's cot. A morning glory that had survived the flames now twined around one of the exterior posts. A tiny wren busily shoved twigs into a rusty can that had once held horse liniment, and a dirt dauber's nest clung to one of the few overhead rafters.

Life finds a way.

She should have felt something. But there was nothing left here that meant anything to her.

The house was no better.

The rainstorm Curly Joe Adkins had testified to at the hearing must have slowed the flames, judging by the lack of charring on those walls still standing. But what the fire had missed, vandals had stolen. Grandpa's old boots, dishes and utensils, the horseshoe hat rack beside the back door. Even the heavy black pot that had hung on the hook in the big rock fireplace had been taken.

Gone. Everything. Whatever might have bound her to this place had been burned away or stolen three years ago. Not even the smell of scorched wood hung in the air.

Feeling sad and weary—yet oddly free—she walked toward the creek to help Ty lay her grandfather in his resting place beside Mama and Grandma. Once that task was complete, she could leave without looking back.

Grandpa's "someday" dream of a ranch was no more. From now on, what remained of her childhood home she would carry within her heart, for there was nothing left of it here.

Chapter 21

———◆———

Resting his forearm across the top of the shovel, Ty
watched Lottie pick her way across the shallow part of
the slow-moving creek. He felt a stirring of long suppressed
memories of the day he'd come home to find his home smoldering and his parents dead. He still awoke sometimes, his
nostrils filled with the stink of death and smoke, the image
of their lifeless bodies clinging to his mind. He hoped she
would remember the happier times here, and not this charred
ruin of her childhood.

Dropping the shovel beside the hole he'd dug, he walked
toward her, studying her face as he drew closer, trying to
read her mood. He saw no tears, but her dragging steps and
the weary slump of her shoulders told him she had reached
her limit. It saddened him to see this strong, courageous
woman brought so low. He wanted to grab ahold of her and
kiss her sorrow away. His, too.

Instead, he stopped in confusion when she walked silently up to him without stopping, slid her arms around his
waist, and rested her cheek on his chest.

It moved him, such childlike trust from a woman who
had been so poorly used, and for a moment he didn't know

how to respond or what to say. Then he realized she wasn't looking for words from him. Or kisses. Or to be cajoled into a happier mood. All she wanted was a comforting touch.

He could give her that. After what they'd both been through, he needed one, too. So he folded his arms around her, rested his cheek against her head, and simply held her for as long as she would let him.

She was too resilient to give in to sorrow for long, and in a matter of minutes, that sharply intelligent mind had moved on to other problems. He was sorry for it. He liked holding her, liked having her need him. He suspected it wouldn't happen often.

Lacing her fingers through his, she walked with him back to where the coffin awaited burial. "You brought the shovel from town?"

He nodded.

"You should have brought two. I want to help."

"You can." He pointed toward the bank of the creek. "There's a basket over there. Why don't you rustle up something for us to eat while I finish this? It'll be good practice."

"For what?"

"Being a wife. If I decide to let you marry me."

She gave him a playful shove that he pretended threw him off balance, then headed toward the trees. A few minutes later, she returned with fried chicken, a hunk of cheese, and four slices of bread, which they carried into the shade of a tree beside the cemetery. While they ate, she told him of the two women buried there.

It occurred to him that they had both lost their families at a young age. It changed a person, such a loss coming early in life. Either it made you hold back, fearing future losses—like he often did. Or it caused you to grab on to any connection you could find, which is what Lottie did. She was fearless that way. Not afraid to love or be loved. Anyone she met became part of her new family.

After they finished eating, Lottie carried the basket to the wagon and he went back to digging. Luckily, the soil was more sand than clay, and although the hole had to be big enough to accommodate a full-sized coffin, it only needed to be a few feet deep, since all it held was bones. Still, it was tedious work and the sun grew hotter as the day advanced.

He was four feet down and almost finished when he looked up to find Lottie standing at the edge of the hole. She wore an expression he couldn't define—almost smiling, despite the wobbly chin and tear tracks through the dust on her cheeks. "What's wrong?"

"You made a marker."

Feeling the slide of sweat down his forehead, he dragged an arm over his brow. "The undertaker had a spare. All I did was carve the letters on it. Hope I spelled his name right."

When she didn't say anything, he wondered if he'd overstepped. "I would have gotten a stone, but there was no time to have it engraved. We can get one later, if you want."

"He was my grandfather, and I never even thought of a marker. Yet you did. I love you for that."

He looked away, pleased, but embarrassed. "Well, you were pretty busy, being tried for murder, and all." Not wanting to sweat up the cleanest shirt he had left, he pulled it off and tossed it over a bush, then picked up the shovel again.

She continued to watch.

When he figured the hole was deep enough, he used the flat of the blade to smooth the dirt in the bottom, then stepped back to survey his work. Satisfied it was as level as he could get it, he started to toss the shovel out of the hole.

"Wait." She pointed at the far corner. "It's a little crooked there."

He checked, but didn't see it, and turned back to find that she wasn't looking at it, either . . . but at him. He also noticed the wobble was gone. Her hazel eyes still glittered, but with an altogether different expression. And suddenly he felt like a stud in the auction ring. "You're staring."

"I can't help it. You're so—I never knew—I mean, I *knew*, I've just never seen—Lordy, you're so beautiful."

Beautiful? "I prefer manly." He refrained from flexing

to show just how manly. As he climbed out of the hole, her eyes raked over him in a way that made him feel hotter on the inside than out.

"Oh, you're definitely manly. Maybe too manly."

Was that even possible? Maybe on a woman. He advanced toward her. "What about strong? Handsome? Smart?"

"Oh, yes. Definitely." She gave a breathy laugh. "And sweaty and dirty, too."

That stopped him. "I'll go wash in the creek."

"It's only three feet at the deepest."

"Might do some good."

"I'll help."

———

Lottie didn't question the appropriateness of splashing around in a creek with a half-dressed man within thirty feet of her grandfather's freshly dug grave. This was Ty, the man she loved and would someday marry, not some stranger. Besides, it had been a week of bizarre events. A lighthearted frolic with her almost fiancé would be the least of it.

If it had stayed lighthearted.

Which it didn't.

A few well-aimed splashes quickly turned into rapid-fire two-handed water shoveling that ended in a full dunking when Lottie's feet slipped and she went down in the reeds beside the bank.

Grinning in triumph, Ty stood over her, water streaming down his sculpted torso, drawing her eye to every muscle and tendon of his muscular form—from his very wide shoulders, across his lightly furred chest, down the thin line of dark hair that bisected his belly and disappeared into soaked denims that barely hung on his lean hips. *Oh my.*

He was magnificent. Unabashedly masculine. A magnificent male animal.

Pretending surrender, she raised a hand for help in getting back on her feet. As soon as his hand gripped hers, she yanked as hard as she could.

He didn't budge, other than to smirk. "I may not be as

smart as you, but I ain't stupid. Now you want help getting up, or to swim some more?"

Grimacing, she shook a slimy weed from her hair. "What I want is a bar of soap. I wish Becky had remembered to put one in my valise."

He released her hand. "Wait here." Reaching the bank in two long strides, he walked barefoot toward the wagon, rummaged around in his saddlebag, then came back with several blankets and a scrap of soap. Dropping the blankets on the bank by their footwear, he waded in again and sat down behind her, legs stretched out on either side of her hips. "It's not fancy, but it'll get you clean. Dip your head back to wet your hair then lean forward."

Lottie submerged her head then sat up, wiping water out of her eyes.

He rubbed the bar over her head, working up a lather that smelled like the pomade Reverend Lindz had favored.

"Ow." Lottie flinched when something dug into her scalp. "There are hairpins in there."

"Sorry." He fished out several, set them on a nearby rock, then ran his fingers over her wet scalp to be sure he'd gotten them all.

It felt heavenly. His strong hands were so gentle she hardly felt it when he drew the soap through the long, matted strands, trying to work the tangles out.

"You have pretty hair."

Lottie thought it was ordinary at best, but she didn't argue. She was too entranced. No one had washed her hair since before Mama died. And never a man. She couldn't even keep her eyes open, it felt so good.

After piling the soapy hair on top of her head, he began massaging the lather into her neck, then through the fabric over her back and shoulders and arms.

She almost moaned with pleasure. Muscles knotted from Millsap's attack and the long bumpy wagon ride began to loosen. Tense joints relaxed. Even her headache faded. She felt limp as a rag doll and would have sunk face first into the water if he hadn't been holding her.

"This would work better if you didn't have on so many clothes." His voice rustled past her ear, sending delicious shivers dancing down the back of her neck.

Would it truly matter if she took off her dress? She would still have on her shift and drawers, so all the important parts would be covered. And he was behind her so what could he see, anyway? While she reasoned it out, his talented fingers began working at the row of buttons down the back of her dress.

She should stop him. She was a virtuous woman, and virtuous women never allowed men to undress them unless they were married.

But she was going to marry him, wasn't she? In truth, she had almost married him today. Besides, cleanliness was next to godliness. Grandpa must have told her that a thousand times.

By the time she had convinced herself that it was perfectly acceptable to sit half-clothed in the middle of a creek with the man she was going to marry—someday—her dress was unbuttoned to the waist and billowing in the water below her breasts.

The breasts he was washing now, in fact. She looked down, watched his big hands draw soapy circles over her shift, and felt something clench low in her belly.

Her eyes drifted closed. Her body went lax. Sighing, she tipped her head back to rest against his chest. It was just a bath. And she still had on her shift.

"I love your breasts," he murmured.

Lottie was beginning to, too. She had always thought of them as bothersome—bouncing too much when she rode horses, drawing men's attention when she didn't want it, getting sore when her monthly cycle neared. But under Ty's slow, gentle hands, she was gaining a whole new appreciation of them. How they seemed to swell under his touch and ache in a way that sent jolts of pleasure shooting all the way to her toes. Maybe they weren't only for feeding babies, like she'd thought.

"Lean back again and rinse."

Feeling boneless, yet oddly stimulated, Lottie leaned back and to the side so she could straighten out, her eyes still closed.

With one hand under her shoulders to keep her from going under, he used the other to gently drizzle water over her brow and cheeks and neck and chest. Especially, her chest. And before she became aware that he had moved, she felt his lips close over the nipple poking up through her wet shift.

She sucked in air, let it go on a long, stuttering sigh. It was too much. And not enough. Everything seemed to be spinning out of control, yet she didn't want him to stop. To make sure he didn't, she clapped a hand on his wet head and held him captive while his mouth did the most amazing things.

This couldn't be wrong. Nothing about this could be wrong and still feel so good. "Oh, Lordy," she breathed. "I had no idea."

Low laughter sent warm breath over her wet shift. "You still don't."

"Then show me."

She felt him tense and opened her eyes to see him staring down at her.

His eyes had never looked so blue. He breathed deep, nostrils flaring, his lips parted to show the straight, even edge of his teeth. He looked almost savage. A conquering warrior. The primal male. "You're sure?"

Maybe not. Suddenly a whirlwind of doubts and questions swirled through her head. This was a big step. One her grandfather had warned her against many times. Her brain urged her to think it through, analyze it from all angles, find the logical answer to his question.

But her body screamed, *Shut up! Just feel . . . give in . . . allow emotion to rule you for once.*

A drop of water trickled down his neck, through the dip at the base of his throat and over the hard, rounded muscle below. Unable to stop herself, she pressed her hand against the spot where it had disappeared into the dark hair of his chest. Watched the short, damp curls wrap around her fingers. Felt the hard heavy thud of his heart against her palm. And she smiled. "Yes, I'm sure."

———

Ty didn't know what he would have done if she'd said no. He was already so worked up he was afraid he might jump on her like a randy thirteen-year-old. Buying himself time to calm down, he quickly washed, rinsed, shook water out of his hair, and wiped down his chest with the flat of his hand.

All under her round-eyed stare.

He hoped she wasn't analyzing again. That never boded well, especially in situations like this. Not that he'd ever been in a situation like this. He knew it was her first time, and he had to treat her with more delicacy than he might a paid woman, although he'd always tried to do his best there, too. And he also knew if he didn't slow down, he could ruin this before he even got her primed.

Scooping her up, he carried her to the bank and stood her on one of the three blankets he'd brought. With suddenly clumsy hands, he dried them both with another blanket then spread the third on the ground.

She watched in silence, a worried look in her eyes.

"Maybe you'd rather the wagon," he suggested.

"I don't know. What do you think?"

"Here's fine." Turning her around, he quickly undid the rest of the buttons on her dress then worked it over her hips. It didn't go easy since the cloth was wet and his fingers had turned into thumbs. Luckily her petticoat had tabs rather than buttons. Soon it joined the dress and drawers around her bare feet.

And there she was. Just as God made her. Except for the wet shift. Which molded itself to her body like a lover's hands. He slid a shaking finger under the thin shoulder ribbon. "You want to take this off, too?"

"Should I? I wish I'd done this before so I'd know what to do."

"I'll teach you." Forgetting about the shift, he held out his hand.

She took it, settling onto the spread blanket like she thought it might burst into flames under her butt. "You've done it a lot?"

"Not a lot. Mostly just practiced."

"How would you practice?"

"Never mind. Just lie back and relax."

She did . . . with all the enthusiasm of a virgin on a stone altar. He must be doing something wrong. But ever-hopeful, he kept at it.

When he knelt beside her, she sat up, almost hitting his chin, which was still sore from earlier when she'd clipped him. "Why aren't you taking off your trousers?"

"I didn't want to scare you."

"Scare me?" Her eyes went round as a carp's. She stared at the bulge in his denims. "What are you, a Percheron?"

Words failed him.

Apparently taking his silence as her answer—of what, he was afraid to ask—she lay down again, arms stiff at her sides. "I hope it doesn't hurt too much."

He did, too. Propped on one elbow, he stretched out beside her, reminding himself again to go slow and take his time.

"Not that I'm afraid of pain."

He put a hand on her breast. She started, then settled back. His hand looked dark and alien against the pale shift. Brutish, maybe, but not a hoof. *Slow circles, gentle strokes.* "Who told you it would hurt?" Surely not her grandfather.

"Lucy McMann from church. Oh . . . I like it when you do that."

He doubled his efforts. And kept at it until her breathing changed and she started to move against his fingers. "How about this?" he asked, trailing his fingers over her hip, her belly, and down between her legs.

"Oh, my." She arched, her mouth open. "Don't stop . . ."

He didn't intend to.

She began to move even more, her eyes scrunched closed,

her breath coming in gasps. Then without warning, she lurched up, pushed him onto his back, and began to fumble with the buttons on his trousers.

He was shocked. But not for long. Gripped by the same urgency, he helped. After he kicked them off, she climbed on top of him, straddling his hips.

He tried to help there, too, but with breathless determination, she found her own way to the promised land. The woman was a marvel. She might not have known what to do, but she was a quick learner, God bless her.

For a moment they were out of tempo, but when he gripped her hips to help her along, she pushed him away and took charge with the same wholehearted enthusiasm she brought to everything she did.

His eyes almost rolled back in his head.

Desperate to slow her down before he ended it too soon, he leaned up and tried to kiss her. But by then, she had found her rhythm and rode him like there was no tomorrow, sucking him into a cyclone of arms and legs and mouths and pure, erotic sensation. When she let out a cry, he allowed his own release, and the force of it nearly stopped his heart and singed the hair off the top of his head.

He might have blacked out for a moment. Lottie, too, judging by the lifeless way she was draped over him.

"You okay?" he asked once he caught his breath.

"I think I died."

Ty hoped that was a good thing but hadn't the energy to ask.

For a long time, they lay gasping, still intimately joined, his arms wrapped around her. He couldn't have moved if he'd had to. He could barely even breathe.

If he'd loved her before, he worshiped her now.

After a while, she let out a long sigh. "That was incredible. *You're* incredible and Lucy McMann is a bald-faced liar. When can we do it again?"

He couldn't help but laugh.

She reared up. "What's so funny? Did I do something wrong?"

"You were perfect. Amazing. More than any man could wish for. But I'll need a little time to get my strength back."

"Oh." She lay back down, this time tucked against his side, one arm thrown across his chest. "I guess now is when I should ask you to marry me."

"Because I had my way with you?" In truth, it seemed she'd had her way more than he'd had his. But he wasn't complaining.

"Seems silly not to. Although there are still a few unresolved issues we need to talk through."

"Like what?" Ty bit back a yawn. The last thing he wanted to do was talk.

"Like where we should live, for one thing."

It was a struggle to keep his eyes open. "Where do you want to live?"

"Not here. Too many sad memories. My neighbor asked Sims if I'd consider selling. He's already put in fencing and is running his cattle on our land. If he makes a decent offer, we might want to consider it. What do you think?"

He thought they should nap for a while. "What would you do with the money?" Another stifled yawn made his eyes water.

"We. What would *we* do with the money."

Maybe if he closed his eyes just for a minute . . .

"It wouldn't be much," she went on, twining a finger in the hairs on his chest. "Maybe enough to fix up your uncle's place. If that's what you wanted."

That woke him up. He knew her too well. She was up to something.

"Or we could make a down payment somewhere else," she added.

"Like Greenbroke?"

"Well . . ."

And there it was. Another decision made without him. He was weary of it.

She must have sensed his resistance. Leaning onto his chest, she gave him a worried look. "Try not to get upset."

Too late. "Why do you ask my opinion, Lottie, when you've already decided what you want to do? It's your money. Use it how you want." He started to sit up.

She pushed him back down. And not gently. Why was she mad? He was the one who'd been insulted.

"See? This is what I'm talking about. You're so hard-headed you won't even listen to what I have to say."

When had they talked about him being hardheaded? Ty didn't remember that. And he didn't like where she was headed, either. This was exactly why people should sleep after sex. Talk just led to trouble. Not wanting to get drawn into an argument, he decided to be reasonable. "All right, so talk. I'm listening."

Maybe his tone didn't suit her. Glaring down at him with scary eyes, she said through gritted teeth, "No decision has been made about any of this. And there won't be any decisions until we discuss it rationally and come to a *mutual* agreement."

About what? He blinked up at her and tried not to smile. When she got her color up like this, with her feisty hazel eyes shooting lightning bolts and those perfect breasts pumping against his chest like a bellows, he forgot to remember anything except how beautiful she was. "Sure. Okay. Honey."

She made a snorting noise. But the lightning bolts stopped. Sadly, the pumping, too. "Actually, I did find a place." She settled back, her head on his arm. "And it's only eight miles out of Greenbroke. I wrote you all about it in my letter."

"The one I didn't get."

"Take a look at it. Then we can decide."

"What about my uncle's ranch?" The Devil made him say that. He had no intention of fixing it up. He couldn't. He just wanted her to start pumping again.

Instead, she deflated. "Is that what you want to do?"

"Tell me about the Greenbroke place."

That got her going again. He could see she was working

hard to keep her voice neutral so he wouldn't think she was trying to push him into something, which, of course, she was. But he appreciated the effort.

Hands tucked behind his head, he tried to ignore the press of her pert breasts against his side and listened while she described the Buck ranch, with its five thousand acres of prime grazing land that only lacked a windmill and some fencing—the tall, two-story house that would be perfect with a water closet, a couple of porches, a bit of paint, and new drapes—the sturdy barn with four stalls and paddocks that didn't need that much repair—and the year-round creek that only flooded maybe once or twice a year.

Sounded like a lot of work. But what else did he have to do now that he'd left the rangers?

"And it has trees, Ty. Hickory, blackjack, post oak, and even a few pecans along the creek. And the cows are as fat as any I've ever seen."

"Buck is selling his cattle, too?" He said it as a joke to hide the fact that he was starting to get interested. A man should never give in to a woman too easily.

"He might. He's in no condition to drive them to Missouri."

"Sounds like you've already made your decision."

She stroked a hand along his jaw and down his neck, making nerves under his skin quiver in anticipation. "It's *our* decision, Ty. That's what I wrote in my letter. We do it together or not at all."

When he didn't respond—verbally, anyway—she made a last push. "Just take a look at it before you say no, Ty. That's all I ask."

It wouldn't hurt to let her win this one. And she really was trying to do better, so it would behoove him to be generous. Besides, the place sounded like it had possibilities.

"Okay, I'll go see it. Now take off the shift. And this time I'm on top."

Chapter 22

Ty and Lottie arrived back in San Angela just as the late afternoon stage that would carry them to the nearest train station rolled into town. Leaving her at the Overland stagecoach office with their belongings and enough money to buy tickets to the rail line several hours away, Ty hurried to the livery to return the rig and settle his bill. On the way back, he stuck his head into the sheriff's office, curious to see if Millsap was still in jail—which he was—and to tell the sheriff how to reach them if either he or Lottie were needed at his trial. "Or you can check with Mr. Sims," he added. "He'll know how to find us."

"Glad you reminded me." The sheriff rummaged in his desk drawer. "Ridley thought you'd come by on your way out." He held out a thick envelope. "He left this for you."

Ty noted it was addressed to Lottie, not him, so it probably wasn't his bill. After assuring the sheriff he'd give it to Lottie, he sprinted down the boardwalk as Lottie joined two other passengers boarding the stage.

She gave him a look of relief when he climbed in and settled beside her on the thinly padded bench seat. "I was afraid you'd run off."

Leaning close, he whispered, "After the afternoon we had you'll never get rid of me, no matter how hard you try." He waited for her blush then, grinning, handed her the envelope. "Sims left this for you at the sheriff's office."

While Lottie opened the letter, Ty tried to find a comfortable position for his long legs and big feet. Luckily, there were only two other passengers, both men, and by the time they reached the outskirts of town, their heads were nodding to the rocking, bouncing rhythm of the stagecoach.

Lottie lowered the letter to her lap. Keeping her voice low so the dozing men wouldn't be disturbed, she told him her neighbor, Jerry Krispin, had made an offer to buy Grandpa's land.

"A good offer?"

Frowning, she scanned the second page again. "It's decent. But I'm not sure. What do you think?" She handed him the letter.

Pleased that she was asking his opinion rather than leaving him out of it, he scanned the particulars. It seemed a fair price. Ty doubted other offers would be forthcoming but he wasn't about to make such an important decision for her. He handed the papers back. "Would you ever want to live there again?"

"No," she said, without hesitation. "Until I moved to Greenbroke, I didn't understand how hard our life had been. Sure, there were some good times, but mostly it was a day-to-day struggle. I can't count the times I went to bed hungry. I never want to go back to that."

"Even if we rebuilt the house and barn?"

She gave him a weary smile. "You saw it, Ty. Not even your strong back and determination could make such a poor holding into a successful ranch. But if we sold, it might bring in enough to get us started somewhere else. Somewhere with more potential."

"Like the Buck place?"

She shrugged. "Or up near the panhandle where your uncle's land is."

His uncle's place wasn't an option. But seeing she was

willing to sell her inheritance to help him bring his up to scratch gave him hope. And a willingness to compromise. "Before you do anything, you'd best decide if you want a fresh start somewhere else more than you want to hold on to your grandfather's place."

"I definitely want to start over somewhere else. But I hate selling the land. Not for sentimental reasons, but because it may have value someday." She sighed. "It's so confusing. What do you think I should do?"

"It's your land, honey. Do what works best for you. I'll back whatever you decide."

He watched tears fill her eyes. But she was smiling when she stretched up to whisper in his ear, "I love you, Tyree Benton."

Emotion swelled in his chest. As she pulled back, all he could do was grin, not trusting his voice.

"But it's not just me, anymore," she went on. "It's us."

"Is that a proposal, Miss Weyland?"

More tears. A bigger smile. "I guess it is, Mr. Benton. Will you do me the honor of becoming my husband?"

Husband. Again, words deserted him. Instead, he took her hand in his, not caring if the men on the other bench saw, and laced his fingers through hers. Her hand was so small and soft against his big, callused palm. Elegant, yet strong. Like Lottie, herself. "I'll think about it."

She elbowed him in the ribs.

He laughed. "Okay."

"Okay, what?"

"Okay, I'll allow you to marry me. But let's take a look at the Buck place before we set the date."

"Why?"

"I'll have to figure out how long it'll take to make all those repairs you want done, so we can have the wedding there. Maybe by the creek."

"Truly?" Her grin stretched ear to ear, then words tumbled out faster than he could keep up. "You really mean it? Oh, Ty, thank you! You'll love it, I know you will. It's perfect for us!"

He sincerely hoped so, since he'd already wired the proceeds from the sale of his uncle's place to Griffin at the People's Bank, with instructions to find out what it would take to seal the deal on the Delbert Buck ranch.

A sense of inevitability stole over him. Everything was about to change. Soon a husband, hopefully a rancher, then, God willing, a father, and someday a grandfather. With Lottie at his side, anything was possible. The thought of it made him smile. After so many years with the rangers, being told what to do and where to go next, he was ready to chart his own direction . . . if his wife let him. At least with Lottie, he would never be bored.

Beyond the dust kicked up by the horses' hooves, the day faded and the miles rolled by. They'd be stopping soon at the same little railroad town they'd stayed at earlier. And although Ty wanted Lottie in his bed tonight and every night for all the nights he had left, he knew they were running a risk, both of pregnancy and harm to her reputation. He was determined to protect her from that. Protect her from himself, if necessary.

He glanced at the woman dozing at his shoulder. She would be a challenge, no doubt about that. Smartest person he knew, tenderhearted almost to a fault, courageous, logical yet scatterbrained at the same time, and with an appetite for him almost as strong as the one he had for her.

Had a luckier man ever lived?

A sudden image popped into his head: his parents sitting at the kitchen table over dinner, Ma listing all the things Pa needed to do, and Pa just looking at her as he chewed, a smile playing at the corners of his mouth. Eventually, he would do what she wanted, but in his own time and his own way. He never argued with her about it. He just listened and smiled. And oddly, once Ma got that list out of her head, she forgot about it altogether. It was as if the sharing of it was more important than seeing the deed done. Probably a woman thing. Men saw what needed doing and did it. No lists required.

But something more drove Lottie. Perhaps, in losing her

family at such an early age, she'd lost faith that things would turn out right unless she was there to make sure of it. Maybe she thought if she could control everything and everyone around her, she would have a fighting chance of keeping those she cared about safe. Whatever it was, she was a force to reckon with.

It aggravated the hell out of him sometimes. But he couldn't have admired or loved her more.

————

They arrived in Greenbroke early the following afternoon to find the train platform crowded with folks who had gathered to welcome her home.

Even the Bracketts were there—probably closed up the market early to meet the train—Mr. B. beaming through his smudged spectacles, Mrs. B. alternately dabbing at her eyes and waving her hanky.

As soon as the train slowed to a stop, Becky pushed forward, bouncing between tears and laughter as she waited impatiently for the conductor to drop the mounting step so she could be the first to offer a hug. Which she did, the two of them blocking the step until the conductor told them to move along so the other passengers could disembark.

"I can't believe you're home!"

Lottie couldn't either. Nor could she believe so many people had come to greet her. She couldn't stop grinning.

"We're so glad you're back!" Jane called, sandwiched between an unsmiling Briggs and a man Lottie had never seen, but one she guessed was English, judging by the very proper attire and top hat.

As always, Juno stood apart, separated from the others by choice and profession, but his smile was just as welcoming as the others' and turned his normally somber expression into one of rugged masculine beauty.

Griffin was there, as well. While Lottie greeted her friends, she saw him pull Ty aside and speak to him in a confidential manner before shaking his hand, giving Lottie a final wave, and heading back to the bank.

"Attention, everyone!" Jane called, rising on tiptoe and waving her gloved hand beneath the ruffled edge of her parasol. "Please come to the Social Club for refreshments and a welcome home celebration for Lottie. You're all invited," she added with a pointed glance in Juno's direction.

Brave lady. Folks in Greenbroke could get rowdy, especially when free food and drink were involved.

Sensing a presence looming at her back, Lottie glanced around to find Ty standing behind her with her valise and his saddlebags. "I'll take these by Becky's house then meet you at the club, okay?"

"Don't be long," Lottie called as Becky grabbed her arm and propelled her toward Juno, leaning against the wall of the station.

"It'll probably take the two of us to get him to Lady Jane's," the blonde said with a resolute look in her brown eyes. "But I'm determined that Juno puts in an appearance. For your sake, of course."

"Of course," Lottie agreed, trying not to laugh.

Juno attempted to maintain his distance, but Lottie would have none of it. Throwing her arms around his neck, she gave him a quick hug in front of God and everybody and thanked him for coming. Then, stepping back, she linked her hand through his right arm, while Becky took his left. "We've got you now, my friend," she said with a laugh as they towed him toward the club.

His gaze flicked to a grinning Becky. "I'm afraid you're right."

The day was unseasonably hot and muggy for late June and by the time they reached the club, Lottie was grateful to discard her bonnet and gloves in favor of a cup of cool lemonade.

She couldn't believe all the fuss was for her. Only days ago, her future had looked grim, but now she was home again among her friends and about to start a grand life with the man she loved. She was almost giddy with happiness.

But not everyone seemed in high spirits. Jane looked exhausted, her lively blue eyes ringed with dark circles, and

Briggs was even more stone-faced than usual. In contrast, the Englishman that Jane had introduced as Lord Findlay was excessively attentive to Jane, while mostly ignoring Briggs.

"What's going on with the dandy?" Lottie whispered to Becky by the ladies' punch bowl.

"I'm not sure. I think he might have been Jane's suitor from before and followed her here to ask her to go back to England with him."

"What does Briggs say about that?"

Becky shrugged. "He's not talking. But his eyes are murderous whenever he looks at Findlay. Think he could be jealous?"

Lottie did. But she also thought Briggs would never admit to it. He was almost as bullheaded as Juno when it came to expressing his feelings. "How's it going with you and Juno?"

Becky sighed. "Same as always. I know he cares about me. Just not enough to make a move."

"Keep trying," Lottie urged. "He's a good man."

"What about you and Ty? Things seem a lot smoother between you than when you left."

"They are." Lottie wanted to tell her friend everything. But for the first time, she held back. Nothing was wrong, yet something had changed. She would always think of Becky as the sister she'd never had. But after the events of the past week, especially those hours by the creek next to the cemetery, her feelings for Ty had grown even deeper than any she'd ever had. He was the one she wanted to talk to and be with. But she couldn't shut Becky out. She was important to Lottie, too. "Let's talk later," she suggested. "After we're done here."

But Becky wasn't listening. "Oh, my," she said, her interest focused on something across the room. "Look what the cat dragged in."

Following her gaze, Lottie saw Ty coming in from delivering their luggage to Becky's. And he wasn't alone. Behind him was a familiar and not altogether welcome face. The reverend Nathaniel Lindz.

Lottie glanced at Juno, saw his furious expression, and headed his way before he could slip out the door.

"Deserting us, are you?"

"I've got a saloon to run. Business is always brisk on hot days."

It was a weak excuse but Lottie let it pass. "I thought you'd want to know what happened in San Angela."

"I know you didn't do anything wrong, Lottie. That's enough for me."

It was a moment before she could speak. "I didn't kill him, you know."

"Your grandfather? I know that, Lottie."

"He had rabies." She explained how Grandpa chained himself in the shed and asked her to set it on fire after he died so he couldn't infect anyone else. "I just wanted you to know."

His deep brown eyes softened with sympathy. "I'm sorry." In an impulsive gesture, he reached out and put his hand on her shoulder. "I never doubted you, Lottie. None of us did."

Again, she couldn't speak.

He took his hand away.

They stood in awkward silence until she found her voice again. "I have other news."

"Oh?"

"Ty and I are getting married."

He reared back in mock surprise. "I'm stunned! I had no idea you two were sweet on each other. Or maybe more than sweet," he added with a chuckle, "judging by that blush. When are you tying the knot?"

"That depends on you and Becky. I'm wanting a double wedding."

Amusement faded. "You never give up, do you?"

"Not when I know I'm right. But I can see how anxious you are to get back to your bar rats, so I'll let you escape for now. But start gathering your receipts. I'll be by in a day or two to go over your books and shoot down all your flimsy excuses for putting off what you know is the right thing to do."

"Hell."

With a saucy backhand wave, she sauntered toward the table laden with cookies and cake and sandwiches. Becky stood beside it with Ty and the preacher. Yet she had eyes only for Juno. Even after the saloon owner left the room, her troubled gaze remained on the empty doorway.

Lottie felt a deep regret. Now that she had reached an understanding with Ty, it saddened her that the two other people she loved most seemed determined to miss their own chance at happiness. She needed to find a way to help them.

It was late afternoon when the gathering broke up and Lottie and Ty escorted the Bracketts back to the market. "I can't believe how muggy it is," Ty observed, plucking his shirt away from his sweaty chest.

Mr. B. squinted up at the thunderheads rolling in. "Probably means rain."

"I'm not complaining," Lottie said with a chuckle. "I don't care if it rains or snows or turns blistering hot. I'm just glad to be home again."

Mrs. B. patted her arm. "You poor dear. What you must have suffered. We were so worried, wondering what you were going through."

Lottie knew the kindly woman was hinting to know more. She had every intention of telling the Bracketts everything. But the subject was still a tender one and every time she talked about it, it was like reopening a fresh wound.

She would have to tell Jane and Briggs, too. She'd had no opportunity to speak privately with them earlier with fancy Lord Findlay always hovering in the background. Hopefully, when she went back tomorrow to check on the club books, she'd have a chance to talk to them. All her friends had been so loyal and trusting she felt she owed them an explanation as well as her heartfelt thanks. Which was why she and Ty were walking the Bracketts home now. She wanted the truth to come from her, not through the gossip mill. And once Mrs. B. knew the whole story, everyone in town would soon know it, which would save Lottie from having to go over every painful detail again and again.

Ty must have sensed the downturn in her spirits. Sending her an encouraging smile, he silently gave her hand a reassuring squeeze, then he let it go.

Lottie didn't care if the Bracketts saw. She was just grateful he was close by. It seemed he was always close by when she needed him—shoring up her every weakness, steadying her whenever she faltered. It was such a wonderful, freeing feeling to be loved and no longer alone.

When they reached the market, Lottie knew she couldn't put it off any longer. Following them back into the kitchen behind the store, she asked the Bracketts to sit down. Taking the chair beside Mrs. B., she smiled at the giving couple who had literally saved her life. "I don't know what you heard about why I was arrested."

The Bracketts looked at each other.

Mr. B. shrugged. "We don't cotton to gossip," he said, obviously not knowing his wife as well as he should have.

"Remember when you found me digging through your refuse bin, and I told you I'd been living near San Angela until my grandfather died?"

Both of them nodded.

"What I didn't tell you was how he died." She took a deep breath, hoping to steady her voice, then went over it all again. It was no easier the second time, and somewhere during the recitation, she began to cry.

Mrs. B. handed over her damp hanky. "You wipe those tears away, child. He's no longer suffering. Nor should you."

"Fourteen is mighty young to go through such a thing," Mr. B. muttered.

Ty nodded in agreement, but said nothing.

Lottie dried her cheeks then told them about Grandpa asking her to set fire to the shed after he died so he wouldn't infect anybody else. "'Then you leave this place,' he told me. 'And never look back.' So I did, and ended up here." More tears spilled as Lottie took Mrs. B.'s hand in hers. "And I thank God every day that you found me. I don't know how I would have made it without the two of you."

Now crying, too, Mrs. B. pulled her into a smothering

hug. "You're our daughter, Lottie. We'll always be there for you."

Feeling the press of too much emotion, Lottie gave Mrs. B. a final pat then gently pulled out of the embrace. After pausing a moment to let her nerves settle, she said, "The law assumed I'd set the fire and killed my grandfather. That's why I was arrested for murder and taken to San Angela."

An anxious look came over Mrs. Brackett's face. "But you're back now. Everything's cleared up and you're free?"

"I am."

"Praise be."

Lottie smiled at Ty. "And now for the best part. Ty and I are getting married."

"You don't say!" Mr. B. smacked the table.

Mrs. B. looked from Lottie to Ty and back at Lottie. "You're marrying Ranger Benton?"

"It's Mr. Benton now," Ty said.

"Oh, my. Did you hear, Mr. Brackett?"

"I did."

Mrs. B. started fluttering. "Law's sake. Our little Lottie is getting married."

Lottie gave her intended a broad smile. "If he'll have me."

I've already had you. Resting three fingers on his jaw, Ty mouthed, *three times.*

Heat rushed into her cheeks. *If you want to go for four,* she warned him with a look, *you'd better be good.*

I thought I was good.

The memory of how good he was sent new tingles to all those parts he seemed so taken with, and made her question her decision to stay at Becky's until the wedding.

Chapter 23

An hour later, Ty left her off at Becky's then went to find a room. They'd agreed to sleep apart until the wedding. Silly maybe, but rules were rules, and they didn't want to flaunt conventions more than they already had. Since Lady Jane's was too expensive, that left the Greenbroke Hotel or Sally's old room at the Spotted Dog, assuming a new whore hadn't moved in while they were gone. He probably could have stayed in the storeroom at the market, but the cot was too short and he wasn't that fond of mice and he didn't want to impose . . . or be hovered over, Lottie guessed. After kissing him good-bye, she sent him on his way and went into the kitchen, where she found Becky sitting at the kitchen table with Reverend Lindz. It was apparent they'd been arguing: Becky's mouth was tight as a tailor's stitch and Lindz was scowling.

"Sorry," Lottie muttered and turned back into the hall.

Becky shot from her chair. "He was just leaving."

"I was?"

"You are," Becky said firmly. "You were going to repay Juno, remember? Maybe I'll see you at the Spotted Dog later."

With her glaring down at him, the reverend had no choice but to leave.

As soon as the door closed behind him, Becky sank back into her chair. "Thank heavens you came when you did."

Taking the chair Lindz had vacated, Lottie asked what was wrong.

"He came back thinking we would get married. Can you imagine?"

Lottie could. Especially since Becky had never told him she wouldn't. "You told him no?"

"Not yet. I may have to marry him yet."

"*Have* to?" Good heavens, was she pregnant?

"Not *have* to. I'm definitely not in a family way, since we've never . . . you know. Not that he hasn't tried."

"Don't elaborate," Lottie muttered, a bit shocked that a preacher would contemplate the wonderfully wicked things she and Ty had done. Add another sin to his list. And hers. "So why would you have to marry him?"

"No one else seems to want to."

Ah. Juno. "You're twenty-one," Lottie reminded her. "You have years to bring a certain someone around."

"He's not budging. I even kissed him. And he liked it, I could tell. But he just laid there like a big lump."

"*Laid* there?"

"I've decided to give him one more chance to ante up. If he doesn't come around, I'm washing my hands of him."

"Wait. Start at the beginning. Where was he laying?"

Becky gave her an odd look. "In his bed. Where else?"

"And you were there with him?"

"Not *with* him." Becky waved the idea away "It was the morning I got your telegram that you were coming home. I was so excited I ran straight to tell Juno. Naturally, he was still sleeping—he never gets up before noon, you know. I barged in anyway and woke him up. Did you know he sleeps with a gun? And hardly any clothes?"

"He was naked?"

"Not entirely. Just on top. The rest was covered." A distant look came into her eyes. "His hair stuck out every which way and he had pillow wrinkles on his cheek and a sleepy-sexy look . . ." Her words trailed off on a deep breath. "Oh,

Lottie, I had no idea he was so muscular." Realizing Lottie was gaping at her, she laughed. "He was gorgeous. Except for a nasty bullet scar on his chest. I almost jumped on top of him, then and there."

Lottie wasn't sure how much more of this she wanted to hear. Juno was like a brother to her. The thought of him and Becky—she didn't want to think about it.

"Anyway," Becky went on, "I told him you and Ty were coming home and we should do something. For a moment, he just blinked those brown eyes at me, then he did the most astounding thing. He grabbed me and kissed me!"

"Oh my word."

"I know! Granted, he'd kissed me once before when we'd been drinking and I—never mind that. But this kiss was different. More personal somehow. More honest and spontaneous. And much too short."

"I need coffee," Lottie muttered, rising from her chair.

"Check the pot. There might be some left. Anyway, Juno looked as surprised by the kiss as I was. I asked him what he was doing."

Lottie chided herself as she poured a cup of lukewarm coffee and returned to her seat. This was a private thing between her two dearest friends. She shouldn't be listening. "What did he say?" she asked, despite good intentions.

"That he'd been dreaming when I woke him up and told him to do something, so he did. And that's it. As if it wasn't the most wonderful kiss in the world and I didn't matter to him and it was all a big mistake. I showed him a thing or two."

Lottie's cup thumped on the table. "Oh, Becky! What did you do?"

"I told him my mama always said if you're going to do something, you ought to do it right. Then I kissed him back. For a long time." That dreamy look again. "It was wonderful, everything I'd imagined, and I could tell he thought so, too. It was kind of obvious, the way the sheet—"

"Then what happened?" Lottie blurted out. She had enough lurid pictures in her mind. She didn't need *that* one, too.

"He pushed me away with a guilty look like he'd been caught with his hand in the cookie jar. Which it almost was."

Lottie closed her eyes on that one, but the image still danced behind her lids.

"So we argued a bit," Becky went on, saving Lottie from trying to formulate a response. "He told me to turn my back while he dressed, and we went to his office." With a sneer, she added, "Probably felt safe from further temptation with his dead wife and son watching us from the tintype on the bookcase shelf."

Avoiding that troublesome topic, Lottie asked what they'd argued about.

"Jane and Mr. Briggs. I think they're in love, but Juno says no. Still, I'm sure something's going on with the two of them, and now with Fancy Findlay lurking about, things seem even more tense."

"In what way?"

"When I went to tell them you were coming home, I found Jane and Findlay arguing in the lobby at the club. At least, it looked like arguing, although it could have been surprise. I'm guessing the man wasn't expected, even though they seemed to know each other pretty well. He sure has an eye for Jane. And a glare for Briggs. Jane mostly looks flustered. From what Bea Davenport told me and what I can piece together, Findlay wants Jane to go back with him to England. I think Briggs does, too. But he didn't look happy about it. Probably because she'd be going with Findlay."

"Briggs never looks happy."

"Around Jane he does. Unless someone is rude to her. Then he's as touchy as a teased snake."

"He is rather protective."

"More than protective. The way he hovers around her, and never takes his eyes off of her when she's in the room. Even the way they argue. He's smitten."

Lottie pushed her cup aside. "I agree. But for some reason is afraid to admit it, even to himself."

"Like Juno."

Exactly like Juno.

They were a pair, Briggs and Juno. Both had seen too much death and destruction, and it had changed them. Tempered by circumstance and hardened by cruel experience, they would always be the outsiders looking in, never fully belonging. Their choice, mostly. Sometimes the stranglehold of the past was stronger than the lure of the future. Lottie knew that from what she'd just gone through. The events three years ago had colored everything in her life until she'd been forced to confront it.

"Well, I can't wait on Juno forever," Becky announced. "It seems lately all I do is drift from one day to the next, hoping and waiting. That's no way to live. If Juno doesn't want me, the good reverend will do well enough."

"You would really marry Nathaniel Lindz?"

"I'd prefer not. He's starting to get on my nerves. And I hate that greasy hair restorer he uses, which, I can tell you for a fact, isn't working. But if he's my only choice, what can I do?" She rested her folded arms on the table. "Enough of my troubles, tell me what happened in San Angela."

So Lottie went over it all again, telling Becky more than she'd revealed to the Bracketts, including that awful attack by Ranger Millsap in her jail cell.

"Thank goodness Ty was there to pull him off. I hope you got him so good he'll never be able to get it up again."

Now that she was experienced, Lottie knew what Becky meant and heartily agreed. Hopefully, she and Ty wouldn't have to go back for his trial. She never wanted to see the man again. "But there's some good news in all this," she said. "Ty and I are getting married."

Becky reacted with predictable squeals and hugs and demands that Lottie go over all the details.

She did, and even though it was getting dark and Becky would be late to her job at the Spotted Dog, Lottie told her everything, only omitting the part about her and Ty making love by the creek. That was a private thing, too precious to share with anyone but Ty. "And later this week," she concluded, "Ty and I are going out to the Buck place to decide if that's where we want to settle." Seeing Becky's look of disappointment, Lottie quickly added, "It's only eight miles away. And I'll be in town several days a week to attend my clients, so it's not like we wouldn't see each other all the time."

"You'll still do bookkeeping?"

"Sure. Why wouldn't I?"

"Most men don't want their wives working for others once they have a husband and home to take care of." As she spoke, Becky rose and grabbed her bonnet from a peg by the door. "Probably afraid people will think they're not good providers."

That silly male pride again. "Ridiculous. I like bookkeeping. Besides, I need to keep an eye on our investments." But the nagging thought arose. What if Becky was right? What if Ty wouldn't want her working away from the ranch?

"I'm sure you'll work it out." Becky's voice held only a trace of doubt, and maybe a hint of wistfulness. "It's obvious Ty would do anything for you. Well, I'd best run. See you in the morning."

Lottie sat at the table long after Becky left, mulling over what she had said. Marriage was starting to sound more complicated by the day, especially if it meant giving up her hard-won independence and struggling through all those domestic chores she wasn't very good at. She was beginning to wonder if it was worth it.

Then she remembered the feel of Ty's hands running over her, and how his strong body trembled beneath her touch, and the way his smile made her heart stutter and her limbs grow weak. It was definitely worth it. *He* was worth it. She had never felt so treasured or protected as when she was with Ty. She couldn't—wouldn't—give that up.

Another impasse. Another delicate negotiation looming ahead.

With a sigh, she rose and headed toward her bedroom. Who knew loving a man could be such a tricky business?

———

The next morning was as unseasonably warm as the day before had been, and felt even muggier, if such was possible.

Lottie awoke tired and cross, having spent a restless night wishing Ty was beside her.

Needing to stay busy so her worries wouldn't overwhelm her, she decided to go to the club first to tell Jane and Briggs about her trial. Then she would go to the bank to see if Griffin had heard anything new about the Buck place and if Delbert Buck was still looking to sell. If anything had changed, Griffin would know. And if he didn't, Humphries would. She hoped Buck would make a counter offer she could live with, and that the proceeds from the sale of Grandpa's place would be enough for a down payment. If not, she could liquidate some investments. But only if Ty agreed to settling there and allowing her to pay for the improvements she wanted. She felt they'd made progress, but he was a stubborn man who didn't push easily . . . a trait she admired when he wasn't pushing back at her. Maybe tomorrow they could ride out and look the place over. Surely he would see the same potential in it that she did.

She found Jane and Mr. Briggs in his office, discussing menu choices. Both looked tired and tense. She was glad that Lord Findlay wasn't there—it would be difficult enough sharing the details of her trial and imprisonment with friends. Having a stranger privy to that, as well as her grandfather's ordeal, would have been awful.

They listened with typical British aplomb—a word Lottie had recently learned from Jane. When she finished, Jane dabbed at her damp eyes with a delicate lace-edged hanky. "Oh, Lottie, how brave you are. I doubt I could have endured it."

"You're stronger than you think," Briggs said staunchly. "You both are."

Was she imagining that faint softening in his expression? Had she finally worn a tiny crack in that stiff reserve?

"And of course, we knew it was all a mistake," Jane added. "You're too sweet a girl to do such a ghastly thing. Anson said so himself, didn't you, dear?"

Briggs looked ready to argue that point, but Lottie quickly moved on to her other news. "Also, Ty and I are getting married."

After well wishes and hugs—only from Jane, of course—Briggs asked when the wedding would take place.

"I didn't want to set a date until I knew for certain the two of you would be able to attend."

He frowned. "Why wouldn't we be able to attend?"

"There's talk that Jane might be returning to England."

"Talk." He shook his head in disgust. "I thought you knew better than to get your information through gossip, Miss Weyland."

Lottie narrowed her eyes at him. "Which is precisely why I'm asking now, Mr. Briggs."

"We'll be there," Jane broke in. "We wouldn't miss it for the world, would we, Anson?"

"Not by choice."

Lottie smiled her appreciation and moved on to a different subject. "Now what about you? Who is Lord Findlay and why is he here?"

Briggs gave her a stern look. "Lord Findlay does not concern you."

"Do be civil, Anson. Of course, she's concerned. She's our friend." To Lottie, Jane added, "I suppose rumors are rampant about that, too."

Lottie admitted she'd heard a few, mostly about Lord Findlay.

"Not surprising," Briggs muttered.

"Oh, dear. What are they saying?"

"That he's an old beau and has come to take you back to England."

Briggs snorted.

Jane sighed.

Lottie knew she was being as nosy as Mrs. B. but she was worried. In addition to not wanting Jane to leave Greenbroke, it was plain to see by the dark circles beneath her eyes that the Englishwoman was unhappy and not sleeping well. "Is it true? He was a suitor?"

"At one time he might have been. But it didn't work out between us."

"She means he deserted her at the first sign of trouble," Briggs said, his voice taut with anger.

Jane gave another sigh. "Please, Anson. You mustn't be too hard on him. Lord Findlay had his own troubles at the time, if you'll remember."

"He was a bloody fortune hunter," Briggs muttered. "Still is."

An ongoing argument, Lottie guessed, noting Jane's half-hearted response and Briggs's obvious disgust.

"But I thought you wanted Jane to go back to England," she said to him.

"I do. But not like this. Lord or no, the blighter isn't good enough for her."

Before Lottie could question that, the door opened and Lord Findlay stuck his blond head inside. Ignoring both Lottie and Briggs, he smiled at Jane. "Ah, there you are, my dear. I was hoping I might take you in to lunch if you're free."

"Of course." She rose, then hesitated and turned back to Briggs and Lottie. "Will you join us?"

Findlay frowned.

Briggs thrust out his chin. "I don't think—"

"We'd love to," Lottie said.

"Excellent." Jane smiled. "We shall see you in the dining room."

After the door closed behind them, Lottie rounded on the ex-soldier. "Why aren't you doing anything?"

"About what?"

"Jane. You're letting him court her right under your nose."

"It's complicated."

"She loves you. You love her. What's complicated about that?"

"Did I not dismiss you weeks ago? Why do you persist in coming back?"

"Coward."

"Interfering twit." He crossed the room and jerked open the door.

Lottie marched through it.

"You're making a terrible mistake, Mr. Briggs. You're going to lose her."

"She's not mine to lose, and never will be. And that's the end of it. Now march."

It was the least enjoyable meal Lottie had ever suffered through. Poor Jane struggled valiantly to keep up a conversation—which Briggs ignored. Findlay offered a comment now and then—which Briggs also ignored. And Lottie couldn't think of a thing to say after her initial responses to Jane's feeble attempts at small talk. It reminded her of those tense meals back home when Grandpa was on a tear about something.

Soon, silence settled over the nearly empty dining room. The air was so stuffy and charged with tension it was difficult to breathe. Lottie ate as fast as good manners would allow so she could escape, until she saw Jane starting to sag. Reluctantly taking up the conversational gauntlet, she turned to Findlay.

"What part of England do you hail from, Lord Findlay?"

"The Lake District. You would like it, Miss Weyland. It's very green and peaceful. Quite restorative, too, don't you think, Briggs?"

"I wouldn't know."

Findlay looked surprised. "You've never been there?"

"Only briefly. I remember little about it."

"But isn't that where your wife resides?"

Stunned silence.

Jane's knife clattered to her plate.

"W-wife?" Lottie gasped.

Briggs set down his fork. His face seemed carved in stone, except for his eyes. They were terrifying—cold and merciless, empty of expression. "It is," he told the baron in a hard, flat voice. "The last I heard."

"You're married?" Jane choked out.

Findlay glanced from Briggs to Jane. Lottie noted no

malice in his expression. Only confusion. "I'm sorry, did I misspeak?"

Ignoring him, Jane continued to stare at Briggs, her face pale with shock. "You have a wife, Anson?"

Something moved behind those glacial eyes—something sad and defeated. "Yes."

"For how long?"

"Twelve years."

"Oh, God." Jane lurched to her feet and stumbled toward the door.

Lottie started up, too, but Briggs waved her back down and marched after Jane with long, determined strides.

Lottie's mind reeled. *Briggs is married. Briggs is married.* But no matter how many times that thought circled through her head, it made no sense.

"Dash it all. I thought she knew." Findlay frowned thoughtfully at the empty doorway. "But it explains a great deal."

She glared at him, rage bubbling in her throat. "Like what?"

"Her infatuation with him."

"What about your infatuation with her?" She didn't know who she was angrier with—Briggs or Findlay.

He looked at her then, regret in his eyes. "I assure you, Miss Weyland, I take no pleasure in hurting the woman I've been in love with for half of my life."

"If you were in love with her, why did you let her leave England in the first place?"

He spread his elegant hands in a gesture of defeat. "I thought she would be safer out of the country."

"Safer? From whom?"

"Her cousin and his wife. I didn't realize it would take so long to clear her name." He gave a mirthless laugh as he carefully folded his napkin beside his plate. "Such a fuss over a lost necklace. I should have known there was more to it than that."

Chapter 24

―――・:・―――

Lottie fled the dining room, but once in the lobby, she stopped, unsure what to do. She wanted to console Jane, confront Briggs, find Ty and cry on his shoulder. But he was gone on some mysterious errand and she was afraid if she saw Becky or the Bracketts they would ask her what was wrong and she would blurt out something she shouldn't. Not knowing what else to do, she headed to the office to work on the books. Numbers always settled her mind.

As she passed down the hall, she heard Briggs's and Jane's voices coming from behind the closed door of Jane's room. What could he say to explain away his silence? And what was Jane to do now that it seemed Briggs was beyond her reach? Thinking about the pain they both must have been feeling made Lottie's chest hurt.

Closing the door behind her, she went to her desk and pulled out the club ledgers, desperate to block the chaos of her thoughts with the order and calmness that working with numbers brought.

An hour later, Lottie heard a noise and looked up to find Briggs looming in the doorway.

"Don't speak," he ordered when he saw her sitting at her

desk. "Not a word." Steps dragging, he crossed to his desk and sat heavily in his chair. Leaning forward, he braced his elbows on the desktop, dropped his head into his hands, and stared down at the neat stack of mail awaiting his attention. "Bloody hell."

Her heart went out to him. How did a person age a decade in the span of an hour? "Do you want me to leave?"

He didn't answer.

"Should I go to Jane?"

"Not now. She's resting."

"Is there anything I can do?"

He gave a bitter laugh and sat back in his chair. "Can you travel through time and undo a terrible mistake made twelve years ago?"

"No."

"Nor can I." With trembling hands, he began sorting through the mail. "Have you finished with the restaurant ledger?"

"I'm sorry I pushed you so hard. I understand now why you've been so aloof with Jane."

"I was never aloof. More's the pity."

"You're estranged from your wife?"

"Bollocks!" He slapped the letters so hard onto the desk they slid off and fluttered in disarray across the floor. Swiveling his chair to face her, he said through clenched teeth, "I will say this only once, Miss Weyland. Not to satisfy your ravenous curiosity, but to prevent you from badgering Jane with endless questions. Am I clear?"

Too shocked to speak, Lottie nodded.

"Yes, I am estranged from my wife. Because the very sight of me drives her into shrieking hysteria, as does any face but those of her keepers. She thinks I killed the child she miscarried, and that butterflies speak to her, and worms crawl beneath her skin. She is clearly mad and has been for the last ten years and quite possibly for most of her life. I was too young and foolish and besotted to realize that before I married her. When she set fire to my father's church, burning to death three innocent people, the magistrate insisted she be committed to an asylum for the criminally insane, where she remains today. I cannot divorce her, and never intended to fall in love with Lady Jane." He sat back, his face haggard, his hands tightly gripping the arms of his chair. "And there you have it."

"Oh, Mr. Briggs—"

He thrust up a shaking hand. "Not another word, Miss Weyland. I mean it. And stop crying."

"I'm so sorry."

"You're dismissed. Go."

This time Lottie went because she couldn't stem the tears coursing down her face, and she couldn't bear to see big, strong Mr. Briggs struggle against his own.

As she stepped outside, a sudden gust came up, whipping her skirts around her ankles and tugging at her bonnet. In the distance, thunder rolled and lightning bounced along a dark line of clouds hanging in the west. She wished it would rain and get it over with. The air was so humid and clammy her dress clung to her back and her hair had gone from waves to frizzy curls stuck to her sweating brow. Even her tears didn't dry.

Hoping to have her emotions under control by the time she talked to Griffin, she headed toward the bank. When she walked by the Western Union office, the two resident checker players were gathering their checkers and taking the board from atop the barrel they used as a table.

"Best stretch a leg, missy," the older of the two warned. "It's coming up a storm right fast."

His opponent nodded in agreement. "And that green tint in them clouds says it'll be a bad one."

They looked gray to Lottie—which perfectly suited this dismal day—but the clouds were definitely moving fast ahead of a brisk wind. She thanked them for the warning and hurried along. Before she'd gone ten paces, the first fat drops began to fall. Soon they were hitting the roof of the boardwalk overhang with a roar.

She changed her mind about going to the bank. Cutting

through a gap between buildings, she hurried down the back street toward the house she shared with Becky.

The rain came down harder, flattening her bonnet and soaking her dress. Her legs kept tangling in her wet skirts. Her walking shoes grew heavy with mud. What a mess. She glared up at the dark clouds churning just above the treetops. Storms usually brought change, but the air was just as warm and muggy now as it had been before the rain started.

An earsplitting boom sent her ducking. Before the sound of it left her ears, a huge flash backlit the trees and houses along the back street.

Alarmed at how quickly the wind had risen and how close the lightning strike had come, she quickened her pace. Lifting her skirts high, she tripped and slipped across the muddy street. She could hardly see where she was going.

More thunder. Another gust sent her staggering for balance. Somewhere behind her, glass shattered. Arms up to shield her eyes from the driving rain, Lottie stumbled on.

The wind built. Something nearby crashed to earth. Branches pinwheeled through the air. Pieces of broken siding windmilled past. The sound of rain and debris slamming into the buildings rose to a deafening roar.

Looking back, she saw a funnel cloud snake down from the roiling sky.

Gasping and terrified, she scrambled up the steps onto Becky's front porch. The door was open, whipping back and forth on its hinges. The floor inside was slick with rain and leaves. "Becky!" she screamed.

No answer.

A crash made the house tremble. Figurines shattered. Something heavy fell in the kitchen. Heart pounding in terror, Lottie raced into her bedroom, ducked into her closet, and yanked the door closed.

Outside, with the sound of a dozen locomotives racing at full throttle, the twister bore down on sleepy little Greenbroke.

Shrieking wind pummeled the house. Thunder made the floor tremble beneath her. Something slammed against the outside wall at her back, and part of the ceiling tore away. It felt like the house was being ripped apart around her.

Lottie crouched in the corner, a blanket pulled over her head as rain poured through the gaping hole where the roof had been. The house rocked and shuddered. Then with a thunderous crack, the wall fell in on top of her.

———

As suddenly as it had begun, the roar of the wind faded. Thunder grew distant. Rain no longer poured through the shattered front windows of the Spotted Dog.

Ty stumbled out of his rented room, one hand clasped over his bleeding arm. Hearing voices coming up the stairwell, he hurried to the railing and looked down into the main room below.

It was a mess, reeking of whiskey from dozens of broken bottles. The painting over the bar had fallen and the nearly nude lady was impaled on a broken chair. Shards of glass littered the floor and counter. But other than the two front doors sagging on broken hinges and the shattered front windows, the building seemed intact.

He turned back toward the upstairs hallway. "Anybody hurt up here?"

No answer.

"Holy hell," a man said from his chair downstairs, his face white as parchment, his whiskey glass still clutched in his shaking hand.

Henry peered over the top of the bar, bits of glass stuck in his wooly hair. "What happened?"

"Twister." Shoving a toppled chair aside, another man crawled out from under a table. "Mean bastards. Lost a good hound to one near twenty years ago."

Juno pushed past those who had crowded into the back hallway. "Is everyone okay?" He looked up at Ty's bloody arm. "You hurt?"

"Nothing serious. Piece of glass."

"I'll tend it," Belle offered, tightening the sash on a flimsy wrap.

"Later. Check on the others." Ty started downstairs, picking his way over bits of broken glass on the stair treads. Urgency made him careless and he almost tripped. He caught himself and hurried on, desperate to make sure Lottie had gotten home from the club all right.

Below, Juno barked out orders. "Everyone okay up there?" he called when the two other whores, Sugar and Red, moved to the railing, trailed by two wild-eyed customers struggling to do up their trousers.

Red nodded. "Except for cuts and bruises and having the Christ almighty bejesus scared out of us. Henry, can you get me Juno's medical kit?"

"Where's Becky?" Ty asked Juno when he reached the main floor.

"With the preacher."

"No, she's not." Groaning, Lindz crawled out from beneath an overturned table, blood dripping from a cut on his head. "I left her at her house an hour ago."

Juno rounded on him. "You *left* her? With a storm coming?"

"Was Lottie there?" Ty cut in, dread crawling up his back.

"I don't know. I didn't go inside. Anybody got a rag?"

"Jesus." Whirling, Ty charged through the broken front door, Juno on his heels.

Ty had faced fear many times since he'd joined the rangers, but nothing scared him as much as the thought of Lottie lying crumpled and lifeless under the shattered rubble of Becky's house. He couldn't—wouldn't—imagine the rest of his life without her beside him.

As he ran down the flooded street, he saw evidence of the storm's fury everywhere he looked—downed trees, shingles stuck into the sides of buildings, signs torn from their chains, roofs torn off, posts supporting the boardwalk overhang sheared in two, shattered windows in every storefront.

Yet somehow, most of the buildings still stood. Hopefully, the bewildered townspeople staggering out of them had suffered only minor injuries, but he didn't stop to find out. Until he reached Lottie and knew for certain she was safe, he couldn't even think about helping anyone else.

The rain had slowed to a soft drizzle, but water still raced down the street where Becky's house stood. It looked as if this part of town had taken the brunt of the storm. Uprooted trees lay across the road. A broken branch stuck through the back wall of the Western Union office, and one house had been reduced to a pile of splinters. Surprisingly, the livery beside it showed little damage except for the missing loft door and a coating of straw that covered everything within fifty feet of the barn.

Lungs burning, he raced on. He would quit cussing. Memorize the Bible. Go to Africa and preach to natives. Just let her be all right. *Please, God.* His heart felt like it was trying to kick out of his chest, but he kept going, sinking in mud to his ankles, and splashing through the water still washing through the ruts in the road.

God, let her be all right.

He reached the market—made himself slow when he saw the Bracketts sitting on the back stoop, clutching each other but showing no blood. He veered toward them.

Juno splashed past, legs pumping.

"Lottie with you?" Ty called out.

Mrs. Brackett stared at him, her face blank with fear.

"Becky's!" The old man squinted through the cracked lenses of his spectacles. "You find her, son," he shouted and waved him on. "You get our girl."

Ty ran on, vaulted a downed tree, then let out a shout when he saw Becky's house was still standing.

Juno was already disappearing through the broken front door. Ty raced up the porch steps and almost plowed into him when he found him standing amidst broken knick-knacks in the ruins of the front room, his face slack.

Ty gaped in shock. The kitchen was gone. Where Becky's room should have been was a gaping hole.

"Sweet Jesus," Juno whispered.

Ty shoved past him. "Becky! Lottie! Where are you?"

No answer.

He ducked into the front bedroom Lottie used. The roof was half gone and the wall below it had partially caved in. He looked under the bed and through the debris on the floor then tried the small closet on the damaged wall. The door was jammed. He pounded on it and called her name.

No response. He ran back into the parlor.

"They're here," he told Juno, praying it was true. "Start looking. Check the yard. I'll dig through the kitchen."

When Juno didn't move, Ty gave him a hard shove. "Do it! Now!"

Ty pawed through rubble for a half hour, calling out every few minutes. But other than the drip of water from the broken pump at the sink and the crunch of smashed crockery underfoot, he heard nothing.

Desperation made his hands shake and his head pound. Blood seeping from the cut on his arm dripped down onto his Levi's and left dark splatters in the mud on his boots. In a fury of frustration, he tore off the tattered sleeve and yanked out the shard of glass.

Fire shot down his arm. More blood welled as he quickly wrapped the torn sleeve around the wound, using his teeth to tie it off. He welcomed the pain, needed it to keep his thoughts focused away from the growing terror in his mind.

"Lottie!" he yelled again. "Becky!"

"They're not outside." Juno stumbled through what was left of the kitchen wall. He looked ravaged, his eyes red-rimmed, his clothes smeared with mud and blood from a dozen cuts on his hands. For a moment, he stared hopelessly at the destroyed kitchen, as if his mind couldn't grasp the totality of the destruction.

"Jesus . . . Becky . . . I never told her . . ." Abruptly, he bent over, gasping, hands gripping his knees. "If I've lost her . . ."

"You haven't!" Ty said savagely. "They're safe. Maybe they went to the club."

"They didn't," a voice said.

Whipping around, they saw Briggs standing amid the

shattered figurines in the front parlor. Kearsey and Pete Spivey, the mayor, were with him.

"You're sure?" Juno asked in a strained voice. "They could have—"

"I'm sure. Other than a few broken windows, the club was untouched, and all are accounted for. Now what do you need us to do?"

Juno seemed to sag.

But with the arrival of help, new strength flowed through Ty. "Tear this place apart. Board by board. They've got to be here somewhere."

———

Lottie burst into awareness with a jerk that made her head spin. She blinked at the door in front of her. Either the wind had stopped or she had gone deaf. Then she heard dripping and felt water hitting her head. She tried to move, but broken boards lay in a tangle all around her, trapping her against the small door.

Door where?

The closet in her bedroom.

Squinting against the rain, she lifted her face to the light filtering through a gaping hole where the ceiling used to be. Half the wall beneath it was gone.

Where was Becky? Ty? Was anyone still there?

"Help!" she called, then flinched when pain blasted through her head. She managed to free a hand and felt her head. A bump above her right ear that matched the one Millsap had given her on the other side of her head. No blood, but it was tender to the touch. She felt beaten to a pulp, dizzy and nauseated, but everything seemed to work and she was alive.

She pushed on the closet door. It didn't move. With groans and creaks, the rubble above her shifted, pressing down on her even more than before. How much longer until it crushed her?

She bucked and twisted. But whatever had her pinned

wouldn't budge. A feeling of suffocation grew, building with every frantic heartbeat.

What if they didn't find her? What if there was no one left to look for her? She'd been through a twister. Had seen the damage it could do. What if all of Greenbroke had been blown away?

God . . . please. Let Ty be safe.

"Help!" she cried. "I'm here!"

Her only answer was the steady drip of water through the broken boards above her head. A sense of hopelessness numbed her mind. Closing her eyes, she gave in to it, unable to bear the horror of her own thoughts.

After a while—hours, minutes—she heard sounds beyond the broken outside wall. "Help!" she called and banged her free hand on the wall.

The voices came closer.

She knocked harder. "Help! I'm in here!"

"Over here!" someone on the other side of the wall yelled. Crashes. Thuds. The sound of boards being tossed aside.

Then Ty's voice, close by. "Lottie, where are you?"

"In the closet in my bedroom. I can't get the door open."

"Are you hurt?"

"I don't think so. But I'm pinned against the door and the boards on top of me keep moving."

Other voices. She thought she recognized those of Briggs and Juno, then footsteps moving away.

"We're going to try to reach you from outside. Is Becky with you?"

"I never saw her. Isn't she with Juno?"

She ducked as something pounded on the outside wall so hard bits of roofing rained down on her head.

"Cover your head if you can," Briggs called from outside. "We'll have to brace the wall before we can enlarge the hole."

A few minutes later, after a lot of banging and cursing, the wall fell away. Ty's face appeared in the opening. "Keep your head covered."

She heard him yanking at the boards trapping her, then

suddenly the weight lifted and he was reaching inside to drag her free.

"Thank God thank God." He pulled her so tight against his chest she felt the thud of his heart.

She clung to him, afraid to let go.

He carried her away from the debris, set her on her feet, and stood back, eyes scanning her face. "You're all right?"

She couldn't speak. Couldn't stop shaking. Then she looked at her hand, saw blood, and panicked when she saw the red-soaked rag tied around his arm. "You're bleeding!"

"Shh. It's nothing. A scratch. How about you?"

"It looks like more than a scratch."

"I'll have Doc tend it. Are you hurt?"

"Scared. A few bruises. Another bump on my head, but nothing bad."

Juno's face appeared at Ty's shoulder. "Where's Becky?"

She stiffened. "You haven't found her yet?"

"We just started looking," Ty said.

But Juno's face told a different story.

Behind him stood Briggs and Kearsey and the mayor, their eyes haggard in their mud- and dirt-smeared faces. But it was the stricken look in Juno's dark eyes that sent terror through Lottie.

"Where could she be?" he asked in a strained voice. "Lindz said he left her here. Could she have gone to the market?"

"I don't think so. I didn't see her. Have you checked her room?" Pushing out of Ty's arms, Lottie stepped toward the house, then froze when she saw the full extent of the damage to the back of the house. The walls were gone. Part of the roof was gone. What was left of Becky's bedroom was a tangle of broken furniture and shattered wood. Panic gripped her throat. "I—I came in just as the storm hit. I called to her, but she didn't answer. Where could she be?"

"We'll find her," Ty said.

Juno looked ready to collapse.

Lottie turned to Briggs. "Jane?"

"Unharmed. The club is fine. She and Findlay are

clearing the lobby and dining room to shelter those who've been displaced." With a gruff order, he sent Kearsey and Spivey back to search the rubble strewn about the backyard.

"But what if she's not here?" Lottie cried. "What if she's somewhere else and you're wasting time looking in the wrong place?"

"Then we'll keep looking until we find out where she is," Ty said. "I promise."

Two hours later, dusk drifted over the littered streets of Greenbroke.

And still, the rain fell. And still, no Becky.

Desperate to keep her mind occupied, Lottie and several other women set up a soup table on the boardwalk outside the Spotted Dog, dispensing beans, stew, and bread to any-one who needed food. The sheriff and Doc Helms went from building to building throughout the town, searching for survivors, while others dug through the rubble. Ty finished helping Mr. B. board up the broken windows at the market, and now stood with a group of tired, dirty men outside the saloon, discussing where they should look next.

Overall, the damage to the town wasn't as bad as it could have been. One house destroyed, several needing extensive repairs. Most of the buildings on Main Street would require new doors and windows, as well as work on their roofs and a new boardwalk. But the structures along the railroad tracks had been relatively untouched, including the water tower, the Social Club, and the Greenbroke Hotel. Fortu-nately, there were few injuries—other than cuts and bruises and one broken leg. Those needing shelter or minor medical attention were sent to the barn where the Greater Glory to God Assembly dispensed soup, bandages, blankets, spare clothing, and enthusiastic spiritual guidance. Neighbors helping neighbors. It was good to see.

By late afternoon, everyone had been accounted for.

Except Becky.

Lottie watched Juno struggle to stay hopeful, but every time he came back to the saloon after a fruitless search, it was apparent he was starting to weaken. Thinking if he ate something, it might revive his spirits, she carried a bowl of stew over to where he sat on the edge of the boardwalk, looking as dejected as Briggs had looked after Lottie had left his office earlier that day.

Sitting down beside him, she held out the bowl. "Eat something."

He looked over and shook his head. "Not hungry."

"Try. You'll be no help to her if you drop from exhaustion."

With little enthusiasm, he took the bowl. But after a few small bites, he set it aside. "You were right, you know."

"About what?"

"I do love her. And have, for a long time. Damnation, I'm such a fool!"

Not caring who saw, Lottie put her arm around his slumped shoulders. "We'll discuss how foolish you are after we find her. For now, eat."

"What if we don't find her?"

"We will." With her free hand, she picked up the bowl of stew and held it toward him. "Eat. Please."

He ate.

Out in the street, several children picked through the wreckage for treasure, seeing the storm as a grand adventure. A little girl squatted down, her skirts dragging in the mud, and peered beneath the collapsed boardwalk. Behind them, Briggs droned on, outlining a strategy for searching the surrounding area. Earlier, he'd sent Ty and other riders to outlying ranches and farms to see if anyone needed help. Now he was dividing the town into grids for a second search, although they'd already checked through each building and under every pile of rubble with no luck. It was as if Becky had been plucked from the face of the earth.

"She thinks I still mourn my wife," Juno said, setting the half-empty bowl aside. "That's why I won't make a move on her. But it's not that." Turning his head, he let her see the tears welling in his eyes. "I failed them, Lottie. I caused their deaths. Now I might lose Becky, too, and I never told her how much she means to me."

Lottie felt like her chest was collapsing under the weight

of grief and fear. Grief for Jane and Briggs and Juno. Fear for Becky.

"Stop that talk," she ordered. "You act like you've lost her, and you haven't. She needs our prayers not our tears."

"You're right." He stared down at the muddy street beneath his feet, his shoulders rising and falling on a deep breath. "You're right."

A dog limped by. Across the street, the little girl was on her hands and knees, trying to reach through the broken boards where the boardwalk had partially caved in. Sitting back, she called to the other children and pointed, but they paid no attention. She peered under the boardwalk again and appeared to be talking. Trying to coax out a lost pet? Or . . .

Becky!

Lottie bolted to her feet. "She's here, Juno!" Calling for help, she charged across the street, shoes sinking in mud past her ankles.

Juno splashed past her, yelling Becky's name.

The little girl jumped up, eyes round with alarm when he dropped down beside her. "Is someone under there?"

"The lady—"

"Becky! Can you hear me?"

"Juno . . ." The voice was faint, but unmistakably hers.

"Hold on! I'll get you out!" He frantically pulled off tumbled boards. Others ran to help and soon the debris was cleared enough that they could see her beneath the broken boards of the boardwalk.

She was lying on her stomach, covered with mud, pinned beneath one of the joists. Her eyes were closed. Air rasped through her throat as she struggled to breathe.

But she was alive.

Chapter 25

While Lottie ran to tell the Bracketts and Jane and anyone else she saw that Becky had been found, the men
carefully carried her to the small clinic on the first floor of
Dr. Helms's house. Lottie knew she'd only be in the way
while the doctor did what he needed to do, but she couldn't
stay away long. Minutes later, mud-spattered and gasping
for air, she ran back down to his house at the edge of town.

He must have seen her coming—as soon as she charged
up the porch steps, he opened the door. "She's sleeping.
Bruised and a sprained wrist and worn out, but she's fine.
Let her rest."

"I have to see her!" Dashing toward the sick room in
back, she burst through the door to find Juno sitting in a
chair beside the bed, holding Becky's hand.

He looked up in surprise, his eyes suspiciously bright in
his weary face. When he saw who it was, he gave a shaky
smile, and whispered, "She's all right."

Needing to see for herself, Lottie moved to the other side
of the bed.

The poor thing looked like she'd been in a saloon brawl.
Someone had tried to brush the dirt out of her beautiful hair,

but there were still clumps stuck here and there. Her face was mostly clean, but bruises were already showing. Her muddy clothes lay piled in the corner, and she wore a clean, oversized nightshirt. Gauze strips bound her left wrist, and a half-finished bowl of soup sat on the table beside the bed.

"Thank God we found her," Lottie whispered.

"Who would have thought to look under the boardwalk? Crazy woman."

"How did she get under there?"

"She said she was trying to get to me, and ducked under it when the storm hit." The wobble in his voice told her he was still trying to get past that.

"She's safe now, Juno. So don't be blaming yourself."

"If I'd taken care of her right . . ." He let the sentence hang.

"Then take care of her now."

"I plan to."

"'Bout time," a hoarse voice said.

They both looked down to see Becky was awake. And smiling. Until she saw Juno's distress. "What's wrong? Are you all right?"

"No," he admitted, blinking hard. "You scared the hell out of me. Don't ever do that again."

They stared at each other for a moment, then Juno let go a long, deep breath. "We need to talk, Beck. You've got a lot to forgive me for. And I hope you will."

Taking that as her cue to leave, Lottie gave Becky's un-injured arm a squeeze, patted Juno's broad shoulder, and went back to the club to see if Ty had returned.

As she walked down the street, she noted that already the town looked better. Much of the mess was being loaded onto wagons and carted away to a huge burn pile outside of town. Mr. Griffin had taped a sign to the bank door saying the governor had sent a wire to Mayor Spivey, offering help and no-interest loans to those needing to make repairs. It gave hope for a better future and had people smiling, despite the hard work ahead.

Greenbroke would survive.

But the club might not, she thought, when she walked into the lobby to find Briggs and Lord Findlay glaring at each other while Jane tried to maintain a semblance of civility. Luckily, the crowd seeking shelter had thinned out now that the danger was past. Only Bea Davenport, who was cleaning up behind the stragglers, was there to see that Jane was on the verge of tears.

Before Lottie could whisk her away to get some rest, Sheriff Dodson came in, asking for help to control the Bar M cowboys who were hunting cattle that had bolted during the twister.

"They're causing trouble?" Briggs asked.

"No looting or mischief like that," the sheriff assured him. "But with whiskey in short supply at the Spotted Dog and the whores taking the day off—begging your pardons, ma'ams—they're acting a bit surly."

"I'll see about that," the ex-soldier said, that steely look in his gray eyes.

After Briggs left, Findlay cocked a brow at Lottie, probably hoping she would leave, too, but she stayed put. Before long, he gave up and wandered out to watch Kearsey put boards over the broken front windows.

"I think things are in hand here," Lottie said, slipping an arm around Jane's waist. "Why don't we escape while we can? I'd dearly love to put my feet up for a while."

"I could use a rest, too," Jane admitted. She asked Bea to bring in a tea tray when she had a chance, then she and Lottie headed back to her office.

"What a horrid day." With a labored sigh, Jane sank into one of the upholstered chairs by the fireplace, while Lottie took the other. "First that ghastly storm, then Briggs and Findlay squaring off every chance they got. I daresay those two will drive me to drink."

"Is this what the English call 'dissembling'?" Lottie gently asked.

Jane looked at her through weary red eyes.

"Briggs told me about his wife," Lottie said.

"Oh." The starch seemed to go out of her. "A terrible thing. I'm so sad for him."

"What about you?"

Jane shrugged one shoulder, as if too exhausted to lift both. "I'm sad for me, too."

Bea stepped in with a tea tray. As she set it up on a footstool in front of Jane's chair, Lottie asked how her family had fared through the storm.

"We lost a plum tree, two cows ran off, and the chickens probably won't lay for a month, but we're fine, thanks for asking."

"A resilient lot, you Americans. No wonder we lost the war."

"What war?"

"I think that's all for now, Bea," Lottie broke in. "But if you see Ty Benton, please let me know." After assuring her she would, Bea left.

Since Jane looked so weary, Lottie served the tea and butter cookies. As she settled back in her chair, she studied her friend. The pretty Englishwoman looked so fragile Lottie was afraid a wrong word might shatter the brittle shell of her reserve. But she couldn't avoid the subject that was on both their minds. "Is there anything I can do, Jane?"

"About what?"

"This terrible mess you and Briggs are in."

Jane didn't pretend ignorance. "I'm afraid there's nothing to be done." Her cup rattled against the saucer as she set it on the table between the chairs. "Obtaining a divorce is very difficult in England, even if Anson's faith would allow it. He feels it would be dishonorable to turn his back on her, especially since he believes her condition is partly his fault."

"Why? Because of the baby she lost?"

Jane nodded. "Anson didn't know she was carrying a child until she lost it. Yet she blames him for the miscarriage. Did he tell you why?"

"No."

Tipping her head against the high back of the chair, the

Englishwoman gave a weary smile. "Poor Anson is so ready to accept the failings of others, yet ever reluctant to see himself in a good light. The vicar was a great believer in the use of guilt to control his high-spirited son. When Anson's wife saw how effective it was, she used that weapon against him, too."

And, apparently, was still using it. "What happened?"

Jane picked up her cup and took a sip. This time when she set it down, it didn't rattle on the saucer and her voice was strengthened by anger. "Their marriage was troubled from the start. She was either clinging to him, or shoving him away, or inventing elaborate schemes to gain his attention. He grew weary of it and decided to put some distance between them by signing on with the British Light Infantry. It sent her into a rage and they had a terrible row. When he started to walk away, she became almost frantic to make him stay, begging him to prove he still cared for her by making love to her. Against his better judgment, he did, hoping it would ease her worry. She lost the baby the next day."

Horrified, Lottie pressed a hand to her mouth.

"The doctor said these things happen, especially in early pregnancy. He assured Anson it wasn't his fault. His wife was convinced it was. She followed him to his father's church one evening and set it on fire to punish him. He had already left. His father and two others were not so fortunate. She's been in an asylum since."

Lottie shook her head. First Juno and now Briggs. What was it about crazy women and fire?

Jane looked at her through haunted eyes. "You know how he is, Lottie. Honor and duty are all to him. Because of a battlefield promise, Anson brought my wounded brother across two continents so he could die at home. Do you think a man like that would cast aside his marriage vows because of an unstable wife?" Jane shook her head. "It's not in his character. So as long as she lives, there is no hope for us."

Lottie couldn't bear the thought of them being apart for the rest of their lives. They were so perfect for each other. "What are you going to do?"

"I haven't decided." Then, characteristically changing

subject when things became too emotional, Jane put on a determined smile. "But enough of my woes. Let's get you settled, shall we? You won't be able to stay at Becky's until repairs are completed, so I've already set aside our best room for you . . . as our guest."

Lottie was touched. She thought she'd have to move back into her old room at the market, even though since she'd left, the Bracketts had begun using it for storage again. Staying at Lady Jane's Social Club would be the height of luxury compared to a crowded, mouse-infested storeroom. "I can pay," she insisted, hoping it wouldn't be too much. Between her arrest and trial and now the storm, she hadn't done much bookkeeping lately.

Jane dismissed the idea. "I wouldn't hear of it. You're family. Have you any clothes? We could alter some of my dresses, although you're quite a bit taller."

Lottie assured her she would find something at the Led-better house since her room was barely damaged. She mentally reminded herself to look for clothes for Becky, too. "I was heading over there now to see what I can find." And hoping to cross paths with Ty. Surely he would be back soon.

"Then I shan't keep you. I may retire early, so if I'm not about when you return, Kearsey will show you to your room."

Thanking her again, Lottie left. When she walked into Becky's bedroom a few minutes later, she found Juno digging through the wreckage. Luckily, he'd thought to bring a lamp. It was already getting dark.

"How is she?" she asked him.

"Feeling well enough to worry about how she looks. I'm supposed to find her brush and mirror and a change of clothes in all this mess."

"Have you checked the wardrobe?"

He looked around. "There's a wardrobe in here?"

"Men. Bring the lamp." She picked her way to a tall piece of furniture that had fallen on its side. Prying open the shattered door, she found several dresses inside—soaked, but not ruined—and one wet pair of shoes. The bureau that had held Becky's unmentionables was smashed, as well, and shifts and underthings were scattered through rubble. Lottie gathered what was usable and added them to the pile of dresses. "When I take these by Doc's, I'll wash her hair."

"I already did."

Lottie glanced at him, thoughts of Ty washing her hair in the creek making her cheeks hot. How quickly they had both fallen.

"Don't look so appalled. I didn't do anything improper."

She laughed and raised her brows. "Why not?"

"She's hurt, that's why."

Was he blushing? It was hard to tell in the dim light.

"I told her everything," he said. "Yet it didn't seem to matter to her."

What *everything*? Lottie waited, but he didn't elaborate. "That's our Becky. When she loves, she loves with her whole heart."

His lopsided grin made him look years younger. "Thank God for that."

Taking the lamp, Lottie carried it to her room. She located her valise. After filling it with what clothing of hers she could find, she added the items salvaged from Becky's room, snapped it closed, and carried it back into Becky's room where Juno was still digging through the mess in the dark. She studied him from the doorway. "Jane has given me a room at the club. After Doc lets her go, Becky can stay with me until we decide where to stay."

Juno picked up a wet chemise, studied it for a moment, then slipped it into his pocket. "She's staying with me."

"At the Spotted Dog? Would that be proper?"

He straightened to look at her. In the lamplight, his face was all angles and shadows, his mouth set in a tight line. "Becky stays with me," he repeated with quiet emphasis.

Lottie set down the valise and crossed her arms. "Do you intend to marry her, Juno?"

He seemed to find that amusing. "Yes, Ma. As soon as the circuit judge comes through town."

"But what about our double wedding?"

With a snort, he went back to digging.

Taking that as a sign that he was done with that subject, she picked up the valise. "I'll discuss it with Becky."

"Discuss all you want," he said. "But she's staying with me. And leave the lamp."

It was full dark when she reached Doc's office. This time, he wasn't there to open the door, so she marched back to the room where Becky was and dropped the valise on the floor beside the bed. "I want us to have a double wedding."

Becky grinned. "You're upset. That must mean you've been talking to Juno. Can you believe he finally asked me to marry him? And all it took was almost being sucked up in a tornado, getting a sprained wrist, and spending a fun afternoon in the mud under a smashed boardwalk. Who would have guessed he'd be so agreeable?"

"Agreeable as a rented mule." Sinking down onto the foot of the bed, Lottie opened the valise and began separating Becky's things from hers. "Wouldn't you like a double wedding? Everybody there, dancing, merriment, and all the rest?"

"Sounds nice, but I'll leave that to you and Ty." Picking up a muddy, low-cut dress, Becky studied it for a moment, tossed it aside, then reached for another. "I need new clothes. Something more matronly, I think."

"But it would be such fun." Lottie knew she was fighting a losing battle but she hated giving up. "And it wouldn't cost that much if we shared expenses."

"I don't want to wait. By the time all the repairs are finished and the plans are made, I'm liable to be pregnant." She laughed at Lottie's look of shock, but sobered when Lottie didn't laugh with her. "I've already waited too long. And now that I finally have Juno corralled, I'm not letting him get away. The man's as skittish as a blind foal. With reason, it seems."

"What reason?"

"Probably a good thing his wife is dead, or I'd punch her in the face for what she did to him. Did you find any shoes?"

Lottie almost threw them at her. First, Jane's revelations

about Briggs's wretched marriage, and now Becky hinting that Juno's wife had done something equally terrible to Juno. What was wrong with these people? "What did she do?"

"She blamed Juno for everything—even his son dying. Said he never should have left them alone. And she was the one who set the fire! Can you credit that?"

Lottie knew Juno had been out of town setting up his freight business when their house burned, leaving his wife and son sheltering in a drafty barn. What she didn't know was that his wife had deliberately set the fire. "Why would she do such a thing?"

"She was loco, that's why. Juno didn't know how loco until she shot him."

"Shot him!"

"In the shoulder. Oh, Lottie, you should see the scar. He would have died if the doctor hadn't been there. And his poor little boy lying cold on his bed." Lifting a corner of the sheet, Becky dabbed at her brimming eyes. "Just talking about it made Juno half-sick. Me, too. But no matter what his wife said," she added fiercely, "Juno didn't harm that boy!"

"What *exactly* did she say?"

"That his neglect had killed the only thing she'd ever loved and now he'd killed her, too. Then she put the pistol she'd just used on Juno to her temple and pulled the trigger."

"Oh my Lord!"

"Right there in front of Juno and their dead son. So you see why I don't want to wait on a double wedding . . . or to wait getting him into my bed. Oh, don't give me that look, Lottie Weyland. I finally got a rope on him and we're getting married as soon as possible so I can get pregnant—God willing—and start building better memories. That's understandable, isn't it?"

It was. Lottie wanted to start her life with Ty as soon as possible, too. If the storm had taught her anything, it was how quickly everything could be snatched away. She'd already spent too much time plotting a future that might never come. She wouldn't put off living and loving any longer. As soon as she saw Ty, she'd tell him she didn't care where they lived, or what they did . . . other than spending what years they had left with each other.

"You're right." Rising, she bent and kissed Becky's forehead. "I'm so glad you're safe and that you and Juno have worked it out. I know you'll be deliriously happy together. All I ask is that you don't marry without me there to blubber into my hanky and wish you well."

"I would never."

"Good. Now I've got to find Ty and tell him I don't want to wait on a big wedding, either."

By the time she reached the club, it was so late much of the town had settled for the night.

And still no Ty.

With dragging steps, she followed Kearsey up to her room. She felt drained and exhausted, every muscle aching and stiff. At least the headache that had plagued her since she'd been knocked on the head was starting to fade. First Millsap and now a falling ceiling. She should start wearing a helmet.

Kearsey must have seen her weariness. He slowed to show her the luxurious room Jane had assigned to her, then led her straight to the washroom next to the water closet at the end of the hall.

Setting her valise beside the tub, he turned with a smile. "Take all the time you need, Miss Weyland. Most of the other occupants on this floor have turned in for the night, or are downstairs at the gaming tables and won't be up for a while. However, the kitchen is still open. Shall I have one of the maids bring a late dinner tray to your room, in say . . . an hour?"

"That would be wonderful."

"Be sure to send back with her any clothing you want washed overnight. And when you're finished with the tray, just set it outside your door."

"Thank you for taking such good care of me, Mr. Kearsey."

"It's my pleasure."

He turned on the water and showed her how to adjust the

temperature, then set a cake of French milled soap and a towel as thick as a sheep's pelt on a stool beside the oversized copper tub. "Will there be anything else, Miss Weyland?"

"Have you seen Mr. Benton this afternoon?"

"Not since Mr. Briggs sent him to check on others in the area."

"If you do, tell him not to leave until I speak to him."

"Of course."

After locking the door behind him, Lottie pulled her least muddy dress from the valise—in case Ty came by later—then quickly undressed and sank into the tub. It felt heavenly. Muscles relaxed. Soreness faded. The last of her headache drifted away on the scented steam wafting around her. After washing, she soaked until the water cooled, then reluctantly climbed out. She could get used to living rich. She might even have a talent for it.

When she left the washroom a few minutes later, she saw a woman in the hallway, her hand on the latch of a closed door. Just standing there, looking at the door. She wore a satin brocade robe and long dark hair hung in loose waves down her back. She looked ghostly. And undecided. At the sound of the washroom door closing, she turned with a start. In the dim light from the wall lamps, her eyes looked like huge blue marbles in the pale oval of her face.

"Jane?" Curious why the Englishwoman would be so far from her first floor bedroom at this late hour, and in such a state of undress, Lottie walked toward her. "What are you doing up here? Is something wrong?"

As she drew closer, she saw an odd look on Jane's face and the way her gaze darted almost guiltily to the closed door. And suddenly Lottie knew. "That's Briggs's room, isn't it?"

Jane hiked her chin and faced Lottie with grim resolve. "Yes, it's Anson's room. I know how it looks and what you must think of me, but I love him, Lottie. I always will. And after I leave for England it might be decades before I see him again. If ever. I hope you can understand. And forgive me."

"Of course I understand. And there's nothing to forgive." Lottie closed the distance between them. "So you've made your decision? You're going back?"

"In a few weeks. Once I settle my affairs here."

"Without Briggs?"

Lifting a trembling hand, Jane brushed away a tear. "I have no choice, Lottie. I can't stay and see him every day and know we'll never be able to have a life together. It would destroy me."

"You could do what you're doing now. No one need know."

Her smile was sad. "Anson would know. He can't tolerate deception. It would eat away at him until there was nothing left but resentment and the need to escape. Like with his wife. I couldn't bear that." Her eyes glittered in the lamplight. Her face was a mask of pain. "So I shall take what I can get. And use what little time we have left to store up memories to last a lifetime. Is that so wrong?"

"Loving someone is never wrong." Setting down her valise, Lottie pulled Jane into a tight hug. "I understand and I don't judge you. I would never judge you, Jane. Or Briggs. I love you both." When she released her and stepped back, they were both crying. "Do what you will, dear friend. With my blessing."

Blinking hard, Lottie picked up her valise and walked on to her room, her heart as heavy as a stone in her chest.

As she stepped inside, she heard an odd noise, and turned to see Ty slouched in one of the two chairs flanking an ornate table by the window. His head was tipped back, mouth slightly open, big hands clasped over his belt buckle and his long legs outstretched and crossed at the ankles. Snoring.

Leaving her valise next to the saddlebags he'd dropped at the foot of the bed, she moved quietly across the room.

He looked exhausted. And dirty. And the makeshift bandage around his arm showed traces of fresh blood. She wondered if he'd eaten. If he'd been waiting long. If he would wake up if she crawled into his lap and put her arms around him to reassure herself that he was alive and well and the terror that had gripped them this awful day was finally over.

Before she could find out, a knock sent her hurrying back to the door.

She opened it to find a uniformed maid holding an overloaded tray covered with a white napkin. "Your dinner, ma'am. With an extra plate. Shall I put it on the table by the window?"

"I can take it." Not wanting to flaunt the impropriety of having a man in her room at this hour, Lottie angled the tray through the half-opened door. "Are there extra towels in the wash room?"

"Yes, ma'am. Mr. Kearsey sent some up, thinking Mr. Benton might be needing them for his bath."

So much for propriety. "Thank you. When I'm finished, I'll leave the tray and items for the laundry in the hall."

"Very well, ma'am."

Lottie kicked the door closed and turned to find Ty blinking sleepily and scratching his dark, tousled hair. "Lottie." Spotting the tray, he sat up straighter. "Is that food?"

"It is. And by the weight of it, Kearsey sent enough for a small army."

"I told him I was hungry." Rising, he took the tray from her hands and set it on the table by the window. "Smells good."

She made a face. "Regrettably, you don't."

"That bad?"

"Kearsey left clean towels for you in the wash room."

"The food will get cold."

"Not if you bathe fast. And since when do you care anyway? When you're hungry you'll eat anything, cold or not. I've seen you."

With a labored sigh, he picked up his saddlebags. "I better not come back and find all the food gone."

Lottie laughed. Imitating a flirtatious move she'd seen Becky do a dozen times, she flipped a curl off her shoulder. It probably would have worked better if her eyes hadn't been puffy from crying and her hair had been dry. And curly.

Feeling brave, she smiled coyly. "Oh, I daresay there'll be something here for you to nibble on."

He blinked at her, those astounding blue eyes warming her from across the room. Then he dropped the saddlebags, crossed the room in two long strides, took her face in his hands, and kissed her.

And, oh . . . what a kiss. Soft and gentle, at first. Then firm and demanding. Then slow and sweet, his tongue dancing along hers, his hands moving up into her damp hair, then stroking down over her shoulders to her breasts.

Her knees actually wobbled. Her head swam. Her heart beat so fast she thought she might faint.

"You're not wearing a corset," he whispered against her lips.

"I don't own a corset."

"I'll buy you one."

"Why?"

"So I can unlace it. With my teeth. For starters." Taking his hands away, he shot her a wicked grin full of promise, picked up the saddlebags again, and slipped out the door.

Lottie struggled to calm her breathing. She hadn't been kissed often—well, hardly ever. But she was certain Tyree Benton was the best kisser who ever lived.

Chapter 26

———

Fifteen minutes later, Ty returned—smooth-shaven, wet-haired, and wearing clean clothes except for a red spot spreading on his sleeve. Moving to the tray on the table, he pulled off the napkin and grinned when he saw a plate piled high with roasted beef, potato wedges, steamed carrots, and green beans with bacon. "Man food," he said, approvingly. "God bless Kearsey."

"Your arm is bleeding."

"It's just a scratch." Pulling out one of the chairs, he motioned for her to sit.

"A scratch that's still bleeding. Did you have Doc Helms look at it?"

"Tomorrow. I promise. Have a seat."

"You could be dead of blood loss by tomorrow. Let me look at it."

"Can't we eat first?"

Was that a whine in his voice? "At least let me bandage it. Eating dinner with a man who's bleeding isn't that appetizing."

He had to remove his shirt, which awakened all those

breathless feelings she'd battled the first time she'd seen his bare naked chest. The man was a work of art.

She felt him studying her as she ripped off a ruffle from one of her clean petticoats, made a bandage, and tied it around his thick bicep. After reluctantly helping him don his shirt again, she took the seat across from him.

"You've been crying," he said.

She gave a shaky smile. "A little."

"Why? Is everything all right?"

She didn't want to talk about the heartache Jane and Briggs faced. Or dwell on the terrifying events of the day. Or talk about the uncertain future. They were alive and safe and all she wanted to do was rest in his arms and listen to the sure, steady beat of his heart. "Everything is fine now that you're here." Seeing he wasn't convinced, she reached across the table and put her hand over his. "And I'm so happy and grateful I'll be spending the rest of my life with the man I love."

"I hope you're talking about me."

She pinched his hand, then sat back. "Eat. You look hungry."

The blue in eyes seemed to darken. "I am. But I'll start with supper." He set the extra plate in front of her. "Take what you want. I'll finish the rest."

After serving herself, she pushed the still-overflowing plate back across the table.

He dug in. Silence, except for the clink of their forks against china. She enjoyed watching him. He ate like a man who hadn't been fed in a week, as passionate about food as he was about her. Not that she was complaining. Doubtless it took an abnormal amount of food to fuel such a big frame, especially for an active man barely into his twenties. And she certainly wanted him hale and hearty. She only hoped he wouldn't be too upset when he learned she was a poor cook.

He cleared half of his plate before he spoke. "How's the bump on your head?"

"Which one?"

He looked up, regret in his eyes.

"Better," she said, sorry she had reminded him of Mill-sap. "Both of them. How's yours?" The bandage Doc Tillips had put on his temple was gone, but with that wave of hair covering his brow, she couldn't tell if the cut had closed. Since there was no blood, she guessed it had.

"I'm fine." He continued eating.

She loved his neck. Especially when he swallowed. All those muscles and tendons and that bobbing Adam's apple—

"Becky's doing okay?"

She took a deep breath and let it go. "Bruised but happy. She and Juno are getting married. Must be something in the water."

"Worked for us." His smile told her he was thinking about the creek at her grandfather's place. She was, too. Struggling to control her errant thoughts, she stared down at the long thick carrots on her plate, but that only sent her naughty mind to places it shouldn't go. "Briggs said he sent you to check on the Bucks. Are they all right? You were gone a long time."

"The storm missed them. Nice folks."

"They are." She waited, hoping he would say more.

He didn't.

She picked through her green beans for bacon, then gave up and set down her fork. "How'd you like their place?"

"You're right. It has a lot of potential." He pointed to an untouched slice of roast beef on her plate. "You going to eat that?"

"Take it."

He did, devoured it in four bites, then started on her green beans.

They'd have to plant a garden, she decided. A really big one. "More potential than your uncle's place?"

"I hope so."

"Why do you say that?"

"Because I sold my uncle's place. Can I have your roll?"

She bounced it off his chin. "You sold it? Why?" She had hoped to hang on to it as a hedge against future oil exploration in the panhandle area.

"To make a down payment on the Buck place. Although

I guess we should start calling it the Benton place from now on."

Lottie stared at him. Did that mean what she thought it did? "You want to buy the Buck place?"

"Already did. Griffin's holding the papers at the bank for us to sign. Happy birthday and Merry Christmas for the rest of your life, by the way."

"Truly? You bought it? It's really ours?"

"It is."

She would have jumped across the table, but she doubted her legs would hold her. "Oh, Ty. I love you so much."

"I love you, too. Now stop crying. I'm trying to eat."

As she wiped her face, it occurred to her that he'd made this momentous decision without consulting her. And he'd done it without using any of her money. She wasn't sure how she felt about that. But she wouldn't give up on the idea of a full partnership. "What about the improvements and repairs?"

"I'll get to them in good time."

"What if I sold Grandpa's ranch?"

"Then I'd get to them sooner."

"You'd let me pay for them?"

"You're the one who wants them." Apparently unable to withstand her onslaught of questions, he set down his fork, propped his elbows on the table, and clasped his hands above his plate. "I don't care where we live, honey, as long as we're together. And since it's clear you won't be happy anywhere but in Greenbroke, I signed the papers on my uncle's land while we were in San Angela and I sent the money to Griffin to make a down payment on the Buck ranch." He gave that lopsided smile she loved. "I may not be as book smart as you, Lottie, but I know what I'm doing. And the most important thing I can do is make sure you're happy. So yes, I bought the Buck place. And yes, you can pay for the improvements if you want. Are you happy now?"

Deliriously. "You did all that for me?"

"For you and the pecans. They're really tasty." He picked up his fork again. "Now can I finish my supper?"

But her mind was already racing away. "We'll do the water closet first. Or maybe the windmill. The porch."

He watched her as he chewed, an odd smile twitching at the corners of his mouth. "Making a list, are you?"

"If that's okay with you."

"And if it isn't?"

"I'll find a way to convince you."

He forked up a bite of carrot. "Shouldn't be hard. Wear the yellow dress. It worked before."

Joy swelled in her chest until she thought she would burst with it. How had she snagged a man like Tyree Benton? What had she done to be so blessed?

"Becky and Juno are getting married."

"You already said that. When?"

"Soon." And why not? Life waited for no one. Not for Jane and Briggs. Not for her and Ty. They all could have died today, but they didn't. It was like the storm was giving them a second chance.

An idea took shape. She weighed it, studying it from every angle, filling that balance sheet in her mind with all the pros and cons it presented.

If they truly loved each other, why wait?

"Do you love me, Ty?" she blurted out. "Truly love me?"

"I'm letting you marry me, aren't I?"

"I'm serious."

He studied her over a green bean hanging from his fork. "Of course I do. Why do you even ask?"

"Because I've changed my mind."

He lowered his fork and sat back. "About what?"

"Getting married."

A look of alarm came over his face.

"I don't want a fancy wedding," she rushed on before he could interrupt. "I don't want to wait, either. I want us to get married as soon as we can."

"What about all those decisions you said we had to make?"

"We can figure them out as we go along." She tried to

explain. "I'm tired of planning and worrying and fretting about a future that might change when the next storm blows through. I want to be more spontaneous. Less structured. Less fearful."

"Fearful? You?"

"I say we get married and start living. Soon. Tonight."

"We can't get married tonight."

"But we can start living."

He studied her in silence. She could almost see the thoughts bouncing through his head and knew the moment of realization. "I don't have any preventatives."

"Any what?"

"You could get pregnant."

She clasped her hands. "Oh, I hope so." Pictures flashed through her mind. A rangy little boy with big feet and eyes the color of turquoise gemstones and hair as dark as boot-black. A daughter, lining up her dolls for their lessons. Maybe a hound dog. And a barn cat. And Ty . . . always and forever. She barely refrained from leaping across the table and throwing her arms around him.

"Okay." Picking up his fork, he resumed eating.

Okay? That was it? His only response to her momentous decision? Not decision, she reminded herself. Suggestion. She didn't want him to think she was running roughshod over him again.

He must have read her thoughts. Grinning through bulging cheeks, he finished chewing, swallowed, then said, "Food builds stamina. I think we should go for four this time."

With those words, she did jump into his lap, and proceeded to stuff carrots into his mouth as fast as she could. Between laughter, threats, and his attempts to dodge her, they soon had food smeared on their faces, in their hair, and over their clean clothes.

"We'll need another bath," he said, once he stopped laughing long enough to speak.

Her breath caught. "Together?"

"That copper tub is pretty roomy."

She licked a gob of carrot from his eyebrow. "You being

the big, strong man you are, I doubt it would be roomy enough for both of us."

"We'll manage."

"Someone might see us."

"Not if we close the door. I thought you wanted to be spontaneous."

"I do, but not spontaneously scandalous."

"Your decision."

Was that a dare? Lottie looked deep into those flame-bright eyes and saw a mischievous boy. And a kind, honorable man. And a love as strong as her own. Why should she fret about anything with this man beside her? The only thing that would ever hold them back was time. And she didn't want to waste a minute of it.

"Let me go first." Fishing a green bean out of her meager cleavage, she climbed off his lap. "Then you can follow."

He pushed back the chair and rose. "How about I go first, then you follow? As it should be between a man and his wife."

She narrowed her eyes. "Is that so?"

"Or we could race."

"And wake up the entire hotel?"

Devilment danced in his eyes. "Then let's compromise. I'll be first in the tub, and you can be first the rest of the night." He waggled his brows. "How's that sound?"

Images rushed into her head. Heat flooded her body. It sounded like the kind of compromise she could support. Repeatedly. Maybe even in the tub.

Laughing, she opened the door. "After you, Mr. Benton."

Epilogue

———•———

L ottie got her double wedding. But instead of standing
with Ty beside Becky and Juno in a church or before the
circuit judge, the four of them said their vows one July morning under the pecan trees by the creek at the newly purchased Benton place.

A barrel from the market, which Mrs. B. dressed up with
flowers and a lacy shawl, made a beautiful altar. Ty and Juno
and Mr. B. turned lumber discarded after the storm into
benches, which they set in rows before the altar with an aisle
in between. It wasn't fancy, but the scent of summer flowers
sweetened the air, birdsong added to the music of the creek,
a gentle breeze rustled through the leaves of the shady canopy
overhead, and the cloudless sky matched Ty Benton's eyes.

In Lottie's mind, it was the most beautiful day ever.

Reverend Nathaniel Lindz performed the ceremony. He
had accepted Becky's defection so well it took him less than
two weeks to find a new choir director and fiancée—Sugar
Maples, lately of the Spotted Dog—a sweet, pretty girl, as
primed for evangelical manipulation as he was desperate to
provide it. An excellent match, Lottie thought.

Sugar's musical talents were less excellent. But what her

rendition of the "Bridal Chorus" from Wagner's opera *Lohengrin* lacked in accuracy, she more than made up for with volume, pounding with bird-scattering enthusiasm on the piano tied in the back of the buckboard that had carried it all the way out from the Spotted Dog.

Becky thought it was the sweetest thing she'd ever heard. Apparently, she was as insensitive to pitch as Sugar was. But Lottie enjoyed it, too.

Mr. Brackett proudly walked both brides down the grassy aisle—Lottie on one arm, Becky on the other. Anson Briggs stood as best man for the two grooms, while Lady Jane Knightly served as bridesmaid to both brides.

Neither Lottie nor Becky would have had it any other way.

Most of the town came to the ceremony, even Lord Findlay, who remained gracious throughout—probably a stretch for an English baron, but Lottie appreciated the effort. He wasn't really so bad—he just didn't fit. Bea Davenport, Fred Kearsey, Cook, and several other workers from Lady Jane's came to celebrate the nuptials, in addition to serving the excellent luncheon prepared by the club's kitchen staff.

Even Humphries came, and brought with him a boxy camera that he set up on a tripod. Apparently, he was quite the photographer. Mr. Griffin had hired him to take photographs throughout the day—his gift to the brides and grooms. Lottie hoped Humphries could work the focus slide with that squint. She would hate to have everything come out blurry.

Belle, Red, and Henry were there from the Dog, mostly in support of Juno, but also to cheer on Sugar in her musical debut. Their arrival raised eyebrows among the stuffier attendees, but with Ty and Briggs looking on—and Juno's donation of a crate of whiskey from the saloon—no one openly objected, especially when soon after the ceremony ended, the three of them returned to the Spotted Dog and business as usual.

Two things happened that afternoon that promised weeks of fodder for the gossipers. The first came during the vows when Reverend Lindz turned to Juno and asked, "Do you, Junius Alphonse Darling, take Rebecca Gay Carmichael—"

The rest of his question was lost in an eruption of raucous laughter and mocking catcalls.

Juno's face turned red with embarrassment, although he should have expected some ribbing since he'd never allowed anyone to know his full name. Lottie could understand why—he was anything but "darling." Yet she admired the grace and restraint he demonstrated in the face of such teasing.

The second revelation came at the conclusion of the delicious wedding luncheon the club staff set out beneath the trees. Lottie knew it was coming, but that didn't lessen her sorrow when Lady Jane rose to speak.

"I wish to make an announcement, if I may," Jane called out.

Expectant faces turned her way. In the months since Jane had arrived in Greenbroke, she had gained many friends, both for her uniqueness, and for her generosity after the storm. She had become a fixture in the town, rather like that special keepsake set on the highest shelf and out of harm's way, there to enjoy but not to touch. Lottie wondered if anyone else noted how distracted she seemed of late, shining with happiness one minute, then sinking into sadness the next. Findlay must have wondered about it, yet he remained ever attentive. Briggs was more stone-faced than ever, revealing little of the turmoil Lottie knew was tying him in knots inside—the stalwart soldier who had won the battle but lost the war.

After the diners settled, Jane cleared her throat then began. "It is said that Texans are a tough, independent people who don't easily suffer fools, newcomers, or city slickers. But from the first day I arrived in Greenbroke, you have welcomed me and shown only kindness and support. That has meant more than I can say."

"Hear, hear," several voices called. Other listeners raised their cups in acknowledgment. "I love you, Lady Jane," one drunken cowboy shouted, before the elbows of his friends toppled him from the bench.

"However," she went on, "I have been called back to England, so I will be leaving in a few days." Hearing murmured protests from those who hadn't heard she was leaving, she put on a strained smile. "I am sad to go. And I shall never forget each and every one of you." Her gaze moved over the faces turned her way, paused on Lottie for a moment, then moved on. "But the good news is that Mr. Briggs will be staying to watch over the club."

Briggs acknowledged the protests and teasing groans with a thin smile.

"So, until we meet again . . ." Jane raised her glass of lemonade. "God bless you all. I shall love you always."

More cheers.

Jane sat down, her face tight with emotion . . . until Lottie saw Briggs reach beneath the tablecloth to take her hand in his. The look that passed between them nearly broke her heart. Lottie feared that after Jane and Findlay boarded the train for the first leg of their long journey back to England, she would never see her ladyship again. She wondered how Briggs could bear it.

The gathering lasted until late afternoon when the whiskey ran dry and the sun dipped toward the horizon. Needing to return to Greenbroke while they still had enough daylight to show them the way, folks began to offer their good-byes.

Becky and Juno led the way back to town in a beribboned buggy, dragging strings of shoes and tin cans in their wake. Jane followed with Briggs and Findlay, and falling in behind them, tipsy revelers rode on horseback and in wagons, some still singing the latest bawdy wedding song.

Lottie waved until the last guest crossed the creek and disappeared over the rise. Silence settled over the clearing. With a deep sigh, she slipped an arm around Ty's waist. "I can't believe it's over."

"Over?" Looping an arm over her shoulders, he smiled down at her. "I'd say it's just beginning."

She leaned into him, reveling in the strength of the arm holding her close and the warmth of the body against hers. "Is it real, Ty? Are we truly married?"

"We are. You're stuck with me now." Bending down, he brushed his lips against hers, then drew back to study her face. "You're crying again."

"I'm happy."

"I'm happy, too, but I'm not crying about it."

"You might yet."

"Oh?"

Lottie took a deep breath for courage. "What if I told you I still want to bookkeep?"

"Now? You want to talk about this now?" When she didn't answer, he thought for a moment, then shrugged. "I guess I could live with that."

"And I want to be full partner."

"Sure. We can start pulling fence tomorrow. Wear thick gloves."

"And I can't cook."

He reared back. "At all?"

"Grandpa did the cooking at the ranch. But I can open cans."

"Well, that's half of it. I guess we can hire out the other half."

Smiling through grateful tears, she reached up and pulled his head down. "I'm going to love being married to you, Tyree Benton," she whispered against his lips.

"Then let's get started, Lottie Benton." And before she could argue about who should follow whom into the house that was still torn up from all her changes and decorating projects, he scooped her up in his arms and carried her through the doorway into their new home.

Laughing, Lottie kissed her way up his strong neck. Her grand life had finally begun.

FROM AWARD-WINNING AUTHOR
KAKI WARNER

Where the Horses Run

The Heroes of Heartbreak Creek

Wounded in body and spirit after a shootout, Rayford
Jessup leaves his career as a lawman and uses his gift
with damaged horses to bring meaning to his solitary
life. Hired by a Scotsman in Heartbreak Creek to purchase thoroughbreds, he travels to England, unaware
that a traumatized horse and a beautiful Englishwoman
will change his life forever...

"A compelling, radiantly written romance."
—*Library Journal*

**"This beautifully rendered love story is tough and
tender—just what Warner's fans have come
to expect from this gifted storyteller."**
—*RT Book Reviews*

facebook.com/kakiwarner
facebook.com/BerkleyRomance
penguin.com

Penguin
Random
House

FROM AWARD-WINNING AUTHOR
KAKI WARNER

Behind His Blue Eyes

The Heroes of Heartbreak Creek

Ethan Hardesty wants to bring a railroad through Heartbreak Creek, Colorado, but hardheaded Audra Pearsall refuses to sign over the final right-of-way—no matter how persuasive or handsome Ethan might be. But when violence and fear stalk the canyon, Audra doesn't know who to trust—until the man she thought was her friend proves to be an enemy, and the man she resisted becomes her hero...

PRAISE FOR THE NOVELS OF KAKI WARNER

"Warner's warm, witty,
and lovable characters shine."
—*USA Today*

"A must-read...captures the imagination
and leaves you wanting more."
—*Night Owl Reviews*

kakiwarner.com
facebook.com/kakiwarner
facebook.com/BerkleyRomance
penguin.com

M1447T0514